D0015556

The Collected Stories of Max Brand

The Collected Stories of Max Brand

CENTENNIAL EDITION

Edited, with Story Prefaces,
by Robert and Jane Easton

Introduction by William Bloodworth

University of Nebraska Press, Lincoln and London

Acknowledgments for the use of
previously published material
appear on pages 340–42.
Introduction copyright © 1994 by
William Bloodworth. Story
prefaces copyright © 1994 by
Robert and Jane Easton. © 1994
by the University of Nebraska
Press. This book is published by
arrangement with the Golden
West Literary Agency. All rights
reserved. Manufactured in the
United States of America. The
paper in this book meets the
minimum requirements of
American National Standard for
Information Sciences –
Permanence of Paper for Printed
Library Materials, ANSI Z39.48-
1984. Library of Congress
Cataloging in Publication Data.
Brand, Max, 1892–1944. [Short
stories. Selections] The collected
stories of Max Brand / edited
with story prefaces by Robert
and Jane Easton : introduction
by William Bloodworth. –
Centennial ed. p. cm.
ISBN 0-8032-1244-5 (alk. paper)
1. Western stories. I. Easton,
Robert Olney. II. Easton, Jane
Faust. PS3511.A87A6 1994
813'.52 – dc20 93-43938 CIP

To William J. Clark who helped so much

Contents

ix Editors' Preface

xi Introduction

1 John Ovington Returns (1918)

17 Above the Law (1918)

71 The Wedding Guest (1934)

88 A Special Occasion (1934)

103 Outcast Breed (1934)

147 The Sun Stood Still (1934)

160 The Strange Villa (1935)

209 The Claws of the Tigress (1935)

217 Internes Can't Take Money (1936)

236 Fixed (1936)

252 Wine on the Desert (1936)

261 Virginia Creeper (1937)

277 Pringle's Luck (1937)

290 The Silent Witness (1938)

296 Miniature (1939)

309 Our Daily Bread (1940)

317 Honor Bright (1948)

335 The King (1948)

340 Acknowledgments

Editors' Preface

Faced by a wealth of choices — nearly nine hundred stories varying in length from short-shorts to 90,000-word novels, by the man who wrote under the name of Max Brand and some twenty other pseudonyms but whose real name was Frederick Schiller Faust — we chose stories we considered best, along with some we considered especially important or representative of the many genres in which he wrote. The selections are arranged chronologically so that a reader may see Faust's development as a writer and person. But if you prefer a different approach, you may skip here and there, and perhaps wind up like the reader who sat down to read one Faust story and read five.

We begin with the very early 'John Ovington Returns,' which in our view opens the way to all Faust's nonwestern fiction, some two hundred pieces, and also sheds light on his other work. For our second selection we chose another early story, his first western, 'Above the Law.' From these two we move directly to his most prolific period, the 1930s, when he produced his most mature works. In the preface to each story we tell how that story relates to Faust's life and other work.

This writer was killed on the battlefield as an overage volunteer correspondent in World War II, but new collections of his work, based on previously published magazine material or unpublished manuscripts, have continued to appear. Counting both new collections and reissues of books published during his lifetime, Faust has averaged a new book every four months for the past seventy-four years, which may qualify him for the *Guinness Book of World Records*. But what will his place be in American and world literature?

Until recently Faust's image has been incomplete. But with increasing publication of new biographical and critical material, as well as work by Faust himself heretofore generally unavailable – crime and science fiction, fantasy, historical romance, western stories, poetry – the picture is becoming clearer. We see a protean figure of giant dimensions appearing in many guises, appealing in different ways to a wide variety of audiences. We hope this book – Faust's 221st – will help clarify his emerging image. William Bloodworth's introduction takes a decisive step in that direction.

Robert and Jane Easton

Introduction

This book is a collection of stories by the writer who from 1917 to his death in 1944 published popular fiction under the pseudonym 'Max Brand.' His real name – Frederick Schiller Faust – was not particularly convenient in 1917. The name Max Brand, however, was wonderfully suited for popular stories, especially westerns. Faust published his fiction under a variety of other pen names as well. *The Claws of the Tigress*, excerpted in this volume, originally appeared under the name 'George Challis,' which Faust and his agents preferred for his historical adventure pieces. A few stories, including two published in *Harper's* in 1934 and part of this collection, were published under Faust's own name.[1] He also wrote and published poetry, generally as Frederick Faust.

Max Brand, pen name and public cover, has shielded Frederick Faust's life from close observation. Born in Seattle in 1892, he grew up poor and desperate in California's San Joaquin Valley. 'I grew up tall, gangling, crushed with shame because of dodged bills at local stores,' he once told his daughter, 'learning to withdraw from children of my age, thrown utterly into a world of books and daydreaming, daydreaming, daydreaming.'[2] By the time he reached thirteen both his parents had died. At age nineteen he worked his way into the University of California, where he discovered a talent for writing, turning out an amazing quantity of poems, essays, and plays. As a student he also learned to drink heavily and resist authority. In 1915, partly because he had criticized the president of the university in print, the Berkeley faculty refused to grant him his degree. He then spent several hectic years trying to get into the Great War and establish himself as a poet at the same time. He failed at both efforts but in New York City learned that he could produce popular stories for pulp magazines like *All-Story Weekly*, *Argosy*, *Detective Story Magazine*, and *Western Story Magazine*.

In 1917 he married his college sweetheart in California, moved with her to New York, and continued his pulp writing. While he wanted fame as a poet, his success came in the millions of words he produced for the pulps, especially in the form of western stories. In the early 1920s though no more than thirty years old, he suffered a heart attack; his self-imposed cure was to work harder and live faster. In 1926 he moved to Italy with his growing family, living for the next twelve years in a rented villa in Florence. His prose often earned him over seventy thousand dollars a year. During those years he turned out an average of over three thousand words of salable fiction daily. He would work all morning to write three lines of poetry and all afternoon to produce twenty-five pages of his latest story. He spent every dollar he earned – and more – on his lavish style of life. He was more than generous with friends, relatives, and struggling writers in need. Often he drank heavily.

After 1932, when pulp magazines began to fail, Faust turned to other magazine markets and eventually to Hollywood. Between 1938 and 1944 he worked as a screenwriter for M-G-M, Columbia, and Warner Bros. and formed close associations with Thomas Mann, Aldous Huxley, Richard Aldington, and other writers lured to Hollywood. In 1942 Warner Bros. teamed him with William Faulkner to work on the screenplay for *The de Gaulle Story*.[3] He continued to publish stories and novels, yet he was never satisfied with his accomplishments and claimed to be embarrassed in particular by his popular fiction. He yearned to write poetry on the scale and in the style of the classic Europeans he admired: Homer, Dante, Chaucer, Shakespeare. He felt unsatisfied, incomplete, unable to direct himself toward true literary achievement. The 'inside story' of his life, he said in 1939, was 'one of an aspiration gone wrong.'[4] He was anxious to make more money than the one thousand dollars per week the Hollywood studios were paying him, though earning the money made him feel that he had sold his artistic soul.

The writer who had missed action in an earlier war wanted to report the experiences of American infantrymen in World War II. Faust convinced *Harper's* to make him a war correspondent. With a bad heart, almost fifty-two years old, he ended up with the Fifth Army in Italy, not far from his old villa in Florence, shortly before the beginning of a major Allied offensive on May 11, 1944. Within a few hours after the fighting started that night, he was killed by a shell fragment.

Throughout his complicated personal life, Faust hid from public view his role as a writer of fiction. No one, certainly not Faust himself, revealed the true identity of Max Brand until 1938, when one of his book publishers wrote about him in a *Publishers Weekly* article.[5] The combination of intentional anonymity and multiple pen names has always made it difficult to describe and assess Faust's place in American literature. He is familiar to many readers today only as the writer of western novels that since the mid-1940s have filled the paperback bookracks in drug stores, bus depots, and convenience stores – places where American readers have sought the entertainment of novels. His stature in the eyes of the general public is similar to that of Zane Grey or Louis L'Amour. As a result, when critics and scholars have written about Faust, they have stressed his role within the rise of the popular western. Russel G. Nye in *The Unembarrassed Muse* (1970) and John Cawelti in *The Six-Gun Mystique* (1971) and *Adventure, Mystery, Romance* (1976) both view Max Brand (or Frederick Faust) as a key in the development of the popular western. Faust's work followed and built upon the popularity of Owen Wister, Zane Grey, and other early writers of western romances and adventures.[6] Recent scholars, especially Christine Bold in *Selling the Wild West* (1987) and Cynthia S. Hamilton in *Western and Hard-Boiled Detective Fiction in America* (1987), offer sophisticated ways of understanding Max Brand, but they still see him primarily as a writer of westerns. While scant attention has been paid to Faust's other work, he is well placed – in the guise of his most famous pen name – within the tradition of western stories.[7]

The reputation of 'Max Brand' as a writer of westerns may have less to do with Faust's publicity efforts than with the great resurgence of interest in westerns after World War II. He left behind almost two hundred western novels, virtually all of which had been originally published in pulp magazines between 1918 and 1938. Faust died at the beginning of the paperback era, which delivered his work to a new generation of readers. As a result, he has been over-recognized as a writer of westerns. His talent in other areas of fiction has gone unnoticed except by a faithful but generally uncritical following of fans and collectors. It is not widely known, for instance, that in the mid-1930s Faust wrote gripping crime stories with a hard-boiled tone and urban settings. The stories in this book may help to set the record straight.

In reality, Faust was a writer of enormous and diverse talent. He was also a writer tormented deeply by his own genius and ambitions, and generally unable to appreciate his own ability to write prose fiction. His life, full of dramatic intensity and psychological conflict, deserves attention in and of itself.[8] But his stories, particularly his short stories, stand out as small monuments of achievement in a literary career that was overwhelmed by an enormous number of published words.

Ironically, the sheer quantity of fiction Faust produced has given critics reasons to neglect him or to see his work as the product of outside forces rather than true creativity. After all, he published over nine hundred works of fiction in his lifetime. William F. Nolan, author of *Max Brand: Western Giant* (1986),[9] a bibliographical checklist, points out that during a mere three years in the early 1930s, Faust published more than five million words or the equivalent of seventy-five novels. Faced with such numbers, recent scholars have tended to sort through presumably representative texts – mainly westerns – in search of evidence to support a single theme. Often that theme is a hypothesis concerning the importance of external influences on Faust's life. Christine Bold, for instance, wrote of Faust's divided allegiance between money and art, a division evident in his two literary roles: commercial writer and classical poet. The internal struggle within Faust thus informs the narrative technique of his westerns. 'The split between Faust and Brand, between classicist and hack, which Faust assumed was completely absent from his stories, actually gives his novels a distinctive dimension,' Bold stated.[10] Cynthia Hamilton claims deep psychological origins for many features of Max Brand, especially the kind of underdog hero his westerns often incorporate into 'intensely personal myths' that are 'relevant to those on the bottom of the socio-economic heap.' In Hamilton's view, such traits in Brand westerns derive from Faust's own childhood, especially from ambiguous feelings about his father.[11]

Such approaches to Faust's fiction, from the outside in, so to speak, and with emphasis on his westerns, are provocative and illuminating. But they tend to give greater credence to the effects of external forces than to Faust's own powers as a writer. Moreover, the focus on a single apparent theme, as evidenced by Max Brand westerns, shortchanges the diverse reality of Faust's fiction. He wrote in many genres, and his works express a variety of themes. Efforts to reduce Faust's image to a single dimension are therefore questionable. The eighteen selections in this book show far more divergence from one another than they do similarity. The reality of Faust is a constant sense of multiplicity in his life and his works. His many pseudonyms are only the outward sign of this multiplicity. If there is an overall unifying element in Faust, it is simply his talent for storytelling.

In 1918, shortly after the beginning of his career as a writer for Frank A. Munsey's pulp magazines (especially *All-Story Weekly* and *Argosy*), he complained to a friend about the difficulty of writing serials. The serial writer, he explained, had to drag in new characters and complications and use 'a thousand tricks' to make the narrative long enough for the typical five to eight installments in a magazine. But short stories were different. 'After all, they're rather fun to write,' he said. No padding was required. 'All you have to do is concentrate on a snappy beginning and a smash for the close.' [12]

Snappy beginnings and smashing conclusions are not the ordinary criteria for great short fiction. But Faust's use of such terms suggests a narrative effect that he could achieve more fully in short stories than in longer fiction. The stories collected here bear testimony to this fact. In his frequent attention to small details of character and scene – such as the movement of the horse at the end of 'Miniature' – Faust deserves to be appreciated on grounds beyond sheer numbers. His incredible productivity and the facts of his life have always invited hyperbole. Faust is 'The Fabulous Faust,' 'Western Giant,' or 'The King of the Pulps,' as though he were a key figure in some sideshow of American literature that is located far from center stage. In reality, and perhaps in spite of his amazing productivity, he was a surprisingly careful practitioner of fiction.

The stories in this book will certainly enhance the legend of a writer whose talents can be seen in a wide range of styles and genres. Some of the stories were written for pulp magazines like *Argosy* that depended for commercial success on the direct marketing of issues packed with fiction. 'John Ovington Returns,' 'Above the Law,' 'The Strange Villa,' 'Outcast Breed,' and 'The Claws of the Tigress' were all pulp stories. Writing for the pulp magazines appealed to Faust; the absence of tight editorial policy meant that he was free to invent narratives and characters without worrying much about standards of taste. Much of his pulp work, however, did not take the short story form. In this collection only 'John Ovington Returns' was originally a short story, published in 1918.

The other four pulp stories were originally published as single-issue novelettes.

Two *Harper's* stories – 'The Wedding Guest' and 'A Special Occasion' – reveal Faust's ability to produce work that is consciously literary in imagery and situation. The earnings from such stories, however, were not great, especially in view of the time they took to produce. His interest in writing them, therefore, was more limited than his talent to write them. In fact, his interest was limited to 1933 when 'The Wedding Guest' and 'A Special Occasion' were written: a year in which Faust faced a declining pulp market and considerable uncertainty about his future as a writer. Writing *as a vocation* was, after all, the central fact of his career in fiction. His typewriter was the sole source of his income and the basis of the hope, never realized, that he might some day be able to write nothing but poetry. His need for money did not encourage him or his agent to pursue high-brow magazines of his day, even though his *Harper's* stories suggest that he could have done so with considerable success.[13]

Most of the stories in this collection were neither pulp nor high-brow in their origins. *Cosmopolitan, Collier's, Good Housekeeping,* and *The American Magazine* were so-called 'slicks.' Printed on glossy paper, they not only looked different from the pulps but they relied much more on advertising revenue for financial success. As a result, the slicks preferred to reserve plenty of space to advertise products to their middle-class readers. The slicks also maintained tighter editorial control than the pulps, which Faust did not like. Yet by the early 1930s he knew that the visibility of the slick magazines could expand his own market. Despite some carping on his part about the demands of editors, Faust produced excellent short work for what he called the 'hard paper' magazines. The slick magazines seem to have provided an effective compromise between Faust's pulp imagination and the controlled prose he was capable of producing for *Harper's*. Such stories are well represented in this collection.

In 1919, at age twenty-seven, Faust had explained to a friend how difficult it is for a young writer to base a story on character. 'Now, of course, we all know that character work is the highest thing fiction can aspire toward,' he said, 'but really, nobody under forty years of age can possibly draw a convincing character. . . . The best way for a beginner is to start with a narrative idea and make the characters fit in with the story rather than start with the characters and fit the story to them.

Truly, the latter is the better way – but not until we're forty plus.' That Faust followed his own advice can be seen in the strong, moving plots of his work. He was a teller of stories, a writer capable of a new narrative idea almost every day of his adult life, a person who took great joy in sitting around with magazine editors and other writers to 'talk story.'[14] True to his earlier perception, as he moved beyond age forty he found that he could, when called upon, write stories 'the better way,' founding them more on character than on plot. The difference in this regard is clear between an early western like 'Above the Law' (1918) and the equally action-packed spy story, 'The Strange Villa' (1935). While the western hero (Black Jim) is of some interest because of his presumed violent nature, his emotional responses are less developed than are those of Anthony Hamilton, the espionage hero. Yet even in Faust's most mature fiction, he is still the teller of stories, the writer who knew almost instinctively that good characterization must be based on the events of a narrative.

On occasion, Faust was able not only to write good stories but also to incorporate in them significant elements of then-current American attitudes and cultural events. The basic themes of a story like 'Our Daily Bread,' for instance, are poverty and anti-Semitism, the latter serving as an antagonist which the story itself seeks to defeat. In many of the stories Faust wrote in the 1930s, the Great Depression looms in the background.

While all the magazine stories here are worth the attention of students of American literature and popular culture, 'Internes Can't Take Money' is a particularly interesting example of Faust's style and influence. Published in *Cosmopolitan* in 1936 at the height of the Depression, it is a vintage, nonwestern Max Brand story that reveals Faust's clever manipulation of popular images and attitudes at a propitious historical moment. 'Internes Can't Take Money' skillfully fits together Dr. James Kildare's personal concerns about money, the ethics of the medical profession, big-city ward politics, the criminal underworld, and details of medical procedure – all presented at the height of the Great Depression.

The tone of the story is established early through Kildare's fear that his poverty as a hospital intern might force his return to the country farm where he was raised. 'The future to him was a great question mark, and New York was the emptiness inside the loop of the mark. Add a few strokes to the question mark and you get a dollar sign.' Kildare is not affluent. His economic dread, reflective of the times, stands in contrast to the well-moneyed politicians and criminals in the areas around the hospital where 'there were men who lived according to a new standard of morality about which Kildare knew nothing.' Kildare notices this new kind of morality even in the 'perfection' of the clothes worn by characters such as Hanlon. The melodramatic resolution of the story brings together medicine and the morality of the street, a reconciliation suggested early when Kildare illegally operates on a wounded hoodlum with the assistance of the injured man's associates. The people of the street and the saloon pay homage to Kildare in their physical attention to him after the operation:

> Jeff and another man – he who had worked with the retractors – were rubbing the blood from Kildare's hands with painful care. He surrendered his hands to them like tools of infinite value in the trust of friends. A warmth flowed like strong drink through his brain.

In *Playing Doctor,* subtitled *Television, Storytelling and Medical Power,* Joseph Turow points out how post–World War II attitudes toward the medical profession were profoundly affected by popular stories, beginning with 'Internes Can't Take Money.' Everything else followed: not only the movies and television stories about Dr. Kildare, but also *Marcus Welby, M.D., Medical Center,* and even *M*A*S*H.*[15] The influence of Faust's piece upon two generations of stories about doctors, primarily stories from other media, says little about the literary qualities of his fiction but certainly verifies the historical impact that a contemporary reader can sense in the details of Faust's story.

Gore Vidal once said that it is the peculiar fate of American writers not to achieve fame but to become celebrities. In the case of Max Brand, however, the opposite is true. Max Brand was famous but Frederick Faust was never a celebrity. In fact, the writer who made the name famous – Frederick Schiller Faust – took rigorous measures to protect himself from public view. Even to his own children he told elaborate stories to conceal his writing of magazine fiction. By 1937, when Paramount released the first Dr. Kildare movie, *Internes Can't Take Money,* starring Joel McCrea and Barbara Stanwyck, some people knew that Faust was Brand. But this knowledge, even when spread by *Publishers Weekly* the next year, did little to disrupt the security that Faust had created for himself. The greatest irony of his career is the contrast between the popularity of Max Brand and the privacy of Frederick Faust.

The stories in this book, which honors the centennial of Faust's birth, will certainly help readers understand both the popular appeal of Max Brand and the broad, complex talent of Brand's creator.

William Bloodworth

NOTES

1. Faust published his work under a total of twenty different pseudonyms. His fiction appeared under the names of Frank Austin, George Owen Baxter, Lee Bolt, Max Brand, M. B., Walter C. Butler, George Challis, Martin Dexter, Peter Dawson, Evan Evans, Evin Evan, John Frederick, Frederick Frost, Dennis Lawton, David Manning, Peter Henry Morland, Hugh Owen, and Nicholas Silver. He used two other aliases for ghostwriting and some of his college prose, and a twenty-first name, Henry Uriel, was used for one poem published after his death.

2. Frederick Schiller Faust to Jane Faust, November 25, 1939. This letter and many others are in the collection of Faust's papers at the Bancroft Library, University of California, Berkeley.

3. See Joseph Blotner, *Faulkner: A Biography* (New York: Random House, 1974), 1123–24, and Frederick R. Karl, *William Faulkner: American Writer* (New York: Weidenfeld and Nicolson, 1989), 678–79.

4. Ibid.

5. Edward H. Dodd, Jr., 'Twenty-Five Million Words,' *Publishers Weekly*, March 26, 1938.

6. Russel B. Nye, *The Unembarrassed Muse: The Popular Arts in America* (New York: Dial Press, 1970) and John G. Cawelti, *The Six-Gun Mystique* (Bowling Green, Ohio: Bowling Green State University Popular Press, 1971) and *Adventure, Mystery, Romance: Formula Stories as Art and Popular Culture* (Chicago: University of Chicago Press, 1976). Also see William Bloodworth, 'Max Brand's West,' *Western American Literature* 16 (1981): 177–91.

7. There is some dispute, however, over the centrality of Max Brand to the western tradition. In 'Max Brand's West,' I argue that Max Brand westerns generally do not participate in the same kind of western myth-making that westerns by Zane Grey and others do.

8. Robert Easton's *Max Brand: The Big 'Westerner'* (Norman: University of Oklahoma Press, 1970) is an excellent treatment of Faust's turbulent life.

9. William F. Nolan, *Max Brand: Western Giant* (Bowling Green, Ohio: Bowling Green State University Popular Press, 1986), 1–2.

10. Christine Bold, *Selling the Wild West* (Bloomington: Indiana University Press, 1987), 92.

11. Cynthia S. Hamilton, *Western and Hard-Boiled Detective Fiction in America: From High Noon to Midnight* (Iowa City: University of Iowa Press, 1987), 115–16.

12. Faust to G. W. Fish, November 1, 1918, cited in John Schoolcraft, 'The Fabulous Faust: His Life and Letters,' an unpublished manuscript in the Faust papers at the Bancroft Library.

13. Faust was nevertheless eager to place some of his stories in high-quality magazines and willing to be identified as someone other than a writer of pulp fiction. For this reason, he allowed the *Harper's* stories to be published under his real name in 1934. From 1936 to 1938 he again allowed himself to be identified as the author of magazine fiction in the case of three stories published in the *Saturday Evening Post* and two in *The American Magazine*. From early 1938 until his death in May, 1944, no further stories appeared under his real name: everything was published under the Max Brand byline. However, several weeks after his death on the front lines in Italy, his fourth and final *Saturday Evening Post* story, a serial, was credited to Frederick Faust.

14. Howard V. Bloomfield, editor of the Munsey Company's *Detective Fiction Weekly* in 1933 and 1934, told me in a 1986 interview that one of Faust's greatest joys when he was in New York City was to spend hours on end at a restaurant discussing ideas for new stories. 'Talk story' was Bloomfield's term for the activity.

15. Joseph Turow, *Playing Doctor: Television, Storytelling, and Medical Power* (New York and Oxford: Oxford University Press, 1989), especially the first chapter, 'Internes Can't Take Money,' 3–24.

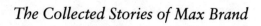
The Collected Stories of Max Brand

John Ovington Returns

Faust had been writing professionally little more than a year when this story appeared in *All-Story Weekly* (June 8, 1918). It shows both his experimentation with fantasy, a field which attracted him, and his fondness for myth, folk tale, balladry, and a reality beyond ordinary reality. Poetry sparkles through the prose, as in much of his work. We see his love of history from which much of his later historical fiction would flow. 'John Ovington Returns' also presages a fantasy novel published posthumously, *The Garden of Eden* (Dodd, Mead, 1963), perhaps the most unusual western novel Faust ever wrote, in which not a shot is fired nor a blow struck by fist. There are also elements of fantasy in many of Faust's later works outside the western, such as *The Smoking Land* (Capra, 1980) – sometimes called his only science fiction novel.

In 'John Ovington Returns' we find autobiography, too. The twenty-six-year-old author had just informed his beloved young wife that he was about to leave her and their two-month-old daughter and go off to war, much as the fictional John Ovington informs the woman he loves. Characteristically, Faust had exactly fifty cents in his pocket when this story brought him sixty dollars (at the rate of a penny a word). With typical optimism he abandoned wife and child in a New York City apartment, confident he could support them with stories written while he was in uniform. Dorothy Faust's reactions are not recorded but can be imagined.

Faust's fiction shows he could write almost any kind of fiction successfully, but by his own testimony he didn't write so much as dream. 'If I think, I can't write,' he once said. 'I have to dream.' Dreaming helped him open doors to what his analyst C. G. Jung called the collective unconscious, that world of archetypal experience and power from which we may draw our greatest strength and truth.

This story was written by 'Max Brand,' a pen name Faust had begun using for his prose the year before. He reserved 'Frederick Faust' for poetry published in the popular *All-Story Weekly* as well as in the highbrow *Century Magazine.* 'John Ovington Returns,' in short, shows both the kind of writer Faust was and the kind of writer he would become.

THE OLD servant stopped and faced him. The light from the candle he carried flickered across his bald head as he nodded wonderingly, and John Ovington hardly repressed a smile.

'You are quite sure you were never in the house before?' asked Hillton.

'No,' said Ovington, 'I was never here before, but somehow it seems to me that a big amber-colored vase with black figures tracing down the sides should stand by that window. It's just a fancy, but rather unusual in its clearness.'

'The Ovingtons are an unusual family, sir,' said Hillton, and he raised his candle so that its light fell more fully on the sternly carven face of his new master. After his moment's scrutiny he shook his head as one who gives up a problem.

'A vase like the one you speak of stood there ever since the house was built, but last week Mrs. Worth broke it while she was cleaning the room. Every week I have the rooms cleaned, sir, but for the past year they have never been used, none except the kitchen and Mr. Ovington's bedroom where he lay sick for so long.'

'And died?' said Ovington.

'And died, sir. He wouldn't trust any one save me. I wrote the letter which brought you here, and I signed it for him.'

'I shall never forget that letter,' said Ovington. 'And that is the room where I sleep now?'

'The master has always slept in that room since the family came here to live,' he answered. 'Now I think you have seen the whole house, Mr. Ovington.'

'But isn't there a room behind those folding doors?' asked Ovington.

'That is the library, and it hasn't been opened these past fifteen years. Fifteen dreary years, sir. It must be fearful thick with dust.'

'And why has it been closed all this time?'

'That was the time when young Master Ovington died, and since then the master couldn't bear to go into that room. For the family pictures hang there, and he couldn't stand to look on them, he having lost his heir. The family name ended with him, as he thought. It was only through the lawyers that we traced the line to you, sir, through your great-grandfather, John Ovington, the man who disappeared.'

'So I understand,' said Ovington. 'But let's have a look at the room.'

Hillton drew in his wrinkled lips anxiously.

'To-night, sir?'

'Why not?'

'It's a fearsome place to go into at night with all the great, stern old Ovingtons painted and hanging on the wall. It's most like a graveyard, sir, with the ghosts up and sitting on their tombs. I'm sure you will not like it to be there at night, Mr. Ovington.'

'Tut!' smiled Ovington, and he laid a reassuring hand on the old man's shoulder. 'We'll risk the dust and the family pictures.'

It was only after much reluctant fumbling and many sidewise glances as if in hope that Ovington's resolution would die away that Hillton finally produced the key. The lock had set so fast that it required a great effort for Ovington to send it gritting back. He swung the door wide and stepped into the high, dark room. The wavering of the light behind him made him turn to Hillton, who stood outside the door, the candle fairly shaking in his hand.

'Come, come!' laughed Ovington. 'After all, it's only a room with nothing more dangerous in it than shadows.'

'No, sir,' said Hillton, 'I'm not afraid. But it's a strange house and a strange people.'

He entered slowly, the candle held high above his head, peering about at every step.

Into the highest shadows of the raftered ceiling the wavering candle-light hardly reached, but it shone on the ponderous table, thickly dusted, and into the black throat of the fireplace, and picked out the long row of portraits receding dimly on either side of the room. Among them were a few dressed in the ruffs of the Tudor period. Others appeared in somber Puritan gray, straight faces under tall hats. Among these one caught Ovington's eye. He took the candle from Hillton and held it close to the portrait.

He almost thought for a moment that he was dressed for a fancy ball and stood before a mirror, for it was his own face which returned his gaze with a half scowl and a half sneer, the same strong nose, thin cheeks, and unflinching eyes. He blinded himself with his hand and looked again, but the resemblance persisted. He felt that his forehead had grown very cold.

'And who is this, Hillton?' he asked, wondering if the servant would notice the resemblance.

'That is your great-grandfather, whose name was John Ovington, like your name,' said Hillton, forgetting his uneasiness as he talked. 'He was the strangest of all the Ovingtons, for he rode away one day and never came back, and that is the last people ever heard of him. And all that was many and many years ago. So long that my father could not remember.'

He led the way to the window and drew aside the curtain, loosing a cloud of choking dust. Outside the moon glimmered on the garden terraces, which stepped down to a tree-covered hollow, but the other side of the valley rose dark and steep, with a great square house topping it.

'That is the Jervan house,' said Hillton, and his pointing hand trembled in the moonlight. 'That is the house where Beatrice Jervan lived, who was the sweetheart of our John Ovington in those old days, but John Ovington went across the seas and fought in France. So when he came back Beatrice Jervan loved him no longer, and they say that he would have forced her to marry him, for he was a stark, fierce man; but she fled away in the night with another man. And John Ovington waited for them at a forking of the Newbury Road as they fled on their horses. He stopped them and would have made them turn back, but the man drew a horse-pistol and shot him through the shoulder and rode on with Beatrice Jervan, and God knows what became of them both. We only know that a granddaughter of that couple married back into the Jervan family, and now there is a Beatrice Jervan over there again in that house; and over here' – he laughed tremulously in the moonlight – 'is a John Ovington again.

'Well, when the man rode on with Beatrice that other John Ovington rose up from the road where he had fallen and called after them: "I have failed this time, but I shall not fail twice. I shall come again. I shall wait for you in this place, Beatrice Jervan, and carry you away with me forever."

'But that he never did, for shortly afterward he went and took ship in Boston Harbor and went across the sea to other countries. And he was your great-grandfather. All that he left was this picture on the wall and a little cedar chest of his papers which sits on that shelf next to the brass-bound Bible. He was the last of the old family, for after him his cousin took the name and the inheritance.'

Through a long moment Ovington stood staring at the opposite house.

'I am going to stay here and read some of those papers,' said he at last, 'so you can leave the candle, Hillton.'

'Will you sit here all alone, sir, on your first night?'

He folded his hands in his anxiety, and when Ovington nodded he turned and went falteringly from the room, shaking his head solemnly as he walked.

II

On top of the papers in the small chest lay a miniature of a girl. It had evidently at one time been a bust painted by an artist of some skill, but the lower part of the picture was rubbed and faded beyond the recognition of any form. Only the face remained clear. The hair drew back from the forehead in the severe lines which pleased those grim old New Englanders, and the eyes drooped demurely downward, but no moral preceptor could lessen the curve and the lure of the red lips. It seemed to Ovington that the eyes might at any moment flash up and yield him unknown depths of light and mockery.

He dropped the miniature to his knee and sat for a time looking straight before him. When he had rallied his thoughts he commenced to turn over the papers. They were all letters written in a woman's hand, and despite the yellowing of time and the fading of the ink, he could make out the words with little effort. Arranged in the order of their receipt the letters told their own story of the love between Beatrice Jervan and John Ovington.

There was a long group covering the period of the wooing, and then came the time when Ovington decided to go to the war, and this letter:

I could not say it last night. I needed quiet so that I could think it all out clearly, and now I know what I wanted to say. You must not go to the war, John, dear.

I know that glory is a wonderful thing, but a good wife is a wonderful thing, too, John, and would you care to win glory and lose a wife? Not that I am sure you would lose me; but I love happiness, dear, and I am afraid of pain; and if you were thousands and thousands of miles away, what would I have to remember you by? It is so hard to remember a man by his silences, John!

Dear, will you try to please me in this? And then I will try to please you all the days of my life. But the sea is so broad, and the French shoot so straight – and I do so love laughter, John! Come to me to-night, and I know I can change your mind.

He rose and walked with the candle until he faced the picture of John Ovington. Yes, that was the face of a man able to defy the charm of sudden glances and slow smiles. He went back to the letters. They diminished rapidly in length, and then came this:

If you want me, you must come and fight for me, Captain John Ovington. There may be dreadful fighting on the plains of France, but I think you will find enough war here on the hills of Connecticut. He has yellow, curling hair, John, and wide, blue eyes, and a gentle voice and a ringing laugh, and he's as much of a man as you are, almost. If you want me, you must come for me. It may be too late. I can't tell.

Then came a short note:

You need not come. It is too late!

But John Ovington had decided to come back and try, and after his return were two letters, the last:

If you will not come to see me, John Ovington, I shall come to see you; though if I do that I know that mother will faint.

I think I have never seen so grave a man as the John Ovington I met on the bridge the other day. Have you truly forgotten me? All grave men are not silent, John Ovington. I have a plan to discover if you can really smile.

I will be by the fountain in the garden to-night if it is not too cold.

And John Ovington had evidently changed his mind that night and gone to the garden and made desperate love, hoping against hope, for the last letter said:

Vincent Colvin has been with me all this morning. I am going to ride away with him to-night. I have not forgotten, but I promised myself to him long ago, and now I shall keep the promise. My father objects, so we are going to go out for a ride from which we shall never come back, and we will take the Newbury Road. Oh, my dear, it breaks my heart to ride out of your life. It has all been so strange, so maddeningly dear and painful. Must this be good-by?

He read no more that night, but he sat a long time at the window watching the night mist creep up the valley, tangling among the trees, and at last setting a gray veil across the window-pane.

The next morning the challenge of the keen October air drew him out into the open. In the stables he found a great black charger and had him saddled. The groom eyed him dubiously as he lengthened his stirrups to suit his western fashion of riding, but when he swung into the saddle and started down the path with his broad hat curling up in front to the wind and his cloak fluttering behind him, while his powerful pull on the reins held down the horse to an uneasy prance, the groom grinned with open admiration.

'I reckon an Ovington,' he said, 'is always an Ovington.'

But as he took the road down the valley Ovington could not forget the adventure of the previous evening, for the Connecticut hills rolled up on either side, a remembered beauty of yellowing browns, gold, and crimson running riotously together and all the trees still shining with the touch of the night mist. And the great lift and sway of the gallop set his heart singing in unison with the hoof-beats. He could not tell how far he had ridden, for every bend invited him on and on down flaming vistas.

He passed from the main road on to a narrow path which, after a quarter of a mile, surged to the left, and around a quick turn he thundered across a stream on a narrow foot-bridge, a frail structure which tottered and shook under him. At the same time he heard the clatter of hoofs coming toward him down the same path and in a moment a racing brown horse flashed about the curve and dashed onto the bridge.

It was far too narrow a path for two horses to edge by each other. He brought his mount to a rearing stop.

When he looked again the brown horse stood head to head with his black, and he was face to face with the loveliest girl he had ever seen, but a remembered beauty – yes, the face of the miniature, a spray of autumn leaves at her breast stirring as she panted.

'This is a real escape, isn't it?' she cried, and her voice carried more mirth than fear.

'I guess it's an escape,' he said quietly, after another moment of staring. 'Here, there is not room for two to pass. I'll back off the bridge.'

But when he drew on the reins the black horse reared straight up, and when he came down stiff-legged the little bridge wavered and groaned.

'Don't do that!' she cried, truly frightened by this time. 'I'll back off.'

She moved her horse back cautiously, step and step, and he followed, but when they came onto the path again he still blocked the way and the puzzled searching of the eyes made her flush slightly.

'Your name is Beatrice Jervan,' he stated.

'Yes,' she said.

'And mine is John Ovington.'

She clapped her hands in delighted discovery.

'Are you really the new John Ovington? Let's shake hands and be friends. We're neighbors, you know.'

He rode beside her and took her hand. He knew that she was saying: 'But you are a stranger here. How did you know my name?'

He smiled vaguely on her. 'Can you tell me how old this bridge is?'

'Yes,' she said, wondering. 'It is said to be a hundred and fifty years old. But I doubt it.'

'Well,' he said, 'I feel as if I had known you for one hundred and fifty years.'

'With that soft hat and that riding-cloak,' she laughed, 'you look as if you might be a bandit of that period.'

'With that smile,' he said, 'you look as if you might be a woman of almost any period. May I ride with you?' he continued. 'If I may I'll try not to say any more foolish things like that last one.'

'It doesn't matter,' she said; 'it's the October air that makes one happy without knowing just why. Of course you may ride with me if you care to.'

They made back across the bridge again and up onto the road. As they broke into a canter he fell back a little to watch the lilt of her perfect horsemanship.

'If you ride so far back I can't talk to you,' she complained, 'and then you'll think I'm stupid.'

'You don't have to talk,' he said. 'I'm perfectly entertained, and be-sides — '

But she spurred her horse to a wild gallop and the rest of his sentence was jolted from his mind as he pursued. The long stride of the black brought him beside her in a few seconds.

'You ride well,' he shouted as he reined in to her pace, 'but you see you can't escape me.'

She slowed down rather sullenly.

'I have never been passed before on these roads,' she said.

'Not passed,' he corrected; 'merely caught.'

She accepted the comment with a cold glance. He rode a little behind her, perfectly happy and perfectly silent. A keen wind rose and whirled down the valley to meet them. Sometimes the force of the gust seemed to sway her back in her saddle. From stirrup to head she gave in grace-ful lines to the sway and lunge of the gallop, and Ovington ground his teeth to keep from singing aloud. It seemed hardly a moment before she checked her horse.

'Our ways part here,' she said, then smiling: 'Are you always silent, Mr. Ovington?'

He raised his hat without replying, wheeled, and spurred up the hill, and she remained for a breathing space watching the play of his broad shoulders as he rode.

III

Through the next ten days he wandered about the place uneasily. He could hardly define his own mood. He felt vaguely that he was waiting, but he had not the slightest idea for what. But on the tenth day a letter came and he knew. He recognized the handwriting, but before he dared to tear it open he went first to the little cedar chest and compared the two scripts.

They were identical.

The letter began without prelude just as that other letter came to that other John Ovington a hundred and fifty years before:

If you will not come to see me, John Ovington, I shall come to see you.

A red mist came before him. He felt himself trembling like a child, and it was some time before he could resume the reading. Without a single variation the letter repeated the time-yellowed manuscript of the cedar chest.

I think I have never seen so grave a man. All grave men are not silent, John Ovington. I have a plan to discover if you can really smile. I will be in the garden to-night if it is not too cold.

'I will not go,' he said aloud, as if to convince himself against himself. 'I will not let this damned riddle ruin me as it ruined a John Ovington four generations before me.'

He commenced to pace up and down the room. According to the old story he should go to that garden to-night and make desperate love to her. And according to that story he was lost in the end, fate played against him.

Ovington tried to rally his reason. He tried to convince himself that this was all a weird dream, but the two letters lay convincingly side by side. Had the spirit of the old John Ovington truly come back to try the old task again? Would there be for him the same agony of heart and mind? He covered his face with his hands and groaned aloud, for he saw again the spray of autumn leaves stirring at her breast.

After supper he went into the library to fight out the night there, but the old portraits leered down at him, the little cedar chest loomed like a silent oracle of sorrow. He rose at last and went out to pace the terraces of the garden.

His foot sounded hollowly over the little bridge across the river, but he did not notice it. Unconsciously he wandered up the path on the other side of the valley, through the opening of the hedge of evergreen, and onto the velvet lawns of the Jervan estate.

A light laugh only a few feet away startled him into vivid consciousness. He found that he stood near a circle of shrubbery, in the center of which a fountain splashed and showered, and through the light falling of the spray he heard the thrilling velvet of Beatrice Jervan's voice:

'Go away now, Vincent. I so want to be alone.'

And a pleasant voice answered:

'Have I wearied you to-night, dear?'

'No,' she answered, 'but I am tired of saying pretty things and hearing them, just for a little while. I am hungry for the quiet and the chill of this air. Please go back to the house and tell them that I am taking a walk through the garden. They will understand.'

'And I shall see you later? And you are not cold?'

'You will see me later. I am not the least cold.'

'*Au revoir* a little while. Dear, I am full of strange thoughts to-night. It is almost as if you were slipping away from me. I have reached out to you a hundred times, and my heart has closed on nothing. What does it mean?'

'Fantasy!' she said, and as she laughed the sound broke and ran trilling down like the musical chuckle of a bird. '*Adieu.* You need not fear. I shall stay true to our plan. *Adieu.*'

Ovington heard the man's lightly treading step pass away over the lawn, the shrubbery brushed against him noisily, and then the silence slipped back over the place and the faintly moving air shook the fountain into light showerings of spray, felt rather than heard, like the pulse of a heart. And a great yellow moon floated up through the branches of the eastern trees, took the changing tracery of the black limbs, and now drifted abroad into the pathless heaven, so that her light, peering slant over the shrubbery looked on the silver nodding head of the fountain.

And deeper and deeper slanted the light until he saw it glimmer like a dark star in the hair of Beatrice.

She raised her head up to meet that light. It fell upon her face like a sculptured smile, and Ovington stood breathless, watching, waiting, with a musical dread in his heart. Then the dark fur which clung against her throat shifted and the shadow of the lifted eyes changed. He stepped into the circle of the shrubbery and stood before her, and she, looking up, saw the black outline of his head against the rolling moon.

'You are for all the world like a man come down from the moon,' she said, and her voice was so low that she seemed to be talking to herself rather than to him.

He stood for a long moment before he could speak.

'And who,' he asked, 'is dear Vincent?'

'Vincent is a very nice boy,' she answered, 'who has yellow curling hair and wide blue eyes and is as much of a man as you are, John Ovington.'

He dropped into the stone seat beside her and leaned forward, his hands clasped and his eyes on the ground. He was so perilously near her that she could mark the tensed lips and the frowning forehead of his profile, but the wide brim of his hat put all the rest of his face in shadow. She watched his strongly interlaced fingers.

'So you are a silent man, John Ovington?'

'I am thinking very hard,' he answered.

'Yes, you are troubled about something?' He felt the perfume and touch of her breath as she leaned swiftly toward him. And as she leaned she saw the interlacing fingers grind together. A tremor shook her that was half fear and half delight.

'I suppose,' he began at last, 'that you have watched the sun glinting in Vincent's yellow hair?'

'Of course,' she said.

'And your fingers have touched it where the sun has fallen?'

'That,' she said, 'is a secret.'

'I am quite sure I have no use for Vincent,' he said.

In the pause the wind went rushing past them and ran on through the far-off treetops, whispering and muttering.

'And I suppose,' he went on, 'that you could not begin to count the moments you have spent looking into Vincent's wide, blue eyes?'

'I am sure that would be hard to reckon,' she said gravely.

'I think I could hate Vincent,' he mused. 'Do you like him a great deal?'

'I'm sure I dislike confessionals.'

'It is rather hard,' he said at last.

'What is hard?'

'To play against fate, and to come into the play with the stage set against me.'

'I don't understand!'

But watching those gripping fingers she did understand, and the shaking of the fountain counted out the waiting seconds until he spoke again.

'It would have been so easy in any other setting,' he said. 'For instance I might have seen you first at a tea-table, saying the silly things that go with tea.'

'I hate tea,' she said fervently.

'Or I might have seen you at the end of a long ride instead of the beginning. I might have seen you with your hair tumbling roughly and your hat askew, and your figure slumping wearily at every stride of the horse. You would not have mattered then, very much.'

She looked up to the moon, but it seemed too bright, too searching, now, and she dropped her eyes hastily back to his hands.

'But even as it was,' he said, 'I could have stood out against you if it had not been for the spray of autumn leaves at your breast.' He nodded solemnly. 'That was what did the harm. It was hardly fair, do you think?'

'They were only autumn leaves,' she said, 'and anyway I don't understand why you are so solemn.'

'That is fibbing,' he remarked unemotionally, 'and it is not even a white fib. You know perfectly well that the stage was set, and that I had not a chance when I came blundering on to the boards, a mere supernumerary in the last act. But, knowing all this, why did you send me the note? I don't like bear-baiting when I am the bear.'

She looked away from him suddenly into the shadows of the shrubbery. Then, almost desperately:

'Is this mere neighborliness, John Ovington? Can a man meet a girl once and then talk as you are talking?'

'Does it seem impossible to you, Beatrice?' he muttered. 'Does it really seem so strange to you? Tell me frankly.'

'I don't know,' her lips framed, but without sound.

'Your face is so in the shadow,' she said in a very low voice, 'that I cannot tell whether or not you are smiling to yourself.'

'I don't dare to look up to you for fear that you would understand too clearly. But tell me truly, why did you write that note?'

'I cannot tell. I sat down before a piece of paper and the words came of themselves. I don't know what I wrote. I am sorry if I hurt you.'

'And I cannot tell why I came here to-night,' he answered, 'for I determined to stay away, but my steps guided themselves. Here I am. It is not you or I who speak here to-night, Beatrice, but old forces greater than we. We are puppets in the game. We are the guests of chance. Do you not feel it?'

'I cannot say,' she said, 'but everything seems changed. It is as if I knew you for a long time. When you speak I remember your words from long ago. And my heart is cold and strange. And – and – I wish you would go, John Ovington. I am afraid of you.'

'I cannot go yet,' he answered bitterly, 'for I sit here and see as plainly as if I were looking at you, the stir of your breast, and the moonlight white and cold along your throat, and the unconscious smiling of your lips, and the unsearchable shadows of your eyes.'

He turned to her fiercely and his left hand gripped the back of the stone seat as he leaned over her.

'Can't you make them clear and plain and readable? Can't you make me feel that I have no hope? That you are completely lost to me? That I have no share in your soul? Why do you torment me with this damnable ghost of hope, Beatrice?'

She made no answer to the compelling whisper, but through a long moment she met his eyes and into the silence once more the shaking of the fountain beat like a pulse. Then she shrank a little away with a

musical tremor of sound, and her hand fell palm up across her eyes. He
drew her to him, rich with the soft warmth of her body.

His lips touched her throat. A sob formed there. He kissed the tremu-
lous hollow of her hand. At once it fell away helplessly. He crushed
the parted lips. At once her breath came brokenly and moaning to his
ear, and while the thunder of his heart shook both their spirits, she
whispered:

'God help me! God help me!'

Thereat he rose suddenly and turned away with bowed head, for at
the moan of her voice the thought of the yellow, rustling papers of the
cedar box came upon him like a drift of the last leaves of dead autumn.
Then he knew that she was by his side.

'It is not ended yet,' she was saying. 'If we are the guests of chance
now, oh, be strong and become the master of it all! Find out the way.
There is always one road home. John, I trust in you.'

When he was able to raise his head she was gone, and a mist that
drew across the moon made all the play gray and cold.

He reached his house again and stood a long time before the picture
of John Ovington until it seemed that the hard half sneer of the pictured
smile was meant for him, and when he slept that night the mockery of
the smile followed him.

IV

But when he rose the next morning and looked over the shimmer of
color running on the hills, a new hope swelled in him and a confidence
of power. But as the day drew on the thought of the papers in the cedar
box depressed him.

In the middle of the afternoon Hillton brought him a letter. Once
more he knew the contents before he broke the seal, but as he read the
expected words a sick feeling of suspense came over him.

Vincent Colvin has been with me all this morning. I am going
to ride away with him to-night. I have not forgotten, but I promised myself to him long ago, and now I shall keep the promise. My
father objects, so we are going out for a ride from which we shall
never come back. We will take the Newbury Road. Oh, my dear, it
breaks my heart to ride out of your life! It has all been so strange, so
maddeningly dear and painful. Must this be good-by?

Once the letter was finished the suspense left him. Automatically he ordered his trunk packed and arranged his affairs as if he were about to go on a long journey. At sunset he went for the last time to look at the picture of the other John Ovington.

The smile twitched the lips and the sneer was doubly bitter.

After that he rode the black horse down the Newbury Road. He hardly knew what position to take, but when he came to a branching of the road the black horse of his own accord drew down to a walk. He had ridden him under the black shadow of an oak by the roadside before he remembered Hillton's story:

'And John Ovington waited for them at a forking of the Newbury Road.'

He would have ridden out and found some other waiting-place as he remembered, but a grim determination came up in him and he sat his horse motionless. He remained there for perhaps an hour. The moon came up and ran white along the road. Then a clatter of hoofs beat far away.

Colvin came first as they rounded the last turn, a large man riding strongly on a gray horse. They were a hundred yards away when Ovington rode out from beneath the tree, his hand raised.

Colvin brought his horse to a stop on grinding hoofs.

'Who the devil are you, sir?' he shouted. 'What do you mean by stopping me?'

'I haven't the least wish to stop you,' said Ovington calmly, 'but I intend to stop Beatrice Jervan to-night. As for you, you may ride to hell, for all of me.'

He could see Colvin's face set with fury.

'What authority have you for this?' he demanded, still partially controlling his voice.

'The authority of good sense,' smiled Ovington, 'which says that it is both too late and far too cold for a girl to be out riding.'

'Damn your impertinence,' cried Colvin. 'Get out of the road or I'll ride you down like a dog!'

'Ah,' said Ovington, 'you talk well, Colvin. But there is an older score to settle between us than you dream of. You must ride this way alone to-night.'

'You fool,' shouted Colvin, 'if you must have it, take it!'

As he spoke a revolver flashed in his hand, but as it dropped to the level Ovington spurred his black suddenly forward.

With his left hand he struck up Colvin's arm, and the revolver roared past his ear. With his right arm he seized Colvin about the waist and drew him bodily from the saddle.

As he swayed a moment struggling on the saddle-bow, Ovington swung his right hand free and struck. The blow fell behind Colvin's ear and he collapsed without a sound.

Ovington flung his limp body to the ground.

'You have killed him!' whispered Beatrice. 'Flee! Flee!'

'He's merely stunned,' said Ovington. 'Turn your horse. We ride another way this night.'

She reined her horse away and raised her riding-crop.

'Keep away,' she cried in a choked voice. 'I am afraid! Keep away. He has my promise – I shall not leave him!'

He laughed short and hard.

'Promise?' he said. 'Do you think that words will stop me to-night after I have conquered destiny at last? Do you dream that words will stop me? Then one way with both!'

As he spoke he rode upon her. The riding-crop fell upon his shoulder, but he did not notice it. He swept her from the saddle into his arms and crushed the parted lips fiercely against his own.

'Dearest,' he said, 'after four generations of waiting, I have returned for you and won you away from fate.'

Suddenly her straining body gave to him; he heard a murmuring and changed voice at his ear:

'Ride! Ride! He is stirring on the road. He is awakening!'

And as they spurred up the road he turned his head and saw the gray horse and the brown fleeing side by side far away with loose shaken bridle-reins and empty saddles.

Above the Law

Faust's first western story, 'Above the Law' originally appeared in *All-Story Weekly* (August 31, 1918) and until now has not been reprinted. Like 'John Ovington Returns,' published three months earlier, it shows a young author experimenting with a new genre, one he would use extensively during his career because it yielded quick income in an increasingly popular field. His editor and mentor at *All-Story Weekly*, Robert H. Davis, urged him to follow the example of Zane Grey, whose western stories were bestsellers and whom Davis had also published. But here, at the beginning, and throughout his western fiction as well, Faust shows a distinctive difference. This is a western story only because it is set in the West. It could take place anywhere, and this is why most of Faust's western fiction is unique. He rarely attempted what is generally called 'realism.' Instead, as author Jon Tuska expresses it in the second edition of the *Encyclopedia of Frontier and Western Fiction* (in preparation), Faust wrote 'fantasy, allegory, parable, [and] fairy tale' that happened to be set in the West. Or, as Robert Sampson put it in Volume One of *Yesterday's Faces* (Bowling Green Popular Press, 1983), 'The Brand stories exist in a singularly pure level, free of time's limits, in a world more open, more dangerous, more intense than our familiar present.'

The 1918 screen adaptation of 'Above the Law' starred Jewel Carmen and Henry Woodward (two notables of the day). It was the second in a long line of Faust stories that were adapted for the screen and featured major players. It was released by Fox under the title *Lawless Love*. Faust gives the impression that the story is set in California, and though it was actually photographed in the Huntington Lake region of California, the film was set in Arizona.

This is a timeless tale of two people finding love and new identities. Jerry is a self-reliant outsider, rather like Faust himself, and from any viewpoint an unusual western heroine. Faust was creating Dan Barry (*The Untamed,* Putnam, 1919), his first western antihero, at the same time he was creating Jerry, his first western antiheroine. When Jerry finally meets Black Jim, he too is an outsider. Like Barry, Black Jim resembles 'a powerful and sinisterly beautiful beast of prey.' Both embody the atavism that connects many of Faust's fictional characters with the animal world.

Likewise, both are western versions of Achilles, the Homeric super-warrior, and are typical of Faust characters based on classical models. Characteristically, too, in his first western story we encounter references to the works of Shakespeare, Malory, and Scott, three of Faust's favorite authors. Critics may question these references, but there was more high culture on the western frontier than one might believe. And the American slang characteristic of 1918, if almost gratuitous, is also almost Elizabethan in its flavor. This story expresses the conflict between Faust's desire for loving domesticity and his need for adventurous male freedom, a conflict which persisted in his later work.

I

HER EYES were like the sky on a summer night, a color to be dreamed of but never reproduced. From the golden hair to the delicate hands which cupped her chin, a flowerlike loveliness kept her aloof from her surroundings, like a rare pearl set in base metal. Her companion, young and darkly handsome, crumpled in a hand, scarcely less white than hers, the check which the waiter had left. In the meantime he gazed with some concern at his companion. Her lips stirred. She sighed.

'Two dollars for ham and – in jay dump,' she murmured. 'Can you beat it, Freddie?'

'He sort of sagged when we slipped him the order,' answered the dark and distinguished youth. 'I guess the hens are only making one-night stands in this country.'

'They've got an audience, anyway,' she returned, 'and that's more than more could draw!'

She opened her purse and passed two bills to him under the table.

'Why the camouflage?' he asked, as he took the money.

'Freddie,' she said, 'run your glass eye over the men in this joint. If they see you pay for the eats with my money, they'd take you for a skirt in disguise.'

A light twinkled for an instant far back in her eyes.

'Take me for a skirt?' said Frederick Montgomery in his most austere manner. 'Say, cutey, layoff on the rough stuff and get human.'

Her lazy smile caressed him. 'Freddie,' she purred, 'you do your dignity bit, the way Charlie Chaplin would do *Hamlet*.'

Mr. Montgomery scowled upon her, but the dollar bills in the palm of his hand changed the trend of his thoughts at once. 'Think of it, Jerry,' he groaned, 'if we hadn't listened to that piker Delaney, we'd be doing small big-time over the R. and W.!'

'Take it easy, deary,' La Belle Geraldine answered. 'I've still got a hundred iron men – but that isn't enough to take both of us to civilization.'

Montgomery cleared his throat, frowned, and raised his head like a patriot making a death speech in the third act. 'Geraldine,' he said solemnly, 'it ain't right for me to sponge on you. Now you take the money. It'll get you back to Broadway. As for me . . . I . . . I can go to work in one of the mines with these ruffians!'

La Belle Geraldine chuckled. 'You couldn't do it without a make-up, Freddie. And, besides, think of spoiling those hands with a pick-handle!'

Mr. Montgomery regarded his tender palms with a rather sad complacency. 'There's no other way out, Jerry. Besides, I can . . . I can. . . .' His voice trailed away drearily, and La Belle Geraldine regarded him with the familiar twinkle far back in her eyes.

'You're a born hero, Freddie – on the stage. But we're minus electric lights out here, and the play's no good.'

'We're minus, everything,' declared Freddie, with heat, overlooking the latter part of her speech. 'This joint hasn't even got a newspaper in it, unless you call this rag one.' He pulled out a crumpled paper, a single sheet printed raggedly on either side. Geraldine took it and regarded it with languid interest.

'The queer thing,' she muttered, as she read, 'is that I sort of like this rube gang out here, Freddie.'

'Like them?' snorted her companion, as he shook down his cuffs and tightened his necktie. 'Say, Jerry, you're talking in your sleep. Wake up and get next to yourself! Pipe the guy in the corner piling fried potatoes on his knife with a chunk of bread.'

She turned her head. 'Kind of neat action, all right,' she said critically. 'That takes real courage, Freddie. If his hand slipped, he'd cut his throat. Don't be so sore on them. As parlor snakes, they aren't in your class, but don't spend all your time looking at the stage set. Watch the show and forget the background, Freddie. These boys may eat with knives and get a little too familiar with their revolvers, but they strike me as being a hundred percent men.'

'You always were a nut, Jerry,' yawned Montgomery. 'For my part, give me the still small voice, but not the wilderness. I can see all the rough nature I want in the Central Park Zoo.'

He pushed back his chair.

'Wait a minute, Freddie. Hold the curtain while I play the overture. I've got an idea. Listen to this!'

She spread out the Snider Gulch *Clarion* and read:

'Attention, men of Snider Gulch, it's up to us! The citizens of Three Rivers have organized to rid the mountains of Black Jim. Prominent miners of that town have placed two thousand dollars on deposit, and offered it for the capture of the bandit, dead or alive. Men, is Snider Gulch going to be left behind by a jerk-water shanty village like Three Rivers? No! Let's get together. If Three Rivers can offer two thousand dollars for the capture of Black Jim, Snider Gulch can offer three thousand easy. We've got to show Three Rivers that we're on the map!'

'How's that for a line of talk, Freddie?'

'What's the point?' he queried. 'What do you get out of that mono-logue?'

'Wait a minute, the drums are still going out in the orchestra and your cue hasn't come yet. But before I get through I'm going to ring up the curtain on a three-act melodrama that'll fill the house and give the box office insomnia.'

She went on with the reading.

'We can't expect to land Black Jim in a hurry. The reward money will probably get covered with cobwebs before it's claimed. The men who get it will have their hands full, that's certain. If they can even find his hiding-place, they will be doing their share of work.

'There are a number of theories about the way he works. Some people think that he lives either in Snider Gulch or Three Rivers, and does his hold-ups on the side. No man has ever seen his face because of the black mask he wears over his eyes. All we know is that his hair is black and that he always rides a roan horse. But that ought to be enough to identify him.

'Some hold that he hides in some gulch with a lot of other outlaws. They don't think he leads a gang because he always works alone, but they believe that other gun-men have found his hiding-place and are living near him. If that is the case, and Black Jim can be found in his home, we will clean out the bandits who have given our town a black name.

'If Black Jim is caught, he will surely hang. He hasn't killed any-one yet, but he's wounded nine or ten, and if he's ever pressed hard there's sure to be a lot of bloodshed. However, it's up to the brave men of Snider Gulch to take the chance. If they get him, they'll prob-ably get the rest of the gun-fighters who have been sticking up stages (which is Black Jim's specialty), and robbing and killing lone miners and prospectors, which is the long suit of the rest of the crowd.

'In conclusion, all we have to say is that the men who get the money for Black Jim's capture will earn it, and our respect along with it.'

She dropped the paper.

'Now do you see, Freddie?'

'I'm no psychic wonder, Jerry,' he answered with some irritation. 'How can I tell what act you're thinking of? Wait a minute!' He gaped at her with sudden astonishment. 'Say, Jerry,' he growled, 'have you got a hunch that *I'm* going to go out and catch this man-eating Black Jim?'

She broke into musical laughter.

'Freddie,' she said, when she could speak again. 'I'd as soon send you to capture the bandit as I'd send a baby with a paper knife to capture a machine gun. No, deary, I know you want to get out of here, but I don't want you to start East in a coffin. It costs too much!'

'Slip it to me easy, Jerry,' he said, 'or I'll get peeved.'

'Don't make me nervous,' she mocked. 'I don't ask you to do any-thing rough except to put on clothes like the ones the guys around here are wearing – heavy boots, overalls, broad-brimmed hat, red bandanna around the neck.'

He stared at her without comprehension.

'Do you think they'll pay to see me in an outfit like that?'

'They ought to, and it's my idea to make them. It's a nice little bit for us both, Freddie. First act starts like this. Stage set: A western mining town, Three Rivers. Enter the lead – a girl, stunning blonde, wears corduroy walking skirt.'

Montgomery grinned but still looked baffled.

'You hate yourself all right,' he said, 'but lead on the action.'

'Nobody knows why the girl is there, and nobody cares, because they don't ask questions in a mining town.'

'Not even about the theater,' groaned Montgomery.

'Shut up, Freddie,' cut in La Belle Geraldine. 'You spoil the scene with your monologue stunts. I say, the swell blonde appears and buys a seat on the stage which starts that afternoon, running towards Truckee. She kids the driver along a little and he lets her sit on the seat beside him. As soon as she gets planted there, she begins to talk – let me see – yes, she begins to hand out a swift line of chatter about what she can do with a revolver. Then she shows him a little nickel-plated revolver which she carries with her. He asks her to show off her skill, but she says "Nothing stirring, Oscar." Finally they go around a curve and out rides a masked bandit on a roan horse. Everybody on the stage holds up their arms as soon as he comes out with his gun leveled.'

'How do you know they would?' said Montgomery.

'Because they always do,' answered Geraldine. 'Nobody thinks of making a fight when a masked man on a roan horse appears, because they know it's Black Jim, who can shoot the core out of an apple at five hundred yards, or something like that. Well, they all hold up their hands except the girl, who raises her revolver and fires, and though she used a blank cartridge the gun jumps out of the grip of the bandit as if a bullet hit it. Then he holds up his hands and everybody on the stage cheers, and the girl takes the bandit prisoner. The stage turns around and carries them back to Three Rivers. The people of the town come to look at Black Jim. . . .'

'And they see I'm not the guy they want. Then the game's blown.'

'Not a hope,' said Jerry. 'They don't know anything about this man-killer except the color of his horse. They'll take you for granted.'

'Sure,' groaned Montgomery, 'and hang me to the nearest tree, what?'

'Take it easy, Freddie. There's *some* law around here. You just keep your face shut after they take you. They'll wait to try you the next day, anyway. That'll give me time to cash in the reward. I'll be fifty miles past before they get wise. The next morning when they come in to stick a rope on your neck, you simply light a cigarette and tell them it's all a mistake. Let 'em go to Snider Gulch to the hotel and they can find a hundred people to recognize you as a ham actor. Tell them you were merely trying a little act of your own when you stuck up the stage and that your partner flashed the gun from the driver's seat. Say, kid, the people of Three Rivers will see the laugh is on them, and they'll buy you a ticket to Denver just to get rid of you. I'll meet you there, and then we'll trot on to Broadway, savvy? It's a dream!'

'A nightmare,' growled Montgomery, though light entered his face. 'But still. . . .'

'Well?'

'Jerry, I begin to think it wouldn't be such a hard thing to get away with this! But what if you couldn't get me out of the tow? What if they started to lynch me without waiting for the law?'

'That's easy,' smiled Geraldine. 'Then I step out and tell them it's simply one grand joke. All we would have to be sorry about is the money we spent on your horse and clothes and gun. It's a chance, Freddie, but it's a chance that's worth taking. Two thousand dollars reward!'

Montgomery's eyes hardened.

'Jerry,' he whispered, 'every stage that leaves Three Rivers has a lot of pure gold in the boot. Why not play the bandit part legitimate and grab the gold? It's a lot simpler, and there's no more risk.'

Geraldine studied him curiously.

'You've got the makings of a fine crook, Freddie. It's in your eye now.'

He colored and glanced away.

'It's no go, deary. If we cheat these miners with my little game, at least we know that the money comes only from the rich birds who can afford to put up a reward. But if we grab the cash in the boot, how can we tell we aren't taking the bread and jam out of the mouth of some pick swinger with a family to support?'

She finished with a smile, but there was a suggestion of hardness in her voice.

'Jerry,' he answered, 'you're certainly fast in the bean. I'd go a ten-spot to a Canadian dime that you could make up with one hand and darn stockings with the other. We'll do it your way, if you insist. It'll be a great show.'

'Right you are, Freddie. You've got the face for the act.'

They had to spread a hundred dollars over a horse, a revolver, and Montgomery's clothes. He spent most of the day shopping and at night came home with the necessary roan, a tall animal which was cheapened by bad ring-bones. His clothes, except the hat and boots, were very inexpensive, and he managed to buy a second-hand revolver for six dollars.

While he made these purchases, La Belle Geraldine, now registered at the 'hotel' under her real name as Annie Kerrigan, opened a conversation with the girl who worked in the store. She proved diffident at first, with an envious eye upon Jerry's hat with its jaunty feather curled along the side, but in the end La Belle's smile thawed the cold.

'She handed me the frosty eye,' reported Jerry to Montgomery that evening, 'until I put her wise on some millinery stunts. After that it was easy. She told me all she knew about Black Jim, and a lot more. People say he's a big chap – so are you, Freddie. His complexion is dark – so is yours. One queer thing is that he has never killed anyone. The paper said that and the girl said it too. It seems he's a big-time guy with a gun, and when he shoots he can pick a man in the arm or the leg, just as he pleases. I don't suppose you can hit a house, at ten yards, Freddie, but it's a cinch they aren't going to try you out with a revolver – not as long as they have a hunch you're Black Jim.'

That night Montgomery learned all that could be told about the stage route and the time it left Three Rivers. By dawn of the next day he and Jerry were on the road towards Three Rivers by different routes.

II

The happiness of women, say the moralists, depends upon their ability to preserve illusions. Annie Kerrigan punched so many holes in that rule that she made it look like a colander. Illusions and gloom filled her earlier girlhood in her little Illinois home town. Those illusions chiefly concerned men. They made the masculine sex appear vast in strength and illimitable in mystery.

She remembered saying to a youth who wore a white flower in his lapel and parted his hair in the middle and curled it on the sides: 'When I talk to you, I feel as if I were poking at a man in armor. I never find the *real* you. What is it?'

The youth occupied two hours in telling her about the real you. He was so excited that he held her hand as he proceeded in the revelation. When he left, she boiled down everything he had said. It was chiefly air, and all that wasn't air was surrounded with quotation-marks so large that even Annie Kerrigan could see them. So she revised her opinion of men a little.

In place of part of the question-marks she substituted quotations.

As she grew older and prettier, she learned more. In fact she learned a good deal more than she wished to know about every attractive youth in her town.

So Annie Kerrigan started out to conquer new worlds of knowledge.

Her family balked, but Annie was firm. She went to Chicago, where she found the stockyards – and more men. They smiled at her in the streets. They stared at her in restaurants. They accosted her at corners. So the mystery wore off.

About this time Annie was left alone in the world to support herself. She starved for six months in a department store. Then an enterprising theatrical manager offered her a chance in a third-rate vaudeville circuit.

Before that season ended she had completed her definition of men. In her eyes they were one-half quotation-marks and the other half bluff. Every one of them had his pet mystery and secret. Annie Kerrigan found that if she could get them to tell her that secret, they forged their own chains of slavery and gave her the key to the lock.

In time she held enough keys to open the doors of a whole city full of masculine souls. But she never used those keys, because, as she often said to herself, she wasn't interested in interior decoration. The exceptions were when she wanted a raise in salary or a pleasure excursion.

In this manner Annie Kerrigan of many illusions and more woes developed into La Belle Geraldine with no illusions: a light heart and a conscience that defied insomnia. She loved no one in particular – not even herself – but she found the world a tolerably comfortable place. To be sure, it was not a dream world. La Belle Geraldine was so practical that she knew cigarettes stain the fingers yellow and increase the pulse. She even learned that Orange Pekoe tea is pleasanter than cocktails, and that men are more often foolish than villainous.

Without illusions, the mental courage of Jerry equaled that of a man. Therefore she commenced this adventure without fear or doubt of the result. It was a long journey, but her lithe, strong body, never weakened by excess, never grown heavy with idleness, shook off the fatigue of the labor, as a coyote that has traveled all day and all night shakes off its weariness and trots on, pointing its keen nose against the wind. So she went on, sometimes humming an air, sometimes pausing an instant to look across the valley at the burly peaks – and far beyond these, range after range of purple-clad monsters, like a great hierarchy whose heads rise closer and closer to heaven itself. She found herself smiling and for no cause whatever.

She had estimated the distance to Three Rivers at about ten miles.

Yet it seemed to her that she had covered scarcely a third of that space when the road twisted down and she was in the village. It was even smaller than Snider Gulch. The type of men to which she had grown accustomed during the past few weeks swarmed the street. They paid little attention to her, even as she had expected. Mountains discourage personal curiosity.

The six horses were already hitched to the stage and baggage was piled in the boot. After she bought a passage to Truckee, her money was exhausted. If she failed, the prospect was black indeed. She could not even telegraph for help, particularly since there was not a telegraph line within two days' journey. She shrugged this thought away as unworthy.

When the passengers climbed up to select their seats, Geraldine remained on the ground to talk with the driver about his near leader, a long-barreled bay with a ragged mane and a wicked eye. The driver, as he went from horse to horse, examining tugs and other vital parts of the harness, informed her that the bay was the best mountain horse he had ever driven, and that with this team he could make two hours' better time than on any of the other relays between Three Rivers and Truckee.

She showed such smiling interest in this explanation that he asked her to sit up on his seat while he detailed the other points of interest about this team. Her heart quickened. The first point in the game was won. As they swung out onto the shadowed road – for the cañons were already half dark, though it was barely sunset – she made a careful inventory of the passengers. There were nine besides herself and all were men. Two of them, sitting just behind the driver, held sawed off shotguns across their knees and stared with frowning sagacity into the trees on either side of the road, as if they already feared an attack. Their tense expectancy satisfied La Belle Geraldine that the first appearance of her bandit would take the fight out of them. The others were mostly young fellows who hailed each other in loud voices and broke into an immediate exchange of mining gossip. She feared nothing from any of these.

The driver worried her more. To be sure his only weapon was a rifle which lay along the seat just behind him, with its muzzle pointing out to the side, a clumsy position for rapid work. But his lean face with the small, sad eyes made her guess at qualities of quiet fearlessness. However, it was useless to speculate on the chances for or against the masked and waiting Montgomery! The event could not be more than half an hour away.

They had scarcely left Three Rivers behind when she produced the small revolver from her pocket. The driver grinned and asked if it were loaded. It was a sufficient opening for Geraldine. She sketched briefly for his benefit a life in the wilds during which she had been brought up with a rifle in one hand and a revolver in the other. The stage driver heard her with grim amusement, while she detailed her skill in knocking squirrels out of a tree top.

'The top of a tree like that one, lady?' he asked, pointing out a great sugar pine.

'You don't believe me?' asked Jerry, with a convincing assumption of pique, 'I wish there was a chance for me to show you.'

'Hmm!' said the driver. 'There's a tolerable lot of things for you to aim at along the road. Take a whirl at anything you want to. The horses won't bolt when they hear the gun.'

'If I did hit it,' said Jerry, with truly feminine logic, 'you would think it was luck.'

She dropped the pistol back into the pocket of her dress. They were swinging round a curve which brought them to the foot of the long slope, at the top of which Montgomery must be waiting.

'I hope something happens,' she assured the driver, 'and then I'll show you real shooting.'

'Maybe,' he nodded, 'I've lived so long, nothin' surprises me, lady.'

She smiled into the fast-growing night and made no answer. Then she broke out into idle chatter again, asking the names of all the horses and a thousand other questions, for a childish fear came to her that he might hear the beating of her heart and learn its meaning. Up they drudged on the long slope, the harness creaking rhythmically as the horses leaned into the collars, and the traces stiff and quivering with the violence of the pull. The driver with his reins gathered in one hand and the long whip poised in the other, flicked the laggards with the lash.

'Look at them lug all together as if they was tryin' to keep time!' he said to Geraldine. 'I call that a team, but this grade here keeps them winded for a half an hour after we hit the top.'

The rank odor of the sweating horses rose to her. A silence, as if their imaginations labored with the team, fell upon the passengers. Even Geraldine found herself leaning forward in the seat, as though this would lessen the load.

'Yo ho, boys!' shouted the driver. 'Get into that collar, Dixie, you wall-eyed excuse for a hoss! Yea, Queen, good girl!'

His whip snapped and hummed through the air.

'One more lug altogether and we're there!'

They lurched up onto the level ground and the horses, still leaning forward to the strain of the pull, stumbled into a feeble trot. Jerry sat a little sidewise in the seat so that from the corner of her eye she could watch the rest of the passengers. One of the guards was lighting a cigarette for the other.

'Hands up!' called a voice.

The driver cursed softly, and his arms went slowly into the air; the hands of the two guards shot up even more rapidly. Not three yards from the halted leaders, a masked man sat on a roan horse, reined across the road, and covered the stage with his revolver.

'Keep those hands up!' ordered the bandit. 'Now get out of that stage – and don't let your hands down while you're doin' it! You-all there by the driver, get up your hands damned quick!'

III

A great tide of mirth swelled in Jerry's throat. She recognized in these deep and ringing tones, the stage voice of Freddie Montgomery. Truly he played his part well!

She crouched a little toward the stage driver, whipped out the revolver, and fired – but a louder explosion blended with the very sound of her shot. The revolver spun out of her fingers and exquisite pain burned her hand.

Her rage kept her from screaming. She groaned between her set teeth. This was an ill day for Frederick Montgomery!

'For God's sake!' breathed a voice from the stage behind her. 'He'll kill us all now! It's Black Jim!'

'Down to the road with you,' cried the bandit, in the same deep voice, 'and the next of you-all that tries a fancy trick, I'll drill you clean!'

Warm blood poured out over her hands and the pain set her shuddering, but the white hot fury gave her strength. Jerry was the first to touch the ground.

'You fool!' she moaned. 'You big, clumsy, square-headed, bat-eyed fool! They'll stick you in the pen for life for this!'

'Shut up!' advised a cautious voice from the stage, where the passengers stood bolt upright, willing enough to descend, but each afraid to move. 'Shut up or you'll have him murdering us all!'

'Sorry, lady,' said the masked man, and still he maintained that heavy voice. 'If I had seen you was a girl, I wouldn't have fired!'

'Aw, tell that to the judge,' cried Geraldine. 'You've shot my hand off! I'll bleed to death and you'll hang for it! I tell you, you'll hang for it!'

He had reined his horse from his position in front of the leaders and now he swung from his saddle to the ground, a sudden motion during which he kept his revolver steadily leveled.

'Easy in there!' he ordered, 'and get the hell out of that stage or I'll blow you out!' He gestured with his free hand to Jerry. 'Tear off a strip from your skirt and tie that hand up as tight as you can! Here, one of you, get down here and help the lady. You can take your hands down to do that!'

But there was another thought than that of La Belle Geraldine in the mind of the practical stage driver. His leaders stood now without obstruction. He had lost one passenger, indeed, but the gold in the boot of his stage was worth a hundred passengers to him. He shouted a warning, dropped flat on his seat, and darted his whip out over the horses. At his call the other passengers groveled flat, which put the thickness of the boot between them and the bullets of the bandit. The horses hit the collars and the stage whirled into the dusk of the evening.

To pursue was folly, for it would be a running fight with two deadly shotguns handled by men concealed and protected. The masked man fired a shot over the heads of the fugitives and turned on Jerry. She was weak with excitement and loss of blood and even her furious anger could not give her strength for long. She staggered.

'I'm done for, all right,' she gasped. 'As a bandit, you're the biggest cheese ever. My hand . . . blood . . . help. . . .'

Red night swam before Jerry's eyes and, as utter dark came, she felt an arm pass round her. When she woke from the swoon, her entire right arm ached grimly. She was being carried on horseback up a steep mountain side. The trees rose sheer above her. She strove to speak, but the intolerable weakness flooded back on her and she fainted again.

She recovered again in less pain, lying in a low-roofed room, propped up on blankets. A lantern hung against the wall from a nail and, by its light, she made out the form of the man who stooped over her and poured steaming hot water over her hand. He still wore the mask. She closed her eyes again and lay gathering her wrath, her energy, and her vocabulary, for the supreme effort which confronted her.

'So you did your little bandit bit, did you?' she said at last with keen irony, as she opened her eyes again. 'You had to pull the grandstand stunt with a fine audience of ten to watch you? You had to. . . .'

'Lie still, don't talk' he commanded, still in that deep and melodramatic bass which enraged her. 'You have a fever, kind of. It ain't much. Just keep quiet an' you'll be all right.'

It was the crowning touch! He was still playing his part!

'Deary,' she said fiercely, 'this is the first time in my life I ever wished I was Shakespeare. Nobody but the old boy himself could do you justice – but I'm not Billy S. and I can only hint around sort of vague at what I think of you. But of all the tin-horn sports, the ham-fat, small-time actors, you're the prize bonehead. Honey, does that begin to percolate? Does that begin to get through the armor plate down to that dwarfed bean you're in the habit of calling your brain?'

He went on calmly pouring the hot water over her hand. She had not credited him with such self-control. He did not even blush as far as she could make out. It made her throat dry with impotence.

'An old woman's home, that's where you belong,' she went on. 'Say, you're wise to keep that mask on. You'd need a disguise to get by as a property man on small-time. Deary, you haven't got enough bean to be number two man in a monologue.'

He stared at her a moment and then went on with the work of cleansing the bullet wound in her hand. Evidently he did not trust himself to speak. It was not a severe cut, but it had bled freely, the bullet cutting the fleshy part between the thumb and forefinger. To look at it made her head reel. She lay back on the pile of blankets and closed her eyes.

When she opened them again he was approaching with a small bottle half full of a brownish-black fluid, iodine. She started, for she knew the burn of the antiseptic. She tucked her wounded hand under her other arm and glared at him.

'Nothing doing with that stuff, cutey,' she said, shaking her head. 'This isn't my first season, even if I'm not on the big-time. You can give that bottle to the marines. Go pour that on the daisies, Alexander W. Flathead, it'll kill the insects. But not for mine!'

She saw his forehead pucker into a frown above the mask. He stopped, hesitated.

'Take it away and rock it to sleep, Oscar,' she went on, 'because there's no cue for that in this act. It won't get across – not even with a make-up. Oh, this will make a lovely story when I get back to Broadway. I'm going to spill the beans, deary. Yep, I'm going to give this spiel to the papers. It'll make a great ad for you – all scare heads. You can run the last musical comedy scandal onto the back page with a play like this. Here! Let go my arm, you big simp – do you think. . . .'

He caught her wrist and drew out the injured hand firmly. She struggled weakly, but the pain in the hand unnerved her.

'Go ahead – turn on the fireworks, Napoleon! Honey, they'll write this on your tombstone for an epitaph.'

He spread her thumb and forefinger apart, poured some of the iodine onto a clean rag, and swabbed out the wound. The burning pain brought her close to a faint, but her fury kept her mind from oblivion. She clenched her teeth so that a tortured scream became merely a moan. When she recovered, he was making the last turn of a rather skillful bandage. She sat up on the blankets.

'All right, honey, now you've played the music and I'll dance. What's the way to town from here?'

He shook his head.

'Won't tell me, eh? I suppose you think I'll stay up here till I get well? Think again, janitor.'

She rose and started a bit unsteadily toward the door. Before she reached it his step caught up with her. She was swung up in strong arms and carried back to the blankets. While she sat dumb with hate and rage, he took a piece of rope and tied her ankles fast with an intricate knot which she could never hope to untie with her one sound hand.

'You'll stay here,' he explained curtly.

'Listen, deary,' she answered between her teeth, 'I'm going to do you for this. I'm going to make you a bum draw on every circuit in the little old U.S. I'm going to make you the card that doesn't fill the straight, that's all. Get your shingle ready, cutey, because after this all you can get across will be a chop-house in the Bowery.'

'Lie still,' growled the deep voice. 'There ain't any chance of you getting away. Savvy?'

He turned.

'Deary,' she cried after him, 'if you don't cut out that ghost voice stunt, I'll. . . .'

The rickety door at the back of the shack closed upon him.

'I never knew,' said Jerry to herself, 'that that big Swede could do such a swell mystery bit. He ought to be in the heavies, that's all.'

She settled herself back on the blankets again more comfortably. The last sting of the iodine died away and left a pleasant sense of warmth in her injured hand. Now she set about surveying her surroundings in detail. It was the most clumsily built house she had ever seen, made of rudely trimmed logs so loosely set together that the night air whistled through a thousand chinks.

Two boards placed upon sawhorses represented a table. A crazily constructed fireplace of large dimensions was the only means of heating the shack. Here and there from pegs and nails driven into the wall hung overalls, deeply wrinkled at the knees, heavy mackintoshes, and two large hats of broad brim. On the floor were several pairs of heavy shoes in various states of dilapidation. In the corner next to the hearth the walls were garnished with a few pots and pans. On the table she saw a heavy hunting knife.

There were three doors. Perhaps one of them led to a second room. To know which one was of vital significance to her. If it was the door through which the masked man had disappeared, then he was still within hearing distance. If that were true, she could hardly succeed in reaching that knife upon the table unheard, for she would make a good deal of noise dragging herself across the floor to the table. She determined to make the experiment. If she could cut the bonds and escape, she made no doubt that she could find the road to Three Rivers again, and even to wander across the mountains at night with a wounded hand was better than to stay with this bungler. Moreover, there was something in his sustained acting which made her uneasy. She knew his code of morals was as limited as the law of the Medes and the Persians and of an exactly opposite nature. On the stage, in the city, she had no fear of him. He was an interesting type and his vices were things at which she could afford to shrug her shoulders. But in the wilderness of the silent mountains even the least of men borrows a significance, and the meaning he gave her was wholly evil.

She commenced hunching herself slowly and painfully across the floor toward the table. Half, three-quarters of the distance was covered. In another moment she could reach out and take the knife.

A door creaked behind her. She turned. There he stood again, still masked and with his hands behind him. He started. His mouth gaped. She made another effort and caught up the knife. At least it was a measure of defense, even if it were too late for her to free herself.

'Jerry!' he said, in a strange, whispering voice.

She eyed him with infinite disgust.

'Playing a new role, Freddie, aren't you?' she sneered.

He merely stared.

'You're versatile, all right,' she went on. 'First the grim bandit, and then the astonished friend. Say, deary, do you expect "warm applause"? No, cutey, but if I had some spoiled eggs, I'd certainly pass them to you.'

'Jerry, you're raving!'

She gritted her teeth.

'I'm through with the funny stuff, you one-syllable, lock-jawed baby. Now I mean business. Get me out of this as fast as they hooked you off the boards, the last time you tried out in Manhattan.'

'Do you . . . have . . . will. . . .'

'Bah!' she said. 'Don't you get next that. I'm through with this one night stand? Drop the curtain and start the orchestra on "Home, Sweet Home." Talk sense. Cut this rope. I'm starting and I'm starting alone.'

'For God's sake, Jerry.'

'Lay off on that stuff, deary. If words made a cradle, you'd rock the world to sleep.'

'How . . . how did you come here?'

She stared at him a moment and then broke into rather sinister laughter.

'I suppose you've been walking in your sleep, what? I suppose I'm to fall for this bum line, Freddie? Not me! You can't get by even in a mask, Mr. Montgomery.'

'Geraldine.'

'Can the talk, cutey. You can tell the rest to the judge.'

'But how can I help you?' he asked. He turned and she saw his hands tied securely together behind him!

While she still stared at this marvelous revelation, the door opened again and another Montgomery strode into the room. He was the same build as the other man. He wore the same sort of mask. His hair was black. He could not be Montgomery. It was only when they stood together that she felt a significant difference in this man. Seeing Jerry with the hunting knife in her hand, he crossed the room and leaned above her.

'Give me the knife,' boomed the musical bass voice.

She shrank back and clutched the heavy handle more closely.

'Keep away,' she cried hoarsely.

'Give me the knife.'

'Black Jim!' breathed Jerry, for the first time wholly frightened, while her mind whirled in confusion. 'Is the whole world made up of doubles or am I losing my brain? Keep off, Mr. Mystery, or I'll make hash of you with this cleaver!'

She held the knife poised and the man observed her with a critical eye.

'Fighter,' he decided.

He leaned forward and his hand darted out with the speed of a striking snake. She cut at him furiously, but the hand caught her wrist and stopped the knife while it was still an inch from his face. He shook her hand, and the numbing grasp made her fingers relax. The knife clattered on the floor and he carried her back to the pile of blankets. When she opened her eyes, she saw Black Jim loosing the hands of Montgomery.

'No use in we-all stayin' masked any more,' said the bandit. 'I've been down an' seen the other boys. I thought maybe they'd vote yes on turnin' the girl loose again. I told 'em she was too sick to see anything when I brought her in. I told 'em I'd blindfold her when I took her out to the road again. But they-all sort of figure she'd be able to track back with a posse followin' jest a sense of direction like a hoss. They vote that she stays here, an' so it makes no difference what she sees.'

He finished untying Montgomery's hands, and drew off his mask.

Her faintness left Jerry. She saw a lean-faced man with great, dark eyes, singularly lacking in emotion, and forehead unfurrowed by worries. Montgomery, likewise withdrew his mask and showed a face familiar enough, but drawn and colorless.

'All I'm askin',' said Black Jim, 'is have you got anything against me?'

'I?' queried Montgomery, and he drew a slow hand across his forehead as if he were partially dazed.

'Yes, you,' said the other, and the dark eyes dwelt carefully on Montgomery's face. 'If you've got any lingerin' suspicion that there's something coming from you to me, we'll jist nacherally step out an' make our little play where there's room.'

'Not a thing against you, my friend,' said Montgomery with a sudden heartiness for which Jerry despised him. 'You had the drop on me and I guess you had special reasons for wanting that stage.'

The outlaw shrugged his shoulders.

'I got to go out again,' he said, 'an' I'm goin' to ask you to watch this girl while I'm gone.'

'Glad to,' said Montgomery.

Black Jim turned, paused, and came back. 'If anything happens to her, my friend.' He hesitated significantly. 'The boys seemed to be sort of excited when I told them about her bein' in my cabin,' he explained. 'If they-all come up here, don't let 'em come in. You got a gun!'

He stepped to the door and was gone. The eyes of Jerry and Montgomery met.

'Quick!' she ordered. 'Talk out and tell me what has happened, Freddie, or I'll go crazy! I'm half out of my head now!'

'It's Black Jim!' he said heavily.

'I knew that half an hour ago. Your brains are petrified, Freddie. Start where I'm a blank. How'd you come here?'

'He held me up!'

'Black Jim?'

'Yes. I was waiting behind the rock with my mask on. I heard a horse coming up the road from behind and, when I turned, I was looking into the mouth of a pistol as big as a cannon. I put up my hands. I just stared at him. I couldn't speak. He said he was sorry he couldn't leave the job to me. He said there were two things clear to him. He went on thinking them over while his gun covered me. Then he told me that he couldn't leave me alive near the road. He had to take me up to his camp. Then he came up behind me and tied my hands behind my back. Jerry, I felt that if he hadn't thought me one of his own sort, he'd have dropped the curtain on my act forever!'

He shuddered slightly at the thought.

'He made me ride before him up here,' he went on, 'and he put me in this cabin. As far as I can make out, we're in a little gulch of the mountains. It's a sort of bandits' refuge. When we rode over the edge of the hill and dipped down into the valley, I saw some streaks of smoke down the cañon. There must be a half dozen places like this one, and some of the outlaws in every one. What'll we do, Jerry, for God's sake, what will we do?'

'Shut up!' she said fiercely, and her face was whiter than mere exhaustion could make it. 'Lemme think, just lemme think!'

Montgomery had no eye for her. He strode up and down the room with a wild expression. He seemed to think of her as an aftermath.

'What happened to you? Was it Black Jim again?'

'I pulled my gun and shot in the air. He shot the pistol out of my fingers and put my hand on the blink. I fainted. He brought me up here. That's all.'

Her thoughts were not for her troubles.

'I'm going to make a break for it!' he cried at last. 'Maybe I can get free!'

'And leave me here?' she asked.

He flushed, stammered, and avoided her eyes.

'It doesn't make any difference,' he muttered. 'I couldn't find my way out, and maybe they'd take a pot shot at me as I tried to get away. It's better to die quick than starve in the mountains. But, my God, Jerry, what'll he do when he finds out that I'm not an outlaw like himself?'

'Stop crying like a baby,' she said. 'I've got to think. There's only one thing for you to do,' she said at last, raising her head, 'and that's for you to play your part as he sees it. You can act rough. Go down and mix with them – but be here with me when Black Jim is here. They can only kill you, Freddie, but me. . . .'

Her eyes were roving again.

'Maybe I can do it,' he said rapidly, half to himself. 'Pray God I can do it!'

Her upper lip curled. 'You're in a blue funk – a blue funk,' she said. 'Freddie, here's your one chance in a lifetime to play the man. Do you see *my* condition? Do you see the little act that's mapped out ahead for me? It's as clear as the palm of your hand. He brought me up here because he thought I'd die if he left me in the road. Even his heart was not black enough for that! But once he had me here it wasn't in his power to send me away again. That's what he meant when he said he had talked to the "boys." They wouldn't let me go because they thought I might be able to find the way back and bring a posse after them. Don't you see? They have me a prisoner. And you're all that I have to protect me.' She stopped and moaned softly. 'Why was I ever born a woman?'

He moistened his lips.

'I'll do what I can,' he mumbled, 'but – did you see that devil's eye? He isn't human, Jerry!'

'I might have known,' she murmured to herself, 'I might have known he was only a stage man.' She said aloud: 'There's one chance in a thousand left to me, Freddie, but there's no chance at all unless you'll help me. Will you?'

'All that I can . . . in reason,' he stammered miserably.

'It's this,' she went on, trying to sweep him along with her. 'You had your eyes open when you came up here. Maybe you could find the way out again. Freddie, you said on the road today that you loved me. Freddie, I'll go to hell and slave for you as long as I live, if you'll fight for me now. Tell me again that you love me and you'll be a man!'

His lips were so stiff he could hardly speak in answer.

'I didn't tell you one thing,' he said. 'When we came over the top of the hill, at the edge of the valley, we passed an armed man. They keep a sentry there.'

She pointed with frantic eagerness.

'You have your gun at your belt! That will free us, I tell you. It is only one man you have to fight.'

He could not answer. His eyes wandered rapidly around the room like a boy already late for school and striving miserably to find his necessary book.

'Then if you won't do that, cut the rope that holds my feet and I'll go myself!' she cried. 'I'll go! I'd rather a thousand times die of starvation than wait for the time when the eyes of that fiend light up with hell-fire.'

'Black Jim,' he answered, and stopped.

She loosened her dress at the throat as if she stifled.

'For God's sake, Freddie. You have a sister. I've seen her picture. For her sake!'

He was utterly white and striving to speak.

'He would know it was me who did it,' he said at last, 'and then. . . .'

Voices sounded far away. They listened with great eyes that stared at each other but saw only their own imaginings.

The voices drew closer.

'The door! The door!' she whispered. 'Lock the door! They're coming – the men he warned us about!'

He was frozen to the spot on which he stood.

'Hello!' called a voice from without.

'Montgomery!' she moaned, wringing her hands.

At last he walked hastily to the door.

'You can't come in here,' he answered.

'Why the hell not?' roared one of them.

'Because of Black Jim.'

A silence followed.

'Is he in there?'

'No, but he wants no one else to come in while he's gone.'

They parleyed.

'Shall we chance it?' 'Not me!' 'Why not?' 'Let's see his woman.' 'Sure. Seein' her doesn't do no harm.' 'Who's in there?' 'It's the pal he brought up.' 'Are we goin' to act like a bunch of short horns?' asked a deeper voice. 'I'm goin' in!'

A dozen men broke into the room. At the first stir of the door Jerry dropped prone to the blankets and feigned sleep. The crowd gathered first about Montgomery, searching him with curious eyes.

'Here's the new lamb,' said a lithe, white-faced man, and he grinned over yellow teeth. 'Here's another roped for the brandin'. Let's pass on him now, boys!'

A chuckle, which rang heavily on the heart of Montgomery, ran around the circle, but though his soul was lead in him, his art came to his rescue. After all, this was merely a part to be played. It was a dangerous part, indeed, but with a little effort he should be able to pass before an uncritical audience. He leaned back against the wall and smiled at the group. It required every ounce of his courage to manage that smile.

'Look me over, boys,' he responded, 'take a good long look, and in case you're curious, maybe you'll find something interesting on my right hip!' He broke off the smile again. For one instant the scales hung in the balance. What he said might have been construed as a threat, but the smile took the sting out of his words. After all, a man who had been passed by Black Jim himself had some rights among them.

'You're a cool one, all right,' grinned a man who was bearded like a Russian, with his shirt open, and a great black, hairy chest partially exposed, 'but where'd you get that color? Been doing inside work?'

'Mac's the name,' said Montgomery, easily, for the last remark gave him courage, 'and some of the boys call me Silent Mac. I'm a bit off color, all right. That's because some legal gents got interested in me. They got so damned interested in me they thought I shouldn't be out in the sun so much. They thought maybe it was spoiling my complexion, see? They fixed a plant and sent me up the river to a little joint the government runs for restless people. Yep, I've just had a long rest cure, and now I'm ready for business!'

A low laugh of understanding ran around the group. A jail bird has standing in the shadow of the law.

'You'll do, pal,' said the yellow-toothed one.

'You can enter the baby show, all right,' said another. 'I'm the Doctor.'

'I've heard of you,' said Montgomery, as the crowd passed him to examine Jerry.

'Know anything about the calico?' one asked Montgomery.

'Not a thing,' answered the latter carelessly, 'except that Jim picked it off the stage.'

'And a damned bad job, too,' growled he of the beard. 'Where's he goin' to fence her up in a corral like this?'

'Bad job, your eye!' answered one who leaned far over to glance at her partially concealed face. 'She's a looker, boys – she's a regular Cleopatra.'

They grouped closely around her.

'Wake her,' suggested one, 'so's we can size her up.'

One who stood closer stirred her rudely with his foot. She sat up, yawning, rubbing her eyes, and smiled up to their faces.

'Turn me into a wall-eyed cayuse!' muttered one of them, but the others were silent while their eyes drank.

Montana Pete, with a mop of tawny hair falling low down on his forehead, dropped to a squatting position, the better to look into her eyes.

'Well, baby blue-eyes,' he grinned, 'what d'you think of your new pals?'

'Oh,' she cried, with a semblance of pretty confusion, 'I . . . I . . . where am I? Oh, I remember!'

'Boys,' said Montana Pete, rising, 'we ain't the kind to have a king, but I'm all for a queen! What?'

'Sure,' said the Doctor. 'There ain't nothing like the woman's touch to make a home.'

They roared with laughter.

'Look out! She's remembering some more and here comes the waterfall!' called another.

Jerry, in order to get time to plan her campaign, broke into heartrending sobs. The bearded man, who rejoiced in the name of Porky Martin, now came forward again.

'Lemme take care of her,' he said. 'I had two mothers, six sisters, an' fourteen sweethearts. I know all about women!'

He dropped to one knee and put his arm around her.

'Take it easy, kid. You're runnin' loose now an' we'll give you all the rope you want, except enough for hangin' yourself. Look around you, kid, here's enough men to make a jury and you got a home with every one. Am I right, boys?'

'Let me . . . alone!' wailed Jerry, and she shuddered under the caress.

'Huh!' growled Porky Martin. 'She's proud, damn her.'

'Give her time, give her time,' said the Doctor. 'The kid's hurt. She don't savvy yet, boys, that she's in a real democracy where everything's common property.'

'No more foolin',' advised Montana Pete. 'Jim'll be coming back any time. He'll sure be glad to find us here, I guess not.'

'Who's Black Jim?' snarled Porky Martin. 'I've stood for enough of his nutty ideas. I say to hell with Black Jim. We've had enough of him!'

'Say that to him,' said Montana easily. 'I won't hold your hands, Porky. Take it easy, kid' – this to Jerry – 'we ain't all swine.'

'Wha' d'ya mean?' said Porky in a rising voice.

Jerry trembled, for she knew that if the men began fighting over her, her fate was sealed.

'You ain't deer, I reckon,' said Montana Pete, with obvious scorn.

'Let me go!' cried Jerry, not that she hoped for freedom, but because she thought there was some chance of changing the issue. 'Let me go! I won't tell about you! I swear I won't!'

She extended her hands, one slender and white, and then the other in its ominously stained bandage, first to Porky Martin and then to Pete.

'Look at that,' said Pete. 'We're a fine gang to stand around makin' life hell for the kid.'

He dropped to one knee beside her.

'We'll give you a square deal, you lay to that, but we can't let you go. There ain't no hope of that, understand.'

She shrank against the wall, her sobs coming heavily at intervals.

'What I say is this,' orated Porky Martin. 'What do you make out of Jim bringin' in two people in one day – and one of them a woman?'

'Why, you poor fat head,' said the Doctor soothingly. 'Mac over there was blockin' one of Jim's plays an' to get him out of the way Jim took him up here. Anyway, Mac's one of us. What's bitin' you? She was hurt. Besides, maybe Jim wanted that woman's touch around his house.'

'Aye,' said Porky, 'but there's a lot more to be said about that. As far as I go, I'm sick of this feller who stays away from the rest of us – never even gets drunk with us – and now he gets a woman!'

'Look out!' warned a voice. 'I think. . . .'

Several heads turned to the open door which framed Black Jim. His eyes ran slowly from face to face until they settled on Montgomery. The men stirred uneasily.

'I told you-all to keep these out,' he said calmly to Montgomery. By his contemptuous gesture he might have been referring to dogs of the street.

'They said you'd changed your mind,' Montgomery explained.

'I ain't ever done that yet,' said the bandit. 'Hope you've enjoyed yourselves, boys.'

'Look here,' said Porky Martin, blustering. 'What we want to know is about the calico here . . . we. . . .'

'I told you about her before,' said Black Jim softly, 'and you sat around an' hollered an' said she was to stay here. It's too late to get rid of her now. She's seen us all. She could identify every one of us.'

'We ain't askin' you to send her off,' said Porky, 'but as long as she's goin' to stay here we don't see no nacheral reason why she has to hang around here in one cabin. We're boostin' for a lot of changes of scenery.'

'We?' asked Black Jim and he frowned.

'You heard me before, damn you!' He was half crouched with the fighting fury in his face. The rest of the men moved quickly back, leaving an open space between the two. Porky's hand tugged and writhed about the handle of his revolver as though he found difficulty in drawing it, but Black Jim made no movement toward his weapon. His soft, dark eyes dwelt without change on the face of his opponent. Jerry watched, utterly fascinated. She saw Montgomery staring in the background. The rest of the men stood closer to Porky, as if they sympathized with him, and their eyes were fixed with a sort of mute horror on Black Jim. An instinct told her that the moment he made a motion towards his revolver every gun in the room would be out and leveled at him. Yet, when the strange sympathy troubled her throat, it was not for the bandit who faced the roomful of enemies, but for the crouched, tense figure of Porky Martin. His big beard quivered. She saw his jaws stir. A strange, gurgling sound came in his throat, and yet he could not draw his revolver.

'My God!' breathed the Doctor.

It was as if some spell broke with his voice. A dozen breaths were audible in quick succession. Porky Martin drew a long pace back and half straightened. His hand left the butt of his revolver, and then both hands moved in slow jerks up toward his head. The gurgling rose louder in his throat. It formed into gasping words.

'Jim – don't shoot – for God's sake!'

The whole of that great body shook. A moment before he had been the most awe-inspiring of them all, and the center of Jerry's fears.

'Hypnotism,' she murmured to herself, but she did not believe her own diagnosis.

'Take your hands down, Porky,' said Black Jim. 'I ain't asked you to put 'em up there.'

In spite of this permission, the big man's arms remained as if fixed in air.

'Get out,' ordered Black Jim, and gestured toward the door.

Porky started sidewise, edging past Black Jim as if he feared to take his eyes off him. At the door he whirled and bolted suddenly into the dark. The order of the bandit had apparently been directed at Porky alone, but all the rest obeyed, each man moving silently, keeping his face with religious earnestness toward Jim and his hand on his revolver until he came to the door through which each vanished with startling swiftness. They were all gone. Montgomery alone remained. Jim faced him.

'Get out,' said the bandit, 'an' tell the rest of 'em that there's a dead-line drawn at the edge of the trees. They can cross it when they get tired of livin'.'

Jerry made vain motions to him with lips and hands to stay and wondered why she dared not speak out, but his eyes were not for her. Like the rest he moved sidewise, and darted out into the night. Black Jim turned to Jerry and she set her teeth to make her glance cross his boldly. There was a subtle change in his expression. He jerked a hand toward the door.

'That last man,' he said, 'did you really want him to stay?'

'Yes,' she said faintly, 'I'm afraid!'

To her astonishment he nodded slowly.

'Yes,' he said, 'they-all ain't much more'n cattle.'

With that he disappeared into the next room. He came back at once bearing a holstered revolver which he dropped beside her carelessly.

'They're a rotten gang, all right,' he went on, 'and that last man – why did you want him to stay?'

Under the direct question of his eyes, her own dropped till they fell upon the revolver butt, significantly protruding from the holster.

'You don't need to tell me,' he said gently. 'I guess you thought you'd be safer with two. But that pale-faced one ain't a man. He's a skunk. I told him to keep 'em out.'

She did not answer. Her head remained bowed with wonder. Montgomery had been no protection to her. Even now there were twelve grim men who were twelve dangers to her. Yet in the presence of this man-queller, she felt unutterably safe. She glanced at her injured hand and smiled at her sense of security. Black Jim retreated. He came back with a great armful of logs.

Hunger and weariness fought like drugs against the stimulus of fear. She found herself drowsing as she stared into the growing blaze of flames. Her ear caught the chink, the rattle, and the hiss of cookery. Then she watched as through a haze the tall figure of Black Jim, swart against the fire. Through her exhaustion, her suffering, and her fear, that shadowy figure became the symbol of the protector.

v

He came before her again carrying a tin plate that bore a steaming venison steak flanked with big chunks of bread and a cup of black coffee. She tasted the coffee first and it cleared her mind, pumped strong blood through her body again. Another woman would have roused to a paralyzing terror when her faculties returned, but she was used to men and she was not used to the fear of them. After all, what difference was there between this man and those she had known before? She had felt helpless indeed when the twelve filled the room. She had seen and she should never forget a certain flickering light of hunger in their eyes. They were dangerous, but that element of danger she did not see in Black Jim. Some men are dangerous to men alone. Others threaten all nature, born destroyers. She knew that Black Jim was of the first category. Nothing told her except a small inner voice that chanted courage to her heart. Consequently, when the hot coffee gave her strength, she sat erect, propping herself with her sound hand.

'I say!' she called. He started where he sat before his food at the table, lifted his head, and stared at her. 'What about these hobbles, deary?' she went on. His eyes widened, but he answered nothing. 'Cut out the silent treatment, cutey,' said Jerry, her courage rising, 'and this rope. You've got your stage guarded. There's no fear that I'll jump through the curtain to get to the audience. I can't run away. I'm not very slow, but bullets are a little faster. So drop the hobbles, Alexander. They're away out of date.'

He sat with knife poised and ear canted a trifle to one side as if he strained every effort to follow the meaning of her slang. At last he comprehended, nodded, and set her free with a few strokes of a knife.

'It's all right to let you go free,' he said, 'but you got to remember that this shack may be watched from now on. You could get away any time. I won't stop you. But outside you'll find maybe no bullets, but some of the boys who were in here a while ago. Savvy?'

She understood, but she shrugged the terror away, as she would have shrugged away self-consciousness on the stage.

'All right, Jimmy,' she said cheerfully, 'I savvy. Lend me a hand, will you?'

She reached up with a smile for him to assist her to her feet. His astonishment at this familiar treatment made his eyes big again, and Jerry laughed.

'It's all right, cutey,' she said. 'You've got a funny name, but you can't get by as a nightmare as far as I'm concerned. Not without a make-up. Can the glassy eye, and give me your hand.'

He extended his hand hesitatingly, and she drew herself erect with some difficulty, for she had remained a long time in a cramped position.

'It's all right to feed some Swede farmhand in the corner, Oscar, but not La Belle Geraldine. Nix. It isn't done. There's no red light on that table, is there?'

'Red light?' he repeated.

'Sure. I mean there's no danger sign. Say, deary, do I have to translate everything I say into Mother Goose rimes? I mean, may I eat at the table, or do I have to stay on the floor?'

He regarded her a moment with his usual somber concern. Then he turned and carried a stool to the table and brought her food to it.

'This is solid comfort,' declared Jerry, as she settled herself at the board, and she attacked the venison with great vigor.

There were certain difficulties, however, against which she had to struggle. Her right hand was useless to manage the knife, but she was able to steady the fork between the third and fourth fingers. With her left hand she tried to cut the meat, but progress in this way was highly unsatisfactory. In the midst of her labors a brawny hand carried away her plate.

She looked up with a laugh and surrendered her knife and fork.

'After all,' she said, 'you flashed the gun that put my hand to the bad. So it's up to you to do the prompting when I break down.'

He raised his eyes a moment to consider this statement, but he failed to find the clue to its meaning, went on silently cutting up the meat, and finally passed it back to her. Dumbfounded by this reticence, Jerry kept a suspicious eye upon him. Among the people with whom she was familiar, silence meant anger, plots, hatred. Evidently he turned the matter over seriously in his mind, for his gaze was fixed far away.

'Lady,' he said at last, meeting her inquiry with his dull, unreadable eyes, 'was you-all born with that vocabulary, or did you jest find it?'

Jerry rested her chin upon a clenched white fist while she smiled at him. 'You're wrong twice, Solomon,' she answered. 'An angel slipped it to me in a dream.'

'A dream like that is some nightmare,' nodded Black Jim. 'Would you-all mind wakin' up when you talk to me?' He chuckled softly.

'Say, Oscar,' said Jerry, 'I'd lay a bet that's the first time you've laughed this year.'

He was sober at once. 'Why?'

'The wrinkles around your eyes ain't worn very deep.'

He shrugged his shoulders and confined his attention to his plate for a time, as if the matter no longer interested him, but when she had half forgotten it he resumed, breaking into the midst of her chatter: 'Speakin' of wrinkles, you don't look more'n a yearling yourse'f. I would ask, how old are you, ma'am?'

The instinct of the eternal feminine made her parry the question for a moment. 'I'm old enough,' she answered, 'but take it from me, I don't have to wear a wig.'

'Hmm!' he growled, considering this evasive return. 'What I want to know is where you-all got to know so much?'

'Know so much?' repeated Jerry. 'On the level, Oscar, or speaking with a smile? I mean, do you ask that straight?'

'Straight as I shoot,' he said.

She leaned back, curiosity greater than her mirth. 'Honest,' said La Belle Geraldine, 'you've got me beat. You've got me feeling like a toe-dancer in the mud. You're the original mystery, all right. To hear people talk of you, you'd think Black Jim put the "damn" in "death." But if I just met you at a dance, I'd think you were so green you didn't know the first violin from the drummer.'

'Speakin' in general,' replied the bandit carefully, 'I get your drift, but even if I begin allowing for the wind. . . .'

'Meaning the way I talk, I suppose,' broke in Jerry.

'Even allowin' for that,' went on Black Jim, 'I don't think I could shoot straight enough to ring the bell. You've got me side-stepped.'

'Go on,' said Jerry, 'I'll keep them amused till you bring on the heavy stuff. What do you mean?'

'Well,' drawled Black Jim, 'you look a heap more like a picture of a lady I once saw in a soap ad than anything else. You're all pink an' white an' soft, with eyes like a two-day calf.'

'Go right on, Shakespeare,' murmured La Belle Geraldine. 'You can't make me mad.'

'When I brought you up here,' said Black Jim, 'I figured that when you come to, you'd begin yellin' an' hollerin' an' raisin' Cain. I was sort of steelin' myself to it when you opened your eyes a while ago. Lady . . .' – here he leaned across the table earnestly – 'I was expectin' a plumb hell of a time.' He grinned broadly. 'I got it, all right, but not the kind I thought.'

'I sure panned you some,' nodded Jerry. 'I thought. . . .' She stopped. To tell Black Jim that she thought she was talking to Frederick Montgomery when she recovered from her faint would be to expose that worthy. Once it were known that he was only a temporary bandit, his days in the valley would be short indeed. In his pose as a man-killer, an ex-convict, a felon in the shadow of the law, he was as safe as a child in the bosom of his family. Otherwise, a dozen practiced fighters would be hot on his trail. 'I was just sore,' concluded La Belle Geraldine, 'to think I had balled up everything by flashing a small-time act on a big-time stage.'

The pun amused her so that she broke into hearty laughter. The sound reacted on both her and the bandit. Though he fell silent again and scarcely spoke for the next hour or more, she thought that she could detect a greater kindliness about his eyes.

He went about cleaning up the tin dishes with singular deftness. When he concluded, he turned abruptly upon her.

'Time to turn in. You sleep there. I bunk in the next room. S'long!' He turned at the entrance of the other apartment. 'How's your hand?'

'Doing fine,' smiled Jerry. 'S'long, Jim!'

VI

She was still smiling when she slipped down among the blankets. For some time she lay there wondering. By all the laws of Nature she should not have closed an eye for anxiety. She pictured all the dangers of her position one by one, and then – smiled again! She *could* not be afraid of this man. The very terror he inspired in others was a warm sense

of protection around her. The weary muscles of her body relaxed by
slow degrees. The wind hummed like a muted violin through the trees
outside. She slept.

When she woke, a fire burned on the hearth brightly again, and the
room was filled with the savor of fried bacon and steaming coffee. Black
Jim sat at the table draining his tin cup. Jerry sat up with a yawn.

'Hello, Jim!' she called. 'Say, this mountain air is all the dope for hard
sleeping, what?'

He lowered the cup and smiled back at her. 'I'm glad you-all slept
well,' he drawled, and rose from the table. 'I'm goin' off on a bit of a
trip today,' he said, 'but before I go I want to tell you. . . .'

'My name's Geraldine,' she answered, 'but most people shorten it up
to Jerry.'

'Which I'd tell a man jest about hits you off,' he answered. 'You ain't
seen much of the valley. I suppose you'll want to explore around a lot,
an' you can go as far as you like, but jest pack that shootin'-iron with
you by way of a friend. Come here to the door and I'll show you how
far you can go.'

She followed him obediently and, standing at the entrance to the
shack, looked out over the silver-misted valley. Four guardian peaks
surrounded a gorge about a mile and a half long and half a mile wide,
narrowing toward the farther end where the entrance gap could not
have been more than a hundred yards in width. The shack of Black Jim
huddled against the precipitous wall of rock at the opposite extremity
of the valley and stood upon ground higher than the rest of the floor.
Great trees rose on all sides, and what she saw was made out through
the spaces between these monsters.

'Where are the others?' she asked.

He waved his hand in a generous circle. 'All around. Maybe you
could wander about for a month and never find where they stay. But if
you meet 'em they'll be gladder to see you than you'll be to see them.'

'And if I stay right here,' she asked him, 'would I be in danger from
them?'

'They came last night,' he said grimly, 'but I got an idea they won't be
in no hurry to come again. At the edge of those trees is a deadline. They
know if they come beyond that they're takin' their own chances. If you
see 'em come, make your gun talk for you.'

He stepped through the door and she followed him a pace into the open air. The big roan horse, lean of neck and powerful of shoulder, stood near, his bridle reins hanging over his head. Black Jim swung into the saddle.

'Jest hobble this one idea so it don't never get outside your brain,' he said. 'The men in this valley are only up here because they wanted to get above the law – and they are above it. The only law they know, the only law I know, is to play square with each other. Partner, I've busted that law by bringin' you in here. Accordin' to all the rules there ain't no place for anyone here exceptin' the men that's beyond the law. I dunno what they'll do. Maybe it's war. Maybe it ain't. Rope that idea and stick a brand on it. S'long, Jerry. An' don't get near that gap down to the far end of the valley.'

He spurred the roan through the trees and disappeared, leaving Jerry to listen to the rapidly diminishing sound of the horse's hooves. Then the silence dropped like a cloak about her, save for the light humming of the wind through the upper branches. She went back and buckled the revolver with its holster about her waist. She felt strangely as if that act placed her at once among the ranks of those who, as Black Jim said, were 'above the law.'

A great impulse to collapse in the middle of the floor and weep rose in her. All that life of gaiety, of action, of many butterfly hopes, was lost to her. Years might pass before she could break away from this valley of the damned. Perhaps she might actually grow old here, away from men, away from the lure of the footlights. Hopelessness tightened about her heart and Jerry began to sing while the tears ran down her face. After all, she was trained to fight against misery, and she fought now until the tears stopped and her voice was sure. The very sound of the song was a cure to all ills.

She set about examining the cabin with the practical mind of any one who had had to make a home of a dressing-room in a theater and who can give a domestic touch even to a compartment in a Pullman. The main room could be made more attractive. When her hand healed, she could cut some young evergreens and place them here and there. That floor could be cleaned. Those clothes, if they had to hang on the wall, might at least be shaken free from dust and covered with sacking. She turned her attention to the adjoining room.

Here was the bunk of Black Jim, covered with a few tumbled blankets. Another pair of lanterns sat in a corner. More clothes lay here and there about the floor. Beyond his room lay the horse shed. She turned back to examine Jim's belongings. What caught her eye was a little pile of books upon a rudely-made shelf. She took them down one by one. Here was the explanation of the bandit's mixed English, sometimes almost scholarly and correct, but again full of Western vernacular. It was a cross between the slang of cowboy and mountaineer and the vocabulary of the educated. There were six volumes all told. The first she opened was Scott's *Red Gauntlet* which fell open at 'Wandering Willie's Tale.' Next came a volume of Shakespeare's greatest tragedies – *Othello, Macbeth, King Lear,* and *Hamlet* – then *Gil Blas,* a volume of Poe's verse, and another of Byron's, and finally quaint old Malory's *Morte d'Arthur.* 'Can you beat it?' whispered Jerry to the blank wall. 'And me – I haven't read a single one of 'em!'

How he had got them she could not imagine. Perhaps he took them with other loot from a stage. At any rate, they were here, and their presence made her strangely ill at ease. There is a peculiar reverence for books in the minds of the most illiterate. It is a superstition which runs back to the days when the written word had to be copied by hand and a man was esteemed rich if he possessed three or four manuscripts. That legendary reverence grew almost to worship in the early Renaissance and, when the invention of John Fust finally brought literature within the grasp of the poorest man, the early respect still clung to ink and paper – clings to it today.

Of books Jerry knew little enough and consequently had the greater respect. In school she had gone as far as *The Merchant of Venice,* but blank verse was an impassable fence which stood between her and the dramatic action. When she started out on her own gay path through the world, she found small time for reading and less desire. Books were all very well, and the knowledge which might be found in them was doubtless desirable, but for Jerry as unattainable as the shining limousines which purred down Fifth Avenue.

Her first impulse when she saw this little array of books was a blind anger whose cause she could scarcely discover. It seemed as if the reading of those books had suddenly placed the bandit as far away from her as he was away from the law. But when the anger died away a tingling excitement followed. Perhaps through these books she could gain the clue to the inner nature of Black Jim. If these were his only books, he might be molded by the thoughts he found in them. Therefore, through them, she might gain a power over him which, in the end, would avail to bring her safely from the valley. With this purpose before her, Jerry formulated a plan of campaign.

She must in the first place make the bandit like her. When this was done, all things would be possible. But she also knew there was much work before her until this end could be accomplished. His gentleness had not deceived her. It was the velvet touch of the panther's foot with the steel-sharp claws concealed. Those claws would be out and at her throat the moment she attempted an escape, or even a rash movement. In the meantime she must work carefully, patiently, to win first his re-spect, and then, perhaps, his affection. It was dangerous to attempt this. Yet it was necessary, and once this was done much might be accom-plished. Possibly she could persuade him to attempt flight with her. If so, there was a ghost of a chance he might be able to fight off the rest of the bandits and take her away from the valley.

The eyes of Jerry brightened again with even this faint hope to urge her on. All that day she did what she could, with her one hand, to clean and arrange the rooms. By nightfall she was utterly weary but expec-tant. The expectancy was vain. Black Jim arrived long after dark and she heard him moving about in the shed as he put up his roan. It was her signal to commence the cooking of supper. She waited with bated breath for his entrance and his shout of surprise when he saw the changes she had worked in a single day, but when he did come it was in silence. He gave no heed either to her or her work.

Jerry fumed in quiet as long as she could, then her plans and resolu-tions gave way before anger. She dropped a big pan, clatteringly, to the floor. Black Jim, who sat near a lantern at a table reading and calmly waiting for his meal, did not raise his head from his book.

'Say, Lord Algernon,' she cried, 'wake up and slide your eye over this room! Am I your hired cook, maybe? Am *I* the scrubwoman at eight per?'

He let a vague and unseeing eye rove toward her, and was immedi-ately lost in his book again. She repressed a slight desire to pick up the pan from the floor and hurl it at him.

'All right, deary,' she said, 'go on dreaming this is a play, but the *finale* is going to take you off your feet. The silent treatment is O. K. for some, cutey, but if you keep it up on me, this show will turn out wilder than a night of *Uncle Tom's Cabin* down in New Orleans.'

She resumed her cooking in silence. Black Jim had not favored her with even a glance during this oration. That evening was a symbol of the days to come. He ate in silence, without thanks or regard to her. Apparently now that her wound was no longer troubling her greatly, his attitude was changed. She felt it was not that he was indifferent. She had simply vanished from his mind. He had cared for her hurt. He had warned her of the dangers she might find in the valley. He had armed her against them. Thereafter she ceased to occupy his thoughts, for his code was fulfilled.

She fumed and fretted under this treatment at first, and still attempted to follow out her original campaign of winning Black Jim to her side. In all respects she failed miserably. She attempted to read his books. The verse wearied her. The vulgarity of *Gil Blas* stopped her in twenty pages. She could not wade through the opening exchange of letters in *Red Gauntlet*. Her mind turned back to Montgomery many times during the first ten days, but he never appeared and then she forgot him.

Black Jim was never at home during the day. He either rode out on the roan or else he went off on foot and returned at night with game, so that they never lacked meat. Cooking, short walks through the trees, endless silences, these things occupied the mind of La Belle Geraldine.

Yet she was not unhappy. She was of the nature which loves extremes and to her own astonishment, growing every day, she discovered that the hush of the mountains filled her life even more than the clattering gaiety of the stage. Slight, murmuring sounds which would scarcely have reached her ear a month before, now came to her with meaning – the thousand faint stirs which never cease in the forest. Heretofore she had never had a thought which she did not speak. Now she learned the most profound wisdom of all when the mind speaks to itself and the voice is still.

Whatever of the old restless activity remained in her found a vent in the ceaseless study of the bandit. She picked up a thousand clues little by little, but they all led in different directions. At the end of a month she felt she was farther away from the truth than she had been at the first. All that she really knew was what he had told her. He lived above the law. She knew him well enough to see he was not a criminal because of hate for other men, or even because he loved the thrill of his night riding. He simply avoided that other world of men because it was a world where life was constrained by a thousand rules.

To her mind he was like a powerful and sinisterly beautiful beast of prey which hunts where it will through the forest and, when it is pressed in its haunts by man, turns and strikes him down. She carried the animal metaphor still farther. She saw it in his singular silence, which was not reticence, but the speechlessness of a man to whom words are of no use. She saw it most of all in the singularly fathomless eyes. They never mocked her. They were simply veils through which she could not look.

The face changes expression only because man lives among fellows, whom he wishes to read his emotions, his anger, his pleasure, his contempt. Therefore his features grow mobile. Black Jim lived alone. When he was with men and wished to express an emotion, he did not pause to express his will in anything save action. At first, when the endless chatter of La Belle Geraldine disturbed him of an evening, he simply rose and left the cabin to walk through the woods. It was not long before she understood why.

The clock which ticks out our lives in the cities of men had no place in his house. He rose in the morning early because, like an animal again, he could not sleep after the light came. He felt no measuring of time by which to check and control his actions. He ate at any hour, now and then, once a day, often four times. Jerry fell into his habits through the strong force of a near example. The ticking of the clock no longer entered her consciousness and, in its place, flowed the broad and tideless river of life.

VII

The deadline which Black Jim said he had drawn around his cabin certainly had its effect, for never after the first day did she see one of the bandits. Now and again she caught the sound of distant firing when they practiced with their guns. Three or four times she heard drunken singing through the night as they held high festival. Otherwise she knew naught of them or their actions, though her mind retained the grim gallery of their portraits. The day would surely be when Black Jim should fail to return from one of his expeditions, and then. . . .

That day came. She waited till late at night, but he did not appear. She could scarcely sleep and, when the morning came, she sat in the cabin guessing at a thousand horrors. A voice took up a song in the distance, and then came closer and closer. Jerry stood up and felt for her revolver with a nervous hand. The voice rose clearer and clearer. She could make out the words:

'Julia, you are peculiar;
Julia, you are queer.'

Jerry dropped her hands on her hips and drew a long breath, partly of vexation and partly of relief.

'It's Freddie,' she muttered.

'Truly, you are unruly,
As a wild Western steer.
Some day, when we marry,
Dear one, you and I;
Julia, you little mule, you,
I'm going to rule you,
Or die.'

The song ended as the singer approached the edge of the open space before Black Jim's cabin. Jerry stepped through the door to see Montgomery standing in the shadow of the trees.

'Yea, Jerry!' he yelled. 'Is the gunman around?'

'He's not here,' she answered. 'You don't have to be afraid of anything, Freddie.'

'Oh, don't I?' came the reply. 'Didn't he make this a deadline, La Belle Geraldine? Suppose he should come back and find me on the other side of it? Not me, Jerry. I like life too well!'

'Where've you been?' said Jerry, approaching him 'and what in the *world* have you been doing, Freddie?'

For as she drew closer she found herself looking upon a Frederick Montgomery who, voice alone, remained the man she had known. A vast stubble of black beard and whiskers, unshaven for full two weeks or more, obscured the fine outline of his features. His broad hat, pushed back from his forehead, allowed a mop of tangled hair to fall down almost to his eyes. Overalls, soiled and marred with wrinkles, a shirt torn savagely across the side, muddy boots, and the heavy revolver completed his equipment. Jerry was aghast.

'What's the matter?' asked Montgomery. 'Some hit, this costume eh? It isn't make-up, kid. It's the real thing.'

'And I suppose you're the real thing under it?' said Jerry in deep disgust.

'Sure,' said he, easily. 'Stack all your chips and put 'em on me, kid. I'm the real stuff!'

'Why haven't you been around?' asked Jerry sharply, and bitter anger took her breath. 'You knew I was left here at the mercy of Black Jim. And you haven't done a thing to help me! Why?'

'Why?' repeated the other, but not peculiarly embarrassed. 'There's a reason, kid. I've been too busy living.'

'Too busy getting dirty, you mean,' snorted La Belle Geraldine. 'Go make yourself decent and then come back if you want to talk with me! But if you've got dirt in your mind, Freddie, water won't help you.'

He growled deep in his throat and she stepped back a pace. She had never heard such an ominous sound from him before: now she scanned him more closely. It seemed to her that his eyes were sunken and shadowed significantly.

'Don't try that line on me any more, Jerry,' he answered. 'You could get by in the old days, but it won't do up here.'

'Won't it, deary?' asked Jerry, with a rather dangerous sweetness.

'Not a hope, kid,' answered he. 'I'm through with all that stuff. Down in the States a jane could pull that line now and then and get by with it, but up here it's a man's country and it's up to you to side-step when anything in pants comes along.'

'As a man,' returned Jerry, yet for some reason she did not feel as brave as her words, 'as a man, cutey, you come about as close to the real article as a make-up will let you. But I'm behind the scenes and it won't quite do, Mr. Montgomery, it won't quite do.'

He scowled but he softened his tone as he answered. 'Look here, Jerry,' he said, 'I didn't come here looking for a fight. Am I your friend or am I not?'

'Do you remember how you backed out of the room when Black Jim simply looked at you, Freddie?' she asked gently.

'Sure I do,' he growled, 'but you can't hold that against me, Jerry. There isn't a man of the bunch who would take a chance face to face with Black Jim. He ain't human, you ought to know that. The only difference between him and a tiger is that he uses a gun. He's just. . . .'

'Cut it out, Freddie,' she broke in. 'I'm tired of you already. Ring off. Hang up. You're on the wrong wire.'

'Say, kid,' he said with gravity, 'do I gather that you stand for that man-eater?'

'Take it any way you like,' she said coldly.

He laughed. 'Of course you don't,' he went on disagreeably. 'You're simply kidding me along. What if I could show you the way out of the valley tonight, Jerry?'

She caught her breath.

'The way out? Freddie! Are you playing me straight?'

'I don't know,' he said, with a trace of sullenness, 'but this is my night on duty at the gap.'

'Then I'm free!' she cried. 'I'll start as soon as it's pitch dark and. . . .'

'Wait a minute,' he interrupted, 'don't run away with yourself. If you disappeared, Black Jim would know I let you pass and when he found out that his. . . .'

'Stop there,' she said. 'Freddie, what do you mean . . . do you think. . . ?'

'Lay off on that, Jerry,' returned Montgomery. 'You're a swell dancer, but you can't get away with heavy stuff like this. You've been all alone with him here, haven't you?'

She touched her hand to her forehead and wondered at its coldness in a vague way. 'Why should I care?' she murmured. 'Let him think what he will.'

'But I'm still strong for you,' Montgomery was saying. 'Don't get white and scared, kid. I don't hold it against you, much. What I say is, why not get rid of Black Jim? You can take him off his guard. Say the word and I'll hang around at night and you can signal me when he's asleep. Then I'll come and do the work. It'd be a risky job, but for your sake, kid, I'd. . . .'

'You've said enough,' she answered, summoning her courage and fighting back her disgust, for here was her one chance to gain freedom. 'If you're afraid of him, why not go with me? What's your idea? Do you really intend to stay here? Freddie, you haven't become one of those swine!'

He laughed heavily. 'Swine?' he repeated. 'Say, kid, did you ever see swine with this stuff hanging around in their hides?' He slid a hand into his hip pocket and brought it out again full of gold pieces of three denominations. He poured it deftly back and forth. 'Take a slant at it, Jerry. Listen to 'em click! One little job I pulled last week brought me this and about twice as much more. Easy? Say, it's a shame to take the coin. It's like robbing the cradle. Do you think I'd leave this game even to go off with you, Jerry? Not till I'm blind, kid! Get wise! Say the word and we can pull a stunt on Black Jim that'll give us the cabin and all the loot stacked up in it.' His eyes glittered. 'How much *has* he got stowed away in there, kid?'

She retreated another pace. He was half a dozen yards away now.

'I don't know,' she murmured. Fear was growing in her, and horror with it. In sudden desperation she held out her hand to him and cried: 'Freddie what is it? You were pretty clean when you first came up here. What has changed you? What's happened?'

'What's happened?' he asked, dully, as if he could not follow her meaning.

'Yes, yes! Open your lungs – taste this air. Isn't that enough in itself to make a man of you? And the scent of the evergreen, Freddie – and the nearness of the sky – and the whiteness of the stars. . . .'

'And the absence of the law, kid,' he broke in. 'Don't forget that. A man makes his own law up here, which means no law at all. We're above it, that's what we are. Stay here a little longer and you'll get it, too!'

She stared at him with great eyes while her mind moved quickly. She was beginning to understand, not the gross-minded brute which Frederick Montgomery had become, but the singular influence of the wild, free life. Of those other twelve and of Montgomery, the open license made animals. There *was* a difference between them and Black Jim. She had felt the touch of the animal in him, too, but in another manner. The others were like feeders on carrion. He was truly a great and fearless beast of prey. The solemn silences of the mountains imparted to him some of their own dignity. The mystery and the terror of the wilderness were his.

'Above the law?' she said. 'No, you're beneath it. I wish . . . I wish I were a man for half a minute – to rid the world of you all!'

She turned and fled back to the cabin.

'Jerry! Oh, Jerry!' he shouted from the edge of the clearing where the deadline of Black Jim still held him.

She turned at the door.

'Have you made up your mind about it finally?' he asked.

She shuddered so, she could not answer.

'Then, by God, I'll have you, if I have to get Black Jim first, and I'll get his other loot when I get you!'

He disappeared among the trees and she went back into the cabin, weak at heart and filled now with a strange yearning for the return of Black Jim. The vultures, she felt, circled above the valley, waiting for her. He was the strong eagle which would put them to flight.

Evening drew on. He did not come. Night settled black over the valley and the white stars brushed the great trees that fringed the cliffs. Still he did not come. The hearth fire remained unlighted. The damp cold of darkness numbed her hands and her heart. She waited, bowed and miserable. He was delayed, but delay to Black Jim could mean only death. No other force could take all this time for his return. This grew more certain as the hours passed. In that gloom every minute meant more than whole hours during the day.

At last she made up her mind. Montgomery – not the light-hearted man she had known, but a hot eyed beast – threatened her. Not he alone, but perhaps all of the other twelve were so many dangers. Now that Black Jim was gone, she was helpless in their hands. By the next day they would know of his long absence and come for her – for her and for the rest of the loot, as Montgomery had said. She must get away from the valley that night.

The sentinel was there, to be sure, but that sentinel was Montgomery and she felt there was a fighting chance she could pass him safely in the gap. If necessary, she could fight, and perhaps she could handle a revolver as well as he. Perhaps she could surprise him. He would not be expecting it and, if she could get him under the aim of her revolver, she knew he would not play the role of hero. Once out of the gap there was an even chance for life. She might wander through the mountains until she starved to death. On the other hand she might find a road and follow it to town. She weighed the chances in her own practical way, rose from the stool, saw that her cartridge belt was well filled, strapped a canvas bag full of food on the other hip, and left the cabin.

She kept as closely as possible to the center of the valley, for she felt that the habitations of the gang must lie close to the wall, on which side she could not know. As she approached the gap, she went more and more slowly, for here the valley began to narrow rapidly, and the chance she might encounter one of the twelve grew greater. At every step she feared a discovery, for it was impossible to guess what lay immediately before her. The valley floor was not only thick with great trees, but mighty boulders. They had evidently been split by erosion from the cliffs around and lay here and there, a perfect hiding place for a veritable army. The keen scent of wood smoke reached her nostrils. She paused a moment, uncertain from which direction it came, for the air was still. Then she turned to the right and stole on with careful steps. Each crackling of a twig beneath her feet made her heart thunder.

The scent of smoke grew fainter, ceased, and came again. A murmur like the sound of voices brought her to a dead halt to listen. She heard nothing further for a moment and went on again until a great rock, full forty feet in height, blocked her progress and she began to circle it. As she turned a corner of the great rock, she stopped short, and dropped to the ground. The big rock and several smaller ones close to it lay in a rough circle, and in the center of the space smoked a pile of wood, which would soon break into flames. Already little crimson tongues licked along the edges, quivered, and went out, to be replaced by others. By the dim light of this rising fire, she made out shadowy figures one after another, nine in all, and could not see all of the circle.

'Start it yourself, Porky,' said a voice.

A snatch of flame jerked up the side of the pile of wood and flickered a moment like a detached thing at the top. By that light she saw the big, bearded fellow leaning against a rock just opposite her.

'Not me,' he answered. 'Mac will be back maybe. If he don't come, I'll start the ball rollin'. Gimme time.'

The fear which made her drop to the ground still paralyzed Jerry, so that she heard these things as from a great distance. With all her heart she wished for the strength to creep back from the rock, but for the moment she was incapable of movement. The clatter of a galloping horse drew up to the rocks and stopped. Montgomery entered the circle and threw himself down beside Porky. A general silence held the group. The fire flamed up and clearly showed the round of somber faces as they turned to Montgomery.

New heart came to Jerry, for Montgomery had evidently abandoned his place in the gap and now the way of her flight lay clear. She rose cautiously from her prone position to her hands and knees and began to draw softly back.

'Did he come through?' asked a voice.

'Just passed me,' answered Montgomery, 'and he was riding hard. The roan looked as if he'd covered a hundred miles today.'

Jerry paused, all ears, and her heart leaped. They must mean that Black Jim had ridden through the pass. The shadow of the rock concealed her perfectly and unless someone actually walked upon her, through the aperture between the two big boulders, there was practically no chance they could discover her presence. Black Jim had returned and now she connected his return to the valley, for some unknown reason, with this assemblage in the night. She could not forget the threat which Montgomery had made earlier in the day.

'Put it to them straight, Mac,' said Porky to Montgomery. 'Give 'em the whole idea, just the way you talked it over with me. They're set to listen. I sort of prepared the way.'

'All right,' agreed Montgomery. 'I'll tell you where I stand. I'm tired as hell of having Black Jim walk all over us. I say, if we're men, we've got to put an end to it, savvy?'

Another of those little ominous silences fell on the circle.

'It appears to me, partner,' drawled Montana, 'that you're talkin' a powerful lot, when a man might say you're only jest landed among us.'

'He ain't askin' you to come in on the plan,' broke in Porky aggressively. 'Neither am I. Jest listen, an' if you don't like the idea a mighty sight, nobody's goin' to hurt you for staying out.'

'Nacherally,' agreed the Doctor, 'but kick out with your hunch, Mac.'

Jerry went cold, yet she edged a little closer for fear that a single, low-pitched word might escape her.

'I haven't been here long,' said Montgomery, 'but while I've been here I've learned enough about Black Jim for him to make me sick.'

'He generally makes folks feel that way,' said a voice, and a chuckle followed, which broke off short, for Porky was glowering from face to face.

'You remember what he did the day after he brought the girl into the valley?'

'I reckon he brought you-all in about the same time,' said the man of the pale face and yellow teeth, grinning.

Montgomery frowned back. 'He took me from behind,' he said savagely. 'I didn't have no chance to get at my gun, or maybe the story wouldn't be the same.'

'Go on, Silent,' encouraged Porky. 'Don't let 'em throw you off the trail.'

'All right. You remember he came down here and told us all he had a deadline drawn around his cabin at the edge of the trees and if any of us crossed it he was no better than dead meat?'

A general growl rose, for the memory angered them to their hearts.

'We all were pretty still when he spoke,' said Montgomery, 'and my way of looking at it, we acted like a bunch of whipped dogs.'

'Kind of smile when you say that, partner,' said the pale-faced man, 'or pretty soon maybe you'll be riding your idea to death!'

'I'm telling you what it seemed to me,' said Montgomery. 'I say, what right has Black Jim got to make rules up here? This valley is above the law, isn't it?'

'It ain't the first thing he done,' said Porky. 'He's been makin' laws of his own all the time, an', by God, I ain't the man to stand for it no longer, which I say, Black Jim is always a bluffin' from a four-flush.'

'Me speakin' personal,' added the Doctor, 'I got no use for a man that won't liquor up with the boys now an' then. It shows he ain't got any nacheral trust for his pals.'

'I say it's come to a show down,' said Montgomery. 'Either we've got to move out and leave the valley to Black Jim, or he's got to move out and leave it to us. Am I right?'

'All savin' one little thing,' drawled a voice. 'You-all seem to be for-gettin' that Black Jim ain't partic'lar willin' to move for anybody. Ef it comes to movin' him, he'll have to be carried out feet first, in a way of speakin'.'

'And why not move him that way?' asked Montgomery.

Once more the breathless silence fell. Jerry could see each man flash a questioning glance at his neighbor and then each pair of eyes fell glowering upon the fire. A little gritting sound caught her, and she found she was grinding her teeth savagely. All her wild, loyal nature revolted against this cool and secret plotting.

'Because it ain't no way possible,' said the Doctor, 'to ride Black Jim without buckin' straps an' a Spanish bit.'

'Maybe not for one man,' said Montgomery softly, 'but here's twelve can all shoot straight and every one knows his gun. Can Black Jim stand up against us all at one time?'

'Maybe not,' said the Doctor, 'but he ain't no gun-shy paint-pony, an' before we're through flashin' guns, some of us are goin' to start out on the long trail for the happy huntin' grounds. You can stack your chips on that, partner!'

'Then, by God!' cried Porky, starting to his feet with such suddenness that the others shrank a little, 'if you're goin' to quit cold, me an' Silent Mac'll take on the game by ourselves, and we split the loot between us. There'll be a lot of it. He don't never spend it any ways I can see – no liquor, no gamblin', no nothin'. Boys, the stuff must be piled up to the roof!'

Without hardly knowing what she did, Jerry drew the revolver from her holster and drew a deadly bead on Porky's breast. She checked her-self with horror at the thought that a single pressure of her finger would bring a man to his death. Three or four others rose around the circle.

'If it comes to a show down, Porky,' said one of them, 'we'll stack our chips with yours. I'm ag'in Black Jim, an' I'd jest as soon tell him so from the talkin' end of a gun.'

'Me, too,' said another, and a clamor of voices rose in affirmation.

Jerry began to draw back, head whirling.

'Then there's no time like tonight,' called Montgomery, 'and I tell you how we can work best.'

He lowered his tone as he spoke and, as Jerry drew back behind the jutting angle of the rock, she heard only a confused murmur. There she crouched a long moment, thinking as she had never thought before. The way out of the valley lay clear before her. If she rose and walked on, she would be free within ten minutes and in fifteen escape beyond the reach of pursuit. The other alternative was to turn back to the cabin of Black Jim and warn him of the danger which threatened. If she did this, it meant she would be involved in the same fate which was soon to envelop the solitary bandit.

Thirteen men that night would attack him. When he fell, she would be the prize of the victors. Jerry moaned aloud. Then she rose, still crouching, and hurried off among the trees towards the gap of the valley. Terror drove her faster and faster. When she reached the last rise of ground, she broke into a stumbling run. In another moment she stood at the farther end of a narrow pass, and paused an instant to catch her breath. Before her the ground pitched steeply down, down to freedom. On that outward trail she would be headed again for happiness, for the applause of the gay hundreds, for the shimmer of footlights, which had been to her like signal fires which led finally to fame. She looked back to the valley. It was black as death. She looked up and there were the cold, white stars, very near. One of them seemed to burn in the top of a tall pine, a lordly tree.

A great weakness mastered Jerry, and she dropped to her knees, her shoulder pressing against the cliff which fenced the gap. Perhaps the thirteen were even then prowling toward the cabin of Black Jim. Perhaps Jim was stooped over the hearth, kindling the fire. Perhaps he even thought of her, at least to wonder carelessly where she had gone. Big tears formed in her eyes and ran hotly down her cheeks. She threw her arms up toward the pallid stars, and her hands were fiercely clenched.

'O God,' she said, whispering the words, 'tell me what's the big-time thing to do! How'm I going to put over this act right? I've been on the small-time so long I don't know what to do! I don't know what to do!'

Surely there was an answer to that prayer, for her tears ceased at once.

She rose and looked once more longingly down the slope that led to liberty. Then she turned and went back into the double night of the valley. She went on at a swinging step and hope came to her as she walked. Surely the crew of Porky and Montgomery would deliberate some time longer, laying their plans for the attack. She had heard enough to know they feared Black Jim worse than death and they would not be the men to take greater chances than necessary. She might reach the cabin before them. Once or twice she started to run, but she stopped and swung into a walk again for she must not exhaust her strength. There might be need for it all, before the night was done.

IX

She grew more and more cautious as she approached the farther end of the valley and, for a time, hesitated at the edge of the circle of trees around the cabin, watching and listening. She found nothing suspicious. When she moved a little to one side, she saw a shaft of light fall from a window of the house. It was a golden promise to Jerry, and her heart beat strongly again with hope. Once with Black Jim she felt at that moment as if they could fight off the whole world between them.

She went tiptoeing across the open space like a child stealing up to catch a playmate by surprise. At the open door she stood a moment, peeking around the corner and into the interior. The shock of discovery unnerved her even more than the plot she had overheard, scarcely an hour before. By the lantern light she saw Black Jim standing with folded arms beside her bunk. He stared down at an array of woman's clothes which was spread out on the blankets. She saw a long, rose-colored scarf, a dress of blue silk that shimmered faintly in the dim light, light shoes on the floor, a small round hat, and there were other articles at which she could only guess, for they were not all exposed.

'Jim!' she called softly, and then stepped into the doorway.

He whirled with a clutching hand on the butt of his revolver. He was pale but a deep color poured into his face and his eyes wavered to the floor under her shining glance. 'I thought you were gone,' he said. 'I thought. . . .' He raised his head and went to her with outstretched hand. 'Jerry,' he said, as she met his grasp, 'I was thinkin' awhile ago that I didn't care for anything livin' except the roan. But I reckon I'd have missed you!'

The confession came stammeringly forth. Jerry pressed his hand in both of hers. 'You're just . . . you're just a dear,' she said, and in a moment she was on her knees, turning over the finery, article by article. Tears brimmed her eyes again. 'I thought you never noticed me,' she said, turning to him. 'I thought I was no more than the blank wall to you, Jim!'

'A man would be blind that didn't see your clothes was getting some worn, Jerry,' he said, and she saw that his eyes were traveling slowly over her from head to foot, as if to make sure she had really come back to him. It thrilled her with a happiness different from any ever known in her life. She forgot the danger of the thirteen gangsters and the warning which she had come back to give Black Jim at such a peril to herself. She leaned over the clothes to conceal the hot color in her face and to fight against a sudden sense of self-consciousness. It was more like stage fright than anything else, yet it was different. It was not the fear of many critical eyes. It was an awful knowledge that her own searching vision was turned back upon her soul and every corner of her heart lay exposed. And still that quivering, foolish, childish happiness sang in her like the murmur of a harp string.

She felt a slight touch at her side. Black Jim had opened the canvas bag and glanced at the contents. He stepped back, a frown and a smile fighting on his face.

'You did start on the out-trail, Jerry?' he asked.

She remembered now with horrible suddenness all she had come back to tell him. It brought her slowly to her feet, white, tense.

'I *did* start,' she answered. 'You were gone so long. I thought you were hurt – killed – and that I was left here at the mercy of. . . .' She stopped and then hurried on. 'I started to go down the valley and on the way I came to the same crowd of men who were in this room the night you brought me here. They were around a fire. I hid beside the rock and listened to their talk. They were threatening you, Jim! They plan to come up here tonight and attack you – because of the gold you have – and me! They were all there. They hadn't even left a man to guard the gap!'

'Which left you plumb free to go on out of the valley,' said Jim, half to himself, and entirely disregarding the rest of her speech.

'We must leave at once!' she cried. 'We must try to sneak off down the valley before they arrive to make their attack. . . .'

'But you come back here to tell me,' he went on, musing, 'when you might have got away.'

She caught him by the arm and shook it savagely.

'Wake up!' she called. 'Listen to me! Don't you understand what's going to happen?'

'I didn't think there was no man would do that,' he said, 'leastwise, not up here. But now a woman has done it – for me!' For the wonder of it he shook his head slowly. 'Jerry, I've been consider'ble of a fool!'

'Yea, Jim!' called a voice from the night.

'Git down!' whispered Black Jim, and dragged her to the floor. 'Keep low when the bullets start comin', an' stay down. Hell is just startin' around here!'

'Don't go!' she pleaded, clutching him. 'They want you to go out and then they'll shoot at you from the shelter of the trees.'

His faint chuckle answered her.

'After all, Jerry, I'm not a *plumb* fool!'

He ran softly to the door and swung it open.

'Who's there?' he called. Then he whispered to Jerry: 'I can see four of them among the trees, an' Silent Mac an' Porky are standin' by the deadline waiting for me to come out. Watch them from the other side of the cabin. They might try to rush from that side.'

'Come out!' answered the voice of Montgomery. 'We got to see you, Jim, or let us come across your deadline.'

Jerry ran to the narrow window on the farther side of the room and peered out cautiously. The new-risen moon shed so faint a light she could see nothing at first.

'What d'you want with me?' she heard Black Jim say.

Now, as she strained her eyes, she made out one, two, three dim figures moving behind the trees. The cabin was surrounded on all sides.

'We need you, Jim,' answered Porky's voice. 'They's a passel of men camped in the gap. When day comes, they'll start cleanin' out our valley.'

Black Jim chuckled. 'Jest a minute, boys,' he called. 'Wait there, an' I'll be with you.' He crossed hurriedly to Jerry.

'They're on this side, too, Jim,' she breathed. 'They have us surrounded! It's death to us both, Jim! There's no escape!'

'Remember this!' he whispered. His hand closed on her shoulder. 'Whatever happens, keep close to the floor. They got us trapped. Maybe there ain't any hope. Anyway, it'll be a fight they'll remember. . . .'

'I will! I will!' she answered, and her voice trembled, for he seemed to have caught at her whole soul with his hand, 'but before it begins – I've got to say – I've got to tell you. . . .' She stopped, then went on with a great effort. 'Jim, before we die. . . .'

'Hush!' he said. 'There ain't goin' to be no death for you!'

'Before we die,' she pressed on, 'remember that I love you with all my heart and soul, Jim!'

'Jerry, you're talkin' loco!'

'It isn't much to be loved by a small-time actress, and I've never once been behind the lights on the real big time. But, oh, Jim! I wish I was keen in the bean like Cissy Loftus, because then. . . .'

Slowly, fumblingly, his arms went around her and tightened.

'Jerry!' he whispered.

'Yes?' she answered in the same tone.

'It seems to me. . . .'

'Dear Jim!'

'It won't be so partic'lar hard. . . .'

'Dear . . . dear old Jim!'

'To pass out now. But it's too late to ask for a new deal. This deck's already shuffled and stacked. Jerry, we'll play a straight game even with a fixed deck. An' . . . an' I love you, honey, more'n the roan an' my six-gun put together!' He gathered her close with powerful arms, but the kiss which touched her eyes and then her lips was gentle and reverent.

'Are you sleepin', Jim?' called a voice.

He turned and went with drawn revolver to the door, still ajar. From behind him, Jerry could see Montgomery and Porky standing in the moonlight.

'I ain't sleepin',' replied Black Jim, 'but I'm figurin' why I ain't shot such hounds as you two, without warnin'!'

As if he had pressed a spring which set automata in motion, they whirled and leaped behind trees.

'Take warning!' called Black Jim. 'I could have bagged you both with my eyes shut, an' the next man of you that I see I'll let him have it!'

For reply a revolver barked and a bullet thudded into the heavy door. Black Jim slammed it and dropped the latch. A series of wild yells sounded from the trees on all sides and a dozen shots rang in quick succession. After this first venting of their disappointed spleen, the bandits were silent again. Jerry poised her revolver and searched the trees carefully. A hand dropped on her arm and another hand took away the revolver.

'If there's shootin' to be done,' said Black Jim, 'I'll do it. The blood of a man don't wash off so easy, even from soft white hands like yours, Jerry!'

'Then when you shoot, shoot to kill!' she said fiercely. 'They are trying for your life like bloodhounds, Jim!'

'Kill?' he repeated, taking up his place at the small window with his revolver raised. 'Jerry, I've never killed a man yet, no matter what people say, an' I'm not goin' to begin now. Why, a bullet in the leg or the shoulder puts a man out of the way jest as well as if it went through the heart. Git down closer to the floor!'

His gun exploded. A yell from the edge of the trees answered him, and then a chorus of shouts and a score of bullets in swift succession smashed against the logs. Through the silence that followed they heard a distant, faint moaning.

Black Jim, running with his body close to the floor, crossed the room to the window on the other side. Almost instantly his gun spoke again, and a man screamed in the night among the trees.

'Too high!' she heard Jim saying. 'I meant it lower.'

'They're beaten, Jim!' she called softly. 'They don't dare try to rush the cabin. They're beaten!'

'Not yet!' he answered. 'Unless they're plumb crazy, they'll tackle us from the blind side. There ain't any window in the shed, Jerry!'

x

From three sides of the house he could command the approaches through the door and the two slits in the wall which answered in place of windows. On the side of the shed where the roan was stabled, there was not the smallest chink through which he could fire. Jerry sat twisting her hands in despair.

'Take the ax, Jim,' she said at last, 'and chop away a hole in the logs. They're all light and thin. You could make a place to shoot from in a minute!'

He started to fumble about in the dark for the ax. But the weak side of the cabin was too apparent to be overlooked by the besiegers. Before the ax was found, a great crackling of fire commenced outside the shed and a cry of triumph rose from the men without. The sound of the fire rose; the roan whinnied with terror. Black Jim slipped his revolver back into his holster, and turned with folded arms to Jerry.

'So this is the *finale*,' she said with white lips. 'Where's our soft music and the curtain, Jim?'

'Let the girl out!' shouted the voice of Montgomery. 'We won't hurt her! Come out, Jerry!'

'Go on out, honey,' said Black Jim.

She went to him and drew his arm about her.

'Do you think I'd go out to them, Jim?'

'I don't think,' he said. 'I know. There's nothin' but death in here!'

A gust of wind puffed the flames to a roar up the side of the shed outside, and they heard the stamping of the roan in an agony of panic.

'There's only two ways left to me,' she said, 'and dying with you is a lot the easiest, Jim. Give back my gun!'

'Honey,' he said, and she wondered at the gentleness of his voice, 'you're jest a girl – a bit of a slip of a girl – an' I can't noways let you stay in here. Go out the door. They won't shoot.'

'Give back my gun!' she repeated.

She felt the arm about her tremble, and then the butt of a revolver was placed in her hand. The fire hissed and muttered now on the roof of the cabin. Red glimmers of light showed and filled the interior with a grim dance of shadows.

'I never knew it could be this way, Jerry,' he said.

'Nor I, either,' she answered, 'and the day I make my final exit is the day I really began to live. Jim, it's worth it!'

Through another pause they listened to the fire. Outside Montgomery was imploring the girl to leave the house and, as the fire mounted, an occasional yell from the crowd applauded its progress.

'Seein' we're goin' out on the long trail together,' said Black Jim, 'ain't there some way we can hitch up so's we can be together on the other side of the river?'

She did not understand.

'I mean, supposin' we were married. . . .'

She pressed her face against his body to keep back a sob.

'Seems to me,' he went on, 'that I can remember some of a marriage I once read. Do you suppose, Jerry, that if me an' you said it over now, bein' about to die, that it would mean anything?'

'Yes, yes!' she cried eagerly. 'We're above the law, Jim, and what we do is either sacred or damned.'

'The part I remember,' he said calmly though the room was hot now with the rising fire, 'begins something like this, an' it ain't very long. Is Jerry your real name, honey?'

'My real name is Annie Kerrigan. And yours, Jim?'

'I was never called nothin' but Black Jim. Shall I begin?'

'Yes!'

'I, Black Jim, take thee, Annie. . . .'

'I, Annie, take thee, Black Jim,' she repeated.

'To have and to hold. . . .'

'To have and to hold.'

'For better or worse. . . .'

'For better or worse.'

'Till death do us part. . . .'

'Jim, dear Jim, can *that* part us?'

'Nothin' between heaven an' hell can, honey! Annie, there was the ring, too, but I ain't got a ring.'

The room was bright with the firelight now. She raised her left hand and kissed the third finger. 'Jim, dear, this is a new kind of marriage. We don't really need a ring, do we?'

'We'll jest suppose that part.'

The roan made the whole cabin tremble with his frantic efforts to break from his halter.

'An' old Roan Bill goes with us,' said Black Jim. 'Everything I wanted comes with me in the end of things, honey. But he ought to die easier than by fire!'

He drew his revolver again and stepped through the doorway into the shed. Jerry followed him and saw Roan Bill standing crouched and shuddering against the wall, his eyes green with fear. Black Jim stepped to him and stroked the broad forehead. For a moment Bill kept his terrified eyes askance upon the burning wall of the shed. Then he turned his head and pressed against Jim, as if to shut out the sight. With his left hand stroking the horse gently along the neck, Jim raised his revolver and touched it to the temple of Roan Bill. Another cry broke from the crowd without as if they could look through the burning walls and witness the coming tragedy and glory in it.

'Old pal,' said Black Jim, 'we've seen a mighty pile of things together, an' if hosses get on the other side of the river, I got an idea I'll find you there. So long!'

'Wait!' called Jerry. 'Don't shoot, Jim!'

He turned toward her with a frown as she ran to him.

'The wall, Jim! Look at the wall of the shed!'

The thin wall had burned through in many places and the wood was charred deeply. In several parts the burning logs had fallen away, leaving an aperture edged with flames.

'I see it,' said Black Jim. 'It's about to fall. Get back in the cabin.'

'Yes,' she answered, fairly trembling with excitement, 'even a strong puff of wind would blow it in! Listen! I see the ghost of a chance for us! Blindfold Roan Bill so that the fire won't make him mad. We'll both get in the saddle. Then you can beat half of that wall down at a single blow. We'll ride for the woods. They won't be watching very closely from this side. We may . . . we may . . . there's one chance in a thousand.'

He stared at her a single instant. Then by way of answer jerked the saddle from a peg on the wall of the cabin and threw it on the roan's back. Jerry darted into the cabin and came out with the long scarf, which she tied firmly around the horse's eyes. In two minutes their entire preparations were completed and a money-belt dropped into a saddle-bag. Jerry was in the saddle with the roan trembling beneath her, and the reins were clutched tightly in one hand, a revolver in the other. Black Jim caught up a loose log-end, fallen from the wall.

'There in the center,' she called. 'It's thinnest there!'

'The minute it falls start the roan,' he said. 'I'll swing on behind as you pass!'

With that he swung the log-end around his head and drove it against the wall. A great section fell. He struck again. A yell came from with-out as another width crushed down, and Jerry loosened the reins. At the very moment that Black Jim caught the back of the saddle, the roan stepped on a red-hot coal and reared away, but Jim kept his hold and was safe behind the saddle as the horse made his first leap beyond the burning timbers.

'They're out! This way!' shouted a voice from the trees, and two shots in quick succession hummed close to them.

Fifty yards away lay the trees and safety. The roan lengthened into a racing stride. A chorus of yells broke out around the house and Jerry saw a man jump from behind a tree, and the flash of a revolver in his hand. The long arm of Black Jim darted out and his gun spoke once, and again. The man tossed up his arms and pitched forward to the ground. Still another revolver barked directly before them and she saw, by the light of the flaming house, the great figure of Porky Martin, half hidden by a tree-trunk. A bullet tore through the horn of the saddle.

The woods were only a fraction of a second away from them. Martin stood in their path. Once more the revolver of Black Jim belched and, as they plunged into the saving shadow of the trees, she saw the outlaw stagger and clutch at his throat with both hands.

'To the left! To the left,' said Black Jim, 'and straight down the valley for the gap!'

A week later a golden-haired girl rode down a broken trail on the side of one of the lower Sierras. By her side walked a tall man with quick, keen eyes. When they broke from the edge of the forest, she checked her horse and they stood looking down on the upper valley of the Feather River.

Far away the water burned jewel-bright under the sun, and almost directly below them were the green and red roofs of a small village. Here the trail forked, one branch winding west along the mountainside and the other dropping straight down toward the village.

'Which way shall it be?' she asked. 'I don't know where the west trail leads, but this straight one takes us down to the village, and that means the law.'

'Jerry,' he answered, 'I've been thinkin' it over, an' it seems to me that it'd be almighty hard to raise kids right above the law. Let's take the trail for the village!'

The Wedding Guest

This story shows Faust's full maturity as a writer. During the 1930s and 1940s, when the promise of financial success of earlier years was in many ways fulfilled, Faust had several hundred magazine stories and seventy-three hardback books behind him. Twenty-seven films had been based on his work. In the 1920s Faust had written about a million words a year, mainly for pulp magazines because they bought nearly everything he produced at rates up to five cents a word. Occasionally he had written crime or contemporary urban romance or historical adventure stories, but his primary output had been westerns. A weekly issue of *Western Story* might carry three contributions by him under different names. There had been little incentive to change procedure since he wrote prose primarily to support himself and his family.

In 1925, after suffering a severe heart attack, he moved with his wife and their young daughter and son to Europe to escape the tensions of New York. In 1926 he fulfilled a long-held dream of living in Florence, the city where the Renaissance was born and home to such poets as Dante and Petrarch. He thought the city might inspire the poetry he felt was at the heart of his creative life. He wrote poetry every morning with what he considered his best effort, and prose in the afternoon and evening with what he called his left hand. At first there was reason to think he was on the right course, since his first book of poems, *The Village Street* (Putnam, 1922), had received critical praise. But the product of his long labor at an epic poem in Homeric style, *Dionysus in Hades,* found few readers when published in 1931 in a world fraught with economic distress and rising dictatorships.

By 1934 the erosion of Faust's pulp magazine markets by the Great Depression forced a crucial change. To maintain his level of income he had to satisfy what remained of his former markets while establishing new ones. He decided to try the higher-paying slick-paper magazines such as *Collier's*, *The Saturday Evening Post*, and others, which paid thirty cents or more a word. They required a different kind of writing but presented his work to a larger, more sophisticated audience. 'It is not exactly the goodness of the writing that counts,' he told a friend. 'What matters is the attitude and ideas.'

Rising to the occasion, he published nearly two million words annually. Like General Motors, he produced a product for nearly every kind of buyer – but he typed it all with two fingers on his Underwood upright. It was hard work, but it meant artistic growth as well as market transition. Sensing his unrealized potential, his literary agent, Carl Brandt, bet him five dollars he couldn't publish a 'serious' story.

In response Faust wrote 'The Wedding Guest.' The story appeared in *Harper's* (January 1934) and earned him $250 plus the five from Brandt (though Faust grumbled that during the time required to write it he could have made $2,000 in other markets). The story, nevertheless, marks the emergence of the complete man and writer. It reveals Faust's knowledge of and love for Europe, especially France, where he had lived before settling in Italy. Yet 'The Wedding Guest' represented a new dilemma: he found he could publish serious prose and make his reputation that way instead of – or in addition to – writing poetry. This story has the poetry which came from the heart of his creative life and which, for the most part, was expressed better in his prose – as here – than in his verse. That 'The Wedding Guest' is one of a very few stories to carry Faust's name rather than a pseudonym reveals, perhaps, Faust's own assessment of the story.

W HEN I WAS IN PARIS, Olympe Arouet wrote to me:

Dear Paul, now you are in France, but May is still cold in Paris. Do come into the summer and visit us. Besides, I have a need to see you. That is a need very much. Will you come?

I had probably not seen Olympe more than six times altogether, but these were spread through ten years, and, since I had been a Christian name to her father, I suppose she had inherited the fashion of using it. Jean Arouet had been an entomologist, and in his torture chambers, which he called his 'studies,' I had seen a praying mantis clamp a cricket in its hinged saws and turn its pointed little face to me as if inviting my attention before it began to eat. Jean Arouet was proud to claim that blood of Voltaire ran in his veins but, making a good modern transition, where Voltaire had plagued little humans in the name of Man, Jean Arouet speared insects in the name of Science. He was a tall, lean, bending man with so many things on his mind that he never could keep his eyes steady. He talked very well, though his French was too fast for me most of the time; but anyway it was not for his conversation that I went to see him. He had collected not only a great many insects but also a number of good American bonds, and that was where I came in as his broker.

When I received that letter from his daughter it was not of the dead man I thought or of Olympe's grave face with its high cheekbones and sober eyes. She was carrying on her father's work, I understood, and that meant she would still be dressed in gray high-collared smocks. Jean Arouet said that she had the eye and touch which makes for perfect dissection under the microscope. Yet I saw her less vividly than I saw Provence; for a spirit that is neither France nor Italy comes out of that land, and I had breathed of it. Some countries are old and dead: Provence is old like the sea. I don't mean Avignon alone, but even the open country, whether it undulates slowly or lies in strange colored flats. It is a land that is never wholly seen, but the thought of it comes over the mind in a pleasant mist and strangeness, not of twilight and night only, but even of the midday when the distances withdraw into the shimmering of that strong sun.

All of this Provence, which can be tasted and remembered but never spoken, spread warmly out from the page of Olympe's letter. 'May is cold in Paris'; but every month is cold in Paris, after Provence. 'Besides, I have a need to see you. That is a need very much.' Well, she was ten years younger than I, and twenty-five; with high cheekbones — that type, in which the skull shows a little through the face, steps rapidly out of girl-hood, out of womanhood, into the long, seasonless and virgin aridity. And yet an ardor that was truly Provençal came out of that one twisted phrase: 'That is a need very much.'

It kept me hurrying all the way; it was well underlined in my mind by the time I swerved my car off the wide white road and let it roll past the mottled and pale trunks of the plane trees until the curving drive brought me in front of the house. It was not too big to fit comfortably into the eye; the color was more the stain of time than of yellow paint;

and what pleased me most was that I could remember even the details of the coat of arms over the big doors, where a thin-bellied lion, on one side, wagged his tail and stood up and stuck out his tongue at a dragon on the other side. It is always comfortable to remember with exactness; all sorts of melancholy ghosts turn into commonplace reality and the future also seems secure.

It was only the middle of the morning, because I had got on the road almost with the dawn to finish the second stage of the journey, and the servant who opened the door for me was in one of those long, gray, striped coats which save both shirt cuffs and the knees of trousers during housecleaning. Of course this grayness was what I expected, but when I stepped into the big hall I was startled to see flowers all about. The western windows were shuttered against the heat of the day, but through the open door there came light enough to give me a first glimpse, and after it was closed I still saw great vases overflowing with yellow and white and red in the shadows. I was breathing the rich, bittersweet fragrance of roses when a whisper came down the stairs and Olympe walked out of the big, dark arch to me.

I had heard that she was carrying on with her father's work. Work, my eye! The cat was away for good and this mouse was playing. When I had been thinking that this type often steps quickly from girlhood through womanhood into dry, endless years, I had forgotten about the ones who bloom. Part of this was French bloom, on the lips and cheeks, but the living eyes were real and the thin morning gown let some beauty glimmer through.

She put out a hand, not to take mine so much as to grasp a surprising idea. The brightness of it was in her face as she said: 'But, Paul! I didn't remember that you were so big. But, Paul!' She spoke English better than she wrote it, with not many wrong constructions that I can remember, though she had the usual Latin trouble with the short 'i,' and I was glad all up my spine that she deedn't remember that I was so beeg.

She said that we would go into the garden, but just then a young fellow came in and gave me a quarter of a bow and a tenth of a smile and said, 'It has happened, Mademoiselle Olympe.' She introduced me to him and his name was something ending in 'pour' or 'four.' There is nothing so sour as a sour Frenchman, and he was that sourest kind with a sallow skin and cheeks hollowed enough to press down the corners of the mouth. These fellows are all as tough as tool-proof steel but they look consumptive, and in me the look is father to the wish.

When Olympe heard that 'it had happened' she waited a moment, looking at me, considering my will. Already she had made me feel twenty pounds bigger. My business had been going with a limp and a stagger ever since '29, but I stood beside Olympe inwardly feeling myself one of those fabled giants of the Street, inscrutable, weighty, and profound. I could have announced opinions on the farm problem, or anything.

'Have you ever seen the Great Peacock – the moth, Paul?' she said. 'Come upstairs for one little minute. It is so beautiful.'

I was ready to go with her anywhere for more than one leetle meenute, so I followed to the second story and down the open loggia that served for a hall. This gave me a glimpse of the garden behind the house that once had been palms and rounded beds of brown dead grass with frazzled edges, but now it was dazzling in the sun and glowing in the shadow; even the lady of the fountain had come to life and threw a cypress-shaped radiance into the air. Why, the world was no longer dying but living; no, not the world but just old Provence, the beautiful and the guilty.

We went into a bare room with an old deal table in the middle and a little dome of wire screen on the table, and inside the screen was the Great Peacock moth. What could one say of the grays and the browns of the wings, bordered with white, and four black eyes set into them? No, only the pupils were black, for out of the iris colors dissolved and spread the rings of white and black and dull crimson and exquisite rosy brown. It was so big – I had not dreamed that a butterfly could be so big! But there were more things to say that will not come pat in words except that I remember how I wanted to touch the deep brown of it and began to smile with pleasure at the mere thought.

Olympe clasped her hands in excitement so that I saw the light tremble on the red enamel of her nails as she bent over the wire gauze of the prison.

'It is not a prince but a princess, François,' she said to the fellow who was her assistant in the laboratory. 'See how she is feathered with softness, Paul!' I liked that. It made me smile as much as though I had touched the beauty. Feathered with softness! And it looked that way in spite of its size, as though the thin air could float it. 'She is a princess, now, but she is going to be a queen. François, open the window. You've forgotten to open the window.'

François looked at me still more venomously as though I had given the little reprimand, but as he opened the window he told Olympe to remember that the Great Peacock was barely out of the cocoon and that there was still time.

'There! There!' said Olympe gently. She went to the window and held her hands out into the sunshine. The rest of her was exciting enough, but her hands were lovely and perfect now covered with bright gold.

'Now the news is passing out,' she said. 'The wind is carrying it. Do you see that poplar trembling and silvering, Paul? You can hear the whisper spreading.'

She kept her hands spread out in the heat of the sun; her eyes were half closed; she began to laugh, and the laughter was only a whisper too.

'What's the news that's passing through the window?' I asked François.

'The sort of news that the male moths want to hear,' he said. He kept his eyes fixed on the girl and spoke as though it hurt him to give me information. 'There aren't many of them. Only at the feet of the oldest almond trees. But this news will go to them, even against the wind, and they'll come for leagues.'

Olympe had raised her head and, with closed eyes, let the full strength of the sun pour against her face. I was sure she did not hear François continuing, with a slow sneer in his voice: 'One mate, and all the rest are wedding guests. They die the same day. They do not eat. The mouthparts are only vestigial. They always dance round the wedding couple and they always die.'

I think he would have gone on in the same quiet, ironical voice, but Olympe now turned from the window. Somehow I felt that he had not been talking about the moths but telling me that he loved the girl.

We went down into the garden and sat on a bench where the crystal shadow of the fountain kept flowing over our feet. Now that I was close to the garden, I could see that it had not been altered from its old condition very long before. The ragged grass borders had been trimmed to neatness and flowers were blooming even in shadowy places where they could never have grown, so that I began to guess that the whole place had been brightened suddenly by putting potted plants in the ground. Some of the big blossoms had commenced to lean on dying stalks; I could not help thinking of a stage-set and wondering what the action of the play would be, or if it had already commenced with me as an unconscious actor. This sense of unreality that contained me as part of the illusion was not a thing to smile at, for it was like having the print of a book dissolve and widen into the green and gold and blue of nature, all the beauty of summer enlarging from the poor words that had contained it. To give that illusion force and weight, here was Olympe Arouet beside me with the grayness of her old life laid away and a distance of imagination, beyond the distances of time and space, between the moment and the past. Excitement that had commenced to warm my blood when I first saw her now mounted into my brain. I was both spectator and performer; I began to watch and to expect, hoping that I should soon recognize the part that had been assigned to me.

If this seems very extraordinary or fanciful language, nevertheless, the bearing of Olympe was that of one before a great audience, and her expression kept changing as though she were listening to several persons instead of one. I remember casting about for things to talk of, and that I thought of trying the weather, the garden, Provence; but all of these merely made a setting for the girl. She was talking on, and all at once I realized that she had asked me a question. So I said frankly: 'I've not been hearing you very well. I've been too busy looking at you and thinking about you.'

She was very pleased; she began to laugh, with her eyes resting on mine.

'Ah, Paul, how nice of you!' she said. 'I was tired of being listened to and never seen. And so I studied being this way, and now I *am* this way. Do you like it?'

I smiled, and she laughed at herself again. 'I want to be assured and reassured,' she said. 'Like a baby taking its first steps.'

'You're not a baby,' I told her seriously, because I was alarmed. It is high time to be afraid when a girl becomes so extremely naïve. 'But say what it was that made you send for me?' I went on.

'Ah, because I wanted to see you, my old friend. And then besides there is the other thing. But how am I going to talk about that? How am I to say it?'

She caught her face in her hands and looked askance at the fountain, as though she might find help in the brightening and the showering of the water. 'I *must* find a way of saying it,' she murmured.

All at once I was sure that I did not want her to say the important thing which might put an end to my visit. She was in some sort of trouble, no doubt; she was in some sort of money trouble, of money doubt and, though I should be glad to give advice or help, I felt that I wanted to be something more than a broker just then. 'There is plenty of time,' I said.

'Ah, is there plenty of time?' she asked, with a great breath of relief.

'There's all the time in the world.'

'Then I needn't hurry? I can wait – and find the words? Ah, how good that is! Just for a little while, even for a day or two, you will forget Paris and New York, Paul?'

At this she touched my arm and appealed to me with her face raised, so that I saw clearly the edges of the paint on her lips and the black that thickened her eyelashes; yet somehow this artificiality did not seem to me unclean.

'Don't do that,' I said, before I knew that the words were coming.

'What?' she asked, drawing back her hand quickly. 'What have I done, Paul? Ah, you see I have spent so much time with insects that I don't know how to talk to men!'

That made me smile. 'The fact is – ' I began. But then she broke in: 'Don't explain. If you'll keep on smiling, everything is all right, and I don't want you to explain.'

We got to lunch time quickly, for time moves very fast when one is trying to lay hold on every passing minute. Once when I was in Italy I remembered leaving the heat of Florence to go to the Lido, and sitting in the deep shadow of a hotel veranda and never turning my head, for fear the world behind me would not be as happy as my heart, and simply watching the high wall of the sea with white sails climbing it and taking the blue stain of distance as they reached the top. This day with Olympe Arouet was like that. Something like air hunger made me take a deep breath now and then; the cause of happiness was partly in that old Provence and partly in the girl, and as time rushed by me I was afraid to arrest its flight by trying to understand.

The dining room was big and still and cool and dim. François, who sat with us, was almost lost in the shadow except for the gleam of his eyes as he turned them toward me; but Olympe shone in all lights. What we ate I don't remember, but there was a wine of Alsace, well iced, with a thin bouquet and good clean taste. After lunch came siesta time, but late in the afternoon Olympe appeared again in a dress of rough, misty blue. It looked loose and easy and cool, but quite smart enough for Paris. And time began to sweep past me like a wind again until, all at once, the sunset was blooming round the wide horizon.

Then I remembered myself and said, 'It's time for me to get to town and find a room in the hotel.'

'In the hotel? A room in the hotel?' cried Olympe. 'But see this big house – it has always been too full of rooms, and yours is ready for you. The one where you had your siesta. Couldn't you be happy in that room?'

I thought of the tall curtains and the whispering airs and the great jars out of which the flowers rose and leaned. But: 'You know, Olympe, you haven't a chaperon in the house. The room is charming, but of course I can't spend the night here.'

She thought about this for only a moment before she said, 'Well, there's François for a chaperon.'

'That youngster?' I exclaimed.

'Knowledge is what counts, and François knows everything,' she answered. She laughed in a way that I did not altogether like. 'François will be perfect as a chaperon,' she said, 'and of course you are going to stay.'

I felt that it was very wrong, but to give any French girl advice always seems a foolish impertinence. Anyway I stayed. We walked about through the garden a bit longer before Olympe went up to dress for dinner. I followed more slowly, knowing that I was doing wrong but entirely happy about it. I suppose there are few pleasures that are not improved by a small sense of guilt.

Just as I came into the hall a very odd thing happened. The lights flashed on, making the sky beyond the windows a deeper blue, and in the corner of the hall I saw François with his hand still on the electric switch. The fellow watched me across the room like a cat, but as I came to the foot of the stairs I knew that he was smiling. Somehow he was relieved – relieved and triumphant.

I turned about quickly and the smile was indeed on his mouth, insolently persisting.

'What's the news of the Great Peacock?' I asked, to justify the manner in which I had turned.

'Oh, they'll be arriving, perhaps before night,' he said, with a French shrug of his French shoulders.

'Pouring into that room upstairs?' I asked.

'And the other rooms,' said François. 'A lot of the wedding guests lose their way.'

The sneer with which he spoke became unendurable. I turned away, and the memory of his smile followed up the stairs behind me. I could not get the chill out of my blood until I had finished bathing and dressing, because I kept remembering what the girl had said – that François knew everything. Confound him, I began to fear that he did!

Downstairs I found Olympe dressed in white and completing herself with a corsage of flowers. She had blue and yellow and red to choose from but she appealed to me to make a choice. 'But I know what you will pick,' she said, turning her back to cover the three little bouquets from my eyes. 'I have it in my hand now.'

'Show it to me and I'll be honest,' I said.

She held out the red and I nodded at once. 'I thought so,' she said, and I knew that I had made a mistake though I could not see why. But how can any man understand a woman when what seems to us the most faint and devious path may be the broad, straight road to her heart?

François appeared, silent and yellow as always, and made himself useful serving dry vermouth with fragrant, thin shavings of lemon peel dropped into it, while Olympe pinned the miniature red roses at her breast, smiling down at them or at her hands. Afterward she made me sit in a high-backed red chair. The red velvet that lined it was a bit moth-eaten, but that only helped it to look authentic and baronial. She surveyed me from the arm of a smaller chair, saying: 'Have you had a happy day, Paul? There is something in the quiet down here, and a few people like it. Have you been happy?'

I told her that there was a lot in the quiet down there, and that I was very happy. 'Yes, after Paris,' she said. 'Paris is a plus for some people, but it is a minus for others. It's a minus for me.'

Now, as she sat there chatting, her voice soft and her smile continuing, I could feel that she was judging me in relation to that stiff-backed velvet chair which framed me. For the second time I was aware of her criticism and, because of that, perhaps, all at once I knew that I was in love with Olympe Arouet. All the other women I had cared for became as dim as pictures in a family album; the dust of time covered them, throat and lips and hair. I knew also that Olympe had made me love her and that she had called me from Paris for that purpose; but by the very knowing of these facts I was subdued, and by the simultaneous assurance that at this same moment she was not quite sure of the wisdom of her course.

What is a man to do in a time like this? If he tries to be entertaining he is apt to make himself into a grinning ape; if he is silent he is a boor. On the other hand, he may become demonstrative, and that is apt to be the worst of all. I was cold with anxiety, and now I told myself that I understood why François refilled my glass with almost an air of kindness. I could swear that he himself loved Olympe, but already he had ceased worrying about me. I was filled with a very still and deep desire to murder François except that when he was gone I would lose with him the answer to that riddle which he seemed to understand. What he had said about wedding guests going astray – that was what got between me and the taste of the French vermouth.

It was just at this time that the tires of an automobile came grinding over the gravel of the driveway and stopped before the house. A moment later a servant appeared and announced that a man's automobile was out of order and that the chauffeur would have to work at it, but the gentleman asserted he was a friend of the house and sent in his card.

Olympe took it, canted her head a bit to one side, frowned, and then looked up at the man who had stepped into the doorway. He was dressed in rough tweeds. It looked as though the wind had been tousling his hair all day long and his forehead had been polished red-brown by the sun. He was tall but sparely made and his shoulders were a trifle bent. Yet what a man he seemed! Young, I mean, and smiling because he found the world young with him. There was an alertness in his carriage, and the very bend of his shoulders gave him the look of one leaning forward to run. Besides all that – the youth and the impatient hurry of his look – he was more distinguished in that traveling suit than a diplomat in tails with a string of gaudy medals and ribbons across the breast. When Olympe went up and spoke to him, he bowed over her hand in a way that no American has ever been able to bow; no, not trained dancers even. His manners were those of a race which for a thousand years has looked at women as though they were queens of Sheba but which has treated them as though they were not worth a damn.

While Olympe Arouet talked to him I could see her head lifting by degrees, and when she turned toward us again, I knew that she had taken something into her eyes. She introduced him to us with a sort of happy unconsciousness. When he came closer, he seemed much more foreign than at a distance. His head was well made but there was a boniness about the temples and a distinct slant of the eyes. His name I never made out very clearly but it sounded, on the lips of Olympe, something like Borik, or Zborik, or Borikh, and the first name was Crassin, perhaps spelled with a 'k' and a 'z.'

I thought he was a Russian, but he might have been a Magyar or a

Pole or even a Mongolian. All Western tongues were hard for him, as I learned before the evening was over, yet he seemed able to understand Olympe and she certainly understood him from the moment when he began apologizing for his clothes to the time we all sat down at the dinner table. It appeared that his chauffeur had hopes of repairing the car soon, and that it was important for Borik to be on his way again as soon as possible.

How glad I was of that! I wanted to leave the table and help the chauffeur. The engine trouble, it appeared, had developed only a few miles down the road, and then Borik, or Zborik, or whatever his name was, had remembered that many years ago he had come from his far-off country with his father and had visited the house of Jean Arouet.

'But I remember it perfectly well now,' said Olympe. 'You were the tall boy in the uniform. Do you still wear uniforms?'

'Why should we, except on a golf course?' said Borik – at least, that was the meaning I got out of his chopped and broken French. Olympe laughed a good deal at that, and even let her eyes leave his face for a moment to welcome François and me into her mirth, but I could not smile. If only that chauffeur might be inspired to finish his work soon – that was my only thought. Sometimes François and I looked straight at each other. His expression was that of a man listening to faraway sounds, and I know that mine was the same.

Olympe ran on about the visit and the wise, bearded face of Borik's father.

'He is dead,' said Borik, and closed his eyes and smiled.

That hit me – the calm, clear voice more than the words.

He knew the French for 'dead' well enough and he brought it out in his melodious voice with a trifle of Oriental sing-song, caused I suppose by the effort of finding strange words. I hoped the cold blood of this would shock Olympe, and it did. The smile left her face as though a shadowy gesture had removed it. She leaned and stared for an instant; then her trouble disappeared. All this, mind you, took hardly longer than the flicker of an eyelash, but then I saw, or guessed with Olympe, that the eyes of Borik had closed in exquisite anguish. He was tasting that death again, not smiling at it.

It's a small thing to write about. It wasn't a small thing to see. It lasted a second, but that was long enough to take one winging into a strange land where people can look the end of things in the face and keep on smiling. I felt rather dizzy, returning again to that table which

Olympe had made so brilliant and gay that it was like a victory feast — at which François and I represented the losers.

Borik went on talking about his father. I think I understood him more by the words and the murmured sympathy of Olympe, which commented on everything. Just what the situation was I do not know, but there had been some sort of a rising and the castle had been filled with yelling murder. A few of the faithful had dragged Borik away from his father — to save the line — and I suppose it had been some little principality not too obscure for revolution to find it out. And then the father had turned and faced the murderers in a narrow hall, covering the rescue of the boy.

'He stood like this,' said Borik.

With a lift of his hand and his head he showed how the brave old man had stood. The tears began to run down Olympe's face, but a moment later Borik had us out in the wind among the icy rocks of winter mountains, the pursuit laboring behind so close that the nightmare weakness began to come into my knees as I listened. Then Borik was at the verge of a great lake, he was pushing out in a small boat, and as the waves hurled him about, a thick squall ran over the waters and shut him away from the view of his enemies.

'But my father was dead!' he finished.

Jealousy feeds on all things, even the tenderest; but, though I wished Borik any place away from that house, even in hell, I liked him as well at that moment as I have ever liked any man.

I don't mean that Borik spent the entire dinner time talking about his own experiences — and death. He did his gallant best to get François into the conversation and I remember that he told me with a sort of an air that he had seen New York, once — in a picture book! He raised his hand and his eyes and then shuddered; there are a good many people who feel that way about New York, but Borik smiled to show that he was speaking as one ignorant of how to value such a mighty bigness and majesty and ugliness.

After dinner we went into the salon on the way to the garden, where Olympe had suggested a walk, but Borik spied the piano and he brushed the three of us into the garden ahead of him, with his gestures and his bows; afterward we heard the piano and the voice of Borik singing. He had neither range nor strength; some of his notes squeaked and others were shouted; but he did the thing with a strength of race, so to speak, and out there in the black-and-white of the garden by moonlight we felt the wildness of joy and the wildness of sorrow of which music can make one theme.

Olympe sat down on the first bench with François on one side of her and me on the other. She lay back with her head reclining, given up to listening. There was enough wind to blow the shadow of a branch across her, so that she was continually between the moon and the darkness, and this gave an odd effect as though she were drifting away from us toward the music.

'Paul,' she said, 'were you ever in love?'

'Yes,' I answered.

'Tell me about it,' said Olympe. 'Tell me about it, while I listen.'

Tell her about a love affair of mine while she listened to Borik's Oriental music? Well, I told her, clearly, so that François could listen also. I tried to make another night, far away in California, but still farther away in my own mind, live again there in Provence in the untrue beauty of that garden.

She listened devoutly – always more to the music than to me, and once she looked up at me and said, 'Was it like that?' and sorrow that music knows nothing about went through me.

She was using my words, not me.

In the meantime that damned chauffeur might save everything if he would only hurry with his work!

The music ended. Borik stood on the terrace, leaning wearily on the stone balustrade and saying that he was tired. He was so tired that he wanted to lie down and sleep, even if it were only for an hour.

François and I looked at each other suddenly as Olympe sprang to her feet. She had no idea that the evening was to end like this and she went up to Borik and talked eagerly to him. But he merely looked down at his hands on the balustrade and shook his head. I don't know what she had suggested – a walk, a talk; but she was completely indignant over this ungentlemanly behavior. She turned about and said:

'I'm tired also. François, will you show him a room? There is an extra one ready, I think.' She turned back to Borik and said:

'Perhaps I shall not have the pleasure of seeing you again, monsieur. Perhaps your car will be repaired before morning and you will be gone. Therefore, adieu.'

He bowed over her hand, and she went quickly into the house.

When Borik and François were gone, there was no reason why I should remain in that damned garden with the ghost of Borik's singing about me, so I went up to bed in my turn. I passed François in the upper hall and he said, 'But perhaps, after all – '

I let him finish off his idea with his own gesture and went gloomily on.

But then I reached the open door of a room and saw Olympe standing at the window with the moonlight sloping over her. She had thrown over her shoulders a great cloak of figured velvet and, since her hands were on her hips, I thought of the soft, unfolded wings of the Great Peacock.

'Olympe – ' I said.

She turned her head, silently, but I could see that she was smiling, and that was what drew me across the room until I faced her. There was enough in me to have poured out song and poetry but all I could say was, 'I love you!'

She laid a hand on my breast and lifted her head a little. It was not exactly a gesture to withhold me but rather like that of one who supports a book at the proper distance for reading. I noticed then a very thin, an almost impalpable fragrance, and afterward I saw that she was smiling. She was not using me for her mirth but I knew that I stood at a great distance.

I stepped back a little. Her hand remained where it had been, half extended; her smile remained also, and I had to set my teeth and gather my strength before I could walk out of that room. A few minutes later I was lying in my bed, swearing through stiff lips in a whisper. There had been no reason for waiting for a silly convention at such a time. I could see now that the best plan for me would have been to talk as soon as possible – even that morning, or certainly in the evening, and then perhaps I could have drawn her to me forever.

The last I remember of that hour was that my hands were still gripped hard, and I was telling myself that I would have her in spite of Borik and the devil.

When I wakened there was a whispering in the room, a queer hushing noise that made me snap on a light which showed me half a dozen Great Peacock moths fluttering around the room; and I realized that the call of the female had gone out, as Olympe had said it would, and had brought in the searchers. These were some of those wedding guests that had missed the way.

I sat up in bed and looked at the great beauties drawing their uneasy circles closer and closer to the glare of the light. And then I heard a sound like a drawn breath with a choking sob in it out in the hall.

I pulled on a dressing gown, stepped into slippers, and jerked the door open, and saw François close by. The moon had shifted until the light of it slanted through the arcades of the hall, and by that illumination I saw that the face of François was battered and running blood. His clothes were fouled with dust. His coat was ripped open.

He came right up to me. Blood spattered from his lips as he said, 'And you – you slept – you slept, you – '

He meant a great deal of insult, but somehow I was in no humor to resent what he said because it was clear that we had at least one important interest somewhat in common. And then I heard the sudden rattle of a self-starter in front of the house, the whine of a departing motor. A horn sounded, already small with distance.

François leaned a hand against the wall and nodded at me. He laughed, and the laughter did horrible things to his face.

'Now he is gone,' said François. 'He was ready to go, and he has gone. And I – and you – '

He began to laugh again and then went down the hall with a bit of a stagger in his step. His door closed and shut me out by myself in the midst of an unanswered problem. Everything was whirling together in my mind – Olympe, Borik, François, the Great Peacock moth. But I could guess that it was Borik who had started the red dripping down the sallow face of François.

Then I heard a quick, light step farther down the hall. I saw someone open the door of that bare room in which the Great Peacock female was enclosed. I followed and passed in. All the air of the room was one gay confusion, for there were thirty, forty, fifty of the huge butterflies sweeping out of the corners of the room to dance around the central light in the ceiling.

In spite of François there was still sleep in my mind, but the last of it was scattered when I saw that Olympe was there. And with the sight of her that entire day became as dim as something dreamed but never lived, a vision that would melt in the first bright hour of reality. For now I saw her as I had expected to find her when I came down from Paris.

I mean that she had a gray smock over her dress, and from her face every trace of make-up had been removed, so that one could see, as I had expected, the shadowy outline of the skull striking through the flesh, as it were. I had thought that she was beautiful, but she was not even pretty now.

She said: 'Close the door, Paul. But even if you left it open they would not leave.'

'Olympe,' I said, 'I've seen François and – what has happened in the house?'

Now I saw that although her face was as arid and gray as a desert, her eyes held an abundance of light. And I knew that it would never stop welling into them.

Instead of answering me, she said: 'You might even leave the door open to cool the room, because the Great Peacocks won't leave. They're dancing at the wedding feast, you know.'

I stared at her. Comprehension began to come over me suddenly.

'Borik has gone,' I said. 'But you don't mean – Olympe – '

I began to laugh, easily. For the day, you see, was already lost in the intangible part of existence, the dreams.

She spread her hands toward the moths.

'How beautiful they are, the poor dears,' she said.

A Special Occasion

'Virtue can be learned,' Jerry Campbell says in this highly autobiographical selection. Faust himself was continually trying to learn virtue, but apparently did so with no greater success than Campbell, a character caught in a middle-aged morass of disintegrating relationships and fading dreams. Faust's personal life, like Campbell's, was also deteriorating. Campbell has a mistress as well as a wife – as did Faust. Campbell has a drinking problem – as did Faust. Campbell's skills as an architect are being eroded by work that is less than his best, just as Faust feared that the millions of words of prose he was pouring out would erode his ability to write poetry. For these reasons this story may be the most painfully self-revealing of all Faust's stories.

In one passage of 'A Special Occasion,' Campbell sits in despair in his study. 'When he looked about he could recognize only a few of his books which were in light-colored bindings. The Rabelais, for instance, was distinguishable because it was done in unstained Levant morocco, and the polished vellum of a photographic reprint of Caxton's Chaucer shone like a lighted candle; but he could not find Thucydides, the clear-thinker. But even Thucydides, calm and great, would be little help to him. He had forgotten almost everything except the seventh book, and that was an empire's ruin. He had forgotten too much. In his youth he had done his reading; afterward he had bound the volumes and put them away on shelves.' These are Faust's own books and this passage is a cry from his heart.

To be nearer to his agent and his markets, Faust was living periodically in

New York, mingling socially with editors, publishers, writers, and other professional people when the story first appeared in *Harper's* in February 1934. 'A Special Occasion' is set against that background. Like 'The Wedding Guest,' it is a 'serious' story of the kind he rarely attempted, still stubbornly believing the best means for his literary expression was serious poetry. There is no dream-writing here. Faust was digging deep into his own tormented experience and translating it into art. As he later wrote to Grace Flandrau, a fellow writer, 'Now and then in short stories I've barely rubbed elbows with the painful truth, but I've never liked that truth; it's always seemed horrible to me.'

CAMPBELL SAT IN THE LOCKER ROOM after squash and watched the loose flesh over his heart quivering like a jelly. Richards had beaten him. Richards always beat him now, and Cullen would no longer play with him because he was fifty-five and his backhand was no damned good. It never was more than a sort of poke, but it used to connect. He crossed his feet to take the shudder out of his knees and looked down at the folds in his stomach and the delicate rills of sweat in the wrinkles. His windpipe burned down the middle of him. One of these days he would cut out the cigarettes.

Richards, already back from the showers, was at his locker, putting on a pair of glasses with a thin black ribbon hanging down from them. The spectacles dressed up Richards almost more than a suit of clothes and kept one's attention on his tight-lipped mouth. Richards was sixty, but he still played squash because he had a pair of legs under him. He had been a footballer back there in the nineties, and a big fold of muscle hung above each knee.

'I'm giving you a drink tonight,' said Richards.

'Thanks,' said Campbell. 'I'm not drinking. It's a special occasion. My girl comes home. The wife has been up watching her graduate from school.'

Richards took out a bottle.

'I'm giving you a drink,' he said. 'This *is* a special occasion. It's always a special occasion when you get a chance at Bushmill's Black Label.'

'I've heard of the stuff,' said Campbell, 'but I'm not taking it. Nothing tonight. In a house full of women, you know how it is. They hate to see the father with an edge. That's the trouble with women. They don't understand.'

He made a backhanded gesture and looked round the room at the lounging naked men. He breathed the thick smell of sweat and told himself he liked it. How many tons of flesh, in the course of a year, dissolved here in fumes and sweating? Sensible men kept their bodies in a state of flux, building, dissolving. That was nature's plan. Look at the universe of stars, melting into radiation; and somewhere the radiation was regathered to form matter. The astronomers would find that out one day.

Richards uncorked the bottle and gave it to him.

'Give your nose a chance anyway,' said Richards.

Campbell inhaled the fragrance. The alcohol thirst took him hard, just beneath the Adam's apple. He thought of a big trundling automobile like his own, of night, and lights, and a woman. He could always turn off other thoughts and conceive the sort of a woman he wanted, smiling at him.

'It smells weak and too sweet,' he said.

'There's no tick of bathtub gin in it, and it's not your Jamaica rum,' said Richards.

'Rum is all right,' declared Campbell. He frowned, expounding his doctrine: 'There's something honest about rum. Made out of good molasses. It puts it on you gradually. Like putting varnish on a car, all over, coat by coat.'

'Oh, all right,' said Richards. 'I know why you drink rum. We all know why.' He laughed and poured two fingers and a half into two tall glasses. 'You melt some of this in your mouth and try to form good habits. Virtue can be learned.'

When a man is sixty you have to be polite to him. Campbell was at least silent, but he sneered as he breathed of the whisky. He tasted it. 'It's too sweet,' he said. He tasted it again and his anger and his words loosened in his throat. 'It's like a good cognac,' he said. 'It's like a hundred-year-old brandy, by God! It's like Napoleon. Where did you get it?'

'I told you about the case of the Cuban up for murder? You ought to read the papers, Campbell, and you'd find out a lot of good things about me. I took that case to the jury, let in all their damned evidence, and then made a speech about justifiable homicide.'

'You justified murder?' said Campbell dreamily.

'It went over,' said Richards. 'The Cuban paid my fee and felt he owed me something more, so he dug up a case of this Bushmill's. There's a white label too, but this black label spends twenty years in the wood getting older and wiser. You can't buy it unless you know where. It's the finest thing that comes out of Ireland.'

'Barring Irish hunters,' said Campbell. 'I ran into a streak of bad luck three or four years ago and started falling all the time. So I gave it up.'

Richards put back his head and looked at him through half-closed eyes. 'So you gave up – the horses, eh?' said he. 'Have some ice and soda in that.'

'Don't bother me,' said Campbell.

He began to drink slowly, steadily, in small swallows. He kept on drinking until the last of the whisky was down. Then he lighted a cigarette and considered. The whisky was somewhere in the top of his brain, in his heart, pumping out inexhaustible joy through his arteries. 'You don't understand,' said Campbell.

He went over to the bottle and poured a stiff slug into his glass again. Richards lifted a hand and turned a little, hastily, but then he settled back in his chair. Campbell pretended not to notice. 'What don't I understand? About whisky straight?' asked Richards.

'I'm going to tell you something,' said Campbell. 'It's a kind of religion with me. You go back to Rabelais to get the start of the idea. About hearty people. That's the first thing. A man ought to be hearty. A woman too – '

Afterward he knew that he had been talking a good deal. His lips were a little stiff, his eyes felt larger. Richards had the tight face of a judge, and there was not much whisky left in the bottle. Richards had been dressing; he was ready for the street and now he rose.

'Wait a minute,' said Campbell. 'What's the matter? I finished most of that stuff. Look here. I want to pay you for the bottle. What I mean is, it's damn good stuff.'

Richards jerked round quickly. He checked the first words that parted his lips. 'Well, good night,' he said, and went out suddenly.

Campbell brooded while he was taking his shower and dressing, but the familiar happiness began to grow up and brighten that world which a man sees best when his eyes are fixed on nothingness. Going down in the elevator, a number of younger members of the club were pressed about him, and he heard a low voice say, 'The old boy's already on his way.' A soft chuckle answered that remark. Campbell turned with a smile. 'You've had a drink yourself, my lad,' he said. 'Whisky is the staff of the truthteller!'

He saw the eyes of the boy widen a little. 'I beg your pardon, Mr. Campbell,' said the lad. And Campbell said, 'My dear fellow, not at all!'

He looked at his watch when he got into his car, and was shocked. His wife had said that it was a special occasion. Two days before, when she left, she had taken him by the lapels of his coat. Her hands were tight and strong. 'It's going to be a special occasion, Jerry,' she had said. 'You will remember, dear, won't you?'

'Drive like hell,' he said to his chauffeur.

They drove like hell, as soon as the slow, regular pulsation of the downtown traffic let them go. The steady flicker of cars going past him wearied his eyes, so he closed them. Later he discovered with a start that he had been asleep. As he opened his eyes he had a feeling that they were shooting downhill, through flame, but he found that they were merely wheeling softly past the intersection of highways at White Forest. They would soon be home. It was sunset.

This uptilt of the world to the flat once more irritated him as though he had wakened from a happy dream. Fingertips pressed steadily against his head above the ears, it seemed; the unfamiliar taste on the back of his tongue he presently located as Bushmill's Black Label. That made him remember the way Richards had left him at the club, and he reached under the flap of the side pocket of the car to the flask of Jamaica. People hate the truth, he decided. That was why Richards had been hating him with all the color pressed out of his tight lips. But the truth is that men ought to be heartier; women ought to be heartier too. You find the truth back in old Rabelais. 'Drink.' That was what the voice of the oracle of the holy bottle had meant. Be yourself, even the nakedness that alcohol exposes; and if the world doesn't approve, that's because the world doesn't understand – Rabelais, and a lot of other important things.

He took a short pull at the flask, then he took a long one. He took another drink in the way he had learned only a short three years ago, little swallows, rapidly taken, holding the breath. He kept the flask in his hand for comfort and felt the rum work as rum always will, honestly, steadily – no casual flicker but a good strong blaze that warms the farthest corners of the heart.

Then he saw the triangle of lights that announced the house of Cerise Mayberry, over there on the edge of the hills. He tapped automatically on the glass. 'The Mayberry house,' he said, and Jordan turned and

looked at him a tenth of a second longer than he should have dared.
Jordan knew too much; but all chauffeurs know too much. That's the
way they are.

They left the sticky black of the highway and the big, soft tires went
crunching over the gravel of the drive. The dark trees were kindly forms
on either side, sweeping him on. A man's home is where his heart is,
he felt. Cerise Mayberry. He called her 'Cherry.' Cerise is a silly name.
Cherry Mayberry was a nice name; there was really something nice
about it because it fitted her. It had a sort of rhyme to it. More than a
rhyme. Some men have poetry in them. Some haven't. That's all there is
to it.

The car stopped in front of the wooden low veranda, with its three
steps up. He got out. He remembered that the flask was in his hand and
put it back into the side pocket.

Jordan was being chauffeurish. Considering all that Jordan knew, it
was foolish for Jordan to step so far back into his manners and look at
vacancy as he said, 'We're not being late for home – and Miss Louise?'

'I'm only staying a minute,' said Campbell. Jordan was crazy about
Louise. The cook was crazy about Louise. The wife was crazy about
Louise. She was all right. She might even turn out to be hearty if the
wife would keep her hands off now and then. What a girl needs is the
molding influence of a man, the impress of the wider, the bigger life.

Campbell went up the steps and rang the bell. He got out a cigarette
and lighted it. Cerise opened the door and backed up before him into
the safe obscurity of the hall before she kissed him. She came right into
his arms, bending back her head while she lay there for a moment, with
her lips still half-formed after the kiss. Her eyes were loving him.

'Papa, are you blotto?' said Cerise.

He shook himself free. A man ought never to permit flapperisms. The
trouble with Cerise was not that she had been married a couple of times
but that she had grown up to womanhood in the postwar period, and
one could still find in her vocabulary tokens of the days when nothing
mattered.

'Don't be cross,' said Cerise, and went hastily before him through
the door into the living room, slinking a little, looking back over her
shoulder, pretending fright.

He followed her with a firm step. 'I want to talk to you, Cherry,'
he said.

'About Rabelais?' she asked.

He realized that she had only been pretending fear. But one of these days she would know him better.

'One of these days you're gunna know me better, Cherry,' he said.

'Better Cherry?' said the girl. 'There aren't any better cherries. You know that, papa.'

'I don't like it,' said Campbell.

'Of course you don't like it straight,' said Cerise. 'You ought to have lemon juice and things with it. Shall I make you a cocktail?'

'Aw, well. Shake one up,' said Campbell.

He sank into a soft chair and tapped his cigarette ashes on the floor. The great thing about Cherry was that she understood. The worst thing about her was that she didn't understand enough. But you can't ask for the world with a fence round it. Everything has to have a beginning. After a while he would be able to teach her. For one thing, a woman ought not to be so damned expensive. A lot of the clothes they buy are name and nothing else.

Cerise came in again with the cocktail shaker. She went at her work heartily; her whole body shook with the vibration; there was even a tremor in her cheeks, and her fluffly sleeves spread into a pink cloud. Pink was her color. She could not use rouge because of the baby tint of her skin; therefore, except for the eyes and the smiling, her face was rather dim, and one had to look into it closely to see faults. Campbell preferred not to see the faults.

She brought two little base-shaped cups of silver filled with cracked ice so that the cups would frost like the shaker. Then she emptied the ice and poured the drink. It was pink – her color. That was the stain of orange juice in the rum cocktail. He tasted the first one and then he drank three, quickly. If cocktails are to be taken they ought to be drunk before the melting ice has qualified the liquor too much. Cerise had only one; he had taught her never to take more than one because liquor makes the eyes of a woman more unclean than sleep. She sat on the arm of a chair at a little distance because she knew just how to lend herself enchantment. The platinum chain about her throat was merely a line of light; the big emerald of the pendant gleamed like an eye looking this way and that. Her head was tilted back to just the right angle. He liked the consciousness of an art that so perfectly expressed Cerise.

He had been enjoying her silently, like thought, when a football pounced on the little side porch, a door jerked open with force that sent a vibration through the old house and made the two silver cups chime softly together.

'Cerise!' called the voice of young Bob Wilson. 'Oh, Cerise, darling!'

She had got to the door almost in time to stop the last words, but not quite. She opened the door a bit and called over her shoulder: 'Wait a minute, Bob.' Then she faced Campbell.

All he could see was the quick, high lifting of her breast and the green of the emerald, with a price mark tagged on it in his mind. He wanted to kill her, but a man has to take things in his stride, and a good actor improvises to fill a blank.

'I'm sorry I came in so late and stayed so long,' he said. 'Good night, Cherry. And good-by.'

He could see the malice cheapen and tighten her face. What she had to say stiffened her lips. 'Maybe I ought to tell you that a *lady* rang up a while ago and asked if you were here. I think it was your wife.'

He turned slowly from a room he would never see again though he would keep its corners of laughter and breathless silence always in his mind. He knew bitterly that he could never wash himself clean of this yesterday. There was a shadowy half of his thought that told him the uncleanness had spread over others; and if Margaret really had telephoned to inquire for him it meant that she had known about this affair long enough to lose her most vital strength, which was her pride.

He was at the door of the hall before the girl said, 'Ah, to hell with you!'

Campbell got out into his car as quickly as possible and sat back into the cushions with his nostrils widening to take bigger breaths of the cool evening air. As the car turned out cautiously into the highway he had a feeling that thousands of doors were shutting behind him; but in spite of that he knew that he would have to find another road to town so that he might never again see the white, pointed forehead of that house by day or its triangle of lights at night.

The automobile, gathering speed, lurched long and high over a swell in the road; a wave of nausea came up through Campbell and left a cold tingling in his lips. He settled his troubled stomach with another pull at the rum flask. The familiar burn of it put his body at ease before the car turned into his driveway; the trouble in his mind would have to be put at rest in another way.

As for Cerise, he thought, a man can't get something for nothing, and he had been a fool to think that he could go to Cerise and relax like a tired body in a hot bath. She had made a fool of him because he had chosen to be off guard. Merely to be known, merely to be understood is what most of us desire, as though a divine ray will surely dazzle every true observer, as though, in fact, clear understanding would not bring a harvest of sneers and laughter. But the end of all is that one must work and never let the mind be still. He had dodged that truth and lost his happiness with his wife by the evasion. He had wished for gaiety and forgotten that the serious souls are apt to be the gentle ones also; and, though he had known that there was gold to be found in her, he had shrunk from the labor. Now he had come home to her 'special occasion' drunk or half drunk. He spoke the words softly and then tried to rub the thick numbness out of his upper lip. What he would say to Margaret began to enter his throat and his hands.

The car stopped. He got out and looked at the face of his house, all obscured with vines in which the wind kept up a gently rushing sound, like that of water. He looked higher still to where the brow of the building should have risen according to those old plans which he and Margaret had dreamed out together; but through the ghost of the lost idea he saw now the dark tips of trees and the stars.

In the old days, before he had learned how much money can be made out of large contracts and two-family houses, as a young fool of an architect his thoughts had dealt with marble and with noble space. Perhaps he had been young, but not such a fool. Something in the past was worth taking up where he had left it if only he could find the lost way.

When he entered the house he bumped his shoulders on each side of the doorway. That was a bad sign. In the still air his face began to burn. Well, Margaret would give him one of her long, quiet looks.

On a chair he saw the shapeless round of a hat and a blue coat with a collar of soft gray fur. He could remember when Louise had first appeared in it and how it had covered the tall stalk of her body and made him see only her face, like a flower.

He went on down the hall until he saw his wife in the dining room doing something with the flowers on the table. The sight of the glasses, each with its thin high light, and the frosty white of the silver made him feel that his hands were huge, witless things. He would sit silently through dinner, breathing hard; the food would have no taste; it would be something difficult, like pigeons; the women would never look at him; they would keep talking lightly.

He frowned and walked boldly into the room. 'I'm sorry I'm late,

Margaret,' he said. He walked up to the table and dropped the knuckles of one hand on the cold, sleek wood. 'Were you telephoning for me?' He had made up his mind to unmask the guns and face them.

She straightened from the flowers, without haste. It was always as if one sound or a glance had told her everything. Now she stood through a long moment considering him. She was in the rosy shadow of the center lamp, and it made her so young and so lovely that he was moved. He had to start peering before he could reassure himself about the wrinkles round her eyes.

'Yes, I telephoned,' she said. 'Was my voice recognized? I'm sorry for that but I thought that I had to risk something. It's a special occasion in a way, and Louise is still quite fond of you.'

'All right,' said Campbell, nodding as he took it. 'All right. But leaving the girl out of it for a minute' – he moved the thought of her away with a slow sweep of his hand – 'leaving her out, what about you? You've known a good many things for a long time, I suppose?'

She made one of those indirect answers of which she was a master, and he felt she was troubled not by what had been happening in the past but about the way he would accept her knowledge.

'You know that I'm not a radical, my dear,' she said. 'I'm a conservative and I believe that we should carry on with the old things – like households, I mean,' she added quickly.

'All right,' he said. 'I know what you mean, and that the rest is a bust.' But when he had finished saying this she merely continued watching him in an anxious way, and he knew that she was hoping that he also would want to be a 'conservative.' Something was going out of him – the old years – like the swift, dear breath from his body. 'Well, where's Louise?' he asked. He would carry on for the moment and afterward he would confront that blank night, the future.

'Louise took a lantern out to the pasture,' she said. 'She wanted to see Bachelor and Steadfast.'

'I'll go out and find her,' said Campbell, turning gladly.

'Wait a moment. Don't you want a cup of strong coffee?' she asked.

He saw the sense of that. 'Yes,' he said, facing about. 'Some strong coffee. And put something in it, will you?'

That meant morphine. At least he could thank God that Margaret had enough brains not to be horrified by the thought of the drug. She had known, during these last years, that he used morphine after he had been drinking; it helped to take the jitters out of the nerves. But now she kept on in one of her silences for quite a time. He had not been very sure of his 'S' in that last sentence, and perhaps she was going to be disgusted. He could not be sure, because he could not see her face very clearly. Nothing was very clear. He wanted another drink. The silence went on for two or three great seconds.

'Now, look here,' he said, 'I'm not going to have you upstage with me.' He gripped his hands. The tips of his fingers slipped on the wet of the palms. Anger rushed and thundered in him. 'None of this damn' pale martyr stuff. I won't have it. A man takes a drink — why, hell, I won't have you being the offended saint and all that damn' business. Get — get me that coffee!'

She actually waited for another moment.

'All right,' she said. 'I'll bring it to you.'

She went through the swing-door to the pantry, opening it slowly, letting it close so slowly behind her that it made no swishing back and forth. This deliberation made him catch in a deep breath of anger and stir a little so that he saw himself suddenly in the wide mirror above the sideboard, his face deeply set behind the big bright images of the silver. His hand went up quickly to the bald spot to cover the sheen of it. He pulled his fingers down over the soft puffing of his cheeks. He turned his head until he saw the hanging fold of flesh beneath the chin. Even if he got rid of his belly, there was nothing to be done about the face; if he thinned it, there would be more repulsive flabbiness of skin to hang about the eyes and the smile.

Margaret came in with her eyes down on the coffee cup. She had a way of giving a religious solemnity, a processional beauty to her smallest movements.

He took the cup. The phial lay on the saucer beside it.

The little bottle was still sealed, and that meant there was a lot of power within the pinch of a thumb and forefinger, a lot of sleep. He kept on looking at Margaret and stealing toward the truth through darkness until he came into the light of full comprehension. She was watching him as a doctor might watch a patient whose chances are doubtful. Of course she had no real hope, but she would fight to the end to keep the home intact to all appearance. That would be for the sake of the girl. He also had once been very near Louise, but that was back in the old days, at the time when he had won the point-to-point on gray Crucible and little Louise had wept with happiness and pride.

'What's the matter?' asked Margaret, with a gasp in her breathing. 'What are you thinking of?' And she came quickly up to him.

He put out his hand to keep her away, but his hand patted her shoulder. The drink was beginning to go out of him in clouds. It left the familiar weakness in his knees. The chill that came up through the center of him might be fear or exhaustion. An idea began to flicker into his consciousness, dimly and from far away. When he was alone it would be clear. His wife was coming across years of distance to him. Her eyes begged as though she feared a judgment.

'Smile for me, Meg,' he said. 'Then go out and keep Louise occupied for fifteen minutes. I'll be in the library, pulling myself together.'

She left him hesitantly, forcing herself away. As she reached the door, she tried to smile. 'It's going to be all right,' said Campbell. Then she passed into the dimness of the hall. Now that she was turned, seeing her slenderness like that of a girl, the sweetness of the past came over him and the vain desire to return to it. It was a sort of homesickness for which the Germans have a better word – home-woe.

He felt sick; he was weak, and yet his mind worked so clearly that he knew this was an end, not a beginning.

As he had promised, he went into the library, carrying with him the cup of coffee, like the bitter conscience that would have to temper his thinking. As soon as he entered it he regretted having chosen the library because it could never be a place of peace; in those days to which he could make no return he had spent too many hours of struggle and high hope in this room. The big drawing board was still in the corner; he knew every stroke of the unfinished design on it.

He sat down in a deep, soft chair, putting the cup on the little side table. There was no other light than that from the floor lamp beside him. He would have to make up his mind; he would have to finish grappling with that idea which was approaching him from the distance before the coffee was cold.

He was alone. When he looked about he could recognize only a few of his books which were in light-colored bindings. The Rabelais, for instance, was distinguishable because it was done in unstained levant morocco, and the polished vellum of a photographic reprint of Caxton's Chaucer shone like a lighted candle; but he could not find Thucydides, the clear-thinker. The dark red of that leather was lost among sober shadows. But even Thucydides, calm and great, would be little help to him. He had forgotten almost everything except the seventh book, and that was an empire's ruin. He had forgotten too much. In his youth he had done his reading; afterward he had bound the volumes and put them away on shelves.

However, a man should not shrink from being alone. As the panic grew, he wanted to throw open a window and call for Meg, but she could not help; she could not follow where he had to go with his thoughts. It was easier to send the mind back into the past, discovering half-remembered moments of delight, until he arrived, finally, at that picture of the clean-jawed young fighter which stood on the table in Margaret's room. That was the fellow, also, who rode Crucible in the point-to-point. He shrank from that and found himself launched into the future, while his heart sickened. He was not even making money; there, too, he was only a parasite that lived on the past. As for the time to come — well, already he wanted another drink.

So he opened the little bottle and poured it in, to the last crystal.

Then he raised the cup with a strong temptation to pour it all down his throat at a single gulp, covering the irrevocable distance at a stride; but then it came to him that he, who had posed as a connoisseur, ought to proceed with a more civilized deliberation now that he was tasting death. So he only took a good swallow and then lowered the cup gently into its saucer.

The taste was very strong, the bitterness working into the roots of his tongue. The beauty of the thing was that only Meg would know the truth. As for the family doctor, he had understood for a long time that Campbell took morphine and had warned him repeatedly about an overdose.

A soft, warm rushing began in his head, which was proof that even in the single swallow he had taken as much of the drug as made up his ordinary dose. When he took the rest the end would come quickly. He had expected a last-moment panic which might make him break off with the act unaccomplished, but there was no fear at all. He wanted to run to the window and call in Margaret and Louise. He wanted to tell them that he was about to die but that he was unafraid. This, how-ever, would spoil everything; the best was that Louise should find him smiling. As for Margaret, he ought to leave her a note to tell her what a happiness this was; but still the nature of a woman can be sweetened by some regret.

The telephone rang across the hall, not loudly. Coming at this moment, the call made him smile, for in a little time he would have out-stepped even the reach of electricity, and even light leaping forward through millions of years could never overtake him.

The bell was ringing, fading, pausing, ringing, fading, pausing, ringing. In this modern world we supply ourselves with mechanical bodies, with electric nerves that reach round the earth, and it is for that reason that we never can be alone. Someone was calling up to ask them for bridge or a cocktail party, someone inert, unexpectant of anything beyond roast chicken and ice cream and highballs through the evening, someone who could not dream that his telephone call was tapping insistently at the door of death. This fancy charmed Campbell; suppose that he could open the door wide enough, suddenly, to draw that unknown with him into the empty darkness!

Then it occurred to him that the noise of the bell might bring Margaret or Louise suddenly back to the house before the coffee was finished, or at least before the morphine had done its work. So he put the cup aside and went out to the telephone.

When he spoke into the receiver, the voice of Cherry Mayberry sprang out to answer him, like music and a light pouring into his brain.

'I prayed that you'd be the one to answer. Otherwise I couldn't have talked. I would have had to ring off.'

He said, 'I'm busy, Cherry.' Yet he wanted to stand there and listen.

'I know you're busy, but I'll only take thirty seconds. Will you listen, darling? Will you please listen?'

Does one say of a Stradivarius, 'This is a good or an evil instrument?' Well, concerning women also many a wise man has cast away the standards of moral judgment and let the beauty, good or evil, flow into the soul. She was lying; she was panting from the fullness of her lie, never to understand how all-knowing death was now helping him to smile. The sweetness and the breaking of her voice plucked at strings near his heart and made them answer.

'Why, I'm listening,' he had said.

'I sent him away,' cried Cherry. 'I couldn't stand his silly young face. It just made the house more empty. I sent him away. I'm not trying to tell you anything. I'm only saying something. Darling, darling, I'm bad. I've always been bad. Maybe I always *will* be bad. Just tell me that you'll see me once more. I don't care why – just come and damn me – just – '

'Steady!' said Campbell. 'I'm an old man, Cherry. I'm a soft, flabby pulp of an old man, and you know it.'

'I *do* know it,' said Cherry. 'I know you're soggy with booze a lot of the time too. I don't know why I love you. I don't want to love you. But, oh, God, the house is so empty, and I'm so empty and lonely.'

'Hush,' said Campbell. 'Don't be excited.'

'Do you mean it?' she pleaded. 'Do you mean I'm not to be excited?'

'Come, come,' said Campbell. 'This is all nonsense. We'll see about things later on. I have to ring off.'

'Don't ring off. Give me ten seconds more to tell you that – '

Firmly, like one delivering a blow with an edged weapon, he struck the receiver back on the hook and stood a moment half smiling and half frowning. Of course she had been lying and yet not altogether lying either. For if you think of a girl like Cherry Mayberry for a moment, you understand that you are considering a tiger that easily will be urged to strike, as she had struck at him this evening. As for young Bob, well, it was true that there was a certain emptiness about his face, and a girl of experience might prefer more maturity. She cost a lot of money, but then there was a lot of Cherry. She had said she knew he was old and soft; she had said that he was soggy with drink a lot of the time too. That was honesty. Between thieves also there is honesty. And perhaps he had become a habit, insidious and surprising to her, an obsession whose force she could not realize until he had walked out of her house quietly without reviling her, in the calmness of strength. Well, he had her back, and after a break the knot is the strongest place in the cord.

The door of the library, dimly lighted, opened before him the straight road to the end of things. Suddenly he clicked his teeth and turned his shoulder to it. The voice of Louise was coming in laughter toward the front door. It was a young voice as thin and clean as rays of starlight and there was an upward springing in it, as life should be at the beginning.

1934

Outcast Breed

This story first appeared in *Star Western* magazine in October 1934, when sympathetic portrayal of racial minority characters (including persons of mixed blood) in popular fiction was far less common than it has since become. Indeed, as early as 1920 Faust dealt with the problems of love and marriage between Asians and Caucasians in his *All-Story Weekly* serial 'Clung.' (Published in book form under this title by Dodd, Mead first in 1969 and retitled *Ghost Rider* for paperback, 'Clung' was the basis for the film *Shame* [Fox, 1921], starring Anna Mae Wong and John Gilbert.) In 'Outcast Breed' Faust depicts American Indians and mixed bloods with empathy but without sentimentality. He did the same with Blacks, Jewish-Americans, Mexicans, and Mexican-Americans in stories and novels such as 'Master and Man' (*Western Story,* January 5, 1924), 'A Lucky Dog' (*Western Story,* October 22, 1927), *Shotgun Law* (Dodd, Mead, 1976), and *The Song of the Whip* (Harper, 1936).

What might be called Faust's 'American Indian westerns' appeared first as serials and then as books, including *The Rescue of Broken Arrow* (Harper, 1948) and *War Party* (Dodd, Mead, 1973). As Edgar L. Chapman pointed out in 'The Image of the Indian in Max Brand's Pulp Western Novels' (*Heritage of Kansas,* Spring, 1978), these westerns constitute a kind of subgenre within Faust's western fiction. In order to write these twenty or so serials with authenticity, he immersed himself in books by George Catlin, George Bird Grinnell, James Willard Schultz, and others who experienced Indian life firsthand before traditional ways were drastically altered.

Faust's minority group characters are often projections of his youthful self, underdogs struggling for identity in alien surroundings. They are frequently scorned, often confronting grueling ordeals – including, as in this story, an epic fistfight – but finally achieving acceptance and love and 'the end of pain.' Les Harmody, clearly, embodies a Greek hero in Western guise, and John Cameron, with his golden spurs, conjures the image of the fleet-footed Mercury. Cameron's sense of loyalty and honor reflects Faust's own deepest convictions. Ironically, this story was written when these convictions were being severely tested in Faust's personal life. He frequently used the mythic theme of the hero undergoing an ordeal before achieving success and regeneration, but rarely was it done more poignantly, with broader social implications, or with as many autobiographical allusions as here.

I

CAMERON SAW the ears of the rabbit above the rock when he was a hundred yards away. He began to stalk with the care he might have used to get at a deer. Meat in even small portions was so valuable to him and Mark Wayland. As long as the rifle ammunition held out, they had fared well, but it is as hard to get within revolver-shot of desert game as it is to surprise a hawk in the naked sky.

Through the dusty film of twilight Cameron took aim and fired, not exactly at the ears but at the imagined head beneath them, hoping to break off the edge of the rock with the weight of his bullet. But the rock shed the speeding lead as it might have slanted a drop of water. Not one rabbit appeared, but three of them exploded from the shelter, and each ran in a different direction.

Cameron stood up as tall as his toes would lift him. The olive darkness of his face and the brown of his eyes lighted. He smiled a little. It was hard to tell whether it were cruelty or joy or a sort of pity that inspired this smile. And then the revolver spoke to north, west, south, rapidly, the nose of it jerking at each explosion. The first two rabbits skidded along the earth, dead. The one to the south leaped high into the air and that pitiful, half-human shriek which only a stricken hare utters sounded to the ears of Cameron. The pain of that jerked the head of Cameron to the side. Then his fifth shot accurately smashed the backbone of the jackrabbit from end to end.

Before Cameron moved again, halted as he was in mid-stride, he rapidly re-loaded the Colt. It seemed a single, uninterrupted gesture that jammed the five cartridges into the chambers. When the cylinder was filled again, Cameron picked up the game, cleaned it, tied it in a bleeding bundle for the return trip, and then stood straight once more to scan the horizon. A fox or a wolf will do this after the flurry of the fight, when there is dead game to be eaten – a last look towards all possible danger before the feeding begins; and never a wolf had eyes brighter than those of Cameron.

It was during this rapid scanning of the whole circle of the twilight that he saw the glimmer on the head of the mountain, up there between the ears of the height where stood his and Wayland's mine. That trembling gleam could be but one thing – the shimmer of flame!

The shack was on fire. In some way – it was inconceivable – Mark Wayland had permitted the cabin to become ignited. Once the fire caught on the wood – with no water available for the fight – there was nothing to do but shovel earth at the flames. And perhaps the fire would spread into the shaft and burn the timbers; the shaft would collapse; the labor of the many months would be undone, just as they were sinking into the valuable heart of the vein, just as they were writing the preface to a wealthy life, an easy future divorced from the need of labor of sweat and worry.

Cameron, through the space needed for one long breath, thought of these things. Then he stripped the ragged shirt from his back, wrapped the precious meat in it, and slinging the shirt around his shoulders like a knapsack he began to run.

He ran with his eye on the flame-spotted head of the mountain. As for the roughness of the terrain, his feet could see their own way. The half-Indian blood of his mother gave him that talent. Like an Indian, he toed in slightly, his body erect in spite of the weight on his back, his breathing deep and easy, an effortless spring in his stride. There was something of the deer about him, something of the predatory wild beast, also. He would catch his game, if not at the first spring, then by wearing it down. When it was caught, he would know how to kill. For if he had the body and the darkened skin of an Indian, he had the proud features of the white man, and the white man has always lived by blood.

When he came to the end of the valley, he started up the ascent of the trailless slope with a shortened step. The small weight of the rabbit meat was beginning to tell on him, now. The burning of his lungs, the trembling exhaustion of effort, the agony of labor was stamped in the heaving for breath and in his shuddering belly-muscles; but it appeared only as a slight shadow on his face in the sweat that polished the bronze of his body.

So he came to the upper level, the head of the elevation where he and Mark Wayland had found the thin streak of color, long ago, and had begun their mine. He had brighter light than that of the dusk, now. It came from the ruins of the cabin, weltering with flame. And out of the throat of the mine shaft issued a boiling mist of flame and smoke.

The cabin was gone. The labor on the shaft was ruined also. Well, all of this could be reformed, redone. They had the plunder which three weeks of work in the heart of the vein had put into their hands – fifty pounds of gold-dust. Perhaps it would be wiser anyway to take the money to town, turn part of it into hired labor, tools, powder, mules, and return to reopen the work with ten-fold more advantage.

He thought of that as he stood on the edge of the little plateau and saw the flames. The fire made little difference. But where was the figure that he had imagined hard at work shoveling earth? Where was Mark Wayland? Where was that big, stocky body, that resolute face?

'Mark!' he shouted. 'Mark! Oh, Mark!'

He had no answer. A dreadful surmise rushed into Cameron's mind, a sort of darkness, a storm across the soul.

He ran forward past the mouth of the mine, past the crumbling, flame-eaten timbers of the hoist, towards the fiery shambles of the cabin. It had fallen in heaps. The fire was rotting the heaps away. Smoldering, charred logs lay here and there where they had rolled from the shack.

A more irregular shape was stretched on the ground, smoking. He had passed it when something more profound than the sight of the eyes stopped him. He turned back to that twisted shape and leaned over the body of Mark Wayland!

Strong wires had been twisted around the arms, fastening them helplessly to the sides. The legs had been wired together at the knees and also at the ankles. There was a gag crammed into the mouth, distending it wide. Fire had eaten the body.

Someone had come, caught Mark Wayland by surprise, robbed the cabin, bound the victim, and trusted to the fire to rub out the record of the crime. And then Cameron saw that the eyes of the dead man were living.

A cry came from Cameron like the scream of a bird. He snatched the gag from the mouth of Wayland. He picked up the great, smoking hulk of the body in his arms to carry it to the life-giving waters of the creek.

The voice of Wayland stopped him. The voice was calm. 'I'm dead,' said he. 'I'm already in hell. Don't waste . . . motions. Listen to me!'

Cameron laid his burden back on the ground. He broke the wires that bound the captive. With his bare hands he stopped the red coals of fire that ate at the clothes of the victim.

'A gray mustang,' gasped Wayland. 'He was riding a gray mustang with a lopped ear . . . lopped left ear. A big . . . man. . . . Gimme that gun!'

'No, Mark!' shouted Cameron. 'I'll take care of you. I'll make you well!'

'God!' gritted Wayland. 'Don't you see that I'm burned to the bone? My face'll rub away like rot.' And again added, half-sobbing: 'Gimme that gun. . . . A big kind of man . . . a gray mustang with a Roman nose and a lopped left ear. . . .'

'Mark, you've been a father . . . for God's sake let me be a son to you now. Let me try. . . .'

'Are you gonna show yourself a damned half-breed after all?' demanded Mark Wayland. 'Gimme that gun!'

Cameron was stiffened upright on his knees by the insult. But he drew out the revolver and dropped it on the ground. He whirled to his feet and began to run. He realized that he could not run beyond the sound of the gunshot and cast himself down on his face, with his hands clasped over his ears.

But he heard, nevertheless. It seemed as though the noise were conducted to him through the earth. His body drank it in not through the ears only but through every nerve. It was a deep, short, hollow, barking noise. And it meant that Mark Wayland was dead.

It meant that the years were struck away from Wayland. It meant that the years he had spent in rearing and caring for the outcast Cameron could never be repaid, nor that patience in teaching which had endowed Cameron with far more than his preceptor had ever known.

The whole future was snatched away from Cameron, the whole chance of making a return to his benefactor. And all the love that he had poured out towards Wayland would now have no object. It would blow away in the wind. It would be wasted on a ghost.

Cameron lay still on the ground.

But there was one thing to live for. There was the man – the big sort of man, who rode the gray mustang with a lopped left ear. Cameron got up from the earth as a cat rises from sleep at the scent of prey.

The trail could not be followed by night. Cameron spent the darkness in digging the grave. He carried to the grave the dead man with the flame-eaten body and the purple-rimmed hole in the right forehead. Into the pit he lowered the dead man. Over the body he first laid with his hollowed hands a layer of brush, because he could not endure the thought of rocks and earth pressing even on the dead face. Afterwards he filled the grave.

He wanted some sort of ceremony. Instead, he could only give his own voice. And his own voice was too small for the moment. It could not fill the vast space of the mountains and the desert which the dawn was beginning to reveal. Therefore, as he knelt by the grave, Cameron merely lifted to the morning in the east his empty hands and made a silent vow.

Afterwards, he took the revolver and went on the trail.

There were only five bullets in that revolver, now. But he had enough rabbit's meat to last him for a time. He followed the trail across the desert. It took him three days to get to the hills and to the town of Gallop. There the sign disappeared. But if he ever found the trail of that horse again, he would know it. He would know it by the length of the stride in walking, trotting, galloping. He would know it by the size of the hoof prints.

The only description he had of the rider was of a 'big sort of man,' and Gallop town was filled with 'big sort of men.' Therefore, he left the town and cut for sign in circles around it. Every day he made the circuit until at last, on the old desert trail, he found what he was looking for. He had not been able to spot the gray horse in Gallop, but he had found the trail of it leading from the place.

Two days he ran down that trail, for the rider traveled fast. For two days, the flesh melted from the body of Cameron as he struggled along the traces of the unknown. At the end of the second day, he saw a winking fire in a patch of mesquite beside an alkali water-hole. He crawled to that fire on his belly, like a snake, and saw standing nearby, eating from a nosebag, a gray mustang with a Roman nose – a dirty-gray mustang with a yellow stain in the unspotted portion of its hide. And its left ear was lopped off an inch from the point.

By the fire sat a big man with a broad, red face, and red hair. When Cameron looked at him, he smiled, and took a deep breath. The weariness of the two days of running slipped from his body. The tremor of exhaustion passed away from his nerves. His hands became quiet and sure.

Then he stood up on the edge of the firelight. 'Put up your hands,' said Cameron.

The red-faced man looked up with a laugh. 'You won't get anything off of me except a hoss and a half a side of bacon, brother,' he said. 'What's the matter?'

'Stand up!' commanded Cameron.

The red-faced man grunted. 'Aw . . . well. . . .' he said. And he rose to his feet.

'You've got a gun on your hip,' said Cameron. 'Use it!'

'What's the matter?' shouted the other. 'My God, you ain't gonna murder me, are you?'

Fear rounded his eyes. He looked like a pig, soggy with fat for the market. A horror surged up in Cameron when he thought that this was the man who had killed Mark Wayland. As well conceive of a grizzly slain by a swine.

'Look!' said Cameron. 'I'll give you a fair chance. I'm putting my gun up and we'll take an even start. . . .'

This chivalry was not wasted. The man who looked like a pig snatched his own weapon out, suddenly, and started fanning it at Cameron with the flick of a very expert thumb. He should have crashed at least one bullet through the brain of Cameron except that instinct was as keen as a wolf in him always. It told his feet what to do and as he side-stepped he whipped out his own gun.

If he could kill three scattering rabbits on the run, he could kill one red-faced swine that was standing still. Cameron drove a bullet for the middle of the breast. It clanged on metal instead of thudding like a fist against flesh. The revolver, jerked out of the fat fingers, was hurled back into the red face. The big fellow made two or three running steps backwards, gripped at the stars with both hands, and fell on his back.

Cameron picked up the fallen gun. It was whole.

'Here!' he commanded. 'Take up that gun and we'll start again.'

The other pushed himself up on his hands. There was a bump rising on his forehead but otherwise he had not been hurt. 'Who are you?'

'My name is Cameron. Stand up!'

'I ain't gonna stand up. God Almighty saved my life once tonight, but he won't save it twice. Cameron, I never done you any harm. Why are you after me?'

'You've done me more harm than any other man can ever do!' exclaimed Cameron. He came a little closer, drawn by his anger. Hatred pulled the skin of his face taut. 'When you did your murder . . . when you wired him into a bundle and left him to burn in the cabin . . . you didn't know that he'd manage to wriggle out of the fire and live long enough to put me on your trail. But. . . .'

'Wired into a bundle . . . burn in the cabin . . . what are you talking about, Cameron? I never killed a man in my life!'

'What's your name?'

'Jess Cary.'

'Cary, tell me where you got the gray horse?'

'From Terry Wilson, back there in Gallop.'

'What sort of looking man is Wilson?'

'Big sort of feller.'

Surety that he was hearing the truth struck home in the brain of Cameron like the bell-clapper against bronze. He began to tremble. It was as though God had indeed turned the bullet from the heart of Jess Cary; and only for that reason were the hands of Cameron clean.

Back there in the town of Gallop – a big fellow by the name of Terry Wilson – a man who had been anxious to sell the gray horse – that was the murderer of Mark Wayland.

Cameron backed off into the darkness.

II

He had a last picture of Jess Cary glowering hopelessly after him from the small, ragged circle of the firelight. Then he turned and struck back through the night.

There was big Terry Wilson to be reached. But Terry Wilson was a known name in Gallop, it appeared, and men whose names are known are easily found. Terry Wilson would have to die; and then some peace would come to the tormented ghost of Mark Wayland.

This thought soothed the soul of the hunter. During the last two days he had made great exertions following the trail of Jess Cary. So when he reached a run of water in the hills at the edge of the desert, he stopped the swinging dog trot with which he covered ground and lay down to rest. Infinite fatigue made the earth a soft bed. As for the hunger which consumed him, a notch taken up in his belt quieted that appetite. In a moment he was sound asleep.

He had five hours of rest by dawn. Fatigue still clouded his brain, so he stripped, swam in a pool of the stream, whipped the water from his brown body, and then ran in a circle until his skin was dry. After that, he dressed and ran on towards Gallop with the same effortless pace which always drifted him over the trail. A jackrabbit rose from nothingness and dissolved itself with speed. He tipped it over with a snap shot and ate half roasted meat, sitting on his heels at a hot, smokeless fire of dry twigs. Afterwards he lay flat for twenty minutes, sleeping; and then rose to run as lightly as ever towards Gallop.

That night he slept three hours, ran on again, and entered Gallop in the early morning when life was beginning to stir. He had two bullets left in his gun, but two bullets would be enough.

The blacksmith had the doors of his shop open and was starting a fire in his forge. 'Terry Wilson . . . can you tell me where I can find him?' asked Cameron.

The blacksmith looked up from the gloom of the shop.

'Terry Wilson. Sure. He's got the corral at the end of the town. He's the horse dealer.'

The horse-dealer! The lightness went out of the step of Cameron, as he turned away. He had thought that vengeance was about to fill his hand. Instead, it was probable that Wilson was only another milestone pointing down the trail of the manhunt.

He reached the corrals of the horse dealer in time to see a new herd driven through the gates of the largest enclosure. They washed around the lofty fences like water around the lip of a bowl. Dust rose in columns, a signal smoke against the sky. Dust spilled outwards in billows, and in that mist Cameron found a big fellow who was pointed out to him.

'Mr. Wilson,' he said, 'you sold a lop-eared gray to Jess Cary, didn't you?'

The man turned his eye from the contemplation of the horses.

'Jess stick you with that no-account mustang?' he asked.

'Where did you buy the gray?' asked Cameron.

'Tierney,' answered Terry Wilson. 'Will Tierney.' His eye changed as he stared at Cameron. 'Ain't you Mark Wayland's breed?' he demanded.

The question stiffened the spine of Cameron to ice. Something broke in his brain and a mist of red clouded his eyes. He had to force himself to turn on his heel, slowly, and walk away.

It was not the first time he had heard the word. Breed, usually, or half-breed in full, slurring from life of men with no friendliness for any part of Cameron's heritage. Was it always to strike at him like poison in his shadow? And why? He could wish that he had not led such a secluded life with Mark Wayland, riding, shooting, working as hard as any man, and then, in the evening, stretching out beside the campfire with one of Wayland's books.

He knew something of grammar and books; he knew the wilderness; but he knew nothing of men. Of the human world he had had only a few score glimpses as he passed through with Mark Wayland. And now it seemed that the strange insult of the word breed was to be cast in his face from every side.

But why?

His mother's mother had been a beauty of the Blackfoot tribe, a queen of her kind. Was there not honor in such blood? And a chieftain of the frontier had married her. Was not their daughter able to hold up her head even before thrones? Three parts of his blood were white, and as for the other part, he could see in it nothing but glory. Yet the world called him breed as it might have called him cur!

Will Tierney was asleep at the hotel.

'I'll go and wake him,' said Cameron.

'The hell you will!' answered the hotel clerk. 'He'll take your skin off if you wake him up before noon. Tierney ain't a gent to fool with. I guess you know that.'

Cameron left the lobby. He could wait till noon, easily enough. Behind him his acute ear caught the phrase: 'That's a breed, ain't it?'

'Yeah. Walks like one.'

Why? What was the matter with his walk? Had Mark Wayland kept him purposely in the wilderness during those long prospecting trips so that his skin would be tough before he was exposed to the tongue of the world?

He found a tree in the little plaza opposite the hotel and sat on his heels to smoke a cigarette and think. Sun was filling the world. Over the roof of the hotel he could look up the gorge of Champion Creek and see the white dazzle of the cliffs on its western side. There was beauty and peace to be found; but where white men moved in numbers there was insult, cruelty –

The morning wore away. The sun climbed. The heat increased. A magnificent fellow came down the steps of the hotel and strode along the street. There was a flash and a glory about him. He had that distinction of face which is recognized even at a distance. He bore himself with the pride of a champion. And if his blue silk shirt and silver conchos down his trousers and glint of Mexican wheel work around his sombrero made a rather gaudy effect, it would be forgiven as the sheen of a real splendor of nature.

So that was Will Tierney? Cameron could have wished the name on a fellow of a different aspect, but nevertheless he would have to accost the handsome, swaggering giant. He was up and after him instantly, and followed him through the swing-doors of Grady's Saloon on the corner. A dozen men were inside breathing the cool of the place, and the aroma of beer and the sour of whisky.

'Step up, boys!' Tierney was saying. 'Line up. It's on me!'

A trampling of feet brought everyone towards the bar as Cameron stepped to the shoulder of Tierney and said, 'Mister Tierney, you sold a lop-eared gray mustang to Terry Wilson. Do you mind telling me where you got the horse?'

Tierney turned with a sudden jerk. His upper lip pulled back in a sneer that showed the white of his teeth. His eyes were the black of a night that is polished by the stars. He gave to Cameron one glance and then nodded to the bartender.

'Grady,' he said, 'since when have you been letting breeds drink in your place?'

The bartender grunted as though he had been kicked in the stomach. 'Is that a breed? By God, it is! Throw him out! Get out, you damned greaser!'

A bow-legged cowpuncher with a bulldog face and neck shook a fist under the chin of Cameron.

'That means you! Get!' he growled.

Tierney stood back against the bar with one hand on his hip, the other dangling close to the butt of a revolver that was strapped to his thigh. He was laughing.

'You . . . Tierney . . . it's you that I want to talk to!' exclaimed Cameron. 'Where did you get that gray horse? Will you answer me that? It's a fair question.'

'Grady,' said Tierney, 'do I have to talk to the greasers you keep in your place?'

The cowpuncher with the face of a bulldog drove a big fist straight at the head of Cameron. His punch smote thin air as Cameron dodged — right into the sway of another powerful blow. There were a dozen enemies, all bearing down. He tried to shift through them. Hands caught at him. Fingers ground into his writhing flesh like blunt teeth. His gun was snatched away. A swinging Colt clipped the side of his head and half-stunned him.

Then he was through the swinging doors. The sunlight along the street was like a river of white fire that flowed into his bewildered brain. Hands thrust him forward. He was kicked brutally from behind and pitched on face and hands into the burning dust of the street.

'Where's a whip?' called the clear, ringing voice of Tierney. 'We'll put a quirt on the breed dog!'

A whiplash cut across the back of Cameron and brought him swiftly to his feet in time to take another lash across his shoulder and breast. Then a rider plunged between him and the Grady crowd.

The horse was skidded to a halt. A girl's voice shouted: 'What a crew of cowards you are! A dozen of you on one man! A dozen of you! Will Tierney, isn't there any shame in you? Jack . . . Tom Culbert . . . Harry . . . I'll remember that you were all in this!'

They scattered before her words as before bullets. Two or three hurried down the street; the rest streamed back through the swing doors of Grady's saloon. Their shouted laughter beat on the brain of Cameron.

He had dragged off his ragged hat and looked into the gray eyes and the brown, serious face of the girl. She wore a blouse of faded khaki, a well-battered divided riding skirt of the same stuff. But every inch of the horse she rode spoke of money. That was not what mattered. The thing she had done talked big in the mind of Cameron. And it seemed to him that he could look into the beauty of her face as far and as deep as into the loneliness of a summer evening in the mountains.

'It was rotten of them!' the girl flared. 'I don't care what you were doing . . . it's rotten for a dozen to pick on one man.'

He put his hand over his shoulder and tentatively felt the welt which the whiplash had left. It was still burning and growing. He could feel it easily through his shirt.

'I was asking a question of one of them and they didn't want me in there. So . . . .' He made a quick gesture. 'So they threw me out!' he said, and in trying to cover his expression of rage, he smiled.

'Ah?' said the girl. 'The drunken hoodlums! I'm Jacqueline Peyton. Who are you?'

'John Cameron,' said he.

'Cameron's a good name. I like it,' she said. 'I like you, too. I like the look of you, John Cameron. Are you down and out?'

'I've been down just now,' he answered. He turned his head and looked steadfastly at the door of the saloon. 'I'll be up again, though, perhaps.'

'You want to go back in there and fight them? Don't be crazy!' she commanded. 'You come along with me. Dad needs a new man or two, and he'll give you a job. You come along with me.'

She dismounted. She touched his arm and his eyes drew down from the picture of the vengeance which had been growing across his mind.

'Yes . . . I'll go a ways with you,' he said. 'You get on the horse again.'

'I don't ride when a friend is walking,' she answered. 'Come along, John Cameron.'

He walked beside her down the middle of the street.

She was not very tall. Her forehead would touch his chin, just about. That, it appeared, was the right height. She was not heavy and she was not light, except in the quick grace of her movements. She had a voice that he must have heard before. He said that aloud: 'Have I heard you speak before today?'

'I don't know. I'm pretty noisy. I do a lot of talking,' she smiled. 'Have you been around this town?'

'No,' he answered. 'But it seems as though I've heard your voice before. The sound of it strikes in a certain place and makes echoes. It makes me happy.'

She slowed her step and looked up at him with a frown. 'Are you saying that just for my benefit, because you think it sounds nicely?' she demanded.

'Are you angry?' asked Cameron. 'I'm sorry.'

'No, I guess you mean it, all right,' she decided aloud. 'But just for a minute I wondered . . . well . . . let it go! What are you doing in town John Cameron?'

'I'm looking for a man . . . and I think I've found him,' said he.

'Is that good news or bad news for him?' said the girl.

'I have to kill him,' said Cameron slowly.

She looked suddenly up at him again.

'Shouldn't I have said that?' he asked her.

'Great Scott, John,' she answered, 'do you mean that you're out on a blood-trail . . . you . . . at your age. . . .'

'I'm twenty-two,' said he.

'And going to kill a man? Why, John?'

'Because he murdered my friend,' said Cameron.

'Murdered? But there's the law. You can't. . . .'

He lifted his hands and looked down at them curiously.

'If the law hanged him, there would be nothing that filled my hands . . . there would be no feeling . . . there would be no taste,' said Cameron, gently.

'Good heavens!' said the girl. 'You do mean it.'

'You're angry,' said Cameron. 'And that makes me unhappy.'

'Not angry. But horrified. Really on a blood-trail! Are you sure that your friend was murdered?'

'He was tied with wire and left in a burning cabin,' said Cameron. 'And I came back before he was dead.'

They were beyond the edge of the town. The girl halted, looking straight up into the eyes of Cameron, but he was staring past her at the vision from the past.

'He lived long enough to tell me what sort of horse the murderer rode. He told me that and then he asked me for my gun. Then he killed himself.'

'No!' cried the girl. 'No, no, no! It isn't possible that you gave him the gun and let him kill himself!'

'He was burned,' said Cameron, 'until his face was loose with cooking. It was ready to rub away. He was burned like a roast on a spit. That was why I gave him the gun. Before he had to begin screaming with pain. Ah . . . I'm sorry!'

For the girl, making an odd bubbling noise in the back of her throat, had slumped suddenly against the shoulder of the horse.

III

He could not tell what to do, but the sight of her helplessness made him feel strangely helpless, also. He touched her with his hands and his eyes, reverently; and this reverence seemed to restore her strength. She was able to stand straight again. The mare turned her head inquisitively towards the mistress and was pushed away by a touch that was also a caress. The path for the girl's mind had been cleared of everything else so that she could stare at the problem of Cameron.

'*That* is what I saw in your face?' she demanded.

'What else could I do?' asked Cameron.

'I don't know. I only know it was terrible. I never heard of anything so terrible. It makes me want to help you. How can I help you, John?'

'By letting me come to you whenever you're in trouble . . . whenever you need any sort of help. By letting me walk up the road with you.'

'Walk up the road?' she repeated, bewildered.

'This is the happiest thing I've ever done,' he answered. 'Walking up this road with you, I mean.' At this, her eyes avoided him and her color grew warmer. 'That was a wrong thing to say. I've hurt you by saying that,' he declared.

'No,' she said. 'It's not the wrong thing to say. John, I don't think you *could* say the wrong thing.'

He felt his face grow hot. He swallowed, and said after a moment of silence: 'I haven't seen very much of people, and I don't know how to talk.' He walked on beside her. 'But is this a happiness for you, too?'

'Yes.'

'As though when the road climbed that hill, we'd find something wonderful on the other side of it?'

She laughed. 'A sort of road through the sky?' she said.

'Exactly that! How did you happen to think of that? How did you know what I was thinking?'

'I don't know. It's strange,' she said.

He began to laugh and he laughed with her and their voices made together a music of two parts, high and deep, but with only one theme. He was aware of that. It delighted him and it delighted her, also. Their laughter stopped, and they looked at one another with shining eyes. But still they were walking on, and at this moment they passed the top of the hill beyond which, he had said, they might find that the road was laid through the sky.

What they saw was a string of a dozen or more Indians riding across the main trail, blanketed Indians who only lacked feathers in their hair to give them the exact look of the old days. They crossed into the trees and were gone.

'I knew we'd see *something* strange,' said the girl. 'They're heading up towards the new reservation.'

Something had stirred in the heart of Cameron, and he looked earnestly after the vanished file of riders. But now a turn of the trail brought them to the Peyton ranch, suddenly, the confusion of the big corrals, a grove of cottonwoods, and the low, broad forehead of the house itself showing over the rim of the rise.

Her father would be inside, she said. She gave her mare to a boy who loitered near the hitching rack and took Cameron straight into the house. He hung back.

'What's the matter?' she asked.

'My clothes are ragged. They're dusty and dirty.'

'Your skin is clean, and so are your eyes. That's what counts. You come along in and don't be afraid of anything. Father needs a man like you on the place.'

The living room was a big, barn-like place where a dance or a meeting could have been held. Over in a corner, in a leather chair, sprawled a man with gray hair and a grayish, care-worn face. He looked up from some papers spread out before him and rumbled: 'Well, Jack, what have you brought home?'

'John Cameron,' said the girl. 'And he's a lot to bring. He wants a job and you'll give him a place. You *need* him.'

Peyton smiled a little. 'You know how these doggone girls are, don't you?' he asked. 'The newest dress and the newest man are the only things that count!'

Cameron did not smile. He was too seriously and deeply examining the fatherly kindness of that face.

'I want men who can ride and shoot,' said Peyton. 'We have some rough horses and some pretty handy gents in long loops have been helping themselves to the herds. They got one of our own men last week. Can you ride and shoot?'

Cameron laughed. With Mark Wayland, he never had had horseflesh to ride unless it were wild-caught, fiercely savage, vengeful, cruel. 'Yes, I can ride,' he said. 'I can shoot pretty well, too.'

'Good with a rope?'

'I never had one in my hands,' said Cameron. 'But I can learn.'

'Yeah,' growled Peyton. 'Boys can learn how to handle a rope. But only God can teach 'em to shoot fast and straight. Let me see how good you can shoot. Here, come over to this window. . . . Got a gun on you?'

'No.'

'Take this. Look yonder. You see that crow on top of that fence? Knock him off of it.'

'It's not fair, dad!' exclaimed the girl.

'Sure it ain't fair,' said Peyton. 'But there's nothing any closer for him to blaze away at.'

He passed his gun to Cameron, and they saw him stand a little straighter, with his head raised in a peculiar pride and eagerness. Many unfortunate men were to learn the meaning of that lifting of the head before the end of his trail.

He gave to the target a single glance. His hand swept up, bearing the flash of the gun. The nose of it jerked as the weapon exploded. The crow leaped from the fence post and swung into the air.

'Missed!' said Peyton.

'Try again!' cried the girl. 'It was a close one.'

'It will fall,' said Cameron, calmly. 'It is dying on the wing.'

Peyton shrugged. 'What makes you think you hit it? No feathers flew.'

'I always know when the bullet strikes,' said Cameron.

'What tells you?' scowled Peyton.

'I can't say. But I know.'

Peyton glared at the girl and she shrugged her shoulders as she answered the glance. This sort of calm egotism was not to her taste any more than it was to the taste of her father. But now Peyton exclaimed: 'By thunder! Look!'

The crow, flapping hard, circling for height, seemed to fall suddenly from the edge of his invisible tower in the sky. Down he came, blown into a ragged bundle of feathers by the wind, and struck the ground with a thump that was audible to the three watchers. Cameron gave the gun back to Peyton.

'How did you know you'd slugged that bird?' demanded Peyton, almost angrily.

'Well . . . I *feel* which way the bullet goes,' said Cameron. 'I've hunted a good deal when every bullet *had* to be turned into a dead rabbit, or a deer. You learn to feel just where the bullet is going.'

He made this speech with such a simplicity that all at once Peyton began to smile. 'All right, Cameron,' he said. 'I want you on this place. You're hired.'

Hoofbeats swept up to the front of the house, paused. And almost at once there trampled into the room three big men. One of them was Will Tierney.

'There's a dance at Ripton,' called out Tierney. 'Going with me, Jack?'

Then his voice changed as he barked out: 'What's the idea, bringing breeds home, Jack?'

'What do you mean?' asked the girl. She cried it out and made a quick-step away from Cameron.

'Breed?' growled her father. 'Have you got greaser in you, Cameron? By God, you have!'

Big Tierney and the other two men were striding closer. 'Throw him out!' said Tierney. 'Think of the gall of him, coming out here! By God, think of it Jack, what's the matter with you? Can't you see the smoke in the eye?'

Cameron looked not at all at this approaching danger. He considered the girl only and saw her eyes widen with horror and disgust. She caught a hand to her breast as though she were struck to the heart by some memory. He knew what that memory was. It was their walk together up the road.

It would stay in her mind, now, like dirt ingrained in the skin. It would be a foulness in her recollection.

Hands fell on him. But they could do nothing to him compared with the look in the great, stricken eyes of the girl as she turned away from him.

Then Cameron turned towards the others. The two tall, fair-haired men had something of the look of Jacqueline about them. They were her brothers, perhaps.

'Kick him out!' shouted one of them. 'We don't want no damned breeds here!'

'I'll leave the place and never come back,' said Cameron. 'But if you handle me, I'll return and kill you, one by one, I swear to God!'

'D'you hear him, the dirty half-breed!' cried Tierney, and he struck Cameron across the mouth with the flat of his hand. They swept Cameron to the window and hurled him through it. He landed on his head and shoulders, rolled over, and came staggering to his feet.

'And if I have a look at you again,' called Tierney, 'I'll take a whip to you myself!'

IV

In a wind-swept ravine among the hills the campfire blew aside, sharply slanting, fluttering the flames to blueness, making them shrink close to the sticks which were burning. The circle of blanketed figures around that fire was very dimly illumined. Young John Cameron, standing in the center of the circle, near the fire, could be seen more clearly. Instinct had made him select the leader of the party. He had to face the wind in order to look at the old man. He had to stiffen his lips and raise his voice against the blast. Sometimes he was almost shouting. And his breath was short as he came to the end.

'I have told you everything. The white men kick me out of their way like dirt. The white women loathe me. Therefore, I am not one of their people. If I am not a white man, then I am an Indian. Let me come with you.'

There was a slight turning of heads as all looked toward the old man. He rose, tapped the ashes out of his pipe, and stepped close to Cameron. He was very old. The million wrinkles on his face were like knife-cuts, but the eyes, folded back behind drooping lids, were as bright as youth itself.

He laid on the breast of Cameron the tip of a forefinger as hard as naked bone.

'My son,' he said, and the words blew with the wind and entered the mind of Cameron. 'My son, when the heart is sick men turn to new places. But they find no happiness except among their own kind. What is your kind? The white people will not have you. But you have an eye too open and wide. You are not an Indian. We cannot take you. You would bring new ways to us. You are neither white nor Indian. You must live your own life in your own world. Or else you must fight the white men or the Indians until they take you in. All people are glad to have a man of whom they are afraid. Find the best man among many and ask him. He will tell you what to do.'

The wind was at the back of Cameron, helping him, and it was still early night when he came again into the long, winding main street of the town of Gallop. Fire still burned in the forge of the blacksmith. He was still hammering at his anvil when the voice at his door made him look up and see the same agile, light form he had noticed that same morning.

'Will you name the best man in Gallop?' Cameron was asking.

'The *best* man?' The blacksmith laughed. 'Les Harmody is the best man, all right.'

'Where shall I find him?'

'He's in the old Tucker house, down the street. He moved in there the other day and unrolled his pack. Fourth house from the corner, in the middle of the big lot.'

Cameron found the place, easily. His mind was weighted by the sense of a double duty. He had to find Will Tierney and make sure that Tierney was indeed the murderer of Wayland. But when he killed Tierney, it must be not as a sneaking man slayer but as a man of accepted name and race.

Les Harmody might be the man to tell him what to do. He had heard the name before, but he could not tell how or where. Wayland himself must have spoken of Harmody. But the name had always been attached to something great. He was an old man, no doubt, and loaded with the wisdom of the years.

So Cameron tapped with a reverent hand at the door of the shack. A faint light seeped through the cracks in the flimsy wall.

'Come in!' thundered a great voice.

He pulled the door open and stepped inside. The wind slammed the door shut behind him because what he saw loosened the strength of his fingers. He never had seen such a man; he never had hoped to see one.

Somewhere between youth and grayness, young enough to retain speed of hand and old enough to have his strength hardened upon him, Les Harmody filled the mind and the eye. He was not a giant in measured inches or in counted pounds, but he struck the imagination with a gigantic force. He was magnificent rather than handsome. The shaggy forelock and the weight of the jaw gave a certain brutality to his face, but the enormous power that clothed his shoulders and his arms was the main thing. His wrist was as round and as hard as an apple, filled with compacted sinews of power and the iron bone of strength underneath.

He was eating a thick steak with a mug of coffee placed beside it. Gristle or bone in the last mouthful crackled between his teeth now.

'Are you Les Harmody?' asked Cameron.

The other nodded.

'I've come to ask you a question,' said Cameron. He stepped closer to the table.

'You're Wayland's breed, ain't you?' asked the great voice.

Cameron stopped, stiffening suddenly.

'I don't talk to breeds. I don't have them in the same place with me. Get out!' commanded Harmody.

'I go without talking?' said Cameron. 'Like a dog?'

'All breeds is dogs,' said Harmody.

'Dogs have teeth,' answered Cameron, and stepping still closer, he leaned and flicked his hand across the face of the giant.

Harmody rose without haste. His eye measured several things:

Cameron, and the distance to the door which assured him that the victim could not escape. He leaned one great hand on the table and in the other raised the mug of coffee, which he emptied at a draught. He wiped his dripping lips on the back of his hand as he put down the cup.

'I've come to ask a question, and I'll have your answer,' said Cameron. 'I'll have it . . . if I have to tear it out of your throat!'

Harmody did not walk around the table. He brushed it aside with a light gesture, and all the dishes on it made a clattering.

'You'll tear it out of me?' he said softly, and then he lunged for Cameron.

Up there in the mountain camps, patiently, with fists bare, Mark Wayland had taught his foster son something of the white man's art of self-defense. Cameron used the lessons now. He had no hope of winning; he only hoped that he might prove himself a man.

Speed of foot shifted him aside from the first rush. He hit Harmody three times on the side of the jaw as the big target rushed past. It was like hitting a great timber with sacking wrapped over it.

Harmody stopped his rush, turned. He pulled a gun and tossed it aside. 'I'm gonna kill you,' he said through his teeth, 'but I don't want tools to do the job! A greasy breed – a damned, greasy breed – to make a fool out of me, eh?'

He came again, not blindly, but head up, balanced, inside himself, as a man who understands boxing advances. Even if he had been totally ignorant, to stand to him would have been like standing to a grizzly. But he had skill to back up his power. He was fast, bewilderingly fast for a man of his poundage.

He feinted with a left. He repeated with the same hand, and the blow grazed the head of Cameron. It was as though the hoof of a brass-shod stallion had glanced from his skull. The weight of the blow flung him back against the wall and Harmody rushed in to grasp a helpless victim.

His arms reached for nothingness. Cameron had slid away with a ducking sidestep. He had to look on his own fists as tack hammers. They would only avail if they hit the right place a thousand times, breaking down some nerve center with repeated shocks.

The swift blows thudded on the jaw of Harmody, as he swayed around. He tried the left feint and, again, the blow was side-stepped.

Wings were under the feet of Cameron, and he felt them and used them. If only there were more room than this shack afforded – if only he had space to maneuver in, then he could swoop and retreat and swoop again until he had beaten this monster into submission. But he had to keep a constant thought of the walls, the overturned chairs, the table which had crashed over on its side and extended its legs to trip him. And one slip, one fall, would be the end of him.

Those dreadful hands of Harmody would break him in an instant, but every moment he was growing more sure, more steady. He changed from the jaw and shot both hands for the wind. His right thumped on the ribs as on the huge round of a barrel; but the left dug deep into the rubbery stomach muscles, and Harmody grunted.

A second target, that made. And then he reached Harmody's glaring eyes with hooking punches that jarred back the massive head. He reached the wide mouth and puffed and cut the lips. They fought silently, except for the noise of their gasping breath.

And always there was the terrible danger that one of Harmody's blows would get fairly home. Then the devil that was lodged behind his eyes would have its chance at full expression.

A glancing blow laid open the cheek of Cameron. He felt the hot running of the blood down his face.

But that was nothing. Nothing compared with the stake for which he fought. Not merely to endure for a time, but actually to win, to conquer, to beat this great hulk into submission!

He fought for that. He never struck in vain – for the eyes, for the mouth, for the vulnerable side of the chin, or for the soft of the belly – those were his targets.

A hammer-stroke brushed across his own mouth – merely brushed across it – but slashed the lips open and brought a fresh down-pouring of the blood. In return, he stepped aside and tattooed the body and then the jaw of Harmody.

The big fellow was no longer an exhaustless well of energy, but now he paused between rushes. His mouth opened wide to take greater breath. Sweat dripped down his face and mingled with the blood. But the flaming devil in his eyes was still bright.

Exhaustion began to work in Cameron, also. He had to run, to dance, to keep himself poised as on wings. And the preliminary tremors of weakness began to run through his body constantly. He saw that the thing would have to come to a crisis. He would have to bring it to an end – meet one of those headlong charges and literally knock the monster away from him! It was impossible – but it was the only way.

He saw the rush start, and he moved as though to leap to either side. Instead, he sprang in, ducked the driving fist that tried to catch him, and hammered a long overhand right straight against the jaw of Harmody.

The solid shock, his running weight and lashing blow against the rush of Harmody, turned his arm numb to the shoulder.

But Harmody was stopped. He was halted, he was put back on his heels, he was making little short steps to the rear, to regain his balance!

Cameron followed like a greedy wildcat. The right hand had no wits in it, now. He used the left, then, and with three full drives he found the chin of Harmody.

He saw the great knees buckle. The head and shoulders swayed. The guarding, massive arms dropped first, and then Les Harmody sank to the floor.

Cameron stepped back. He wanted to run in and crash his fist home behind the ear – a stroke that would end the fight even if Harmody were a giant. But there were rules in this game, and a fallen man must not be hit.

So Cameron stood back, groaning with eagerness, and saw the loosened hulk on its knees and on one supporting hand.

'Have you got enough?' gasped Cameron.

'Me?' groaned Les Harmody. 'Me? Enough? Damn your rotten heart. . . .'

He lurched to his feet. Indignation seemed to burn the darkness out of his brain, and again he was coming in.

Once more, Cameron stepped in to check the rush. This time his fist flew high – his right shoulder was still aching from the first knockdown – and he felt the soggy impact against the enormous, blackened cushion which covered the spot where the eyes of Harmody should have been shining.

It was a hard blow, but it was not enough to stop Harmody. Before the eyes of Cameron loomed a great fist. He tried to jerk his head away from its path, but it jerked upward too swiftly. The shock seemed not under the jaw but at the back of his head. He fell forward on his face –

Consciousness came back to him, after that, in lurid flashes. He had a vague knowledge that told him he would be killed, certainly. He was dead already. It was his ghost that was wakening in another world.

Then he was aware of lights around him, and the wide flash of a mirror's face. There were exclaiming voices. There was a greater voice than all others, the thunder of Les Harmody. A mighty hand upheld him, wavering. A powerful shoulder braced against him.

He looked, now, and saw his own face, dripping crimson, swollen, purple here and running blood there. He saw the face of Les Harmody beside his own – and the big man's features had been battered out of shape. On the left side there were no features. There was only a ghastly swollen mass of bruised, hammered flesh.

This monster was shouting, out of a lop-sided mouth: 'Here's the fellow that stood up to me – me – Les Harmody! By God, I thought that the time would never come when I'd have the pleasure of standin' hand to hand with any one man. Look at him, you coyotes, you sneakin' house dogs that run and yammer like hell when a wolf comes to town! Look at him. Here's plenty of wolf for you! Look at the skinny size of him that fought Les Harmody man to man, and knocked me down. And then, by God, he stood back and give me my chance to stand once more! I tell you, look at him, will you?'

The big bandanna of Harmody dipped into a schooner of beer. He drew it out, sopping, crushed the excess liquid out, and then carefully sponged the bleeding face of Cameron.

The cold and the sting of the beer helped to rouse him completely.

'Speak up, one of you. D'you see him?' thundered Harmody. There was a murmur. 'Grady, you fat-faced buzzard, d'you see him now? Is he a white man?'

'He's anything that you want to call him, Les.'

'I ask you, is he white, damn you?'

'Sure. He's white, Les.'

'The rat that ever calls him a breed again is gonna have me to reckon with afterwards. No, he don't need no help. He can go by himself. But by God, he'll have fair play, man to man. Listen, kid . . . are you feelin' better? I wanted them to see you, and what you done to me. I wanted the whole damn world to see. Kid, will you drink with me? Can you stand, and can you drink? Whisky, Grady. Damn you, move fast. Whisky for the kid. Here, feller, I've been searching the world for a gent with the nerve and the hands to stand up to me. Here's to the man that done it. Every one of you hombres liquor up on this. Take a look at him. He's a man. He's a M–A–N! Drink to him. Bottoms up!'

There was music in the Peyton house. Joe Peyton thrummed a banjo. Harry and Will Tierney sang. Jacqueline was at the piano, and her father, Oliver Peyton, composed himself in a deep chair with his hands folded behind his head, a contented audience. They had not heard the pounding hoofs of a big horse approach the house, but they were aware of the creaking of the floor in the hall as someone walked toward them, and now the great figure that loomed in the doorway silenced the song in the middle. Oliver Peyton jumped to his feet.

'Hey, Les Harmody,' he called. 'I'm glad to see you, old son. Come in and sit down. You know everybody. What you drinking?'

Harmody accepted the extended hand rather gingerly.

'Thanks, Ollie,' he said. 'I'm not drinking. And for what I've got to say I reckon that standing will be the best. Sorry to break in on you folks like this. Hello, Jacqueline. Hello, Will. Hello everybody. Glad to see you — and sorry to see you, too.'

'What's the matter, Les?' urged Oliver Peyton, frowning anxiously. 'You talk as though you had a grudge, old-timer?'

'By a way of speaking I ain't got a grudge,' said Harmody. 'But in another way, I got a pretty deep one. I've come from a friend, and a better friend no man ever had. You know John Cameron?'

'The breed?' asked Tierney.

Harmody started. 'That's the wrong word for him, Will. I've stood up and told people that "breed" ain't the word for him. But maybe you weren't around when I did my talking. His grandmother was a Blackfoot girl that could of married a chief and done him proud. His father and all his line are as white as white. Understand?'

'Blood is blood,' said Tierney, calmly. 'He's always a breed to me.'

Harmody took in a big breath. 'We'll find a better place to argue it out, one day,' he said.

'Any place and any time would be good for me,' said Tierney, and his bright eyes measured Harmody steadily.

'Quit it, Will!' commanded Oliver Peyton. 'It only riles up Les. Can't you see that? Les, I wish you'd sit down!'

'I'll say it standing,' answered Harmody. 'I've been away in the hills for pretty near a month with Cameron. It takes time to learn to know a friend, but I've learned to know him. On a horse, or on his feet, with his hands or with a gun, I never found a better man. But he's got ideas.'

He paused, when he said this, and ran his eyes over the group, his glance dwelling for a moment on the face of the girl. She had grown pale. 'Jacqueline,' said Harmody, 'maybe you know what news I've got?'

'I can guess it,' she answered.

Her father stared at her.

'I've done a lot of talking and reasoning with him,' went on Harmody, 'but the main thing is that he feels he's given his word, and he's given it to God Almighty. So he'll keep it! Right here in this room he gave his promise!'

'He did,' said the girl through colorless lips.

'What promise?' asked Oliver Peyton.

'When Will and Joe and Harry had their hands on him, he told them that if they threw him out, he'd kill them. He swore to God that he would.'

'What kind of damned rot is this?' demanded Oliver Peyton. 'I heard that, too – but it's rot.'

'Why, he's a crazy fool!' declared young Joe Peyton.

'Harmody,' said Oliver Peyton, 'you mean to say that that fellow . . . that man Cameron . . . that . . . he's going to come on the trail of my boys?'

'He gave 'em a fair warning,' said Harmody. 'There was three of them, and he gave them a fair warning not to handle him. And then they done it. I tell you, Ollie, a promise is a mighty sacred thing to that Cameron.'

'There's a law,' said the rancher, 'and I'll have the sheriff and his men out!'

'Hell, Oliver,' said Harmody, 'you might as well ask the sheriff and his boys to try and catch a wild hawk. I'm telling you the truth. They'll never see hide nor hair of him.'

'You mean that the young snake is down here now?' shouted Peyton.

'He ain't near,' replied Harmody. 'The fact is that he's the kind that never hits below the belt. I've talked and argued with him. I've begged him to think it over because a killing is most usually murder in the eyes of the law. But he can't get it out of his head that he's made a promise to God Almighty to kill the three of 'em. Arguin' won't budge him.' Then he added: 'But he wants you all to be warned fair and square that he's coming after you. You'll kill him, or he'll kill you.'

This struck a silence across the room. Harmody went on: 'You're the special one, Tierney, and he mostly wants to have the killing of you because he says that you sure killed his partner over at their mine.'

'He's a madman,' said Tierney. 'Accusing *me* of murder, eh? All that a mad dog can see is red!'

'He says that there was around fifty pounds in gold dust. And he points out that inside the last ten days you've made a payment on the land where you're going to live with Jacqueline, yonder. You've made that payment. . . .'

'I don't follow all this!' exclaimed Tierney, loudly.

But Harmody said: 'You can't drown me out till I've made my point. You made that payment with thirty pounds of the same sort of gold dust.'

'Will!' cried the girl.

'You damned sneaking blackguard!' shouted Tierney. He strode at Harmody, but Oliver Peyton stepped between and stopped the younger man.

'I know that you're a mighty brave and bright young man, Will,' said Peyton, 'but don't you start anything with Les Harmody. He's just too old and tough to be chawed up by youngsters.'

Harmody backed up to the door.

'I come in here being sorry that I had to bring bad news,' he said. 'But the longer I've stayed here, the more I've felt that the kid is right. There's something damned rotten in the air. Tierney, I think the kid is right about *you* – and if you done that job, God help your soul!'

He was gone through the doorway at once.

Behind him, Tierney was saying: 'Something has to be done about this. A skunk like that breed going about the county poisoning the air with his lies. . . .'

'Will,' said the girl, '*is* it a lie?'

He spun about on his heel and confronted her and her white face.

'Jack, are you *believing* him?' he shouted.

She stared at him for a moment. 'I don't know,' she said. 'I don't know what to believe, except that John Cameron is an honest man!'

She saw everything clearly. It would be a battle of three against one, and poor John Cameron must die unless Harmody threw in with him. Even so, that meant a battle. There was one way to stop the fighting. That was to induce Cameron to leave the country. And if she could find the way to him. . . .

This thought got her out of the room at once. In the corral she caught up her favorite mare and was quickly on the road. Far away – north on the trail or south on the trail, east or west on it, or more likely wandering straight across country, big Les Harmody was traveling now. She turned in the saddle with a desperate eagerness, scanning the horizon, and so made out, very dimly, the movement of a shape over a hill and against the horizon.

She struck out in that direction at once. It was the eastern trail and she flew the mare along it for half a mile. After that she slowed to a walk and, heard distinctly, out of the distance, the clacking of hoofs over a stretch of stony ground. She would have to go very carefully; she would have to hunt like an Indian if she wished to trail this man and remain unheard.

As she came up the next rise, it seemed to her that she heard other hoofbeats behind her; but that was, no doubt, a sheer mental illusion, or a trick of echoes. Before her in the night there was no longer sound or sight of the big horseman. She pressed on at a gallop, giving up all hope of secrecy in her pursuit.

'Les!' she began to cry aloud. 'Les Harmody!'

A deep-throated shout answered her at once. She saw the huge man and the huge horse looming against the stars of the next hummock.

'That you, Jacqueline?' asked Harmody, as she came up. 'What's wrong?'

'Nothing much,' she answered. 'Cameron is after my two brothers. He'll probably kill them or they'll kill him, and that won't make me any richer.'

'What do you want to do?' he asked.

'I want to beg John to leave the country.'

'It's no use,' said Harmody. 'He won't go.'

'I want to try, though. I have to try to persuade him.'

'D'you like Cameron?'

'I like him a lot.'

'Come along, then. A woman can always do what a man can't manage. I've begged him hard to give up this job. He's been like a stone, though.'

They rode on together, leaving the trail presently and plunging into a thicket of brush higher than their heads. Finally, through the dark mist of brush, she could see the pale gleam of a light that showed them into a small clearing where the ruins of a squatter's shack leaned feebly to the side, ready to fall. By the fire Cameron answered the call of Harmody.

'Who's coming with you?' he snapped. 'What made you. . . .' He broke off when he saw the girl. He had been thinner when he last talked to her; but he looked older, now. Across one cheek bone was the jagged red of a new scar which time, perhaps, would gradually dim. He wore better clothes. Perhaps they helped him to a new dignity.

She went straight up to him when she had dismounted, and offered her hand.

'The last time, I insulted you by keeping silent when I should have spoken up,' she said. 'Can you forgive that, John?'

He took her hand, with a touch softer than that of a woman. His grave eyes studied her face. 'They told you the truth,' he said. 'I am a half-breed.'

'It isn't the blood. It's the man that counts,' she answered. 'And I'm beginning to realize what a man you are. I guessed it when we walked up that road together. I knew it when I heard what you'd done to Les Harmody. It's because I know what a man you are that I've come here tonight.'

'Les should never have brought you,' said he.

'She follered me, John,' protested Harmody. 'Don't be hard on me about that. What was I to do? And besides, I thought that she might show you the best way out of this whole mess.'

'That's it, of course,' said Cameron, gloomily. 'I have to be persuaded. But there's no good in that, Jacqueline. There's no good at all. I've given a promise that I'll have to keep.'

She was silent.

'You see how it is?' said the grumbling voice of Harmody. 'Nothing can budge him.'

'There's only one thing I wish,' said Cameron, 'that none of them meant anything to you.'

'Why do you wish that?' she asked him.

'You remember when we walked up the road together?'

'I'll never forget that.'

'If I could keep you from sorrow, I'd like to. You know, Jacqueline, now that I see you here and remember that some of your look is in your brothers, I don't think that I could harm them. But Tierney – I know you're going to marry him – Tierney has to be rubbed off my books.'

'He's nothing to me,' said the girl.

'He has to be. You're marrying him!' exclaimed Cameron.

'I give you my word and my honor, he's nothing to me, tonight. Because I think – I really think – that he did the frightful thing you told me about.'

'You're through with him?'

'Yes.'

'I don't believe that,' said Cameron, sternly. 'If you love a man, you'll never give him up, even if he has a thousand murders on his back.'

'It was never love. It was simply growing up together, and going riding and dancing together, and being encouraged by everyone.'

'Ah?' said Cameron. 'Would a woman marry a man for no better reasons than that?'

She felt the scorn and the horror in his voice. She flushed. 'I'm afraid we do,' she answered. 'John, have you become so hard, so stern? Is there no use, my trying to talk to you?'

'I can listen to you better than I can listen to running water in the desert. Sit down here, Jacqueline. Here by the fire. That's better. I can see your eyes now, you know. Whenever they stir, my heart stirs. When you look up at me like this, my heart leaps like a fish.'

'Hey!' said Les Harmody. 'You can't talk to a girl like that!'

'Can't I?' asked Cameron, startled. 'Have I said something wrong?'

'Not a word!' said the girl.

'Help me to teach him something,' said Harmody. 'All he knows is hunting and reading. He don't know nothing about people. You can't let a gent talk to you like that.'

'Why not? I like it,' said she.

'But doggone it, Jacqueline, unless he loves you, or something like that. . . .'

'I do,' said Cameron. 'Does that make it all right?'

'Hey, wait! Wait!' shouted big Les Harmody. 'What's the matter with you? You've only met her once before.'

'It's true,' said Cameron. 'But that was more happiness in a few minutes than all the rest of my life put together.'

'Well, then you gotta learn not to say everything you think right out loud to a girl. They ain't used to it. You gotta spend a lot of time approaching a woman. You gotta be more doggone particular than when you come up on the blind side of a horse. Ain't I right Jacqueline?'

'Not about John,' she answered.

'Hold on! What's his special edge on the rest of us?'

'I don't know,' said the girl. 'But I like everything he says.'

'Hold on, Jacqueline!' shouted Harmody. 'Hold on, there! If you get ideas into his head, you'll never get them out again.'

'I don't want to get them out again,' she answered.

'Don't say that! I mean,' explained Harmody, 'that if you give him half a chance, he'll start ragin' like a doggone forest-fire.'

The girl smiled up at Harmody. 'You know a lot about girls, Les,' she said, 'but John Cameron happens to know a lot about me.'

She put out a hand and touched the arm of Cameron.

'That's why I've had the courage to come up here tonight,' she said. 'It *couldn't* go on, John, you couldn't take the blood-trail behind my brothers.'

'No,' said Cameron breathlessly, leaning towards her. 'I couldn't lay a finger on them.'

'And Tierney – leave him to the law. There is a law for that sort of man!'

'I can't leave him. I told you that, before. If you were I . . . if you'd been raised by Wayland and then found him dying as I found him, wouldn't you despise yourself if you waited for the law to do your work on the murderer?'

She held her breath, fighting back the answer that rose into her throat, but it burst out in spite of her.

'Yes, I would!' she exclaimed. 'I don't blame you a bit.'

'Quit talking that way!' commanded Harmody. 'D'you know that you'll have him out raisin' hell right away, if you talk to him like that?'

'I'm only begging one thing,' said the girl. 'You've held your hand for a month. Will you wait another month before you take that trail? Will you let the law see what it can do, first of all?'

He dropped his face between his hands and stared at the fire. Les Harmody, making vast, vague signs of encouragement from the background, tiptoed to a little distance. The girl looked up at the giant with a flashing smile of confidence.

And John Cameron had raised his head to answer, the trouble gradually clearing away from his eyes, when the voice of Tierney barked from the edge of the brush: 'Stick up those hands! Fast!'

'What in hell. . . .' began Harmody.

'You're out of this, Les!' shouted the voice of Joe Peyton.

Cameron had risen to his feet. The girl threw herself in front of him.

'Joe, don't shoot!' she screamed. 'Will, don't shoot at him! The poor fellow didn't mean anything – he only has half a brain, Will!'

VI

Will Tierney came out from the brush at a strange, gliding pace, his feet touching the earth softly for fear that he might upset his aim, and his revolver held well out before his body.

'Get away from him, Jack!' he shouted. 'Step away or I'll get him through you, by God!'

Cameron had waited a single second, stunned. His gun belt and gun had been laid aside. His hands were empty, and death was stalking him; but what really mattered was that the girl had called him a 'half-wit.' Had she come merely for the purpose of holding him and Les Harmody helpless while her fighting men came up to wipe out the 'breed'?

He thought of that. Then he turned and dived for the brush. He ran as a snipe flies, dodging rapidly from side to side and yelling: 'Harmody, it's my fight. Stay out of it!'

He heard the scream of the girl, then the guns began to boom. Bullets whistled past his head, right and left; and then the sudden thunder of Les Harmody's voice broke in. The gun-fire continued. But the bullets no longer whirred past him.

The brush crashed before his face. He was instantly in the thick gloom of the foliage, safe for that moment, and he heard the shrill cry of the girl: 'Will! You've killed Les Harmody!'

That voice struck him to a halt. He stood gripping at the trunk of a young sapling until the palm of his hand ached, and behind him he heard Harmody's deep, broken voice exclaiming: 'I'm all right, Jacqueline. Don't worry about me. I'm all right. But I tell the rest of you for your own good – don't go into that brush after Cameron. If you go in there, he'll kill you as sure as God made wildcats! Keep out of the darkness – he ain't got a gun! But he's got hands that are almost as good as a gun.'

They did not press into the brush, but Will Tierney exclaimed: 'Here's hell to pay! It's the breed that ought to be lying here, not Harmody. Les, it's your own fault! If you hadn't got in between me and my aim, I'd have Cameron dead as a bone. He dodged . . . damn him, he dodged like a bird in the air! I never saw such a rabbit!'

'You never saw such a man-eater, either,' declared Harmody. 'And he'll chaw your bones one day, Mister Murderer Tierney.'

'Murderer?' shouted Tierney. 'You mean to say that you believe his yarn about me?'

'Stop talking, Les!' commanded the girl. 'Save your breath. Help me carry him into the shack, Joe – Harry, take his shoulders. Does that hurt you, Les? Gently, boys.'

Back to the edge of the clearing ventured Cameron and from the thick of the brush watched the men carrying huge Les Harmody through the open door of the shack. Will Tierney, coming back into the clearing, kicked some more fuel onto the fire and made the flames jump. This brighter light seemed to be a comfort to him. He walked in an uneasy circle around the fire, staring toward the brush constantly.

In the meantime, the conference inside the cabin could be heard clearly as it progressed. They were examining the wound of Harmody. Once he groaned aloud as though under a searching probe. Then the girl was saying: 'He ought to have a doctor. I'll stay here with him. But he ought to have a doctor by the morning. The three of you go straight for town.'

'I'll stay here with you, Jack,' said Harry Peyton.

'You'll do nothing of the kind,' she answered. 'What if John Cameron knew that there was only one man here?'

'He hasn't a gun,' said Harry Peyton.

'He has his wits and his hands, and that's enough,' said big Les Harmody. 'Jacqueline is dead right. The three of you stay close together all the time.'

Tierney stepped to the door of the shack. 'Bah!' he snarled. 'I'd like nothing better than to tackle him alone. I'd love it!'

'I think you like murder better'n you would ever like fighting,' said Les Harmody.

'When you're on your feet,' answered Tierney, 'I'll give you your chance at me, any time!'

'Thanks,' said Harmody. 'I'll take you up on that, one day.'

'Be still!' commanded the girl. 'The three of you start riding – and start now. Keep bunched. Head for Gallop and get Doc Travis. We don't have to worry about Les for a while. Those big ribs of his turned the bullet a bit. And it's better to have broken ribs than a bullet through the heart. Will . . . you fired to kill!'

'The fool came in my path,' said Tierney. 'What else was I to do? He came between me and Cameron.'

'Who gave you the right to murder John Cameron?' she demanded.

'You talk as though I were a butcher, Jack!'

'I think you are,' she answered.

Strange joy rushed through the brain of Cameron, as he listened.

'Jack,' cried Tierney, 'does it mean that you're through with me?'

'I never want to see your face again!' she replied.

Tierney strode into the shack, shouting something that was lost to the straining ears of Cameron, because all the men were speaking at once. Then, through a pause, Cameron could hear Tierney crying out: 'You prefer a breed, maybe?'

'I prefer John Cameron – I don't care what you call him!' she answered.

Not care? Not care even when he was called a breed? Did she, in truth, prefer John Cameron? He, lingering on the trembling verge of the firelight, the shadows wavering across his eyes, felt a weakness in the knees, a vague and uncertain awe.

The brothers were protesting. Harry Peyton was thundering: 'Jack, you don't mean it! You can't mean it. A dirty half-breed? I'd rather see you. . . .'

'Shut your mouth, Harry,' said the profound voice of Les Harmody. 'Don't you speak to her like that!'

The three men came striding out of the shack a moment later. 'It's no good,' Tierney was saying. 'You can see that she's hypnotized by that rat of a Cameron. Joe, I'm going to have the killing of him.'

'Not if I can get to him with a gun first,' answered Joe.

They went away across the clearing, hastily, and as the brush closed after them, cracking behind their backs, there was a great impulse in Cameron to run forward to the shack and show himself for one instant to the girl he loved, and to Les Harmody who with his own body had stopped the bullets that were intended for his friend.

Some rich day would come when he would have a chance to show Harmody that he was ready to die for him.

He could understand, too, why the girl had called him a half-wit. It had been her first gesture towards stopping the attack of big Will Tierney, to assure him that his rival was a creature of no importance.

But there was something more for Cameron to do than to speak to the woman he loved or to touch the hand of his friend. He had to strike Tierney. If God would let him, he had to strike at Tierney now, and he was on foot, he was weaponless, and there were three men against him, two of whom were sacred from any serious injury at his hands.

As the idea dawned in the mind of Cameron, it seemed at first totally absurd. But he knew that Tierney would probably get out of the country as fast as possible. Tierney had lost his chance at the rich marriage. There now hung over his head the accusation of murder, and there was nothing to hold him in this part of the world except, perhaps, a desire to wipe out Cameron. But the great chances were that Tierney would ride with the Peytons, go as far as Gallop, deliver the message to the doctor, and then slip away towards an unknown destination.

There was no time to catch him, therefore, except on this night. And already the horses of the three were galloping steadily away.

They would turn down through the hills and take the long, straight road offered by Lucky Chance Ravine, which pointed straight on at the town of Gallop. It was his consciousness of the probable course they would follow that taught Cameron what he could do. The riders would have to wind down through the hills to come to the head of the steep-walled ravine. For his own part, he could strike straight across and climb the walls wherever he chose.

As he ran, he made his hands work. He snatched off his shirt, tore it into strips, and began to knot the tough strings together. He could have laughed to think that this was his weapon against three mounted, armed men.

Meantime he had been running as few people can. He had left the woods, slipped through a pass between two hills, and so found himself on the rim of Lucky Chance Ravine. It ran straight east towards Gallop, bordered with cliffs to the north and south, sheer faces of rock.

It was not hard to get down the cliff-face. On the level floor of the ravine, Cameron dodged among the rocks until he came to a narrows where the only clear passage was a ten foot gap between two very large rocks. This was the strategic point for him. It was the thought of this gap through which the riders must pass in single file that had started him for Lucky Chance Ravine. And now he heard the distant clattering of hoofs that moved towards him with the steady lope which Western horses understand, that effortless, pausing swing of the body, slower than any other gallop.

He had very little time for his preparations, but his plan was simple enough. He knotted one end of his clumsy rope around a ragged projection on the side of one boulder, then he crouched beside the other great rock with the loose end in his grip. The slack of the twisted rope lay flat on the ground.

He had hardly taken his place before he saw them coming. He was crouched so low that he could see the heads and shoulders of the two in the lead against the stars, so that they seemed to be sweeping through the sky. Well behind them came the third party. He prayed that the last rider might be big Will Tierney!

He gauged his moment with the most precise care, then jerked up the rope and laid his weight against it. Well below the knees of the horse the rope struck. There was a jerk that hurled Cameron head over heels, but as he rolled he saw horse and rider topple.

As he scrambled to his feet the mustang was beginning to rise, snorting, and the rider lay prone and still at a little distance. Cameron caught the reins of the mustang and led it to the fallen rider. He had to lean close to make out the features of the man in the dull starlight; and with a groan he recognized Joe Peyton.

He thrust his hand inside Peyton's shirt and pressed it above the heart until he felt the reassuring pulsation. Not dead, but badly knocked out.

He got Joe Peyton's gun and flung himself on the back of the horse. It was at full gallop in a moment, speeding after the distant beat of hoofs. He rushed the horse, pressing its flanks with his spurs, and so the leading pair of riders came back to him through the night, growing visible, then larger and larger.

'All right, Joe?' shouted Harry Peyton.

He uttered a wordless whoop for answer, and the leaders sped on, unsuspicious. He could distinguish them one from the other now. Will Tierney was in the lead. Harry Peyton was two or three lengths behind Tierney. Therefore it was beside him that Cameron rushed his mustang, bringing the horse up so fast that Peyton had only time to twist in the saddle and cry out once in astonishment – for he could see, now, the gleam of the bare skin of Cameron.

His cry was cut short; a clip across the head struck with the long barrel of Cameron's revolver dropped Peyton out of his saddle. Cameron, catching the loosened reins of the other horse, jerked the mustang to a halt. And at the same time the yell of Will Tierney flashed across his brain.

Men said that Will Tierney feared nothing human. He must have thought, then, that half-naked Cameron was a devil and not a man; for he dropped himself low over his saddle bow, gave his horse the spur, and raced it towards the distant lights of Gallop. Cameron had a strange feeling that luck was with him; that, having helped him past the first two stages of his night's work, it would not fail him in the last, important moment.

But he found that Tierney was drawing away from him. Big Will Tierney, twisting in the saddle, tried three shots in rapid succession, and missed his mark. But to Cameron there would be no proper revenge in merely shooting a fugitive through the back. That would not repay him for the death of his friend. So he held his fire, and rode harder than before.

In another moment he had his reward. The far finer horse of Tierney had opened up a gap in the beginning, but the much greater weight of Tierney made up the difference after the first burst of speed. His mount began to flag, while the tough mustang that labored between the knees of Cameron gained steadily.

Tierney dodged his horse through a nest of boulders. The mustang followed like a true cutting horse on the tail of a calf. Cameron was not a length behind when Tierney turned and fired again.

And the mustang went down like a house of cards. The earth rose. Cameron's head struck fire through his brain. He fell into a thick darkness and lay still.

When he roused, at last, he was dripping with water. Another quantity of it had been sloshed over him by the figure that stood tall and black against the stars. A groan had passed involuntarily through the lips of Cameron.

'Coming to, kid?' asked Tierney's voice, cheerfully. 'I thought you'd never come around. Feeling better?'

Cameron tried to move, but found that his legs and hands had been bound together with something harder and colder than twine. Then he realized that he had been bound with wire – hard bound, so that the iron ground the flesh against the bones of his wrist and his ankle.

He stared up at the stars and found them whirling into fire. Nearby, there was the sound of swiftly whispering water. And gradually he realized what had happened, and the sort of a death that he was likely to die.

VII

'I'm to go the way that Mark Wayland went, eh?' asked Cameron.

Tierney had been carrying the revivifying water from the creek in Cameron's hat. Now he swished the had idly back and forth, the final drops whipping into Cameron's face.

'Sure you're going the way of Mark Wayland. But to hell with him. Think about yourself!'

'Wayland,' said Cameron, as the confession came from Tierney, 'never did harm to anyone. Why did you murder him?'

'Want to know what he did to me?'

'Nothing wrong!' declared Cameron.

'If you say that again, I'll kick your face in!' said Tierney. 'Listen:

Five years ago, when I was feeling pretty good, I got into a fight with a greaser fool – I never had any use for breeds and greasers.'

'I know,' agreed Cameron.

He was trying to think. Mark Wayland had always said that a good brain could cut a man's way through any difficulty. What device could he find to free himself from the danger of death now? At least, he might keep Tierney talking for a little time. Every moment saved was a chance gained, in that sense.

'This greaser,' said Tierney, 'got me down on the floor of the barroom, and I pulled out a gun and let him have some daylight through his belly. He kicked himself around in circles and took a long time to die. You never heard anything like his screaming. I hung around and listened to the last of it, and that was where I was a fool. There were half a dozen people around but they felt the way I did – that killing a greaser was always self-defense. Then another man came – Mark Wayland. He heard what had happened and started for me. I pulled the gun on him, but he was a little faster.'

Tierney rubbed his right arm. 'Clipped me through the arm so that my gun dropped and then he turned me over to the sheriff. The sheriff didn't want to pinch me, but after Wayland had done the pinching, the law started working. Nothing but murder. And me headed straight for the rope. But I managed to work my way out of the jail, one night. That's one of the good things about this country – their cheesecloth jails.'

He recommenced on the theme of Wayland. 'You were saying that Wayland never did anybody harm. If I'd hanged, that would have been harm, wouldn't it? And living these years, never knowing when somebody might turn up and recognize me – that wasn't harm, eh?'

'Did Wayland recognize you?' asked Cameron.

'I had a mask over my mug. I lay up there behind the rocks and watched you start out hunting. Then I slipped down to the shack and whanged him over the head. It was easy. I wired him up, and touched a match to his clothes to wake him up. He wakened with a holler, too, like the sort of a noise that the greaser made on the barroom floor.'

It was strange and at the same time a horrible thing to look straight into the mind of a man without the slightest sense of right and wrong.

'He wasn't yelling at the end,' remarked Cameron.

'No, he'd shut up as soon as he realized. Too much brute in him. Like an Indian. Pride, and all that.'

Big Will Tierney sat down on a convenient rock and lit a cigarette.

'I thought that he'd break down,' he said, 'when I pointed out what I was going to do – light the cabin and let him roast like pork. But he locked up his jaws and didn't say anything. A queer thing, Cameron. I was almost scared from just sittin' there and looking into the cold of his eyes. It almost made me think of hell, you know.'

'And you went ahead!' muttered Cameron.

'Wouldn't I have been a fool not to? I'd found the gold in the sacks. I needed that money, and needed it damn bad. Old Peyton was too dead set against me marrying his girl unless I showed that I was able to take care of her. He said that he'd never put up the money for me to live easy. He's always seen through me a little. He's the only one of the Peyton family that has until you came along, damn you!'

There was no particular venom in that last speech. He shrugged his shoulders and went on: 'Not that I give a damn about having Jacqueline wise to me. I never cared a rap about her. But I wanted her slice of the Peyton money when it came due. That old swine has a couple of millions. Know that?'

'I knew that he had money. Where did you kill the greaser?'

'You'd like to use that on me, wouldn't you? Why, it was a little side trip made down to Phoenix when I was a kid. If you live till tomorrow, you're welcome to use the news wherever you please.'

Tierney laughed. He had a fine, mellow-sounding laughter, and the strength of it forced back his head.

'But damn the Peyton money,' he went on. 'I'll get along without it. I would have had to play a part with Jacqueline all my life, anyway, and I don't like to do that. Unless I decided to raise so much hell with her that the old man would buy me off with a good lump sum. I've never had to work my way, and I never will have to. Always too many suckers like you and Wayland. They dig out the coin and the wise birds like me get it.' He laughed again.

The brain of Cameron was spinning. 'Tell me something, will you?' he asked.

'Sure. I'll tell you anything you want to know. It's the sort of pleasure that I've never had till now – talking what I please to a fellow who's going to be dead inside of a few minutes. It's like whispering secrets into a grave, kid!' He began to laugh again, highly pleased by this thought.

'Well . . . tell me if you ever had a friend.'

'Friends? I've had a dozen of 'em. Look at the two Peyton fellows. I've got the wool pulled over their eyes a yard deep. Sure I've had friends. I get a friend, use him, chuck him away. That's my idea. Now, let's talk business.'

'What kind of business?'

'The way you're to die.'

'There's the creek.'

'You'd like that,' agreed Tierney. 'Sure you'd like it. But I want to have it longer and sweeter. Maybe you're not like Wayland. Maybe you'll pipe up some music for me, the same as the greaser did?'

'Maybe,' said Cameron, through his teeth.

Tierney stood up and stretched. 'Tell me something. D'you think you broke the skulls of both Harry and Joe?'

'No. They're only a little knocked out,' answered Cameron.

'Too bad,' murmured Tierney. 'They're a pair of wooden dummies, and I'm tired of 'em. But what am I going to do about you, old son? I've got matches. How about lighting you up here and there and watching you roast? As long as you liked Wayland so much, you might as well go to hell the same way he went.' He leaned over Cameron. 'I think I'll have to take that pair of spurs, though,' he decided. 'Where'd you get golden spurs?'

'My friend gave them to me. Les Harmody.'

'The hell he did! Why would Les be chucking away money on a breed like you?'

'He said it was to show that he thought I was as good as any white man.'

'Did he? Well, you're not. Understand? When I've taken these spurs off, I'll show you what I think about you!'

He leaned still farther. With an instinctive reaction, Cameron pulled his feet away, doubling his knees high.

'Good!' said Tierney. 'Going to be some struggling, eh? That's what I want. That's what I like. Put up a good fight, kid! I hate to hook a fish that won't do some wriggling! I'll have you screeching like the greaser on the barroom floor, before I'm through with you!'

He stepped forward to catch Cameron by one foot. His head was low. The target was not unattainable. And Cameron let drive with his heels at the head of Tierney – with the golden spurs of Les Harmody he struck out, making his supple body into a great snapping whiplash.

Tierney, seeing the shadow of the danger at the last instant, yelled out and tried to dodge. But the spurs tore across the flesh of his chin and the heels themselves thudded against the bone of his jaw. He fell on his face.

Cameron came to life, moving as a snake moves. He got the revolver from the holster at the side of Tierney, first. The big fellow already was beginning to move a little as Cameron held the weapon in both hands and with two bullets severed the wires that bound him at the knees and at the ankles.

It was a harder, an almost impossible, task to get a bullet through the wires that confined his two wrists. To manage that, he had to hold the Colt between his feet, pressing his wrists over the uptilted muzzle of the gun until one strand of the wire was against the muzzle of it. But he could not keep the flesh of the wrists from pressing over the muzzle together with the wires.

He managed to get the middle finger of his left hand over the trigger of the gun, another extra pressure and the explosion followed. Hot irons seemed to tear the soft flesh inside his wrists – but his hands were free.

And there was Tierney on his feet at last, staggering a little, then snatching at a second gun as he realized what had happened. Cameron shot low, aiming between the hip and the knee, and saw the big fellow pitched to the side. He struck on both hands, the gun spinning to a distance. Then he reclined there as though he had been struck down by a spear and pinned to the ground.

'By God, it's not *possible!*' shouted Tierney. 'Cameron, don't shoot – for God's sake, don't shoot!'

Cameron went to the fallen gun and kicked it back to Tierney.

'I ought to cut you down and kill you the way you were going to murder me, Tierney,' he said. 'But I'm not going to do that. Wayland taught me a different way of living. There's the gun inside your reach. Grab it up. Fill your hand and take your chance.'

'What chance?' groaned Tierney. 'I'm bleeding to death! Cameron, do something . . . help me! If you try to shoot it out now, I won't lift a hand. It'll be murder. It'll damn your soul to hell. For the sake of God, don't kill me!'

'Look!' said Cameron. 'I'm sitting on the ground exactly like you, now. I'm putting the gun down just the way yours is lying. Now fill your hand and fight – you yellow dog!'

But Tierney, spilling suddenly forward along the ground, buried his face in his arms and began to groan for mercy.

That was why Cameron, his soul sick with disgust, brought Tierney into the town of Gallop with the feet of his prisoner tied under the belly of the horse. A crowd formed instantly. Men ran from the saloons; and some of these were sent off to rouse the doctor and prepare him for a trip.

Tierney, when he saw familiar faces, began to make a frantic appeal: 'Bob . . . Sam . . . Bill . . . hey, *Bill!* Help me out of this. The damned breed shot me from behind. I'm bleeding to death! Bill, are you going to let me go like this?'

He held out his hands in appeal. Cameron rode beside him with no gun displayed. He made a picture that filled the eyes of men, however, and kept them at a distance. For blood had run and dried from a thousand scratches, and naked as he was to the waist, he looked like a savage come back from war with a captive.

Harry Peyton and the gray-headed sheriff appeared at the same time, Harry shouting: 'There he is, sheriff! There he is now. I'll help you get him!'

Harry Peyton had a thick bandage around his head, but otherwise he appeared perfectly well. He was pulling out a gun as he ran. The sheriff stopped that.

'If there's any gun work wanted, I'll call for it,' he said.

The crowd had become still thicker. Men held back from actually stopping the progress of Cameron, but they drew nearer and nearer. 'Are you the sheriff?' Cameron called out.

'I am,' said the other, wading through the crowd.

'Then I'm turning Tierney over to you,' said Cameron. 'I'm charging him with the murder of Mark Wayland.'

The sheriff came up, panting. Harry Peyton was at his shoulder, glowering, ready for battle. 'You let me down, Harry, damn your heart!' snarled Tierney.

'What's this charge of murder?' demanded the sheriff. 'Are you wounded, Tierney? This looks like a damned black night's work for you, Cameron. Hold that horse. Harry, help me get Tierney off his horse. Cut that rope.'

Now that the horses were stopped, the men pressed suddenly close from every side. There was a shout from the rear of the crowd: 'Hang the damned breed! Lynch him!'

Cameron leaned from the saddle and gripped the shoulder of the sheriff.

'Are you going to listen to me?' he demanded. And the green glare of his eyes struck a sudden awe through the man of the law.

'I'm listening to you,' said the sheriff, scowling. 'What's this talk about murder?'

'He killed Mark Wayland. He confessed it to me tonight.'

'Confessed? What made him confess?'

'When he had me lying on the ground and tied with wire – the way he tied Wayland before he burned down the shack at the mine.'

'What kind of a liar will you listen to, Sheriff?' demanded big Will Tierney. 'He shot me from behind. . . .'

'Here's one proof,' said Cameron, and he held out his wrists, with the blood still trickling from them, and the powder burns were horrible to see. The sheriff frowned and a curse of wonder escaped his lips.

'It's true!' he said, suddenly.

'You'll find the wound in his leg, whether he was shot from behind or not,' said Cameron. 'And if you want to know more than that, send down to Phoenix. They've wanted him for murder there for five years. They'll want him still.'

He said it loudly, and the muttering of the crowd was blanketed in a sudden silence. The sheriff said: 'Look at me, Tierney. Is this true? Have you been a damn wolf in sheepskin, all this time?'

'Wait a minute!' yelled Tierney. 'You wouldn't believe a breed against a white man's word, would you? You wouldn't. . . .'

'Shut up,' said the sheriff. 'You're under arrest. Cameron, I can see that I've got to thank you for doing a job that I should have handled myself. Tierney, you look as guilty as hell, and hell is where you'll wind up, with a hangman's rope to start you on the way.'

It may have been that the loss of blood and the successive shocks to his nerves had weakened Tierney, but now at the very moment when he should have rallied himself to make a last desperate appeal to the crowd which might have favored him, his nerve gave way. With one hand he gripped at his throat as though already he felt the rope about it, and slowly turning his head he stared at Cameron – a look that Cameron would never forget.

Then they carried him towards the jail.

The sheriff lingered to say, loudly: 'The next man I hear calling Cameron a breed had better come and call me the same thing. There's no dirt on his skin that soap won't take off!'

It was the same fellow who had yelled for a lynching who now started a new demonstration. Cameron marked him dearly. Perhaps, seeing how the wind was blowing, from this unexpected quarter, the man wanted to bury his other remark under new fervor. But he it was who proposed cheers for 'Cameron, who's all white,' and the crowd, falling into the spirit of the thing, cheered itself hoarse and then drooped back into the saloons to start a celebration.

Cameron himself by that time was riding at the shoulder of the doctor, with Harry Peyton on the other side of him, and Joe Peyton in the rear. The brothers said nothing. They were not the kind to waste words, but neither, Cameron was sure, were they the sort to nourish grudges. And that was how they came back to the shack where big Les Harmody was lying.

When he heard them coming, Harmody shouted a question. The voice of Cameron answered. And a cry of happiness broke from the throat of the wounded man.

There was not much need of talk. When Harry and Joe, who had started with Tierney, returned with Cameron and the doctor, it was a fairly clear proof that everything was altered in the affairs of Cameron.

There was one anxious pause while the doctor made his examination of Harmody, then the medico looked up with a smile.

'Luck and an extra heavy set of ribs have saved you, Harmody!' he said.

An involuntary gasp of relief broke from the lips of Cameron and, hearing that, Harmody held out a sudden great hand towards him.

'Old son!' he said.

Cameron caught the hand and gripped it as hard as he could.

'The two of us, Les!' he exclaimed.

'Fine!' said Harmody. 'But suppose we make it three?'

He looked across at the girl and she, from her place beside the bed, forced her head up until she was looking with great eyes straight at Cameron. She began to smile in a way half fond and half foolish, and Cameron knew that he had reached the end of pain.

The Sun Stood Still

At the age of sixteen and after three years as an orphan, Faust left the Stockton, California, area where he had supported himself by odd jobs and farm and ranch work while living with relatives or employers. Hypersensitive about his lack of parents, status, and money, he moved thirty miles south to Modesto to attend high school. He lived for a time in the home of Thomas Downey, one of Modesto's most respected citizens, its high school principal, and Faust's cousin by marriage. Downey became Faust's mentor, gave him access to his extensive personal library, introduced him to the Greek and Latin classics and, as Faust expressed it later, introduced him 'to the life of the mind.'

'The Sun Stood Still' first appeared in the slick-paper *American Magazine* of December 1934. In this story, Faust used the harsh realities of physical labor, especially those of harvest time, in an innovative way while probing new fictional ground. 'I have in mind a series of stories,' he wrote in a letter from Florence early in 1934, 'to be set in the Central California I knew when I was a youngster, stories a little more seriously done than most of my yarns.' 'The Sun Stood Still' is the first of these. Faust's first story set in the real West, it speaks in terms of everyday realism that retains the transcendent reality characteristic of Faust's work.

In his 1979 introduction to the Gregg Press's edition of *Destry Rides Again* (Dodd, Mead, 1931) Richard Etulain accurately saw the mythic hero as one of Faust's major contributions to the western story. Bill Turner is a mythic archetype in an ordinary setting. He descends to the depths of discouragement, suffers, endures courageously, and emerges to personal regeneration and social acceptance, all in everyday surroundings. 'Life is a hell,' Turner says, 'but real men can live through it.' Like John Cameron in the more fanciful 'Outcast Breed,' he is what Joseph Campbell called 'the hero with a thousand faces' — in other words, any of us. 'The Sun Stood Still' reminds us that though life took Faust out of the San Joaquin Valley, it never took the valley out of Faust's writing.

T HEY SPENT MONDAY MORNING moving the hay press down to the Cooley place and setting it up against the stack nearest the house. It was a good thing to have an easy Monday morning because everyone except Bill Turner went to town on Saturday night and got drunk. Sam Wiley, the boss, drove to Stockton on Sunday evening and at the cheaper beer saloons picked up his crew. Some of them had to be loaded in like sacks of wheat; the others sat up and finished their drunk with whisky on the way home; and the whole gang went about with sick faces and compressed lips on Monday morning.

But the evening before, Wiley had failed to pick up the most important of his men. That was Big George, the best bale-roller in central California, and his absence was a serious loss.

After lunch, they lay around under the fig trees near the Cooley house and smoked cigarettes and talked about what they might do when one o'clock came. But Bill Turner did not smoke; neither did he join in the discussion. He was only eighteen, and his long, skinny body oppressed him continually with a sense of youth. His position was that of roustabout, at twelve dollars a week, and, since his bed was a shock of hay and his food came from the cookhouse, the money was clear profit. He would need it in the autumn when he returned to school to work again toward that higher destiny which was his pride; but all summer that sense of superiority had to be stifled when he was the least member of a hay-press crew.

'We might get Cooley to roll the bales for one afternoon,' suggested Lacey, the power-driver.

Bill Turner moved his head so that he could see the sleek, repulsively self-conscious face of Lacey. The forelock of his long, pale hair was always plastered down with water whenever he washed for a meal. According to his anecdotes, Lacey was an irresistible beau. He had carried his conquests as far as San Francisco and could name the mysterious and expensive places of the Tenderloin.

'Cooley!' said Portuguese Pete, one of the feeders.

'Yeah, Cooley's no good,' said Jumbo, the other feeder.

Bill Turner got himself to one elbow and looked toward the pock-marked face of Jumbo. Except for smallpox he would have been an eminently fine-looking fellow, but that disease had ruined his face as a ten-year sentence had ruined his life.

'Why's Cooley no good?' asked Bill.

Jumbo turned his head slowly, after a manner of his own, and looked at the speaker with his pale eyes.

'Don't you know why Cooley's no good?' asked Jumbo.

Bill thought it over. Cooley had 1,100 acres in wheat and wild-oats hay which ran ten tons to the acre, this year, and it was said that he was going to get $12 a ton. That might mean $20,000 profit, though it was hard to believe that such a flood of money would pour into the pockets of a single farmer. In person, Cooley was sleek and down-headed, and his jowls quivered a little when he talked or chewed tobacco.

'Maybe he's kind of funny,' said Bill thoughtfully, 'but I don't see why Cooley's no good.'

'You've been going to school, ain't you?' asked Jumbo.

'Yes,' said Bill.

'Well, keep right on going,' said Jumbo.

Great, bawling laughter came from the entire crew, with the piping voice of Sam Wiley, the boss, sounding through the rest like a flute through the roar of a band.

Bill Turner gripped his hands hard and slowly rolled over on his back again. His face was hot. Perhaps he ought to spring up and throw an insult at Jumbo; but he knew that he dared not face the terrible pale eye of the feeder. It was not so much the fear of Jumbo that unnerved him as it was a renewed realization that he was not a man. Others – yes, far younger lads than he – could take an intimate and understanding part in the conversation of grown-ups, but in some necessary mystery he was not an initiate.

As he lay on his back, he felt his shoulder and hip bones pressing painfully against the hard ground and he told himself that one day, by dint of tremendous training, he would be robed in great muscles; he would be shaggy with strength.

The thin half-face of Sam Wiley came between him and his upward thoughts.

'Listen, kid. You roll bales for this afternoon. Big George, he's showed you how to tie and everything.'

'My jiminy!' said Bill, laughing weakly. 'I'm not strong enough. Why, I only weigh about a hundred and sixty. I couldn't last it out. Those wheat-hay bales will run up to two hundred and forty.'

Sam Wiley drew back.

There was a silence, and someone cursed softly. Then Jumbo said, 'Yeah, he's *big* enough. He just ain't got it.'

The implied insult was too great to be stomached. Bill sat up suddenly and cried, 'What haven't I got?' He heard his voice shrilling, and he was ashamed of it.

Portuguese Pete chuckled. 'He wants to know what he ain't got!'

'Ah, hell,' said Jumbo, and wearily started rolling another cigarette.

Sam Wiley's face, narrow from chin to brow like the head of a Russian wolfhound, turned again to Bill. He was sun-blackened, except about the eyes, where the wrinkles fanned out in lines of gray. The only thing that was loose was his mouth, which seemed too big for the skull behind it, and that showed all its extra sizes when Wiley spoke.

'You can do it, and I'm gonna give you a shot at rolling bales.'

The outfit could average around 40 tons a day; at 18 cents a ton, that made $7.20 a day for the bale-roller – against the $2 which Bill made as roustabout! Then you subtracted a cent a ton for wear on gloves.

Wiley said, 'I'll pay you your regular two bucks and another dollar thrown in – '

'What!' cried Bill, outraged.

'But if you don't stop the power-driver too much, you get the full rate, kid,' finished Wiley. 'Better go out to the dog-house and look things over. You been in there before.'

Being active and willing, Bill had been favored with a turn at all the important jobs, now and then. He had flogged the power horses around their dusty circle; he had handled the big fork on the stacks or out of the shocks which were run up on bucks; he had stood on the table and built feeds under the instruction of Portuguese Pete or Jumbo; and he had even been in the dog-house of the bale-roller, taught by Big George how to knot the wire in a figure eight with one cunning grasp of the left hand. He looked down at that left hand, now, and wondered if it would betray him in his time of need.

'You get away with it, and I'll keep you on the job,' said Wiley. 'You're a pretty good kid, and Big George is too much on the booze.'

Bill left the shade of the trees. The sun fell on him with a hot weight; his shadow walked before him with short legs. As he crossed the corral, he saw the pigs wallowing in the muddy overflow from the watering troughs. They were growling and complaining; some of them had lain still so long that the sun had caked the mud to white on their half-naked hides. They luxuriated half in heat and half in muddy coolness.

Beyond the barns, Bill crossed the summer-whitened field toward the nearest stack against which the press had been set. The stack burned with a pale, golden flame. Other great mounds rose among the acres of Cooley, some of them filmed over by the blue of distance. Every stack was heavy wheat and oats and when you lift a 240-pound bale three-high you've done something.

The shadow under the feed table promised coolness in the dog-house, but that was all illusion; it was merely dark instead of flaming heat. The wide shoulders of the stack shut away the wind. The big hay hooks of George lay on the scales, to the top of which was tied the box of redwood tags for the recording of weights. The iron rod for knocking over the locking bar leaned against the door. These were the tools for the labor. Bill was weak with fear. He had no shoulders. His arms hung from his skinny neck. He remembered the gorilla chest and arms of Big George, but even Big George had to groan in the hot middle of the afternoon. And this would be a scorcher. In the cool beneath the trees around the house the thermometer stood now at a hundred; it was better not to guess at the temperature in the dog-house or to imagine the middle afternoon.

Sam Wiley in person appeared, leading the power horses. The boss as roustabout made Bill smile a little. The other men came out. Jumbo and Portuguese Pete paused beside the ladder that climbed the stack.

'When you get the bale out, slam that door and lock it fast, because I'm gunna have the first feed pouring into the box,' said Jumbo.

'Aw, the kid'll do all right,' said Portuguese Pete. 'Look at him. He's all white.'

Pete opened his mouth for laughter but made no sound. He looked like a pig gaping in the heat; he had the same fat smile.

Old Buck could be heard off to the left cursing the black derrick-horse, Cap. The power team was being hitched.

'Five minutes to one!' called Wiley.

'Whatcha want, Pete? The stack or the table?'

'I'll start on the stack. But leave the kid alone, Jumbo.'

'Yeah. Maybe,' said Jumbo.

They disappeared upward. The boards of the feeding table sagged above the head of Bill. Jumbo let down the apron of the press with a slam. Hay rustled as he built the first feed. So Bill got on his gloves. He left one hook on the scales. The other he slipped over the bent nail which projected from a beam at his right. Sam Wiley was marking an angle with his heel, kicking into the short stubble.

'Put your first bale here, kid!' he called. 'Build her twenty long.'

It was a terrible distance, Bill thought. If he had to build the stack as big as that, it would mean taking the bales out on the trot and then coming back on the run.

He licked his lips and found salt on them.

'All *right!*' called Jumbo.

Lacey called to his power team. There was a jangling of chains. One of the horses grunted as it hit the collar. The press trembled as the beater rose. It reached the top, the apron above rose with the familiar squeak. The derrick pulleys were groaning in three keys. From far above there was a sound of downward rushing, and the first load from the great fork crunched on the table. It was a big load; a bit of it spilled over the edge and dropped to the ground by the dog-house.

Bill kicked the hay aside because it made slippery footing. He felt sicker than ever.

The beater came down, crushing the first feed to the bottom of the box and pressing thin exhalations of dust through invisible cracks.

Jumbo was yelling, 'What you mean tryin' to bury me, you damn' Portugee Dago?'

The apron slammed down on the feed table again.

Bill looked at his left hand. It would have to be his brains. As for the weighing, the tagging, the rolling, the piling, he would somehow find strength in his back and belly for these things; but if he could not tie fast enough, everything else was in vain. The left hand must be the master of that art.

A word struck into his brain: 'Bale!' How long ago had it sounded in his dreaming ears? Were they already cursing his slowness?

He leaped at the heavy iron, snatched it up, fitted it in, knocked the locking bar loose. As he cast the iron down, the door swung slowly open. He pushed it wide with a sweep of his left arm. Already Tom had the first wire through. Now the second one slithered through the notch on the long needle that gleamed like a thrusting sword.

A good bale-roller ought to tie so fast that he waits for the last strand and insults the wire-puncher by shouting, 'Wire! Wire!' Bill grasped the lower and upper ends of the first one. He jerked it tight, shot the lower tip through the eye, jerked again, caught the protruding tip with his left thumb, pushed it over, cunningly snagged it with the fingers of his left hand, and as they gripped it with his right thumb gave the last twist to the wire. The knot was tied in that single complicated gesture.

The three middle wires were bigger, stiffer. But they were tied in the same quick frenzy – and now he saw with incredulous delight that the fifth wire was not yet through.

'Wire!' he screamed.

It darted through the notch at the same instant and he snatched it off the forked needle.

'Tied!' he yelled, and caught the hook from its nail. He sank it into the top of the bale at the center, and leaned back with his left foot braced against the lower edge of the box. The beater trembled, rose with a sighing sound, slid rapidly upward.

His strong pull jerked the bale out. He broke it across his right knee, swerving it straight toward the scales. With his left hand he caught the edge of the door, thrust the heavy, unbalanced weight of it home, at the same time disengaging the hook from the bale and with it pulling the locking bar in place. He had had a glimpse, as he shut the door, of the down-showering of the first feed, and knew that Jumbo was giving no mercy but was rushing his work even as he would have done if Big George were in the dog-house.

Bill turned the bale end-up on the scales, slid the balance, found 195. The fingers of his right hand, witless behind the thick of the glove, re-fused to pick up a redwood tag from the box. At last he had it. The pencil scraped on the wood in a clumsy stagger. Who could read this writing, this imbecile scrawl? His teeth gritted as he shoved the tag under the central wire.

Then he rolled the bale out. He had to go faster. He had to make it trot the way Big George made a bale step out on legs of its own, so to speak. He put on extra pressure. The bale swerved. It staggered like a wheel that is losing momentum, wavering before it drops. Then, in spite of him, it flopped flat on its side, jerking him over with the fall.

Somewhere in the air was laughter.

He leaped that bale to its side again, hurrying it toward the angle which Wiley had marked on the ground.

'Bale!' shouted Lacey.

Well, that was the finish. He was simply too slow. With his first attempt he was disgraced, ruined, made a laughingstock. And all of those hardy fellows, relaxed in the profound consciousness of a sufficient manhood, were half smiling, half sneering.

He put the bale on the mark and raced back. All was at a standstill. The power horses were hanging their heads and taking breath. Old Buck leaned against the hip of Cap. Jumbo was a statue on the feed table; Portuguese Pete stood on top of the stack, folding his arms in the blue middle of the sky.

The yell of Jumbo rang down at him: 'If you can't use your head, try to use your *feet!* We wanta bale some *hay!*'

But the voice of Jumbo and the words meant less than the sneering smile of Tom, the wire-puncher. He was one of the fastest wire-punchers in the world. Once he had been a bale-roller himself, but now his body was rotten with disease and he walked with a limp.

Bill had the second bale beside the first and was on his way back, running as hard as he could sprint, before that terrible cry of 'Bale!' crashed into his mind again.

'Don't go to sleep at the damned scales,' shouted Jumbo. 'Get them tags in and walk them bales! Here's a whole crew waiting on a thick-headed kid. Are we ever gunna bale any *hay?*'

In the dog-house there was a continual cloud of dust, partly trampled down from the feeding table, partly drifted from the circling of the power team as its hoofs cut through the light hay-stubble and worked into the dobe. Hay dust is a pungency that works deep through the bronchial tubes and lungs; the dobe dust is sheer strangulation.

Life is a hell but real men can live through it. He remembered that. His own concern was to labor through that stifling fog and get the bales out of the way of the feeders. He was doing that now. Sometimes he was clear back to the press and waiting with the iron rod, prepared to spring the locking bar the instant he heard the word 'Bale!' The sun was leaning into the west, slanting its fire through the dog-house. He had laid the whole back row of the bale-stack; now he was bucking them up two-high remembering to keep his legs well spread so that the knees would make a lower fulcrum, always avoiding a sheer lift but making his body roll with the weight.

He laid the row of two-high; the three-high followed. For each of these he had to allow himself a full extra second of lifting time. Big George, when in haste, could toss them up with a gesture, but Bill knew that one such effort was apt to snap his back or knock his brain into a dizziness as though he had rammed his head against a wall. The thing was to rock the bale up over his well-bent knees until the edge of it lodged against his body, then to straighten, lifting hard on the baling hooks, bucking up with the belly muscles and hips and freeing the hooks while the incubus was in full motion. He gave it the final slide into place with his forearms and elbows.

Every one of those three-high bales was a bitter cost. They weighed 200, 220, 240, as the big fork bit into the undried heart of the stack. Bill, himself, a loose stringing-together of 160 pounds. He had not the strength; he had to borrow it from someplace under his ribs – the stomach, say.

Sometimes when he whirled from the stack the world whirled with him. Once he saw two power teams circling, one on the ground and one in the air just above, both knocking out clouds of dust.

When the teams were changed, he caught the big five-gallon water canteen up in his arms, drank, let a quart of the delicious coldness gush out across his throat and breast.

They were baling well over three tons to the hour. That meant a bale a minute tied, taken from the press, weighed, tagged, rolled, piled, and then the run back to the dog-house with the dreadful expectation of 'Bale!' hanging over his head.

It was three hours and a half to four-thirty. He piled three and a half full tiers in that time and then found himself in the dog-house with the great iron bar in place, waiting, waiting – and no signal came.

Tom, the wire-puncher, called the others with gestures. They stood for a moment in a cluster and grinned at Bill.

'You poor fool!' said Jumbo. 'Don't you know it's lunchtime?'

The mouth of Bill dropped open in something between a smile and a laugh. No sound came. Of course, at four-thirty there was a lunch of stewed fruit, hot black coffee, bread, and twenty great, endless minutes for the eating. The men went out and sat in the shadow of the stack of bales – his stack. He followed them. As he came closer to the dark of the shadow, he bent forward, his arms hanging loosely, and spilled himself on the ground.

Half a dozen men were putting shakes on the top of the barn, somewhere, he thought; then he realized that the rapid hammering was in his body, in his brain, as his heart went wild. Out here the air stirred, faintly; it was hot on the eyes and yet it cooled the skin; and every moment breathing became a little easier.

A heavy shoe bumped against his ribs. He looked up and saw Jumbo.

'Why don't you sit up and try to eat your snack, like a man?' asked Jumbo.

'Yeah – sure,' said Bill.

He got the heels of his hands on the ground and pushed himself up against the bale. The rest of the crew were at a distance; their voices came from a distance, also; and the only thing that was near and clear was Mrs. Peterson, their cook, carrying a steaming bucket of coffee.

'Are you all right, Billy?' she asked.

'Yeah,' he said. 'Why, sure. Thanks a lot. I was just taking it easy.'

'Leave the kid alone!' called the harsh voice of Jumbo. She shrank away. 'Women are always horning in!' he added loudly.

Bill was still sipping the coffee when Sam Wiley sang out like a rooster, 'Come on, boys. There's a lot of hay waiting.'

Bill swallowed the rest of the coffee and got up to one knee, gripped the edge of a bale, pushed himself to his feet. The dizziness, he was surprised to find, had ended. He was all right, except that his feet burned and his legs seemed too long.

And then in a moment, with what seemed a frantic hurrying to make up for lost time, the press had started. He finished the fourth tier, built the fifth, and at the end of it found himself teetering a heavy bale on his knees, unable to make the three-high lift. The terrible voice of Jumbo yelled from the stack, 'Hurry it up! Are we gunna bale any *hay?*'

A rage came up in him; he swung the weight lightly into place as Lacey sang out, 'Bale!'

The sun was declining in the west and he remembered suddenly that the day would end, after all. He was not thinking of seven dollars; he was thinking only of the sacred face of night when at last he could stretch out and really breathe.

But the sun stuck there. It would not move. Somewhere in the Bible the fellow had prayed and the sun stood still – Joshua, wasn't it? – while the Jews slew their enemies. Now the sun stood still again so that Bill Turner might be slain.

He still could tie the wires and take the last of the five off the needle. He could get the bale out and roll it. But even the two-high lift was an agony that threw a tremor of darkness across his brain. That place from which the extra strength came, that something under the ribs, was draining dry.

Then, as he came sprinting to the cry of 'Bale!' he heard Jumbo say, 'He *could* do it, Pete, but the kid's yellow. There ain't any man in him!'

Bill Turner forgot himself and the work he was doing with his hands. He forgot the watery weakness of his knees, also, remembering that somehow he had to kill Jumbo. He would devise a way in fair fight.

And suddenly the sun was bulging its red-gold cheeks at the edge of the sky.

'That's all, boys!' Sam Wiley sang out.

And here were the feeders coming down from the stack; and yonder was the familiar cookhouse streaming smoke on the slant of the evening breeze. Someone strode toward him from the stack of bales.

'Look out, kid,' said Tom. 'There comes Big George, drunk and huntin' trouble. That means you. Better run.'

He could not run. He saw Big George coming, black against the west, but he could not run because his legs were composed of cork and water. He got to the scales and leaned a hand on them, waiting. Lacey, wiping black dust from his face, said, 'You poor fool, he'll murder you.'

Big George came straight up and took Bill by the loose of his shirt; he held him out there at the stiffness of arm's length, breathing whisky fumes. It was not the size of George that killed the heart of Bill; it was the horrible contraction of his face and the crazy rolling of his eyes.

'It's you, eh?' said Big George. 'You're the dirty scab that tries to get my place?'

'He ain't got your place, George!' shouted Sam Wiley, running up. 'He only filled in while – '

'I'll fix *you* later on,' said Big George. 'I'm gunna finish this job first or – '

'You can't finish a job,' said the voice of Jumbo.

'I can't do what?' shouted Big George.

'Take off your hat when you talk to me,' said Jumbo.

Big George loosed his grasp on Bill.

'Hey, what's the matter?' he demanded. The magnificence and the fury had gone out from him as he confronted the pale eye of Jumbo. 'Hey, Jumbo, there's never been no trouble between you and me – '

'Back up and keep on backing,' said Jumbo. 'Get your blankets and move. The kid wouldn't run from you, but you'll run from me or I'll – '

It was quite a soft voice, with a snarling that pulsed in and out with the breathing, and Big George winced from it. He shrank, turned, and in a sudden panic began to run, shouting, with his head turned over his shoulder to see if the tiger followed at his heels.

'The kid didn't stop the press today, and he won't stop it tomorrow, Wiley,' said Jumbo. 'If he ain't good enough to roll your bales, I ain't good enough to work on your stacks.'

'Why, sure, Jumbo,' said Sam Wiley. 'Why, sure. Why not give the kid a chance? Come on, boys. I got a heap of fine steaks over there in the cookhouse for you.'

They were all starting on when Bill touched the big arm of Jumbo.

'Look, Jumbo,' he said. 'All afternoon I didn't understand. Thanks!'

The eye of Jumbo, too pale, too steady, dwelt on him.

'Aw, try to grow up,' said Jumbo.

Supper went with a strange ease for Bill. No one seemed to notice the shuddering of his hands even when it caused him to spill coffee on the oilcloth; eyes courteously refused to see this, and the heart of Bill commenced to swell with a strength which, he felt, would never leave him in all the days of his life.

Toward the end Lacey said, 'About three o'clock I said you were finished, Bill. I waited for you to flop. Well, you didn't flop.'

'No,' said Portuguese Pete, 'you didn't flop, Bill.' He grinned at the boy.

'Ah, you'd think nobody ever did a half-day's work before!' said Jumbo.

That stopped the talk but Bill had to struggle to keep from smiling. He was so weak that the happiness glanced through him like light through water.

Afterward he got a bucket of cold water and a chunk of yellow soap. He was the only one of the crew that bothered about bathing at night. Now, as he scrubbed the ingrained dirt and salt and distilled grease from his body, Sam Wiley went past to feed the horses, and the rays from his lantern struck the nakedness of Bill.

'And look at him,' said the voice of Lacey out of nothingness. 'Skinny as a plucked crow, ain't he?'

Bill got to the place where he had built his bed of hay, under an oak tree away from the circle of the other beds, because the snoring of Portuguese Pete had a whistle in it that always kept him awake. Half in the blankets, he sat up for a time with his back to the tree and watched the moon rise in the east beneath a pyramid of fire. He made a cigarette with tobacco and a wheat-straw paper. The sweetness of the smoke commenced to breathe in his nostrils.

Now the blanched hay stubble was silvered with moonlight as though with dew and, as the moon rode higher, turning white, a big yellow star climbed upward beneath it. That must be Jupiter, he thought. When he turned to the west, the horizon was clean, but in the east the Sierra Nevadas rolled in soft clouds. This great sweep of the heavens made him feel it was easy to understand why some people loved the flats of central California. It had its beauty, and the breath of it was the strange fragrance of the tarweed which later on would darken the fields with a false verdure.

He had never been so calm. He had never felt such peace. All the ache of his muscles assured him that at last he was a man, almost.

Then a horrible brazen trumpeting rolled on his ears, seeming to pour in on him from every point of the horizon; but he knew that it was the jackass braying in the corral. Before the sound ended, he put out his smoke and slid down into his bed, inert, sick at heart again. Somehow it seemed that even the beasts of the field had power to mock him.

Through his lashes, he saw the lumbering form of Portuguese Pete approaching with a bottle in his hand. Pete was stopped by another figure that stepped from behind a tree.

'What you gunna do with that?' asked the hushed voice of Jumbo.

'It's good stuff,' said Pete, 'and I'm gunna give the kid a shot.'

'No, you ain't,' said Jumbo.

'Yeah, but I mean the skinny runt lifting those bales – this'll do him good.'

'Leave him sleep,' said Jumbo. 'Whisky ain't any short cut for him. Come along with me and I'll finish that bottle with you. Tomorrow we'll see if the kid can take it, really.'

'You kind of taken a fancy to the kid, ain't you?' asked Pete as they moved away.

'Me? Why, I just been kind of remembering, is all,' said Jumbo.

The Strange Villa

In 1925 Faust had been living in a villa at Menton, France, while, unknown to him, Ernest Hemingway, F. Scott Fitzgerald, and the Murphys were staying not far away at Antibes. While there he drove at breakneck speeds on the Grande Corniche and played roulette at the famous casino at Monte Carlo. He studied Greek so he could read Homer in the original and, feeling condemned to death at any moment by his bad heart, lived every day as fully as possible – including playing golf at the Mont Agel course high above Monte Carlo, where this story opens.

'With Monte Carlo for a setting,' the *New York Times Book Review* said of the Frederick Frost novel *Secret Agent Number One* (Macrae Smith, 1936, from which this story comes), 'Mr. Frost has produced an international spy story that might have come from the pen of Oppenheim himself.' The *Los Angeles Times* commented: 'Fast and full of thrills, and far-flung threads.' The *Cincinnati Enquirer* stated: 'A No. 1 mystery without a relaxed moment in it.'

Apparently none of these reviewers had the slightest idea that Frederick Frost was in fact Max Brand, the well-known writer of western fiction. Similarly, those who read only Faust's westerns are likely to meet here a Max Brand they never dreamed existed. Faust's three related spy novels *Secret Agent Number One*, *Spy Meets Spy* (Macrae Smith, 1937), and *The Bamboo Whistle* (Macrae Smith, 1937) are urbane, witty, and global in reach. Indeed, readers of *Detective Fiction Weekly*, where this story first appeared in the January 5, 1935, issue, voted Faust's spy stories the best of their kind for that year. They feature a sophisticated American daredevil hero, Anthony Hamilton – clearly a forefather of Ian Fleming's James Bond and John LeCarré's Smiley – and two beautiful and formidable heroines. In 'The Strange Villa' we come to know a Monte Carlo that Faust knew intimately and which would eventually play host to a world of rising dictatorships and impending war.

CHAPTER ONE

U P THERE AT SEVENTEEN THOUSAND FEET the moon shone and the stars were scattered, with the plane of Anthony Hamilton flung across them like a flat stone skidding over a pool; but he had to sink out of that clear beauty to the earth and all the warmth of his electrically heated clothing could not comfort him. Two miles beneath him lay a smooth white sea of clouds which meant a low ceiling out of which he must land. Or perhaps clouds and fog continued all the way to the ground and in that case he was probably a dead man. Usually he looked to every detail of preparation himself before stepping into a plane but on this occasion he had left arrangements in the hands of a subordinate and a parachute was missing. To get one meant delay and in the Secret Service of the United States delay is not permitted; lives must be run to a schedule like a train-service, so he had taken the chance. The little monoplane had shot him through the chill of the upper spaces at four miles a minute and here he was over his goal with the main tank empty and the gasoline fading out of the reserve. There again he had been a fool to trust another man's word about the rate of fuel consumption in this new type of engine.

In spite of the fog, he knew almost to a hair's-breadth the exact scene which was clouded over. Just south lay Mont Agel with Monte Carlo at its feet, and just about under him, in the rough of the hills, lay that flat valley where he was expected. If the head of a single mountain had lifted above the white floor, he would have been able to place himself perfectly, but perhaps not perfectly enough to locate that narrow strip of valley. . . . At four miles a minute there is not time for deliberate calculation. He remembered, suddenly, the last time he had teed up a ball on the golf course of flat-topped Mont Agel with a feeling that he could drive off right into the blue of that Mediterranean sky. Now all that beauty was stifled in deadly white; this great, liquid bowl of the sky had at the bottom a dirty sediment into which he had to sink.

He banked and turned, with a slight giddiness, a sense of losing balance, a pressure in his ears; then he dived. It was as though he stood still with the stars flying upwards, turning from dots into dashes of brightness. The air screamed on the struts, whistling a tune as loud as the hurrying drum-beat of the motor. The clouds lifted at him, not the smooth white floor they had appeared from above but high-surging waves, a sea struck to ice in the middle of a storm by one touch of interstellar cold. The waves grew into hills of volcanic crystal; they exploded upwards, and now he dropped like a stone through the upper translucence, through a brief margin of grey, in which cloud-forms appeared, abortive and shapeless, and down into the blind hollow of darkness.

The altimeter showed him a thousand feet and still the wet darkness blew about him. He had the inevitable feeling that the instrument was wrong and that he was about to strike, that instant, on earth which would be turned hard as steel by the force of the impact; but the altimeter must be trusted; that is the first lesson in blind flying. He set his teeth, smiling a little.

Five hundred feet – three hundred –

The bottom of the well was just beneath, and still there was not a gleam, not a glimmer of light. The curtain of cloud dropped its thick fringes right down to the earth. On such a night, even automobiles would be crawling in second along the winding mountain roads.

Something appeared on his left, vague as the first loom of land to a ship at sea. He turned right and felt, rather than saw, the ragged side of a mountain. He was flying level, using that sheer instinct which was one of his greatest gifts in the air. He had readjusted the angle of his propeller blades so that they would take a smaller bite of the thick sea-level atmosphere, but he wished for more power when he felt again that presence of a solid mass on the left. He turned right, and again from another crag to the right once more. He realized, now, that he was swirling about blindly inside the cup of a mountain valley which was very narrow but perhaps three or four miles long. It must be that he had come down on the very goal of his journey. He dropped his one landing-flare. The gleaming line of it flashed, went out. It had struck water.

He sank lower, to two hundred feet, to one hundred – the very sword-edge of danger was at his throat, now, when he saw three dim eyes beneath.

He circled at fifty feet. Hands blacker than the darkness struck up at him. He had slid just over the tops of some trees, but he could make out a cone of radiance extending from those three eyes – a cone flattened on the lower side. That flatness must be the ground.

He shut off the motor and flattened out. Wings beat at him, left and right; more trees. The wheels struck, staggered the plane into a crazy wobbling which he righted with a delicate touch, and then the little monoplane was whispering lightly over grass, slowing, stopping.

Well, the thing was over, and in the Service men must not allow themselves to ponder the strange phases which they add, from time to time, to the history of their past. Anthony Hamilton pulled at a few buckles, shed his heavy flying suit, and stepped out of the plane into the creamy verge of the illumination shed by the three headlights. At this moment one of them went out; the other pair swerved forward and an automobile stopped just before him. The full glare fell on Hamilton and showed him a little older, for the moment, than his twenty-seven years. He had that slight stoop of the shoulders which comes from much bending over books – or tennis-rackets. He seemed a bit grim – for this instant only – but a moment later he was smiling. He was always smiling and this gave him an air of inexhaustible, boyish good-nature.

A big man got out of the automobile and came up to him; the headlights were dimmed at the same moment, leaving only a dusty glow in the fog.

The waxed ends of the big fellow's moustaches were gleaming as he came up to Hamilton.

'This is not a landing field for aeroplanes, monsieur,' said he.

'It is not a highway for automobiles, either,' said Hamilton.

'Monsieur, I am an agent of the Sûreté. May I ask for your paper of identity?'

'Certainly,' said Hamilton. 'Will you take a cigarette from me, at the same time?'

'You are very kind,' said the big man. He took a cigarette from the case which Hamilton offered and himself supplied the light, holding it just a part of a second longer than necessary close to the rather unhandsome face of Hamilton. And Hamilton turned, as a man will, a little to the side as he reached into an inner pocket. He took out a pigskin wallet among whose contents he began to fumble slowly. In the meantime the eye of the big man was occupied by certain characters which became visible along the cigarette, little luminous marks that showed one by one just before the paper curled and charred. The first portion of a signature became visible, letter by letter, before the agent of the Sûreté cried out: 'But you can't be the man! You're twenty years too young! I beg your pardon, Mr. Hamilton.'

'I suppose I ought to thank you for a compliment,' said Hamilton. 'You're Harrison Victor, of course?'

'I am Louis Desaix, of the Sûreté,' said the other, 'and only Harrison Victor in Ohio and a few points east.'

He shook hands, then called: 'Jack! Come here, will you?'

A second man came from the automobile.

'John Carney – Anthony Hamilton. This is the new chief, Jack. Carney's the man to take care of the plane, Mr. Hamilton.'

'How you dropped it down the middle of this well I can't understand,' said Carney. 'We saw the landing flare hit the pool, yonder, and then we waited for the machine to smash and you to bail out and come floating down in the parachute.'

'I *should* have bailed out instead of feeling my way around this room in the dark,' said Hamilton, 'but a fellow at the other end of the line forgot all about the parachute.'

'You came anyway?' asked Harrison Victor. 'You must have known that there was fog here before you started.'

'I couldn't tell that there was fog all the way to the ground. Did you bring out gasoline for the plane?'

They had plenty of it and the two helped Carney carry the tins to the monoplane.

'How is she?' asked Carney. 'I'll have to wait alone here till daylight and I'd like to have something to think about.'

'She's fast as a bullet and nervous as a two-year-old filly,' said Hamilton. 'She takes the air like a bird, but watch her when you make a landing.'

They said goodbye to Carney, who knew where to take the plane, and got into the car. Harrison Victor trundled it over the field, gained the road, and slid through the white smother with increasing speed. He seemed to feel the road by instinct.

'Will you paint the picture for me?' asked Hamilton.

'Show me the part you know, first of all.'

Hamilton leaned a little closer.

'That letter was a beauty. I can recite it.

' "Number 1815" (my number is the same as the date of Waterloo, so it will be easy for you to remember), "Number 1815, you will go at once to Monte Carlo, abandoning all other work. At the Pension Mon Sourir there now resides, or frequently visits, the Number One Secret Service man of Japan. His nationality and name are unknown. Discover both, together with his present purpose in Europe. Our source of information cannot be drawn upon further. It is dead." That was the main portion of the letter. The rest was a sketch of how I should proceed down here and where you would meet me. They might have picked out an easier spot, I suppose.'

'Sometimes,' said Harrison Victor, 'Washington is a little more than three thousand miles away from good sense. But at any rate you're here, and that's a comfort. Officially I heard that you were coming; unofficially I learned that you were the man who did the big job in Okotsk. That was why I was a bit surprised when I saw you.'

'You know in a Russian winter it's easy to grow a beard,' said Hamilton.

'How old are you, really? Twenty-four?'

'Twenty-seven.'

'I was wrong again. It must come from living a lot and not giving a damn.'

'Victor, what have you fellows turned up, down here? What's the Villa Mon Sourir?'

'You know Les Roches?'

'That point which runs out to sea?' Hamilton inquired casually.

'Yes. Mon Sourir is down there in a huddle of pines. An old Italian villa. It's owned now, or rented, rather, on a long lease, by a Californian, a bearded fellow called George Michelson. He has his daughter with him. She runs the place as a pension.'

'What sort of boarders?'

'Usual Riviera run. Polish girl – invalid. German. Czechoslovak. American called Harbor. John Harbor. Vicomte Henri de Graulchier. Just the usual Riviera hodge-podge. No, nicer than usual, most of them. We've looked the place over as well as we could.'

'Have you put an agent in the house?'

'We tried to, but it wouldn't go. We sent out Louise Curran. Know her?'

'No.'

'Ah, you don't know her? Louise is a card and she's turned up some good tricks in her time, for the Service. She went out and tried to get a room, but the place was full up. No vacancies in sight. So I had Bill West go out to take a look at things. You know Bill?'

'He worked for me in Ireland, one summer.'

'Great Scott, are you the man who – '

'Ah, never mind that.'

'I mind, but I'll shut up. You're the whalebone and rubber man who did all the fox-hunting, are you? Ah, well – I sent Bill West out as I say, and he got into the place all right.'

'Find out anything?'

'Yes, he found the Vicomte de Graulchier looking down a revolver at him. Hardy fellow, that vicomte. Fat-looking little chunk, but hardy. Of course Bill had to go to jail as a burglar. He's in for five years, and nothing that any of us can do about it. That's all the forwarder we are about the Villa Mon Sourir. As far as we can make out, the place is innocent, all right. All except John Harbor. And I think that he's the Japanese number one. You never would expect it, either. Sleek, lazy, good-natured blighter. Likes his afternoon Vermouth. But we've caught him cold taking code messages.'

'Got the code?'

'No, it's a hard one to work.'

'Where does he get the messages?'

'In the Casino at Monte Carlo; but we don't know the source of them. We've tried, but we can't tell where he gets his messages. However, we have copies of a lot of them. A whole book of them. Once we decipher the code, the job will be finished.'

'That sounds too easy.'

'Everything is easy in this game – unless you die while you're winning.'

Hamilton said: 'Japan is all out against the rest of the world. She wants the entire East for herself. If she's sent her number one man to the Villa Mon Sourir, hell is going to pop. And I don't think it will be simple to get to the bottom of that hell.'

'We've thought of that in a good deal of detail.'

'Do you know who Japan's number one is?'

'Not even his complexion.'

'No one does,' answered Hamilton. 'We only know one bit of in-formation. Japan's number one is the fellow who induced Theodore Roosevelt to intervene in the Russo-Japanese War. Honestly, you know – to prevent bloodshed, bring world peace nearer, and all that. But his intervention probably saved the skin of Japan. She'd spent her last yen on the job when Roosevelt started persuading Russia towards peace. Wherever Japan's number one is now, you can depend upon it the entire interest of Japan is invested. She wouldn't send him five minutes away from Tokio unless there were some new stars in the sky. This job is vital, Victor.'

'I guessed at most of that. I'm glad to know some more facts, though.'

'Going back to Mon Sourir. You don't find anything extraordinary about the place?'

'Not a thing. Not a single thing except George Michelson's daughter.'

'Well, what about her.'

'The loveliest thing I've ever seen.'

'Ah, I see,' said Hamilton.

'No, you don't see,' said Harrison Victor. 'When I say "loveliest" I mean just that. Perfect.'

'Greek goddess, eh?'

'She's what the Greeks might have produced if they'd kept maturing for another twenty-five centuries. Phidias a little lighter in the bone. I've looked into her because I've looked into everyone in the Villa Mon Sourir. I've found out that she swims the American crawl, went around the rocks and bumps of Mont Agel in seventy-eight honest strokes, flies an aeroplane, drives an automobile like an Italian devil, speaks French, German, Italian, Spanish and – God help me! – Russian, also.'

'Describe her, will you?'

'She's going to be with her father at the Casino, tonight. And that's where I'm taking you. You'll see her for yourself. Luminous as a blonde, mysterious as a brunette. Most damned, exquisite smile.'

'And she runs a little pension on the Riviera?' asked Hamilton.

'You know. Her father isn't so young or so well.'

'What an equipment she has to be the world's number one Secret Service agent,' said Hamilton.

CHAPTER TWO

The architect of the Casino at Monte Carlo is the man who erected the Opera House in Paris, a fellow with an instinct for overloading everything. His attempts at ornateness merely gave a puffed and stuffed effect to his exteriors and his interiors are as overwhelming as an assemblage of fat dowagers. Besides, gilding and regilding cannot brighten Monte

Carlo and all the lights cannot penetrate the grave shadow which enters the mind. The flush and sparkle of after-dinner parties who come in for a dash of play soon passes. Women assume Spartan manners. They never cry out with joy; they never groan or exclaim. They win with austerity and lose with contempt. Besides these casual visitors there are the serious players who sit about the tables equipped with paper and pencil, making rapid notes, busy as bank clerks with their systems. These are the real devotees and their pale, stern faces tell us that Chance is a dark goddess.

Anthony Hamilton, entering in a dinner jacket in the middle of the evening, looked so young, so rich, so American, so flushed with wine and good-nature, that it was astonishing to see such a man without company. His presence was felt at a roulette table at once. Even the serious players looked up at him with a faint gleam of contempt and prophecy as he began to play single numbers. He laid hundred franc bets, three of them, always on the nine, and watched his money whisk away. In the meantime he was spotting the characters from the Villa Mon Sourir who, as Harrison Victor had promised, were gathered at this table. By Victor's descriptions he could identify them easily. The big fellow with the rigidly straight back and the sour face who kept consulting his 'system' and jotting down numbers was John Harbor, the American. The fellow with the short legs and large head, he whose swarthy skin was pricked full of small holes like needle-scars, was the Vicomte Henri de Graulchier. He had the stiff upper lip of a drinker, and his black eyes were continually empty. Yet his dignity was interesting and so was the purity of his English, which retained only a slight oil of the French 'r's.' The very blonde girl was the Pole, Maria Blatchavenski, too thin to be pretty except when she smiled. George Michelson of California wore a beard and moustache, so trimmed that he had a Continental look, but a certain bigness of body and of voice betrayed his Western origin from time to time. He stood behind the chair of his daughter, Mary Michelson, watching her lay her small bets with careful precision. Yes, she was beautiful, yet her beauty seemed to Hamilton a very dull affair; he was about to decide that Harrison Victor's paean of praise was a worthless enthusiasm, when she looked up to her father with a smile. Then Hamilton saw the light; a great deal of it. It was true that she could have been lost in a crowd, but everyone who looked at her twice would be stopped. These were the representatives from the Villa Mon Sourir. As for the agents who worked under Harrison Victor, there was only one present. That was Louise Curran, exquisitely dainty and fresh and good to see. Apparently her 'system' could not occupy all her attention, for every now and then she would lift her hand-bag to powder her nose.

In reality, as Hamilton knew, she was catching in the glass, and memorizing with lightning adeptness whole columns of the figures which John Harbor continually scribbled on a small pad, jerking off the sheets one by one and putting them under the pad. It was in this manner, and with other simple methods, that Harrison Victor had collected quantities of the notations of Harbor. The instant the code was known, a flood of information would pour into the hands of the American Secret Service.

Well, all codes can be solved. That is the old saying but Hamilton did not believe it. In the meantime, what was the source of the information which Harbor was noting down? It might have been almost anything: one of the horns which sounded dimly from the street, the almost imperceptible tremors and fluctuations of one of the lights in the room, the hand movements of some other person, writing at the table, the finger-work of the croupier as he wielded his rake. There were a thousand ways of conveying steady messages such as Harbor was writing down; and that he was scribbling a code there could be no doubt to anyone who considered the sort of numbers he employed. At roulette there is nothing higher than thirty-five, but a typical page of Harbor's notes had read:

'15–331
245–86
99–191
111–232
6–56
73–411'

Under this column of figures appeared a line for addition, but the sum which appeared in the result had, apparently, nothing to do with the column of figures itself.

Studying the calm, still face of Harbor, Hamilton decided instantly that the man himself did not know what he was taking down. The figures were not his short-hand report. They made an unintelligible jargon until they were decoded.

Hamilton, laying his fourth bet on the nine, was surprised by a win. Thirty-five hundred francs was not a great haul, but it was something; eyes lifted to him again from around the table and he permitted himself to laugh with a vacuous joy. It was one of the major triumphs of his art, the production of that laughter, whether it were silent or noisy. He had worked for months perfecting it until, at his will, it could sweep every semblance of intelligence out of his face and sponge all record of thought from his brain. John Harbor seemed overwhelmed by disgust as he stared at the laughing face, so overwhelmed that he rose suddenly from the table, dropped his writing pad into his coat pocket, and left the room.

Hamilton drifted behind him through room after room. The size of the stake he had won furnished him with an excellent excuse for leaving the table at that particular moment. He watched John Harbor go out into the garden and slipped after him.

The fog still covered the night so that the garden lamps shone through enormous halos. The pavement was wet. The palm trees glistened dimly. John Harbor, walking impatiently up and down, tipped one of those gracefully arching branches and cursed the chilly shower of drops that fell on him. He began to brush his coat dry with a handkerchief but still he looked about him until it was apparent that he was waiting to fill an appointment.

Hamilton slipped quietly up behind the palm tree nearest to his quarry and then — he had eyes in his feet like any jungle tracker and the thing should never have happened — he stepped into a hole left where a small paving block had been removed, no doubt for replacement the next day, and pitched forward on his knees. He had trusted to the tree and the fog so entirely that he fell almost in touching distance of Harbor, and that big fellow whirled about with a grunt of fear. He must have been keyed to an electric tension because, as he turned, he snatched out a gun and fired point blank.

The thing was incredible; it could not have happened; but while the brain of Hamilton was disclaiming the possibility of the entire affair his hand was jerking an automatic from the spring holster which supported it under the pit of his left arm. The first bullet had missed him; the second one would not. Still down on both knees and one hand, he shot John Harbor through the head and saw the body fall face down. The impact was like the whack of a fist against bare flesh.

Hamilton, rising, waited for half a second. No footfalls came towards him; from the streets of the town roared and whined the noise of the automobile traffic. At any moment attendants might pour out around him and, in that case, he was a dead man. The first rule of the Secret Service is that its agents receive no government support when they operate abroad. So, for half a second, he contemplated instant flight. The next moment he was leaning over the dead man with swift hands at work. Fountain-pen, wallet, watch he recognized by the first sweeping touch. A hard flat box in the left coat pocket he drew out and found it to be a book, a little volume of Everyman's Library bound in dull green cloth – 'The Journal of the Discovery of the Source of the Nile,' by J. H. Speke, that strange fellow whom the great Burton had hated and envied so. He slid the book back into the same pocket, located the little writing pad with its rustling loose pages beside it, and decided to leave all in place. He looked once more down at the loose body, the hands which grasped inertly at the stones; then he drew back into covert behind the palms. No doubt it was still dangerous for him to linger near the place, but it was very important to discover the persons with whom Harbor had appointed this trysting place.

Another long, long minute drew out; then he heard the quick, light tapping of heels and saw coming straight towards the dead man Harrison Victor's angel of beauty and of grace, Mary Michelson.

CHAPTER THREE

She was tall, with plenty of substance, but he felt that she moved with an indescribable lightness. She shone in on his mind far more than the lamps which made a dazzle in the fog.

He waited to see her take heed of the fallen body but there was no pausing in her approach. She walked straight up to the dead man and leaned over him. Her hands were busy. As she straightened he saw that she was putting into her handbag the little Everyman volume; and with it went the notations which John Harbor had been making that evening.

That seemed cold-blooded enough but that was not all. With her handkerchief – to prevent fingermarks, of course, – she picked up the automatic which had slithered away to a little distance and put it inside the grasp of the dead fingers of Harbor. Then with that swift, light step which seemed a special attribute of virtue, she went back into the Casino.

He followed, after making sure that there was no mark on the knees of his trousers to indicate the place where he had fallen, and he was just coming in from the garden when he saw Harrison Victor pass out through the doorway. He hailed Victor with a murmur and drew him aside.

'Your beautiful angel is one of them,' said Hamilton. 'John Harbor is dead and I've seen her plunder him of his notes of this evening as well as a book; what the book could have to do with the business I can't tell. She was as cool over the dead man as a bird over a fallen seed.'

'Is she one of them?' said the agent of the Sûreté, sadly. 'Well, I've never fallen in love without having it shaken right out of me again. – What killed Harbor?'

'I did,' said Hamilton. 'A damned clumsy, stupid business. But at one time I was on my knees and he was putting bullets past my ears. He was just a little nervous. But the girl, Victor – she's the one for study. If she were honest, she'd be an angel; since she's a crook, she's probably a devil. I have to be introduced to her.'

'You killed Harbor?' murmured Victor, but he added, calm at once: 'I don't know Mary Michelson.'

'Send one of your men to the table where she plays and have him try to nail her stakes; I'll interfere; that will be introduction enough.'

'If you want to go about it – if you don't think that's too much college farce?'

'I believe in college farce,' said Hamilton.

'Farce in the house and dead men in the garden, eh? I'll arrange it as you say, of course.'

Well, it was not strange if Harrison Victor were distinctly cool. Who could tell what disastrous effects the killing of Harbor might have? Before he went in, Victor said: 'I've just had a report from Jack Carney. The fog lifted back there in the valley and as soon as he saw a star he jumped the plane at it. He says that little amphibian swam across the sky like a gold fish across a bowl. In three wriggles it was over the sea and through a lucky rift he was able to get down to the water. He says he still feels as though he had been riding in a thunderbolt; he's bumped a shower of sparks out of the sky.'

Hamilton with this information went back into the game rooms but stopped a moment on the way to have a pony of brandy. There is nothing that loads the air with alcohol fumes as cognac does; if he gave the impression of having had a drop too much it would be as well.

The girl, as he had expected, was back in her place with her father now at her side. If she were a part of an international spy ring, it seemed certain that her father was implicated also. The great forehead, the noble openness of eye in this man denied such a thing but not more clearly than did the beauty of the girl; and Hamilton remembered with a leap of the heart that men and women *can* give their lives to the Secret Service because they are capable of loving danger and their country.

He drifted idly about the table, making his bets two hundred francs, now, and merely laughing in his foolish, silent way when the croupier raked in his money. The girl had just won on the black when a long arm reached from behind and collected her entire bet.

'The lady's money, my friend,' said Hamilton, and gripped that arm at the wrist. He looked up into the face of a tall man who was breathing whiskey-fumes.

'Hello! Hello!' said a very English accent. 'Isn't that money mine?'

'I'm afraid it is not,' said George Michelson.

'Oh, I laid my bet over there,' said the stranger. 'Frightfully sorry!'

He moved off.

'That was nice of you,' said the girl, smiling up at Hamilton.

He favored her with his witless laugh.

'I was watching your system,' he said, 'and I can't make a thing out of it. Deep, isn't it? I've tried systems, but can't keep on any of them for a whole evening. Some idea of my own comes buzzing along and there I go again, chasing butterflies. May I sit down here?'

'Of course,' said she.

He took the luckily vacant chair beside her. She was giving him only a partial attention, the rest going to a consideration of the lists of figures which composed her system; now she was placing a new bet. The lack of makeup, he saw, was one thing that made her beauty a little dim, but the absence of artificial color set off the intense blueness of her eyes; he never had seen anything quite like that blue.

'You're English, aren't you?' asked he.

'No, American.'

'Ah, are you? So am I. Came a bad cropper down in Virginia a while back — schooling a green idiot of a five year old over ditch and timber — and the doctor said I'd better have a change of air and no horses. So over I came to take the old spin around.'

He pointed to a small lump at the side of his forehead. It was quite true that he had had a bad fall from a horse, but not in Virginia. A bullet from an old-fashioned Persian musket had killed the grey Arab mare he was riding as he got out of Teheran towards healthier and less romantic names on the map. Well, that was simply another sentence that belonged to the dead book of the past.

'I know some Virginia people,' the girl was saying. 'Sally Keith, for instance?'

'Do you, really?' He flicked like lightning the complicated card index of his memory. 'Why, this is like an introduction. Sally taught me my manners cub-hunting, ten years ago. Perhaps you've heard her mention me, because she still makes table-talk out of the silly things I did that day. My name is Anthony Hamilton.'

'Perhaps I have heard her speak of you. I'm Mary Michelson. Father, this is Anthony Hamilton, who knows Sally Keith in Virginia.'

The big bearded man stood up and shook hands with a good, strong grip. 'That was a quick eye and hand you used on that sharper, a moment ago,' he said.

It was a very good opening but he could not develop it. They were entirely pleasant but neither of them seemed to want a drink; hints about a motor trip through the back country left them vague; they were not even sure when they would come again to the Casino.

When he left the table he signed to Victor and met him outside the building.

'Have the Michelsons a car?' he asked.

'I have it spotted,' said Victor. 'Any luck?'

'No. I've registered myself as a feather brain, a poor, harmless blighter. That's all. They're charming but they won't be drawn. We've been introduced, and that's all.'

'What do you make of her?'

'Absolutely nothing; she might be a saint, except that I've seen her pick the pockets of a dead man. Put a good man on Michelson's car. Have him fix it so that the machine will break down hopelessly a few miles out of Monte Carlo. And not too near to Les Roches. The moment they start off, send a man to my car and wake me up.'

'Wake you up?'

'I'll be asleep.'

He went to his parked machine. It had a compact body and one of those all-weather tops that go up and down as easily as an umbrella. The seat beside the driver's could be flattened out until it gave almost the comfort of a couch. Hamilton stretched himself on it, closed his eyes, and resolutely toppled himself off the edge of consciousness into the fathomless oblivion of sleep.

CHAPTER FOUR

A voice at his ear brought him at a step back to full possession of his wits. A shadowy arm was pointing and the voice saying: 'There they go – Michelson and his daughter alone in the car.'

He had his own swift machine instantly on the way. It had the long, low hang that he liked and it took corners as though it were running on tracks; so he snaked through the crooked streets of Monte Carlo without ever losing sight of his goal. He was not really out of the city at any time, but merely away from the thickest heart of it. Michelson drove fast but it was child's play for Hamilton's racer to keep in touch.

He wondered whether or not he should have spoken to Harrison Victor about the singular importance which seemed to attach to the copy of Speke's 'Journal.' However, that importance would be no doubt a few mysterious annotations which John Harbor might have made on a flyleaf. Perhaps it was chiefly to receive this book that the girl had the appointment with Harbor; and yet they lived together in the same house, where she must have the leisure to meet him as she chose.

These questions were so small that they were only worth registering; not for long consideration.

They were well out from the city when the tail lights of Michelson's car wavered, then stopped at the side of the street. Anthony Hamilton halted immediately behind them.

Michelson had the hood open and was leaning over the engine, but it was the girl whose hands were busied. 'Ah, Mr. Hamilton! What a chance to meet you here!' said Michelson.

The girl, however, did not lift her head at once from the engine she was examining.

'Not a chance at all,' answered Hamilton. 'You see, there's not much around here for me except weather and wine and roulette, and I wanted to find out where you live. You don't mind, Mr. Michelson? Let me try to be useful.'

'The carburetor's gone,' said the girl, straightening at last. 'Hello, Mr. Hamilton. Will you give us a lift home? We'll have to send garage people to bring in the car.'

'But how could the carburetor go, my dear?' asked the father.

'I don't know,' she answered. 'It's a bit weird altogether.'

'I'll get your things out,' said Hamilton. He was already at work as he spoke, lifting an overcoat and a wrap out of the little automobile. But first his hand had touched the evening bag of the girl – and found it empty! She had disposed of Speke's 'Journal' as quickly as this. The book became, suddenly, of a vast importance. It was instantly the entire goal of Hamilton's search.

He got them comfortably into his car and drove turned in the seat so that he could keep on chattering. But the way to Les Roches was all too short. The car was quickly among the boulders and pines of the little peninsula and now they directed him to stop at a great gate of wrought iron in the middle of a pink wall. The yellow mimosas of the garden within showed vaguely through the mist in the glow of the headlights. The same light, passing down the length of the wall, found the rocks of a beach and the thin hint of waves under the fog. Over the gate appeared the name: *Mon Sourir.*

'We should ask you in,' said the girl, 'but we're responsible for the pension, Mr. Hamilton, and one of our guests is a frightfully light sleeper.'

'You know,' said Hamilton, 'if you have an extra room I'd like to come here. I'd move in tomorrow morning.'

He stood so that the light would fully illuminate the vacuous smile with which he admired her. She showed not the least amusement or contempt.

'What a pity that every room is full, just now,' she said.

'But may I call?'

'Ah, of course you may. Goodnight, Mr. Hamilton. How kind you've been!'

Michelson gave him that hearty handshake again.

'Drop in any time,' he said. 'We both want to see you.'

That was all. Hamilton, watching them through the gate, studied the coat of Michelson with care. There was a slight bulge of the left coat pocket – about such an enlargement as one of the Everyman volumes might make.

Harrison Victor came to his room in the hotel the next morning and sat in a corner smoking a foul black Italian cigar, twisting his moustaches to more delicate points. He looked perfectly the part of Louis Desaix, of the Sûreté.

'There's no note in the papers about the death of John Harbor,' said Hamilton, in the midst of dressing.

'The body's been found, the Villa Mon Sourir consulted, and John Harbor is at the morgue. The papers will carry no articles about the suicide.'

'Suicide?'

'Of course. The gun was found gripped in his right hand.'

'The girl put it there; and his gun was not of the right calibre to make the wound.'

'My dear Hamilton, this is Monaco, where the skies are so blue and the sunshine so golden that people don't want to examine into every ugly little death. The authorities help to smooth things over. Suicides in the Monte Carlo gardens don't help the flowers to bloom. And then it seems that John Harbor was a very obscure fellow. No connections to bother about him. He'll be quietly buried and forgotten. That has happened before.'

A boy brought up a long white cardboard box. Hamilton gave the tip and opened the box when the messenger had left. Inside was a sheaf of pink roses, freshened with a sprinkling of dew.

'Who's sending you flowers?' asked Victor.

'Old fellow, I'm in love. I'm taking these flowers for a morning call. Yes, a *morning* call. Because, last night, I was swept off my feet, overwhelmed, devastated by meeting the beautiful Mary Michelson.'

'You're a cold devil,' commented Victor, without smiling.

'On the contrary, I'm burning with passion,' said Hamilton, yawning.

He was in his morning coat, now, and he turned this way and that to examine his appearance. He was, in fact, a very trim figure, except for that slight stoop and forward thrusting of the shoulders. More than ever he looked, from behind, like a student, and from in front like an athlete.

'You know people don't go in for that sort of thing down here?' asked Victor.

'I'm an outstanding type,' said Hamilton. 'I'm one of those genial young asses who, having been raised in a certain way, never varies a trifle in any habit of his way of life. My mindlessness is so complete that I could never manage to vary my clothes according to my climate. And, this being the morning of the day, morning clothes are required. Also this stick.'

He drew the beautiful, mottled Malacca through his fingertips, admiring its delicate luster and light flexibility.

'And these gloves of yellow chamois cleaned just enough times to fade them white. And the monocle, too. That's a real convenience. It can drop out of my fool face at an embarrassing moment and give me another second to compose my answers. Besides, I have an extra glass in my pocket that turns it into a good magnifying piece.'

'You're an extraordinary smooth article,' grinned Victor. 'Do you never lose your face? I mean, do you always remember which face you're wearing?'

'No,' said Hamilton. 'Years and years ago when I was just a youngster – it must have been four years altogether – I forgot myself completely while I was sitting cross-legged opposite one of those black Sahara Arab sheiks. He showed me my error by reaching for me with a knife.'

'He didn't harvest you?'

'You know, if you sit cross-legged in just the right way, your feet are always free. I kicked the sheik in the stomach and managed to get to his best camel. She was a milk white lamb, and she did all my thinking for me for three days.'

'Are you off, now?'

'Not until you approve of me.'

'You'll get a glance from every eye. You'll be well known to half the people in Monte Carlo before the day's over.'

'If I can keep your attention fixed on my left hand, Victor, I can do wonders with the right. By the way, which was the room of John Harbor, over at the Villa Mon Sourir?'

'On the ground floor, the third door on the left down the main hall.'

'And the girl's?'

'Mary Michelson's? She has the room opening on the second story loggia and looking out to sea. Hamilton, I know that you're a clever workman but I want to remind you that already we have a man in jail for snooping about the Villa Mon Sourir. And Bill West is a clever fellow, too. Awfully clever.'

'Of course he is. But he wasn't in love. You forget, Victor, that all the world loves a lover.'

CHAPTER FIVE

Riviera climate is as unreal as a colored postcard. Beyond the mountains lies the land of the cold Mistral but along the Ligurian coast a fringe of summer remains when all the rest of Europe is overcast with white winter. That golden warmth seemed to Hamilton, on this morning, more like a pictorial effect than ever before, a bit of expensive staging put on by the Casino to content its guests. But the fragrance of the mimosa was real. It carried an honest breath of spring into the air. So he was breathing deep as he drove with the blue sparkle of the sea on his left and that delicate fragrance in his face. Coming down the Avenue de Monte Carlo, he took the Boulevard Albert Premier past the great bowl of La Condamine, and so on by the gardens and palace of the Prince until he came out on the road to Beaulieu. He was taking his ease in the car, with the top down and this warmth of the miraculous summer flowing about him. Okotsk had been a different affair; and in a few days a new order from Washington might fling him half way around the world on a new mission. Even that uncertainty was a delight to him for it was part of the joy of the chase, whether he were the hunter or the hunted.

He turned left, now, into the road which wound among the glimmering boulders of Les Roches, and when he looked out through the trunks of the pine trees the ocean rose as a steep blue wall on either hand, about to flow inwards and close over him. The pink walls of Mon Sourir appeared, and he drove through the open gate with an odd feeling that the panels were closing automatically behind him. The drive circled around a tall cluster of mimosa trees. He stopped his car at the side and rang the bell of the house. The dark fingering around that bell seemed to tell him that the Villa Mon Sourir had abandoned the dignity of a private residence and become a public place.

A butler in grey-striped working jacket and apron opened the door to him. Hamilton gave his card. 'I am calling on Miss Michelson,' he said.

'She is not in, monsieur.'

'Not in? But I'll wait for her. I'm sure she expects me.'

It seemed to him that the square, solemn face of the man forbade his entrance still, but he stepped forward with his witless smile and the butler gave back.

'This way,' he said, and led the way into a little waiting room. The open window of it let him see in a group all the inhabitants of Mon Sourir except Mary Michelson. They were seated in the spicy shade under a pair of stone pines, the gigantic Czech, Karol Menzel, Hans Friedberg with no back to his German head, Ivan Petrolich, the Russian invalid in his wheel-chair, the beautiful young Rumanian, Matthias Radu, sleek and soft as a Levantine, or a woman. The Polish girl, Maria Blatchavenski, was there, at the side of huge George Michelson, and the Vicomte Henri de Graulchier was not seated but sauntered slowly about. He wore a loose tweed coat in spite of the weather and kept his hands in the pockets of it. He spoke with authority that had a caress in it, like one speaking to children and explaining difficult things with a restrained impatience.

George Michelson was saying, at this moment: 'The great southern valley of the Volga is the storehouse, the granary of the country, and if that were held securely – '

But here the butler, crossing the room to the window, said rather loudly: 'Is the light too glaring? Shall I lower the shade, Monsieur Hamilton?'

'It's very pleasant that way, with the sea-breeze blowing in,' he answered. 'Will you put these flowers in water for Miss Michelson?'

The butler carried the long box away and Hamilton, taking a chair and lighting a cigarette, observed that he still could command a view of the interesting group beyond the window. They had altered a little. The hand of George Michelson was no longer raised as though about to emphasize an important point. Pale Maria Blatchavenski no longer sat so eagerly erect. It was as though a stress were removed and the people were relaxing after the strain of effort. The talk was still about Russia, with the vicomte now holding forth in the lead.

'Come, Ivan Petrolich! You are a Russian. Maria, you are almost a Russian – '

'Henri, *no* Polish woman is a Russian. I beg your pardon, Ivan Petrolich, but a Polish woman is removed by thousands of light years from a Russian.'

'Ah, I understand,' said the invalid. His head sank into the cushion at the back of his chair and his pale face was smiling a little. He had almost closed his eyes.

'You are both Slavs,' said Henri de Graulchier. 'And when we talk of race instinct, there is something more important than national boundaries, little national prejudices and blindnesses.'

'Unless one is French, Henri, and then of course it is understandable, it is necessary,' said Friedberg, the German.

'We should argue peacefully,' declared the vicomte. 'And the point that I wish to make is that the Russians are not a melancholy people.'

'Ah, come, come!' murmured Matthias Radu, the beautiful young Rumanian.

'I mean it, and I ask for unprejudiced witness. The Russian is not melancholy. He is simply Asiatic. Because he rubs elbows with the Occident and is different from it, he is erected into a mystery by the western nations. His music, which contains some of the natural wail and minor quality of the Asiatic, strikes the occidental ear as an expression of sadness. The contrary is the truth.'

'These are simply statements, de Graulchier,' said the huge Karol Menzel, the Czech. 'I know a good many Russians.'

'You don't!' said de Graulchier. 'Not at all. Not really know them.'

'Ah, I don't?' murmured Menzel.

'Certainly not. All you know are the educated upper tenth of one percent. And those are the people who speak French and English, drink more Burgundy than vodka, and have been *expected* by their European friends to be mysterious, day-dreaming, melancholy; expected so long that soon they are willing to play the part that is desired. Half Hamlet, half Gargantua. That is your educated Russian – again I beg your pardon, Ivan Petrolich.'

'You always delight me with your aphorisms, Henri,' said the Russian.

'Not aphorisms. I am telling you the truth. Open your eyes to see it. The real Russian, the peasant with his bit of land, is always happy unless he is starving to death. On half a franc, he knows how to make fiesta. There is nothing mysterious about him except the depth of his beard. Admit that I am right.'

'There's no use disputing with him,' declared Karol Menzel. 'Since the days of Napoleon, every Frenchman has argued by Imperial edict.'

They talked on, but there was to Hamilton only one thing of interest in this conversation, and that was the quickness with which it had been changed in temper. When he first looked at the group, it had been tense with attention to the words of George Michelson, who had been declaring that the Volga valley was the granary of Russia, and that if this district were held –

Well, held by whom?

It would have meant a great deal to Hamilton to have heard even ten seconds more of the speech of George Michelson.

But suddenly – as if at a signal – the talk had altered, still flowing smoothly along about Russia, but totally diverted in significance.

In fact, the signal had been given, either by the voice of the butler at the window or by his gesture as he lifted his hand to the shade. It was very significant. It meant that even the servants in this house were deep in the affairs of the masters; it meant that the master, the guests, the menials, every living soul in the Villa Mon Sourir were engaged in working towards a single purpose. What was that purpose? Something which was the will of Japan, no doubt. To be sure, exactly such a hodge-podge of nationalities might be discovered in a dozen pensions or hotels along the Riviera, where the world comes to recapture spring; yet it was noticeable that in this group there were representatives of Rumania, Czechoslovakia, Poland, Germany, France, all nations which bordered on Russia or had some vital interests in its future. Perhaps there were still other representatives – in the kitchen or the garage! Perhaps Esthonia, Latvia, Finland, Sweden had sent men to this conference with Japan's number one secret service agent.

Was he one of those men who sat there talking outside the window? A fellow who had been alive – though only in his early twenties – at the time of the Russo-Japanese War, would now be in his middle fifties, at the least. Friedberg was old enough; so was George Michelson. They were the only ones. No, perhaps the smooth face of Henri de Graulchier made him seem a full ten years younger than the fact.

However, the great probability was that Japan's ace was well hidden from view. He was more apt to be an occasional visitor to Villa Mon Sourir than one who dwelt in it.

A tingling passed through the nerves of Hamilton. For he knew perfectly that dramatic situation in the Far East caused by the swift expansion of Japanese population, Japanese ambitions, Japanese trade. They had a great flood-gate opening for them in Manchuria; and even that bitter land would be a Paradise of opportunity to many of them. But they were not likely to rest content. They needed more and more soil. Their population would be a hundred million, before long – a hundred millions of intelligent, strong, active people, all welded into a single purpose. Who could deny them? The Philippines were close to them, an ideal extension of their empire; Hawaii was not very far away. And if the fringes of China were already crowded with inhabitants – well, the inhabitants could be swept out and place made for the conquering Jap.

But while these great schemes were in progress, the wisest course for Japan was to keep the Russian bear well occupied with domestic problems west of the Urals.

The picture grew in the fertile imagination of Anthony Hamilton. Villa Mon Sourir might be the pregnant nerve-center of the entire brain of Japan, at the present moment. And one wasp-sting, planted on the vital spot, might paralyze the will of a nation of ninety millions.

He rose, walked to the door, and glanced down the hall. The third door down – that was the room of the dead John Harbor. He made up his mind instantly, walked swiftly and softly down the hall, and pushed the door open.

It was no longer a bedroom! It had been turned over night into a livingroom!

CHAPTER SIX

There was no trace that the room ever had been equipped with a bed. A pair of comfortable sofas flanked the fire place. A very good Persian rug with the famous pine-tree pattern on it occupied the center of the floor. On the window there was a pair of curtains of heavy linen, with peacocks embroidered on it in blues and in rich greens. A rather silly bronze group of Zeus and Europa crowned the mantel-piece.

Hamilton closed the door and went back down the hall. There were reasons, of course, which the owners of the pension could give. They would declare that they did not wish to continue in the intimate rôle of a bedroom a chamber which had been rented only so short a time before by a man now dead. But what was really important was that, in this way, they were enabled to wipe out every identification mark of the man who had lived in that place. Not a footstep remained behind him – and the work had been done quickly.

An almost running footfall came up behind him.

He turned and saw the butler bearing down. There could have been many ways to interpret the expression of the fellow's face, but to Hamilton there was only one: it was physical threat.

'What's the way out into the garden?' he asked. 'Awful lot of people out there, but I don't seem to find the way.'

The butler paused. He was breathing a bit hard, and he looked down at the floor as though to disguise the expression which was glowing in his eyes.

'Mademoiselle Michelson, she is coming to see you,' he said.

Hamilton returned to the waiting room and was not surprised to see that group outside the window had disappeared. There remained only the big stone pines, and the sweep of sandy soil, and beyond, the flash of the sun-whitened sea.

He lighted another cigarette, because he needed to think. But before thought, in came Mary Michelson, carrying in the scoop of her arm a bowl that held the great spray of the pink roses.

'*Did* you bring these?' she asked.

'They made me think of you,' said he. 'No blue in them, so they're all wrong. But somehow I thought about you when I saw them. So lovely and fresh, you know. Never can think of anything when I see a florist shop. But today I thought about you. Glad you like them.'

She looked at the flowers and then transferred her smile to Hamilton. 'I do like them a lot,' she said. There was a certain gentleness in her voice that Hamilton had heard before, and he thought he recognized the intonation of a girl addressing a man who was patently a weak-wit.

Consequently he smiled more radiantly than ever.

'You know what I was thinking, Miss Michelson?'

'I'm afraid that I don't.'

'Down at the Metropole they have a new orchestra. All American, like a football team. All champions. There's a fellow there on the slide trombone – you know how a trombone blasts the cotton out of the ears? – but this chap makes it sing. Actually sing. You know, I thought we might trot down there and have a dance or two, one evening. Spot of dinner – and they have some fine old Pol Roger. Absolutely the stuff! Then we could dance a couple of turns. What do you say?'

'How sorry I am that I haven't this evening free!' said the girl. 'You've been in England a good deal, haven't you, Mr. Hamilton?'

'Now, how did you notice that?' asked Hamilton, beaming. 'Went to a school down in Sussex. You know the sort of place. Headmaster all full of algebra and Greek and gardening. Nothing heated except the entrance hall. Boiled in that and froze every other place. Chilblains. Great place for chilblains. Never saw so many chilblains. Hands absolutely purple with them. Good old England! You know – history and all that. Forbears, and that sort of thing. But I'd rather think about it and let the other fellow live in it.'

'Would you?' she said. 'Well – '

She kept on smiling, quietly, thoughtfully. She was seeing all the way through him. Or was it quite all the way? She was all in very crisp white and the reflected light shone on the brown of her throat. Her smiling, he thought, was like an added color to the picture. In her hair there was a special radiance.

'Or, you know,' said Hamilton, 'there's Ciro's, if you like that sort of thing. Wonderful cellar, there. Good music, too. We might trot around Ciro's for a while.'

'There's so much to do here at the pension,' said the girl, 'that I never have my work finished. So I never know.'

'Ah, don't you?'

'No, I really don't.'

'Ah, but look here. You'll come out with me one evening, won't you? Never know what to say when I have to sit and talk. That's the reason they have music. A few fox trots in the air – they give a fellow like me a chance to entertain. You *will* come out with me one evening, won't you?'

'Of course,' said the girl.

'But soon, I mean?'

'I hope so.'

'I know what it is – being busy,' said Hamilton. 'Used to travel with a valet and it wakened me early in the morning to think out something for the fellow to do, all day. Can't give a valet nothing to do. Corrupts them. Ruins them for their next master.'

'Mr. Hamilton, I lead a very simple life here and – '

'A simple life can be the devil, can't it?' interrupted Hamilton, with his smile. 'My Aunt Hester leads the simple life. In a barn. It used to be a barn, at least. At Worcester, Mass. Gets along with three servants. I know all about that. But all I mean is a simple party. Listen to some music. Trot around a little. Enough music to wipe out the silences. I never know what to talk about very well.'

'I think you do – amazingly,' said the girl.

'Ah, do you? That's nice of you. The fact is that I think we could get on. The moment I saw you, I thought we could get on pretty well. If you can put up with a silly ass like me. My Aunt Hester always says that I'm a silly ass.'

He laughed his most vacuous laugh.

'Not at all,' said the girl. 'And of course we could get on. I want to see you very soon – when it can be arranged.'

'The butler has my card, and I scribbled the telephone number of the hotel on it. You wouldn't give me a buzz, would you, when there's time on your hands?'

'Of course I would. I'm so sorry that I have to look after things in the kitchen.'

'Oh, do you? Well, I'll trot along, then. Won't forget me, will you?'

'Of course not.'

'Really, though? That's a promise?'

'Of course it's a promise.'

'That's fine,' said Hamilton. 'It warms me up a lot. It's good to hear. This Riviera – you know – a lot of climate – blue and gold – all that – Casino – only *silly* girls. You know, the ones that won't listen to the music. Just chatter. I'll wait to hear from you, Miss Michelson. Tell you what – I can whang a guitar. Quite a bit. And sing a little. Nothing to write home about. Untrained. But I'd like to sing to *you*, if you can stand it?'

'I want to hear you,' she said.

Her smile had almost worn away before he got out the door. He could nearly hear her comments behind the closed door, as he got back to his long, low-hung racer, and shot away towards Monte Carlo.

From the hotel, he sent for the agent of the Sûreté, Louis Desaix, alias Harrison Victor, who found him lounging beside a window in the westering sun, drinking wine and eating Roquefort with crusts of French bread.

'I had to have you, Victor,' said Hamilton. 'When I found out that they had Chateau Lafitte, 1906 – glorious year, eh? – I knew that if I didn't have company, I'd finish off the bottle all by myself. Chateau Lafitte! 1906! My God, Victor, when you think of the fellows who spend their money for brandy and soda – !'

'How long have you lived in Europe?' asked Victor, touching his moustache ends tenderly.

'That doesn't matter. I only need to tell you that I was raised on a farm. So things go deep. Things like 1906 Chateau Lafitte.'

'Tell me a dash about yourself.'

'Sometime, I'd like to.'

'Sometime, eh?'

'Nothing personal, old fellow.'

'Hell, no,' said Harrison Victor.

He poured some of the wine into a glass, looked towards the sunlight through the glass, and sniffed at the brim.

'Ah, God!' he said. 'Why is it that France is so full of the French?'

'Otherwise,' said Hamilton, 'all the world would want to live here. It's one of the acts of the Almighty. I hope you have a religious nature, Victor?'

'If I didn't, how could I be in the Service?'

'Exactly. I, for one, have a religious nature. In France, I take the French wine and leave the French.'

Harrison Victor tasted the wine and closed his eyes.

Hamilton covered a piece of crust with a green bit of Roquefort and handed it to his assistant.

Said Victor, presently: 'They call Roquefort the drunkard's bread. Now I understand for the first time.'

'There's the pity of it,' murmured Hamilton. 'We never can get drunk.'

Victor sighed. 'What did you find out?' he asked.

'The thing has to do with Russia. Japan's agent number one is probably George Michelson, Friedberg, or Vicomte de Graulchier.'

'De Graulchier is not old enough.'

'Perhaps not. I thought of that, too. But on the other hand, he's the only one of the lot who might be a Jap.'

'Jap? He's perfect French!'

'You may not know all about the Japs. Perhaps you haven't lived in Okotsk. Anyway, tonight I'm going to try to find out.'

'How?'

'By entering Mon Sourir.'

'Hamilton,' said Victor, 'don't do it. Something tells me that those fellows would shoot anyone down like a dog.'

'Not a dog who's in love,' said Hamilton. 'And how in love I am! I've even asked her to spend an evening at Ciro's, and you know that costs like the devil.'

CHAPTER SEVEN

There is hardly a thing in the world so clumsy, so malformed, so apt to speak with a voice of its own at the wrong moment, as a guitar. Anthony Hamilton decided that before he had scaled the pink wall of the garden of Villa Mon Sourir. A light tap brought from the instrument a groaning sound which would not die quickly. The felt in which it was wrapped seemed to retain the sound like moisture and cherish it whole seconds after it should have died.

In addition, the night was clear. Even frost could not have made the stars glitter more brightly and in addition there was a half moon sailing like an ancient ship across the sky and throwing its golden shadow down the sea. From the top of the wall Anthony Hamilton contemplated that beauty without pleasure, partly because light was the last thing he wanted for his excursion, and partly because the top of the wall was guarded with fragments of broken glass, imbedded in the cement. Moreover, he saw a shadowy form approaching him through the little orange trees and he should, of course, have dropped back outside the wall into safety. Instead, being Anthony Hamilton, he dropped down inside the wall and scuttered to the shelter of a black shadow beneath a shrub.

Crunching footfalls came near him from one side; footfalls which were not echoes drew close from the opposite direction. The first man paused not three strides away. The second halted facing him. Hamilton, through the black open-work of the leaves, could see them both against the stars.

'All quiet?' said the first man.

'Too quiet,' said the second.

They spoke in the Czech tongue, which was just a little odd for nightwatchmen on the Riviera and which strained the brain of Hamilton to the utmost. He had hardly more than a book knowledge of that strange language.

'What was that which came over the wall?'

'Nothing. What did you see?'

'A shadow dropped over the wall. I only saw it out of the corner of my eye.'

'A cat, perhaps.'

'Or a man, perhaps.'

'A burglar, you mean?'

'There are better things than money to be stolen here.'

'No one in the world suspects this house.'

'So we think, but the Head, the Master, does not think so.'

'He calls "fire, fire" so often that no one will believe him even when the flames begin to rise.'

'It's better to talk about fire than it is to be burned.'

'Well, what do you want to do?'

'Keep the eyes open and look about.'

'For a man?'

'Yes.'

'Begin here, then.'

They separated. One of them walked straight towards the bush which sheltered Hamilton. He put a hand on the gun which was under his coat. The fellow halted with the leaves of the shrub brushing against his trousers.

'Nobody would try on a night as bright as this,' he said.

'Nobody but a fool.'

'Fools don't matter.'

'Ay, and that's true. Come on, then, but keep your eyes wide open.'

'Do you think I'd sleep on the job when I'm working for *him*?'

'No, because you'd never wake up, perhaps.'

They continued their rounds in opposite directions. It was very odd indeed. Even the French police might like to learn of a quiet little pension which employed two private watchmen to walk the rounds ceaselessly every night, watchmen who talked such good Czech!

Hamilton waited until the footfalls were soundless, and then he walked straight across the garden. He avoided the gravel paths, leaping over them, because the most cunning step in the world, even the velvet paw of a cat, cannot help but make a slight rustling noise when it passes across gravel. The rest of the soil was dug up about the roses and the iris, of which there was an abundance, but Hamilton knew the cunning art of sinking his feet into soft ground without allowing so much as a whisper to sound on the air. In this way, taking long, slow, dipping steps, he crossed the garden and stood in the shadow under the wall of the house.

Voices were speaking inside the place. He could not dissolve them into words and he could not identify the speakers except when a booming laughter, resonant as a note struck on a great gong, came sounding out to him. Only the throat of huge Karol Menzel could have produced the sound. He had made on the mind of Hamilton an impression that grew with the passing of time. He was a sort of smooth-shaven Richard Lionheart, big in body and bigger still in savage potentiality. Among the voices of the men he could distinguish, slightly, the higher pitch of women speaking.

That should mean that the loggia above him would be unoccupied – unless burly Czech watchers made the rounds of the house as well as of the grounds. He looked upwards to estimate the best way of approach.

As convenient as a ladder, the bars of a window climbed in a great, half-decorative scroll towards the loggia above. He gripped the felt covering of the guitar in his teeth, and climbed. He would have been wiser, perhaps, to have left the guitar on the ground below, but in case of a crisis such as might happen, the guitar was really his passport, his accompanying proof and voucher of idiocy.

He climbed very slowly, though even so the infernal guitar gave out certain murmurings and moanings as though ghostly hands were thrumming it. Now he stepped over the low wall of the loggia and entered the shadow cast down from the moon. The cold of danger was in that darkness.

A glance over his shoulder showed him the dusky sea, only flowing with a quicksilver brightness down the path of the moon. A sail blew out of nothingness, stood black against that path and slid away into dimness again; far out a thin line of lights marked the passing of some big passenger steamer.

The loggia was full of chilly little whisperings from the sea-breeze in the vines that overclouded the columns. Some pots of large, strange-shaped flowers stood along the foot of the wall. There was a mat of woven grass and a long bamboo chair for bathing in the southern sun, of course. Beyond, appeared a double door. The glass panes of it winked at him like a dozen black eyes. He tried the handle. It was not locked, and he pulled half the door open, slowly, slowly. In spite of that care the door made a little trembling jingle of sound; and out of the darkness laughing voices were suddenly loud. To his sharpened senses, tongues seemed to be speaking in the very room before him, mocking the stealth of his entrance; but of course that was illusion. By degrees he placed the noise at its proper distance down the stairs. For the inner door of the room was open.

That was ten-fold unfortunate. If he closed the door, a passing servant might notice the change. If he did not close it, he was apt to be seen at any instant as he began his search. One of those queer, senseless panics which he had known before swept over him. As the years went on, his nerves did not grow better. They became distinctly worse and the time might come when he would betray himself by a shuddering palsy of fear in a crisis.

He moistened his lips and took hold of himself with a firm grasp, frowning a little. Then a ray from his pocket torch – it was hardly larger than a fountain pen – cut the blackness like a knife. If by chance he were seized and searched, he would be damned by the possession of that clever little light, perhaps.

The ray glanced over the rough yellow satin of a bed-cover, over the blue wall-hanging at its head; it glimmered across the mahogany top of a table, flashed like a startled eye in the triple mirror on the dressing-table, touched the chairs right and left. In a moment the plan of the room was mapped faultlessly in his memory. He could switch out his light and walk as though by daylight from place to place, secure of not touching any obstacle. In Okotsk he had learned that art of moving in darkness with the surety of the blind.

Under the mattress of the bed, in the drawers of the dressing table, under an edge of the rug, somewhere in the closet, in the adjoining bathroom – through the half-open door he had caught the sheen of porcelain – in any of a dozen places he might be able to discover what he wanted – that little Everyman volume of Speke's famous 'Journal of the Discovery of the Source of the Nile.' It was so important that a dead man's pocket had been picked to obtain it. Now Hamilton was determined to find the true reason of its significance.

He was about to start towards a small, hanging shelf of books near the fireplace when he heard a soft pulsation – a rhythm rather than a sound, which passed down the hall. He shrank back towards the door to the loggia. But it was too late to escape through the door. He was still long steps from it when a thin silhouette appeared against the obscure gloom of the hallway; then the electric lights flashed on.

A grey-headed man with towels over his arm went with a soft whisper of slippers straight into the bathroom. His head was bowed a trifle, thoughtfully. Hamilton, as he disappeared, sank on his knees behind the back of a chair.

The light in the bathroom clicked off; the whispering step recrossed the room; once more it was snapped into darkness; but still Hamilton remained for a moment on his knees, taking breath.

When he rose, making sure that nothing stirred outside the vague gloom of the inner doorway, he took an instant of thought. It might have been that the servant, going on the routine of his work, had seen nothing living in the room. Again, if it were true that every member of the household staff was a trained Secret-Service worker, as Hamilton suspected, the man might have been aware of Hamilton instantly, but have gone on his way with an automatic calm, retreating to cut off the stranger's way of escape. The alarm, even now, might have sounded. Downstairs, not a voice was heard – then a subdued murmur of laughter.

Perhaps they were laughing as they received word that a stranger had dared come among them into the lion's mouth.

Still, Hamilton went straight forward to the hanging shelf of books because there was a decided under-stratum of the bulldog in his nature. A flicker of the torch light he ran across the books in that case and found them all volumes of Everyman, all of them the dull green. And one, just to the right of the middle section, bore the title of Speke's 'Journal'!

CHAPTER EIGHT

He had it out instantly. He was by no means sure that this was the identical volume which he had seen in the possession of dead John Harbor, until he noticed a deep wrinkle at one corner which might have been caused by a fall. He would not have been able to mention that peculiarity if he had been asked to describe the book, but now he remembered it by touch. This was the very volume which he had taken from the coat pocket of Harbor!

He opened it swiftly, not to the text but to the flyleaves, playing the slight radiance of his torch upon the paper, but there was not a mark either in pen or pencil, however faint!

Sighing, he shook his head with a frown and fluttered the pages of the book. A small white slip disengaged itself and fluttered away like an awkward moth. He caught it out of the air. It was a bit similar to those on which Harbor had made his notations. On it appeared the swiftly scrawled column of figures, except that there was no line for addition at the bottom of the sheet.

'336–211
469–172
436–64
464–95
13–281
91–345
456–418
411–260.'

The answer struck him suddenly, with a shock like that of remembered guilt. It was simply a book code and the interpretation of the mysterious numbers which John Harbor had written down in the Casino was, simply, numbers of pages and of words on pages.

He turned to page 336 and, counting from 'we hoped would soon cease to exist' at the top of the page, he got down to word 211. 'Tolerably.'

That word would probably make sense in a message. It was a beautiful start, but of course he had to check the result. Very swiftly, because his trained eye had learned to calculate with a smooth speed, he reached word after word and found himself writing out a sentence:

'Tolerably Burial To To The – '

No, there was no sense in that at all.

He went back and added, to his counting, the title words at the top of the page, on the left, always: 'Source of the Nile' and on the right the sectional topics.

In this way he reached the following word group:

'Indifferent Chiefs The Villagers Fact Men Arrive Customs.'

It seemed to have a vague sense. If it was a collapse telegraphic form of expression it might mean that 'indifferent chiefs' had some sort of relationship to 'the villagers.' But 'men arrive customs' was a stumbling block.

He lowered the book and closed his eyes. Down the stairs the voices were carrying on merrily. A very thin fragrance of tobacco smoke ascended to his nostrils.

Then he started his work all over again. He included, this time, not only the titles at the tops of the pages but also the page numbers, including the numbers as words to be counted. In this manner he got at the following message:

'Opportunity In England Killed Rely On New Diplomacy.'

A fine sweat burst on his face. He set his teeth over an exclamation.

An opportunity in England had been destroyed. They must rely on a new diplomacy!

That made sense, perfect sense. It meant that in a night's work the mass of copied messages which Harrison Victor had accumulated could be turned from naked figures into speaking words. It meant that Tokio *had* been stung to the quick – if indeed Tokio were at the bottom of all this. It meant that he, Anthony Hamilton, had scored another tremendous success – if only the brilliance of his work would be appreciated by the numskulls in Washington. No, all of the brains there were not asleep, and the suddenness of his triumph would be a convincing thing, after Victor and the rest had worked so long!

He felt an imminence of something – a danger coming – and then through the trance of exultation, he heard light footfalls coming up the stairs.

He replaced the slip inside the pages of the book, slid it back into its place on the shelf, and glided to the door. The footfalls were very near, now, but he used a precious second or so of extra time to push the door open silently, and then catching up the infernal burden of the guitar, he stepped out onto the loggia and shrank back against the wall.

At the same time the lights went on inside the room. He could see beautiful Mary Michelson in a dress of clouds of smoke-colored lace, with a red silk wrap thrown over her arm. She was singing softly, smiling as she sang.

Well, however exquisite, she was one of them. She would have to be involved in their ruin, when he managed to compass that. And it would go very hard if, out of the mass of notes in the hands of Harrison Victor, he did not manage to build up a charge against this whole crew of espionage. The French system of justice worked with wonderful precision in dealing with such cases. Sentences were dealt out quickly and no sentence was short.

Mary Michelson, her father, the pale Russian invalid, thin-faced Maria Blatchavenski, overbearing Henri de Graulchier – they would all be erased from the scene at a single stroke!

He retreated to the side of the loggia and was about to swing himself down onto the window bars beneath when he heard a voice saying: 'Well, he could have gone up this way.'

'Where?'

'Along the bars of the window, fool!'

'That's true.'

The two Czechs were murmuring quietly together.

'And then through the door of Mary's room. It's never locked, day or night.'

Very odd that two hired night-watchmen should refer to their mistress by her first name!

The thing was as perfect as a blossoming flower. It was rounded and beautiful and complete. Every man and woman at Villa Mon Sourir belonged to the associated brains of the entire group of international plotters.

The fly in the ointment was that the retreat of the spy was cut off neatly and hopelessly. If he stirred from the loggia, he would be seen by the two men. If he attempted to withdraw into the room – why, there was smiling Mary Michelson who, with one outcry, could bring a swarm of hornets about him.

There was one device left. The childishness of it sat his teeth on edge, but stripping the felt from the guitar, he reclined in the bamboo chair and began to sing, softly, gently touching the strings of the guitar, that popular song about the wavering ocean and the flood of his emotion, with eyes and rise and skies all neatly rhymed in the middle of the chorus.

He had about reached that spot when the door of the bedroom was thrust open and Mary Michelson appeared, with one hand behind her. He could guess what that hand was holding. But at the sight of her, he closed his eyes, put back his head, and gave his whole soul and his whole vocal strength to the silly words of the song.

As the song ended, he saw Mary Michelson sitting on the edge of the loggia wall, smiling at him. Over his shoulder from the corner of his eye he was vaguely aware of two shadowy forms beginning to loom. But the girl's hand moved, and the two half-seen shadows disappeared.

'Mr. Hamilton, *how* did you manage to get here?' asked the girl.

'Over the wall like an alley cat,' he said. 'That was a pretty good one, don't you think? I mean, kind of a good ring and swing to the chorus, you know!'

'Yes, it has a sort of swing,' said the girl, still smiling.

She was watching him, not very intently.

Into the doorway of her room burst the gigantic form of Karol Menzel.

'What's that?' he called.

'My friend Mr. Hamilton dropped in with the loveliest serenade,' said the girl.

'Ah?' said Menzel. 'Serenade? Ah?'

'Ask him out to join the fun,' said Hamilton.

'Won't you come out and join the fun, Mr. Menzel?' asked the girl.

'Fun?' said Menzel. 'No, I won't join the fun. Excuse me, Mary, if you please.'

'Certainly, Karol,' she answered.

The giant disappeared. For the first time, Hamilton was able to appreciate his strength fully. There was something about his hands which called attention to his physical force.

'Oh, by the way, Karol,' called the girl, 'will you tell Henri that I'd like to see him – after a while?'

'I'll tell him,' boomed the voice of Menzel, which was always like a sound out of a cave.

'I say,' said Hamilton, 'you know that song: "Nothing to Tie to?"'

'No, I don't.'

'It's like this:

> "Nothing to hang to;
> Never had an anchor;
> Nothing to sigh to;
> Nothing to tie to – "

Do you like that?'

'It has a nice rhythm,' said she.

'It picks up your feet, what?'

'I think it would,' said she.

'When the old saxophone comes in there – ta-da-ta-deedle-dum! Listen, is that good?'

'Yes, it is,' said Mary Michelson.

She nodded, smiling just a little. She was so lovely that the least bit of smiling cast a great light.

'Here's one of the newest of the new,' said Hamilton.

He leaned back his head and sang, sadly:

> ' "Snow in the sky,
> That's why I cry;
> Everything grey,
> Ever-y day.
> All around
> Only the ground
> Is bright
> And white;
> But when I look up, every day,
> Ev-er-y-thing, is grey!"

What do you think?'

'Ah – well, I don't quite know what to think,' she said.

'Something neat about the words, what?' said Hamilton. 'Look at that bit:

"All around
   Only the ground
   Is bright
   And white – "

I mean, it seems to mean something. And look at the way the rhymes
come in so fast!'

'Yes, the lines *are* short!' she said.

'I was thinking about that song today,' said Hamilton. 'I mean, it was
meant for me, today. You know – plenty of sunshine – mimosa in the
air – the sea bluing itself up bluer than ever. But I was down.'

'Ah, were you?'

'I was! I was wondering what you were thinking about me. Some
people feel that I'm a silly sort of an ass. I was wondering: Do you
think that?'

'No. I think you might be very clever – one of the cleverest fellows I
ever knew.'

He answered, laughing: 'No, not that. Not after what my algebra
teacher said to me in the good old boyhood days.'

'Perhaps the classics were more your line?'

'I got as far as Caesar's bridge,' said he, 'but I never crossed the
blighter.' He was still laughing. 'You know what we ought to do?'

'What do you think?'

'We really ought to go down town and try the Metropole orchestra.
Saxophone player there with a real soul.'

'I'd like to,' said the girl.

'No, but really?'

'Yes, of course.'

'A real party, I mean.'

'That's what I mean, too.'

'All the way from orchids to champagne, is my idea.'

'It's so long since I've gone all the way to orchids and champagne – '
she said.

'Is it? Then we ought to.'

'Yes, I think we ought.'

'And just let the music talk for us.'

'I'd like to just talk about nothing,' she answered.

'The moment I saw you, I knew that there'd be something between us.
You know, sometimes you can tell. Why shouldn't we step out tonight?'

'I'd like nothing better – ' she said.

'But – ' asked Hamilton, anxiously.

'Couldn't we make it tomorrow?'

'Well, why not? But –

> "I never know why
> The nights pass by." '

He sang it with a due wailing earnestness.

'It seems to mean that the nights we miss will never come back,' he said.

'Yes, it does seem to mean that,' she replied. 'Suppose we say tomorrow evening.'

Henri de Graulchier's voice sounded at the door of the girl's room.

'May I come in?'

'Come in, Henri,' she called. 'Mr. Hamilton has just been surprising me with some music. And I was wondering if he wouldn't like to have you show him the house – because I have to go to bed so early? Won't you entertain Mr. Hamilton for a little while, Henri? Ah, but you haven't met. Mr. Hamilton, the Vicomte de Graulchier.'

CHAPTER NINE

It all happened so smoothly and easily that Hamilton hardly realized how he was slid into the hands of the vicomte. Mary Michelson said goodnight to them both with a charming smile but as Hamilton turned away he had a distinct sensation that a telling glance had passed between the girl and the Frenchman. And he knew instantly that he was on trial for his life. When the door closed between them and the girl, he was sure that a distinct chance for mercy had been shut away.

Or could he be sure? Under her smiling there was the bright hardness of steel. She had turned him over to the vicomte for an acid test.

The great form of Menzel appeared in a doorway.

'Come along, Karol,' said the vicomte. 'You know Mr. Hamilton, don't you? Mr. Karol Menzel. Come on, Menzel. Mary thinks that Mr. Hamilton would like to see the house. She had to turn in early. Poor girl hounded by the domestic duties, eh?'

He spoke his very good English, with the slight French oil poured over it. Hamilton could feel it in his throat. Menzel had shaken hands.

'Might have a drink,' he said.

'A drink, of course,' said the vicomte with his fixed smile. A certain difference entered his face when he was smiling. 'Any man who plays single numbers at roulette is sure to like his liquor.'

'Funny thing,' said Hamilton, 'how lucky the nine can be. You know. You find them in fairy-stories. The nines, I mean.'

'Do you?' remarked de Graulchier.

'You know the fairy-stories, of course,' said Hamilton. 'Tom Thumb and all that?'

'Ah? Fairy-stories? Yes, of course. Tom Thumb? Of course.'

He did not know them, it seemed plain. He knew them so little that actually he attached little importance to them. And even in French there are plenty of the tales. Every Frenchman knows Tom Thumb.

Hamilton looked at the pin-pricked face, the long, smooth oval of the face of de Graulchier, and the odd shape and intense blackness of the eyes – a blackness with no shine to it. He remembered the queer effect that a smile had on that face, the sudden alteration, and he realized with a burst of inward light that he was not walking at the side of the real Vicomte de Graulchier. He was not with a Frenchman at all. This short-legged, heavy-shouldered man of an uncertain age was, in fact an Oriental, a Japanese who by the grace of chance was endowed with rather Caucasian features. And, if that were the case, this was the famous Number One of the Japanese secret service. This was the nameless and wonderful man who, at last, had left his post in control of the entire Japanese organization in order to go far abroad and create trouble with his own mind and hands.

Yet his French was perfect. His English was that of a Frenchman. Even the faults in it must have been acquired by infinite and patient practice.

Hamilton, pressing the guitar a little more tightly under his arm, knew that he was walking a path so narrow that one misstep would cast him over a precipice which made the difference between life and death. Henri de Graulchier was walking down the stairs with a singularly elastic step. In fact, from his movements he seemed to be nearer forty than to the sixty which must be the truth.

They went down into the library, where Pierre brought in coffee and cognac. His square of a face retained habitually a look as sour and dry as that of French wine.

Henri de Graulchier said: 'We keep a nightwatchman about. How did you manage to come across the garden without being seen?'

Hamilton winked and held up a forefinger. 'I'm a hunter,' he said. 'When I heard a footstep, I dived into a shadow. The guitar made a moaning sound; and I thought that I was done for. But no, the watchman went on. I got up and skidded for the house. Not on the gravel paths. No, no!' He laughed.

'Ah, not the paths?' said Menzel, looking very straight at him.

'No, no! Too much noise. Over the cultivated ground, stepping with the toe pointed like a dancing master. No sound at all, except what a field mouse might hear. And so – there I was!'

'Well done, Mr. Hamilton,' said de Graulchier, smiling.

'Ay,' grunted Menzel.

'Queer thing, though,' said Hamilton. 'I was half afraid to climb up to the loggia. Really was, on my soul. It didn't seem quite the picture – climbing up there. I wanted to tune up and sing my songs standing down there at the foot of the wall. But then I remembered the nightwatchman, what? The jolly old boy might have collared me and walked me right off the grounds. So I climbed.'

Menzel looked over at de Graulchier.

'Have another cognac?' asked the vicomte.

'Rather!' said Hamilton. 'I can always use a spot of the good stuff after an adventure like this. You don't think Miss Michelson minded, do you?'

'I think she was delighted,' said de Graulchier. 'Music and young girls – the two ideas go well together, eh?'

'Music and young girls?' said Hamilton. 'Hold on – that's good, isn't it?'

'De Graulchier is full of good things,' said Menzel, sourly.

'Music and girls – I'm going to remember that. I could say it, some time.'

'I give it to you, monsieur,' said the vicomte.

'Well, perhaps I ought to trot along.'

'Do let us show you the house,' said the vicomte. 'Miss Michelson asked us to.'

'Thanks,' said Hamilton. 'Imagine turning in at this time of the night, though! Poor girl!'

'She runs the pension and that means a great deal of work with bills, and accounts,' explained Menzel.

'Rotten luck, though,' commented Hamilton. 'Wonderful girl! Wonderful!'

'Let's show you the house, as she suggested. It will fill in a bit of the evening for you,' said de Graulchier. 'This room and the one below, eh, Menzel?'

'They're the best bits,' said Menzel.

'Before the Riviera was a resort,' said de Graulchier, 'the Comte de Volens built this house. Built it big, as you see. Their minds were more spacious, in those days; they needed room for their ideas; and the result was high ceilings and plenty of air. You see how he arranged this room, with the windows opened onto the terrace?'

'Did he put in all the books?' asked Hamilton.

'They came with a later generation.'

'I like books,' said Hamilton.

'Do you?' asked the blunt, heavy voice of Menzel.

'Yes,' said Hamilton. 'They give a nice look to a wall, eh? Always make me think of the time other people have put in grinding.'

'In fact, they cover the wall with time,' said de Graulchier. 'We see their colors, but really we are seeing thought. A fourth dimensional beauty is given to our surroundings by them.'

'Really?' said Hamilton.

He opened his mouth and his eyes a bit and stared.

'Well, well – quite right, too,' he said, and hastily swallowed his glass of brandy.

He looked up in time to see a sardonic smile fading from the lips of Menzel, but the unlighted eye of de Graulchier still reserved a doubt. He was testing his man, but he was by no means sure, it seemed. If that doubt grew – if it increased by a single step – Hamilton was perfectly certain that he was a dead man.

'Fourth dimensional – ah!' said Hamilton, and lighted a cigarette.

'You can find the history of the Volens family by running your eyes over their books. Solid people. Good minds. Read in four languages. And even read a little too much, as you'll see when you come to their Eighteenth Century books. Because there they made the fatal mistake. Their lives were not pleasant enough; they had to garnish their aristocratic minds with democratic ideas. That was the touch of garlic in the salad dressing, you see.'

'Exactly,' said Hamilton, staring more helplessly than ever.

'So many people of today feel the same thing,' said de Graulchier. 'They have possessions, taste, means to employ their minds to the fullest, and yet they insist on adding an extra pungency. They must touch knives and handle fire. They play with the ideas of Karl Marx, make a mystery of him, and so teach the man in the street to look up as though towards a great philosopher. But this is dangerous. For the man in the street wants no ideas except those which he can use like a club to knock down others. Shall we show Mr. Hamilton what happened to the Volens family?'

'I don't think he'd be interested,' said Menzel, shrugging his vast shoulders.

'The way I'll tell the story – yes – I think that that would interest him. Will you come to the room below, Mr. Hamilton?'

'Of course,' said Hamilton, rising with a false alacrity.

He had been under close observation, and now he knew that a gun was to be put to his head.

CHAPTER TEN

They passed down the hall from the library to a door which de Graul-chier opened, revealing a flight of descending steps. Down these the vicomte went with Hamilton behind him and the giant Menzel in the rear.

'A pity that this part of the house isn't used more, in these days,' said the vicomte, leading the way across a lower hall and into a long, narrow room with a vaulted ceiling. 'A little damp, but always cool. A resting place, we might say.'

He laughed a little, something he rarely did. And his voice was surprisingly high and cracked. Only in his laughter did his advancing age appear, thought Hamilton. A switch had turned on one light in a wall-bracket. It made a glare rather than an effectual illumination and allowed the eye to pass through a big open window at the end of the room, and so out over the moonlit, dusky sea. One chair stood before the window.

There was no other article of furniture in the room.

'Observe what I was saying about the folly of dignifying ideas of social reform with the attention of people of good minds. That brought on the French Revolution,' explained de Graulchier, 'and the Volens family was driven out. The comte became an emigré. The revolutionists wandered for a few days through the big rooms of this place and then they withdrew because they were not at home except in their kennels and rabbit warrens. In the meantime, the poor Comte de Volens had taken shelter on board the English fleet and he pointed out to the admiral that this little peninsula would make an excellent foothold on the coast. The English agreed. The Comte de Volens therefore landed secretly, came to the house, and prepared to make a signal from that window – a signal which would be seen at night by the English, who would send a small boat close in to observe the light. But one of those revolutionary rats ferreted out the secret of the comte's presence. He was seized. In that corner of this very room, he was tortured until pain had driven him mad.'

Here de Graulchier turned suddenly and pointed to the corner of the room. And Menzel made a soft, long step towards Hamilton from the rear.

'Why didn't poor Volens talk, then?' cried Hamilton. 'Before I'd take the torture, I'd talk for them – I'd sing and dance for them, too.'

He laughed a little; the sound echoed mournfully through the long chamber.

De Graulchier shrugged his shoulders and glanced towards Menzel. There might have been a thousand meanings in that glance.

'When they learned what the Comte de Volens had intended to do,' said the vicomte, 'they fastened that chair to the floor with bolts – which still hold it in place – and then – they bound him hand and foot, and lashed him into the chair to look as long as he pleased out to sea. For the English never received the signal, never landed, and the Comte de Volens died like a dog – died as a spy *should* die!'

The voice of de Graulchier at this moment boomed suddenly through the room; he fixed his glance steadily on the face of Hamilton. Menzel, keeping directly behind the back of Hamilton made some movement of preparation. And the horror which had come over Hamilton once before, that evening, now surged up in him again.

He could not speak; and yet he had to speak – at once! For half of a terrible second he fought the panic. He could not speak, and yet he had to do something the equivalent of speech.

He walked straight to the chair and sat down in it.

'I hope they gave the poor blighter a cushion to sit on,' said Hamilton. 'Think of the ache of staying here – there isn't even a curve to the bottom of the chair! – '

He could feel, rather than see or hear, the noiseless approach of Menzel from the rear while, in front of him, eyeing him steadily, de Graulchier was studying his face. A quiver of his nostrils, the slightest

change in his voice, and the hand of de Graulchier would make a signal
to the giant.

Hamilton said: 'But after all, Volens was able to die sitting instead of
standing. You know that new song?'

He lifted his chin and half closed his eyes – so that de Graulchier
could examine him even more closely, at will; and Hamilton sang:

> 'Wearily waiting,
> Sitting alo-o-o-ne;
> Wearily sighing – '

'Stop that!' boomed Menzel.

'Oh!' exclaimed Hamilton, starting from the chair. 'Oh, don't you
like it?'

'I do not,' said Menzel.

'Come, come, Karol,' protested de Graulchier.

'Beg pardon, Mr. Hamilton. I mean, the echo in this room – knocks
like a hammer on a fellow's ears, don't you see.'

'Yes, the echo – yes, that's bad,' said Hamilton.

He turned about and flashed his brightest, his most empty smile at
de Graulchier.

'Awfully good of you to spend all this time on me,' he said. 'You know,
I never would have guessed that Mon Sourir had a ghost in it. Looks so
pink and cheerful, you know. Never would have thought that a place
like this had its dead man along with it.'

'Well, shall we go back?' growled Menzel. He looked askance at de
Graulchier, who nodded, and they left the room.

'I used to think that crack in the wall, there,' said de Graulchier, 'was
over some hidden passage.'

'Strange how mistaken a man can be,' said Menzel, with a certain
emphasis in his accent.

'Yes, we can all make foolish decisions,' said de Graulchier. 'But
sometimes it's wisest to suspect everything.'

'Even blank walls?' said the growling voice of Menzel.

But Hamilton, a slight warmth and weakness of relief running in his
blood, knew that he was safe for this moment, at the least. He was not
yet clear of the forest, but de Graulchier had at least missed his first
dangerous spring.

He could understand the vast difficulties which confronted the
vicomte. If he searched Hamilton, for instance, and found nothing; if

Hamilton were really no more than an empty headed serenading fool; then the rough usage would be howled forth to the sky as a frightful outrage. That attention from the French police which of course de Graulchier least wanted to draw would be poured upon him at once and perhaps all his work would be ruined. He had had to try out his suspicions merely by an artistic pressure. Now, perhaps, he was satisfied that Hamilton was no more than he seemed to be.

As they reached the upper hall, Hamilton said: 'I'll have to be coming on.'

'Sorry,' said the vicomte. 'Do come again; but just let us know beforehand. We're expecting to have some savage brutes of dogs loose on the place at night. Wouldn't like to have one of them dine on you, my friend.'

'How can they dine on bones and laughing gas?' muttered big Menzel.

CHAPTER ELEVEN

All the way to the gate, Hamilton paid no heed to the shadowy form which followed him at a little distance, among the orange trees. In the road, a taxi picked him up and whirled him off from the Villa Mon Sourir.

He sank back on the cushion exhausted, eyes closed, breathing deeply of the mimosa-scented air which streamed through the open windows. The treacherous chill of the Riveria night was abroad, now, but he needed that cold to revive him a little.

Yet he kept wondering at himself a little. He had been through a thousand dangers more obvious. It was simply the strangeness of the Vicomte de Graulchier and the deadness of his black eyes that had been wearing down his strength, with great Karol Menzel like a tiger stalking them through the house, ready to strike and kill at a word.

Half an hour afterwards, he had Harrison Victor in his room at the hotel, eating hothouse grapes and drinking a bottle of dry Chablis. Hamilton had exchanged shoes for slippers, coat and waistcoat for a dressing gown. He had the deep windows giving on the sea wide open; the top of trees rolled like more visible waves close at hand, trembling and sparkling under the wind; the gleam of the sea, farther off, merged with the faint shining of the sky.

Harrison Victor said: 'Well – you have news of some sort, Hamilton. Or are you just in a jam?'

'I'm in a jam,' said Hamilton.

'So long as I'm part of the Sûreté, and this is France, how can you be in a jam?' asked Victor, bristling his moustaches with a smile.

'Suppose you find a woman,' said Hamilton, 'young, lovely, generous, good-natured, virtuous, clever, educated – '

'There isn't such a thing,' said Victor.

Hamilton went on: 'Strong, keen, self-possessed – '

'Ah, you mean Mary Michelson?'

'Suppose that the girl warms your heart, and then you discover that her talents are all bent towards a scheme that will smash your country between the eyes and, perhaps, involve the whole world in a war that will make 1914 seem like a fairy-tale?'

'Interesting! I could love a girl like that.'

'Yes, and put her in prison also.'

'Naturally.'

'How would the French act, Victor, towards a beautiful woman? A woman like that?'

'The French can't see beauty in a political enemy.'

'What would they do about her?'

'Devil's Island, I suppose – for twenty years.'

'They might as well send her to hell forever.'

'Of course.'

Hamilton sipped the ice-cold wine and breathed the strange fragrance of it. It was like the mimosa perfume in January – spring and winter combined.

'I hesitate a little,' he said.

'About what?' asked Victor.

'About Devil's Island.'

'Do you mean that you've learned what we want to know?'

'More than we ever dreamed of knowing.'

'About the girl, eh?'

'About everything. Tell me about the Vicomte de Graulchier in the first place. You've looked him up, of course?'

'Yes. Certainly. I've looked up everybody we could trace. Everybody in the Villa Mon Sourir.'

'No doubt that he's the heir to the title?'

'No doubt at all.'

'Gets the title through his father?'

'Yes.'

'What was his father?'

'The usual thing. Country estates, income spent in Paris.'

'What did the father do with his life?'

'Nothing particular. Travelled a little – but lived chiefly in Paris. Wrote a book about the South Seas.'

'Did he ever go there?'

'Yes, for a year.'

'And returned a widower, with an infant son?'

'How did you guess that? Yes, that's the fact.'

'His dead or divorced wife was a Japanese girl, old fellow. This present de Graulchier is half Japanese.'

'Hai!' exclaimed Victor.

'He's the Japanese Number One Secret Service agent,' said Hamilton.

'Not possible!'

'Hasn't he been away from Europe most of the time, recently?'

'Yes, yes. A traveller for years. In Africa, I thought.'

'In Tokio, more likely. He's the great agent, Victor. And he's gathered all of these people about him. We're going to find out for exactly what purpose.'

'Don't string it out. Tell me how!'

'If I tell you, it means that Mary Michelson will be sent to hell.'

'Do you mean that you'd let a woman stand between you and your work, Hamilton? My God, it may mean what you say – the peace of the whole world!'

'Yes,' murmured Hamilton. 'It might mean exactly that. The peace of the whole world!'

He nodded, and began to eat grapes through a long silence, sipping the wine from time to time.

Harrison Victor, starting out of his chair, began to stride up and down the room. Half a dozen times he turned sharply on his companion, words about to explode from his lips, but on each occasion he controlled himself with a sudden effort. He began to grow red in the face, breathing hard.

'There was a time, tonight,' Hamilton said, 'when she suspected me. And if she had acted on her suspicion, I would be dead, now – dead and buried in the sea off Les Roches. Instead, she merely passed me on for further examination; and I managed to pass with a good mark. The great vicomte decided that I *am* only an ass. However, I know that she must go to Devil's Island with the rest – and then perhaps I'll keep one holiday a year in grateful memory of one of the dead!' He broke out, in another voice: 'Victor, what dirty dog's work it all is, sneaking and spying and prying, smiling in the faces of people, stabbing them in the back when the chance comes!'

'Or being stabbed,' said Victor.

'Yes, that's true,' said Hamilton, thoughtfully.

'And when we die,' said Victor, 'it means nothing to the world, except that a fat-faced fellow in Washington pulls one card out of a file and tears it up. If we win any glory, it's never known to the newspapers. If we have any power, we never can parade it.'

'That's true,' agreed Hamilton.

He took a deep breath.

'Well, she has to go,' he said at last. 'Who's the man who works out the code stuff for you?'

'D'you mean that you've got the key to the code?' asked Victor, in a whisper.

'I have. Who has the records of the messages you've managed to catch?'

'Jack Carney.'

'Young for such an important job.'

'An old head on his shoulders. Man – where is the key?'

'In Everyman's Library. Speke's "Journal." Tell Carney to get that in the morning. It's simply a book code. That's all. The first number is that of the page; the second is the word on the page. He counts in the page numeral and the title, each time. That's all.'

Harrison Victor jerked out a handkerchief and wiped his face hurriedly.

'But that will give us a whole library of information!' he said.

'I think that it will,' said Hamilton. 'We'll uncover enough to guarantee a passage for every living soul in Mon Sourir to Devil's Island. And that includes – '

'Come, come!' said Victor. 'There are other women in the world!'

'Of course there are,' said Hamilton.

He leaned back in his chair with his eyes closed.

'See here, Hamilton, this job is going to make you the Number One of the whole United States service! This is the quickest and most brilliant bit that I've ever seen done! Remember that, and forget the girl!'

'Of course,' answered Hamilton, faintly.

'I know she's lovely, but the work she's doing is probably ugly enough. You *will* forget her, Hamilton.'

'Of course I shall,' said Hamilton, 'when I'm dead.'

The Claws of the Tigress

Faust loved history. He unobtrusively made historical allusions in his fiction. In *Hired Guns* (Dodd, Mead, 1948) he disguised the Trojan War as a western story by clothing its heroes in cowboy garb and its heroines in calico. His settings range from the Crusades in *The Golden Knight* (Greystone Press, 1937) to the nineteenth-century South Seas in 'The Blackbirds Sing' (a serial that began July 20, 1935, in *Argosy*), from piracy on the Spanish Main in *The Naked Blade* (Greystone, 1938) to the French Revolution in 'The American' (another *Argosy* serial that began Feb. 27, 1937). Other works touched on a variety of subjects, from slave trading to the Inquisition. Altogether Faust published eighteen pieces of historical fiction.

Among the several thousand volumes in Faust's library, the histories of Herodotus, Thucydides, Tacitus, Froissart, Gibbon, Parkman, Josephus and Bernal Díaz del Castillo, as well as such arcane titles as *A Day in the Cloister* and *The Book of the Sword,* provided information and inspiration to him. 'The Claws of the Tigress' first appeared as a novelette in *Argosy* (July 13, 1935) written under the George Challis pseudonym Faust frequently used for his historical fiction. The story later formed part of *The Bait and the Trap* (Harper, 1951), one of a pair of novels featuring the young firebrand Tizzo, a street waif grown to heroic dimensions. 'My heroes stand twenty feet tall and my heroines bear fifty-pound babies,' Faust once said. An exaggeration, but a measure of what Faust thought humans capable. 'There is a giant asleep in each of us,' he said, 'and when that giant wakes, miracles can happen.' The Italy of Niccoló Machiavelli, a countryside that Faust knew well, forms the backdrop to this story.

CATERINA, Countess Sforza-Riario, high lady and mistress of the rich, strong town of Forli, was tall, well made, slenderly strong, and as beautiful as she was wise. She used to say that there was only one gift that God had specially denied her, and that was a pair of hands that had the strength of a man in them. But if she had not a man's strength, she had a man's will to power, and more than a man's headlong courage.

She was not quite as cruel as Cesare Borgia, her neighbor to the north who now was overrunning the Romagna with his troops of Swiss and French and trained peasants, but she was cruel enough to be famous for her outbursts of rage and vengeance. That sternness showed in the strength of her jaw and in the imperial arch of her nose, but usually she covered the iron in her nature with a smiling pleasantry.

Three husbands had not been able to age her; she looked ten years younger than the truth. And this morning she looked younger than ever because her peregrine falcon had three times outfooted the birds of the rest of the hawking party and swooped to victory from the dizzy height of the blue sky. The entire troop had been galloping hard over hill and dale, sweeping through the soft soil of vineyards and orchards; crashing over the golden stand of ripe wheat; soaring again over the rolling pasture lands until the horses were half exhausted and the riders nearly spent. Even the troop of two score men-at-arms who followed the hunt, always pursuing short cuts, taking straight lines to save distance, were fairly well tired, though their life was in the saddle.

They kept now at a little distance – picked men, every one, all covered with the finest steel plate armor that could be manufactured in Milan. Most of them were armed with sword and spear, but there were a few who carried the heavy arquebuses which were becoming more fashionable in war since the matchlock was invented, with the little swiveled arm which turned the flame over the touchhole of the gun, with its priming.

Forty strong men-at-arms – to guard a hawking party! But at any moment danger might pour out at them through a gap in the hills. Danger might thrust down at them from the ravaging bands of the Borgia's conquering troops; or danger might lift at them from Imola; or danger might come across the mountains from the treacherous Florentines, insatiable of business and territory. Therefore even a hawking party must be guarded, for the countess would prove a rich prize.

The danger was real, and that was why she enjoyed her outing with such a vital pleasure. And now, as she sat on her horse and stroked the hooded peregrine that was perched on her wrist, she looked down the steep pitch of the cliff at whose edge she was halting and surveyed the long, rich sweep of territory which was hers, and still hers until the brown mountains of the Apennines began, and rolled back into blueness and distance.

Her glance lowered. Two men and a woman were riding along the road which climbed and sank, and curved, and rose again through the broken country at the base of the cliff. They were so far away that she could take all three into the palm of her hand. Yet her eyes were good enough to see the wind snatch the hat from the lady's head and float it away across a hedge.

Before that cap had ever landed, the rider of the white horse flashed with his mount over the hedge, caught the hat out of the air, and returned it to the lady.

The countess laughed with high pleasure.

'A gentleman and a gentle man,' she said. 'Here, Gregorio! Do you see those three riding down there? Bring them up to me. Send two of the men-at-arms to invite them, and if they won't come, bring them by force. I want to see that white horse; I want to see the man who rides it.'

Gregorio bowed to cover his smile. He admired his lady only less than he feared her. And it was a month or two since any man had caught her eye. He picked out two of the best men-at-arms – Emilio, a sergeant in the troop, and Elia, an old and tried veteran of the wars which never ended in Italy as the sixteenth century commenced. This pair, dispatched down a short cut, were quickly in the road ahead of the three travelers, who had stopped to admire a view across the valley.

The lady countess and her companions, gathered along the edge of the cliff, could see everything and yet remain screened from view by the heavy fringe of shrubbery that grew about them.

What they saw was a pretty little picture in action. The two men-at-arms, their lances raised, the bright pennons fluttering near the needle-gleam of the spearheads, accosted the three, talked briefly, turned their horses, took a little distance, and suddenly couched their spears in the rests, leaned far forward, and rushed straight down the road at the strangers.

'Rough – a little rough,' said the Countess Sforza-Riario. 'Those two fellows are unarmed, it seems to me. That Emilio must be told that there is something more courteous in the use of strangers than a leveled lance.'

But here something extremely odd happened, almost in the midst of the calm remark of the lady. For the two men who were assaulted, unarmored as they were, instead of fleeing for their lives or attempting to flee, rode right in at the spearmen!

One drew a long sword, the other a mere glitter of a blade. Each parried or swerved from the lance thrust. He of the long sword banged his weapon down so hard on the helmet of Emilio that the man-at-arms toppled from the saddle, rolled headlong on the ground, and reached to the feet of the horse of the lady.

She was on the ground instantly, with a little flash of a knife held at the visor of the fallen soldier.

'Good!' said the countess. 'Oh, excellently good!'

She began to clap her hands softly.

The second rider – he on the white horse – had grappled with hardy Elia. Both of them were whirled from the saddle, but the man-at-arms fell prone, helpless with the weight of his plates of steel, and the other perched like a cat on top of him. His hat had fallen. The gleam of his hair in the bright sunlight was flame-red.

'And all in a moment!' said the countess, laughing. 'Two good lances gone in a trice. Roderigo, you should have better men than that in your command.'

The captain, scowling, and biting an end of his short mustache, swore that there had been witchcraft in it.

'Aye,' said the countess. 'The witchcraft of sure eyes and quick, strong hands. Did you see the lady leap from her horse like a tigress and hold her poniard above the helmet of your friend? Look, now! They are stripping the two of their armor. The big fellow is putting on that of Emilio; the redhead takes that of Elia. Roderigo, take three of your best lances. Down to them again, and let me see them fight against odds, now that they are armed like knights. . . . Ah, what a glorious day – to go hawking for birds and end by swooping out of the sky at men!'

The four men-at-arms were quickly in the saddle and sweeping down the short, steep road; but here the countess found herself too far from the crash and dust of the battle. To gain a nearer view, she galloped after the four leaders, and the armed men, the courtiers, followed in a stream.

Those loud tramplings hardly could fail to be heard by the men in the roadway beneath; in fact, when her ladyship turned the shoulder of the cliff and could look at the scene, she found her four warriors already charging, heads down, lances well in rest, straight in on the pair. And these, in their borrowed armor, with their borrowed lances, galloped to meet the fresh shock.

Six metal monsters, flaming in the sun, they crashed together. The big fellow had lifted one of the men-at-arms right out of the saddle, but the countershock knocked his own horse to its knees; and at that instant the rearmost of the four men-at-arms caught the stranger with a well centered spear that bowled him in his turn out of the saddle and into the dust.

He whose red head was now covered by steel had a different fortune. Riding straight, confident, at the last instant he dropped suddenly to the side, which caused one spear to miss him utterly, while the second glanced off his shoulder. But his own spear caught fairly on a man-at-arms, knocking him over like a ninepin.

'This is jousting!' cried the countess. 'Glorious God, *these* are men!'

He of the white horse, his spear shattered to the butt by the shock of the encounter, whirled his white horse about and went hurling against the only one of the men-at-arms who remained mounted. In his hand he swung not a sword but the old battle-ax which the veteran Elia had kept at the bow of his saddle.

In the hand of the rider of the white horse it became both a sword to parry with and a club to strike; a side sweep turned the driving spear of the soldier away, and a shortened hammer-blow delivered with the back of the ax rolled the other fellow on the road. All was a flying mist of dust, through which the countess heard the voice of a girl crying, 'Well done, Tizzo! Oh, bravely done!'

She had ridden to the spot where the larger of the two strangers had fallen, and leaning far down, she helped him, stunned as he was, to his feet. And now, springing instantly into an empty saddle, he unsheathed his sword and prepared for whatever might be before them.

There was plenty of work ahead.

The men-at-arms of the countess, swiftly surrounding the cyclone of dust, were now ranged on every side in a dense semicircle which could not be broken through. And as Tizzo saw this, he began to rein his white horse back and forth, whirling the ax in a dexterous hand as he shouted in a passion of enthusiasm, 'Ah, gentlemen! We only begin the dance. Before the blood gets cold, take my hand again. Step forward. Join me, gallants!'

One of the men-at-arms, infuriated by these taunts, rushed horse and spear suddenly in on Tizzo; but a side twist of the ax turned the thrust of the spear aside, and a terrible downstroke shore straight through the conical crest of the helmet, through the coil of strong mail beneath, and stopped just short of the skull. The stricken fighter toppled from the saddle and seemed to break his neck in his fall.

Tizzo, still reining his horse back and forth, continued to shout his invitation, but a calm voice said, 'Bring up an arquebus and knock this bird out of the air.'

Not until this point did the lady call out, 'Stay from him. My friend, you have fought very well. . . . Pick up the fallen, lads. . . . Will you let me see your face?'

Tizzo instantly raised his visor.

'Madame,' he said, 'I should have saluted you before, but the thick weather prevented me.'

The countess looked at his red hair and the flame-blue of his eyes.

'What are you?' she asked.

Some of her men-at-arms were lifting the fallen to their feet and opening their helmets to give them air; by good fortune, not a one of them was very seriously hurt. The huge, heavy rounds of the plate armor had secured them from hurt as, oftentimes, it would do during the course of an entire day's fighting.

Defensive armor had outdistanced aggressive weapons. Gunpowder was still in its infancy. The greatest danger that a knight ordinarily endured was from the weight of his armor, which might stifle him when he was thrown from his horse in the midst of a hot battle.

And Tizzo was answering the countess, with the utmost courtesy, 'I am under the command of an older and more important man, my lady.'

He turned to his companion, who pushed up his visor and showed a battered, grizzled face in which the strength of youth was a little softened into folds, but with greater knowledge in his brow to make him more dangerous.

'I am going to take the short cut, Tizzo,' said the other. 'The trust is a two-edged knife that hurts the fellow who uses it, very often, I know, but here's for it. Madame, I am the Baron Henry of Melrose; this is the noble Lady Beatrice Baglione, sister of Giovan Paolo Baglione; this is my son Tizzo. We are on the road from near Faenza, where we've just escaped from the hands of Cesare Borgia, after a breath of poisoned air almost killed me. We are bound back towards Perugia. There is our story.'

The countess rode straight to Beatrice and took her by the hands. 'My dear,' she said, 'I'm happy that you escaped from that gross beast of a Borgia. How could I guess that such distinguished strangers were passing through my territory? Come with me into Forli. You shall rest there, and then go forward under a safe-conduct. My Lord of Melrose — those were tremendous blows you gave with that sword; Sir Tizzo, you made the ax gleam in your hand like your name. I thought it was a firebrand flashing! Will you come on with me? Some of the rest of you ride forward to the castle. Have them prepare a welcome. . . . Ah, that Borgia! The black dog has put his teeth in the heart of the Romagna, but he'll fight for my blood before he has it!'

The countess, talking cheerfully in this manner, put the little procession under way again, and they streamed up the winding road toward the top of the cliff. But all her courtesy was not enough to cover the eyes of Beatrice.

Caterina of Sforza-Riario headed the riders, naturally, and Tizzo was at her right hand, more or less by seeming accident. A little back of the two came Beatrice at the side of Henry of Melrose. And the girl was saying: 'Do you see how she eyes Tizzo? She is making herself sweet as honey, but I know her. She's a famous virago. How can Tizzo be such a fool as to be taken in by her? I don't think she's so very handsome, do you?'

The baron looked at her with a rather grim smile for her jealousy. 'She is not worth one glance of your eyes, Beatrice,' he declared. 'But Tizzo would be a greater fool still if he failed to give her smile for smile. She has three birds in her claws, and if she's angered she's likely to swallow all of us. She never was so deeply in love that she could not wash her hands and her memory of the lover clean in blood. Be cheerful, Beatrice, or you may spoil everything. Smile and seem to enjoy the good weather. Because I have an idea that after the gates of Forli Castle close behind us it will be a long day before we come out again.'

They passed over the green uplands, and sank down into the road toward the walled town of Forli. The city itself was a place of considerable strength, but within it uprose the 'Rocca' — or castle on the rock — which was the citadel and the stronghold of the town. No one could be real master of Forli until he had mastered the castle on the rock as well. And young Tizzo, riding beside the countess, making his compliments, smiling on the world, took quiet note of the mouths of the cannons in the embrasures of the walls.

The drawbridge had already been lowered. They crossed it, with the hollow echoes booming beneath them along the moat. They passed under the leaning forehead of the towers of the defense; they passed through the narrows of the crooked entrance way; they climbed up into the enclosed court of the powerful fortress.

Tizzo was the first on the ground to offer his hand to hold the stirrup of the countess. But she, laughing, avoided him, and sprang like a man to the ground. Like a man she was tall – almost the very inches of Tizzo; like a man her eye was bold and clear; and like a man she had power in her hand and speed in her foot. She looked to Tizzo like an Amazon; he could not help glancing past her to the more slender beauty of Beatrice and wondering what the outcome of this strange adventure would be.

Internes Can't Take Money

In a discussion between Faust and his agent, Carl Brandt, of plots for future stories, Faust began describing the experiences of his friend, Dr. George Winthrop ('Dixie') Fish, an interne in a New York hospital. When Faust said, 'Internes can't take money,' Brandt jumped up, exclaiming, 'There's your title and there's your story!' Thus was born Dr. Kildare.

'Internes Can't Take Money' first appeared in *Cosmopolitan* in March, 1936. Dr. Kildare is a metaphor for the young Faust, a country boy dreaming of making good in the big city. The young hero's dilemma over whether to break a man-made law because of an obligation to a higher moral law reflects one of Faust's own dilemmas: that artistic achievement could somehow excuse personal excesses. It was one of many dilemmas Faust tried to resolve through his writing. 'Work is my salvation,' he once said. Declaring that beauty was the only god he served, he revered strength 'above good or evil,' but could not free himself from the consequences of his actions. His occasional cruelty to his loyal and patient wife Dorothy, and his heavy drinking led to estrangements from Dorothy and from their children and friends and precipitated more than one heart attack. However, Faust produced an immense body of work in twenty-seven years of intense activity, and his marriage did survive.

Faust depended on his friend Edward P. Mulrooney, New York's longtime police commissioner, for information about the city's criminal underworld used in this and subsequent Kildare stories in addition to details provided by Dr. Fish and by his own experiences at Roosevelt Hospital. Dr. Kildare has become a household name thanks to 'Internes Can't Take Money,' four subsequent serials, and five stories in popular magazines. These were made into seven books, fourteen movies, a radio series, a long-running television series, and a second, shorter television series. 'Internes Can't Take Money' may not be one of Faust's best stories, but it certainly is one of his most significant.

J IMMY KILDARE used to get away from the hospital every afternoon and go over to Tom McGuire's saloon on the avenue. He always drank two beers. An interne in the accident room has to have the brains in his fingertips in good order all day long, but two beers don't get very far between a man and himself if he has a bit of head on his shoulders, and Jimmy Kildare had.

McGuire's saloon was comfortable in a dark, dingy way. The sawdust was swept out only once in two days, and the floors were never scrubbed except the evening before Election Day. Just the same, it was a good place. It made Jimmy Kildare think of the barn out on the old farm. The faces of the bums and crooks and yeggs who lined up at the bar were sour, just like the faces of the cows and horses that were lined along the mangers of the barn – long, and all the lines running down except for their arched eyebrows with the fool look of the cows.

When Jimmy Kildare leaned an elbow on the worn varnish of McGuire's saloon it was always easier for him to think of home. The future to him was a great question mark, and New York was the emptiness inside the loop of the mark. Add a few strokes to the question mark and you get a dollar sign.

Jimmy Kildare used to think about that but he never dared to think very far because, when he began to dream, he always saw himself back on the farm in the frosty stillness of an autumn morning where every fence post and every wet rock said to him, 'Jimmy, what are you doing away back here?'

The only times that he escaped entirely from those dreams were when he was working at the operating table, all scrubbed up and masked and draped in white. But even when he was going through the wards and looking into the life or death that brightened or shadowed the eyes of his patients, the old days and the terrible sense that he must return to them used to come over him.

He always wanted more relaxation from his work than those two beers in McGuire's saloon, but he knew that his purse would not stand it. The hospital paid for his laundry. It gave him three meals a day of soggy food. Otherwise, he had to fund himself entirely, except for an occasional lift from famous Doctor Henry Fearson. Fearson from his height had noticed Kildare in medical school and had made it possible for him to carry on when home funds ran out.

Perhaps it was pity that moved Fearson to make those loans. Perhaps it was a quiet belief that there was a talent in the youngster. Kildare never could decide what the motive was, but he loved Fearson. During the interneship Fearson's loans became almost negligible, possibly because an absent-minded genius like Fearson forgot that an interne is an unpaid labor slave. A lot of the other lads were the sons of affluent doctors, and they were always going places on days off, but they never took Kildare and he could not afford to take himself. He wasn't a very exciting companion; he wasn't good-looking; he wasn't stylish.

There was only one day at the hospital for him to write down in red, and that was the occasion when he had assisted at a kidney operation. In the blind red murk the scalpel of the operating surgeon made a mistake and a beautiful fountain of blood and life sprang upward. Jimmy Kildare snatched a forceps and grabbed at the source of that explosion. He reached through a horrible boiling red fog and clamped down. The fountain ceased to rise. Afterward the artery was tied off, and a blood transfusion brought the patient back to life.

That day the great Henry Fearson stopped Jimmy in a corridor and gripped him by the shoulder and said, 'You've got it, Kildare!'

Jimmy shrugged and hooked a thumb. 'That back there? That was just luck,' he said.

But Fearson answered: 'Surgery is like tennis. There's no luck except bad luck.'

Afterward, Jimmy Kildare went to his bare concrete cell and sat for a long time looking at the wall until the wall opened and showed him a brief glimpse of heaven. Then he said: 'Henry Fearson – by God!' and a great promise began to live along his blood stream.

Then the trouble started at McGuire's saloon.

The bartender was named Jeff. He had only one eye. Sometimes he wore a leather patch over it; sometimes he wore a watery glass eye that didn't fit. He was, Kildare gathered, a real force in the precinct because he knew by first name practically every voter in the district. This fellow Jeff never looked at Jimmy Kildare. He always had his one eye fixed on the habitués of the place, for McGuire's saloon had long ago ceased being a money-maker. It was merely a political nerve center vital to McGuire's power in the town.

One day a man in a blue suit and green necktie came into McGuire's saloon when Jimmy Kildare was having his beer. He was a big young man with a blunt, rather fleshy face, like a prize fighter out of training. He said, 'H'are ya, Jeff? Give me a drink, will you?'

Then he dropped to the floor, with his arms thrown wide. The sleeve pulled up from the right arm and showed Kildare that the forearm was cut clean across, well above the wrist.

Jeff, the bartender, put a hand on the bar and leaped over it. He dropped on his knees and began to cry out: 'Hanlon! Hey, Hanlon!'

Jimmy Kildare got out of the saloon and went back to the hospital. An interne who takes supplies out of the hospital is – well, he is a thousand times worse than a burglar, because he is trusted. But Jimmy Kildare took supplies from the hospital. He kept thinking of that young, rather fleshy face, battered, but somehow honest. Not honest enough, of course, or else he would have taken that gaping wound straight to a doctor.

Yet he might not be a criminal who dreaded having a doctor report his case to the police. There were many stories in the precinct of men who died silently, refusing to name their assailants to the officers of the law, and all of those who died in that manner were not thugs. It merely seemed that in McGuire's following and among his enemies there were men who lived according to a new standard of morality about which Kildare knew nothing. And he determined to put from his mind all thought of the letter of the law, remembering only that great silent oath which dwells in the soul of every good doctor – that promise to relieve the suffering ones of this world.

He took from the hospital retractors, sutures, needles, iodine. He went back to McGuire's and found the door locked.

He banged heavily on that door until Jeff looked out at him and said: 'What do you want? Get out of here!'

Kildare said: 'Unless those cut tendons are sewed together properly, Hanlon won't have a right arm. The forearm will shorten. The hand will turn in. There won't be any power in it.'

'Hell!' said Jeff, looking down at him. Then he said: 'All right! All right!' He reached out, grabbed Kildare by the shoulder and dragged him into the family room of the saloon.

Somebody said, 'He's dead!'

Hanlon lay on two tables that had been put side by side. His feet hung over the end of one table.

Kildare said, 'Get out of my way.' A big man barred him, arms spread wide. Kildare kicked him violently in the shins. The fellow howled and hopped away on one foot. Kildare shoved his hand over Hanlon's heart and heard Jeff say: 'Cut it out. This is a kind of a doc. They got them over in the hospital like this. Maybe he knows something.'

Kildare said: 'He's only fainted. Be useful, some of you.' He began to unwrap the towel, exposing the instruments.

'He's come and brought the stuff,' said Jeff. 'Who would of thought!'

Kildare began with iodine. Then he made two men hold Hanlon's right arm. They had put a clumsy tourniquet above the elbow. Kildare got to work on the tendons. He made Jeff and another man hold the retractors that kept the wound gaping for his convenience.

Jeff said, 'It makes me kind of sick.'

The other man said: 'Watch what he's doing, you dumb cluck! The kid's got eyes in his fingers. Watch what they do!'

Kildare put the tendons together one by one, matching the ends with care, and then securing them with mattress stitches, using threads of black silk. You could see the zigzag pattern of the little threads against the cordage of the tendons, all frayed at the cut ends.

Someone said, 'Who did it?'

Another man said: 'Who do you think, dummy? Dennis Innis, of course.'

'He'll get Innis yet,' said another.

'He ain't gunna have no gun hand to get Innis,' said the first speaker. 'There won't be no brains in that right hand of his, even when this slick job is finished. The wits is cut out of it.'

Kildare told himself that he must not think of the meaning behind that right hand. He kept on matching the severed ends of the tendons and making the stitches. Then Hanlon wakened from his trance and began to curse and struggle.

Jeff said: 'You damn fool, this doc is saving your hand. Shut up, will you!'

Hanlon shut up. Suddenly he extended his limp right arm toward Kildare. 'Okay,' he said, and kept his muscles flaccid. Only the loudness of his breathing told of his pain.

When the wound was closed and Kildare stepped back from his work,

Hanlon sat up. Jeff and another man – he who had worked with the retractors – were rubbing the blood from Kildare's hands with painful care. He surrendered his hands to them like tools of infinite value in the trust of friends. A warmth flowed like strong drink through his brain.

Hanlon stared at Kildare, saying, 'Who are you?'

'Oh, go to hell!' said Jeff. 'This is Doctor Kildare. He's a right guy. Oh, go to hell, will you!'

Hanlon smiled. 'Sure,' he said. 'Sure I'll go.' And he looked down at his right hand, which rested on one knee.

For two days Jimmy Kildare did not return to McGuire's. Then habit picked him up and shoved him through the front door. There were four men standing at the bar and Jeff, the bartender, was singing an Irish melody in a husky voice. Two or three of the others kept him company. Jeff broke off in the middle of the song. He went to the end of the bar where Kildare stood and focused on the doctor the blue-gray light of his one eye, warmer, suddenly, than sunshine.

'I thought you was passing us up lately, Doc,' said Jeff. 'What you having? The same?'

'The same,' said Kildare.

The four faces turned and stared.

Jeff was filling the tall glass with beer. He said, to the beer: 'Yeah. Okay. It's him.'

Nobody looked at Kildare any more. They looked, instead, at his image in the mirror behind the bar. Kildare felt their eyes more than ever.

'Go hop on the phone,' said Jeff.

Someone left the room. There was silence as Jeff brought the beer to Kildare.

Kildare tasted it. 'This seems better than usual, Jeff,' he said. He never had used Jeff's name before.

'Yeah, and why the hell wouldn't it be better?' said Jeff. 'Beer comes that way. Good and bad. You know, Doc.'

One of the men sauntered toward Kildare and said: 'I'd like to meet you, Doc. I'm – '

'You back up,' said Jeff. 'Who d'you wanta meet, anyway?'

The man stopped short and turned away, unoffended. He said: 'Okay! Okay!' and went back to his place.

When Kildare had finished his glass of beer, he put the money for it on the bar. 'Well, so long,' he said. 'So long, Jeff.'

Jeff shoved the money back toward Kildare. 'What's that for?' he demanded, with a fierce light in his one eye. 'Now listen, will you? Quit it, will you? . . . And where's your second beer, anyway?'

Kildare felt giddy. 'Why, yes, a second one, please,' he said.

The glass was filled for him. Jeff was scowling bitterly. He shoved the second beer onto the bar with a savage shortness of gesture, disdaining the money with a touch of his hand. But Kildare let the silver lie there.

The door creaked open behind him. 'Hello, Jeff,' said the newcomer, behind Kildare's back.

Jeff, in place of answering, wagged his head toward Kildare.

A big red-faced man with a whisky pungency about him stood beside Kildare at the bar. He wheezed a little as he spoke. His voice was husky but warm.

'I'm McGuire,' he said. 'Pleased to know you, Doctor Kildare. Damn pleased. Like to know more of you out of the same keg. What're you having, Doctor? Don't mean to say you stick to beer, do you?'

'He's gotta work. You know,' said Jeff.

'Yeah, sure. Sure,' said McGuire. 'This is a pleasure, Doctor Kildare. By the way, a friend of yours asked me to give you a letter. He wants you to open it when you get back home. . . . Make mine small, Jeff. Make it right but make it small. Boys, have something with me!'

The envelope was stuffy and soft and fat. Jimmy Kildare went back to his concrete cell in the hospital and opened it in private. He counted twenty fifty-dollar bills.

He sat down on the edge of his bed. A man doesn't have to space out and span out a thousand dollars. It does for itself. And it meant release from prison to Kildare.

For two days Kildare fought himself with all the appetites of his years closing his throat. Then he went back to McGuire's saloon.

Jeff looked at him with brotherly fondness and served him two beers. Kildare put his money on the bar, and Jeff took it, saying: 'You don't need to do that, Doc. But thanks, anyhow.'

Then Kildare pushed the envelope across the table. It was resealed, but rumpled and finger-soiled. 'This is for Mr. McGuire,' he said, and went out.

Afterward, he felt empty but he felt stronger, too. Like a man in training for a fight, fasting before the encounter.

He went right back to McGuire's saloon the next day, and there he

found McGuire himself at the bar in a brilliant checked suit. He looked
at Kildare with trouble in his eye.

'Now, listen, kid – Doc, I mean,' said McGuire, without prelude.
'What the hell? I mean, I got the double of that in my pocket.'

Kildare blushed as he answered: 'You see, I'm an interne. Internes
can't take anything for their work. It's against the rules. If an interne
could take anything, people in the wards would bribe him to get the
extra attention.'

'Wards? Who's talking about wards?' demanded McGuire. 'Hell, I'm
talking about a job in my saloon.'

'I've never done any jobs outside the hospital,' said Kildare, getting
redder than ever. 'It's not allowed.'

'You never did a job in this saloon?' demanded McGuire, with anger.

'No,' said Kildare. 'I never did anything here.'

'My God!' said McGuire. He added, 'Gimme a drink, Jeff.'

But Jeff remained frozen for a long moment. Only by degrees was he
able to thaw out and get into action. Kildare finished his beer and hurried back to the concrete cell, the smell of carbolic acid and the empty
loop of the question mark which embraced his future.

If you work very hard, one day rubs out the other. Kildare worked
very hard and for a long time gave up beer and McGuire's, until a telephone call summoned him, weeks later. He went over to McGuire's
place and found Pat Hanlon at the bar.

'All right, you two,' said Jeff, spreading his hands on the bar like a
benevolent father. Hanlon went to Kildare and took his hand. He held
it for a long time, while his eyes went over Kildare.

'They certainly take it out of you guys at the hospital,' said Hanlon.

'That's just the game,' said Kildare.

'Who wants to play a game where he's always "it"?' asked Hanlon.
'Listen, Doc. Have a drink with me, will you?'

Jeff whispered, leaning across the bar: 'What's it going to be, Doc?'

Kildare said shortly, 'I pay for my own, in here.'

'Come on. Aw, quit it,' said Jeff.

Hanlon said, 'You'll have something with me, brother.'

'I don't drink,' said Kildare, 'unless I can pay for it.' A blind anger
took hold of him. He was staring at the perfection of Hanlon's clothes.

'Aw, quit it!' said Jeff. 'Listen, Hanlon, the kid don't mean it. He
don't mean anything; he just don't know.'

'The hell he don't!' said Hanlon, and turned his back suddenly on
Kildare. He took three steps.

'Are you gunna be a damn fool, Hanlon?' asked Jeff, perspiring with anxiety.

'No,' answered Hanlon. He turned to Kildare again. 'Why be so damn mean?' he asked. 'Look!'

He held out his right hand. He worked the fingers back and forth.

'It's okay, see?' he said. 'I been to see a doc. He said what you done was a masterpiece. He said nobody could of done better. Look – there ain't any scar even, hardly. Now, why be high-hat with me? You could have my guts.'

Jeff interpreted across the bar: 'You hear, Doc? You could have everything he's got. Say something to him.'

Kildare said: 'I can't have anything to do with you. That goes for the whole bunch. I like you all right. When I can help out any of you, I want to do it as long as you don't ask me to take care of a crook.'

'Hanlon ain't a crook!' cried Jeff. 'He's the right-hand man of McGuire, Doc. Hanlon's all right.'

'I'm glad he is,' said Kildare. 'But over there at the hospital they watch us all the time. I'm only an interne. I like you all fine. I can't know you!'

Hanlon's eyes dwelt on the middle section of Kildare's body. 'All right,' he said.

Jeff again leaned over the bar. 'Does that go for me, kid?' he asked.

'Ah – I don't know. I'm going back to the hospital,' said Kildare.

'Am I a thug?' asked Hanlon.

'I don't know,' said Kildare.

'Hanlon!' shouted Jeff.

Hanlon straightened with a quick jerk. 'All right,' he said, still making that cold survey of Kildare's anatomy.

Kildare got to the door before Jeff said, 'Doc, for God's sake!'

Kildare paused. He could feel Hanlon like a leveled gun behind him.

'Listen, Doc,' said Jeff. 'Hanlon has a wife.'

'That's all out,' said Hanlon. 'Quit it.'

'Oh, shut your face, will you, Pat?' demanded Jeff. 'His wife's going to have a baby soon, and there's no doc he can get. Income tax. Hanlon's all right. But income tax. They want him. And they've got the girl watched. They're waiting for him to go back to her. Understand? He's gotta get her a doctor he can trust. Listen, Doc, will you take care of her?'

Kildare said, 'Well, Hanlon, why didn't you tell me?'

So Kildare went. It was a nice little apartment all done up in French-gray. Everything was simple. A new Pat Hanlon entered the world.

Kildare remained by the bed until the effects of the ether wore away from the mother. She kept saying, 'Is it a boy, Doctor?'

'Yes,' he would answer, and her eyes would shine at him, only to grow dim again from the effect of the drug.

Then the baby began to cry, and the sound drew the girl back to full consciousness. She held the baby in the hollow of her arm and crooned over it.

Kildare went back to McGuire's, where Pat Hanlon sat in the back room with his head bowed into his hands. He lifted his head and glared at Kildare.

'It's all right,' said Kildare. 'Your wife is a sweetheart, Hanlon. And now she's got a fine son to keep her company.'

Said Hanlon, 'And how's my girl, Doc?'

Kildare gripped his two hands hard together. He said, 'She's the happiest soul in New York, right now. She wants me to tell you that she loves you.'

Hanlon flung a sheaf of bills on the table. 'Will you for God's sake take some of it?' he pleaded.

'No,' said Kildare.

'Do you despise me that much, Doc?'

Kildare patted the big shoulder. 'I don't hate you, Hanlon,' he said. 'But I'm an interne. I can't take money.'

But Kildare's nerves were still shaking when he got back to the hospital, for perhaps the world did not need any more Pat Hanlons. He sat on his bed after he had made his rounds and looked at the tremor of his hands.

Doctor Henry Fearson had passed Kildare in a corridor, and he had stopped to greet his idol. 'How's everything, Doctor Fearson?'

'Everything? Things never are right except in patches,' said Fearson, and went on.

But the dark of the underworld still clung to Kildare as he sat there. His roommate came in and said: 'Only three months before we get out of this lousy hole. Where do you hitch up after that?'

Kildare lifted his head. 'Fearson says he wants me in his office,' he remarked.

'Fearson? That's a hell of an out for you, brother. Don't you know that?'

Kildare said deliberately, 'He's the finest man and the best doctor I know.'

'Oh, yeah, oh, yeah! We all know that. But he owes money that he shouldn't.'

'What do you mean?'

'I don't know, but they've got him.'

'Why?'

'Something about money. We all know Fearson is a saint, but even saints can be framed. Fearson is framed. They're going to cut his head off. He can go work on a farm in about a month!'

And Kildare thought again of the farm on the autumn morning. He thought of the lofty intellectual brow of Fearson, and that gaunt boy in overalls. He kept on thinking, and the next afternoon he needed his beer.

When he got to McGuire's, Hanlon drew him straight into the back room.

Hanlon said, as they sat down to beer: 'Now listen, Doc. McGuire wants to talk to you. He says you could vote the precinct.'

'I could what?' asked Kildare.

'You don't know what people around here think of you. When you go down the street, does anybody speak? The bums along the pavement, I mean?'

'Yes,' said Kildare. 'They come over to the accident room, too, and ask for me. Yes, they all seem to know me.'

'You been a coupla years around here. You've taken care of a hundred dirty bums, and they've talked about you. You wouldn't take money. You could vote the precinct,' said Hanlon. 'They all know you're a guy that's done something for nothing. McGuire says: "Chuck the regular line. Throw in with him." He can get you five thousand the first year, besides gravy. And then eight thousand, ten thousand and right on up. And twice as much on the side.'

'I'm only an interne,' said Kildare.

'What are you thinking of, with that dreamy look?' asked Hanlon.

'I'm thinking of an apartment all done in French-gray,' said Kildare.

'Aw, hell!' laughed Hanlon. 'You could have ten like that. I mean, McGuire wants to cut you in on something rich. By the way, why don't you come see us? My wife gives me a temperature talking about you.'

'I'd like to see you both,' said Kildare, 'but tell McGuire I'm not a politician. I'm an interne.'

'You want the stuff but you're afraid to take it. Is that right?' asked Hanlon.

'Maybe,' said Kildare.

'What are you afraid of?'

'I'm afraid of dirt that soap and water won't wash off.'

'McGuire's got to talk to you himself,' said Hanlon. 'You certainly are tough. Well, all that's left to me is my own personal angle. I mean, the old girl down there holding the kid and asking what have I done for the doc. Now listen, Doc. Don't be a damn fool. I've got twenty-five hundred dollars – '

'I don't want your money,' said Kildare.

'Meaning it's dirty? Meaning I'm dirty, too?' shouted Hanlon.

'You take it any way you please.'

Hanlon's fist started. But it was only the flat of his hand that struck heavily across Kildare's face.

Kildare came off his chair swinging. Hanlon caught his arms.

'You sap, I gotta mind to wring your neck – I gotta mind to do you in!' shouted Hanlon. 'Get out!'

Kildare got out.

His nose was numb half an hour later, but his hand was steady enough in the operating room.

He was washing up afterward, when he said to his roommate, 'Any more about Fearson?'

'Aw, he's sunk.'

'How do you know?' Kildare asked.

'My old man's on the inside. He told me. They're going to make a goat of Fearson,' said Vincent. 'Money. He's got to pay off, and what the hell money has he got to pay off with when he's cleaned to the gills in the market?'

Afterward, Kildare went to see Fearson in his office. 'Are you in bad shape?' asked Kildare.

Fearson looked at him.

'You mean more to me than anybody in the world,' said Kildare. 'I'd give blood for you. Are they doing you in because you need money?'

'Who's been talking to you?' asked Fearson.

'Somebody. I hope it's a lie. I hope I'm simply making a damned fool of myself.'

'You haven't made a damned fool of yourself. It's true,' said Fearson. 'I played once in my life with crooks. Now they've got me.'

'What are you going to do?'

'I'm going to wait for the knife, that's all,' said Fearson.

'I've got five hundred dollars,' said Kildare. 'I can get my hands on that.'

'I need four thousand in cold cash by tomorrow night,' said Fearson. 'Get that for me if you can.'

He offered no thanks. Kildare went back to his room. He needed no supper. He needed no sleep. He sat at the window and let the light from the next street lamp show him the dingy world of house fronts across the way. Toward morning, he lay down and slept for an hour. His head was ringing all morning as he went about his work. Noon came and he swallowed a few morsels, but the thought of Fearson choked him.

That afternoon he swallowed his pride and made himself go to McGuire's saloon. Only Jeff was there, reading a paper.

'Where's Hanlon?' asked Kildare.

Jeff said, beneath a scowl, 'Hanlon hit you yesterday?'

'That doesn't matter,' said Kildare. 'There's a friend of mine in trouble.'

'Who is he?' asked Jeff.

After a time Kildare murmured: 'You don't know him. Fearson is his name.'

'Fearson? Why, he . . . Sure I know him,' said Jeff. 'Is he a friend of yours?'

'Friend?' said Kildare. 'He's the only friend I have.' Then he added, smiling, 'Outside of you, Jeff.'

'Yeah, I know what you think of me,' said Jeff. 'I know what you think of all of us. Fearson, eh?'

'Where can I find Hanlon? I've got to see him.'

'Hanlon's on the booze again,' said Jeff. 'I don't know where he is. When the news got out what Hanlon done to you, his wife had hysterics. That drove him out of his house. He came here, and McGuire gave him hell. I don't know where Hanlon is. He's been going straight ever since his son was born, but now he's on the loose.'

'You don't think I could find him?'

'Nobody could find him. Even McGuire can't find him.'

Kildare went back to the hospital.

Doctor Reichmann came up to him after surgery. 'What the devil's the matter with you, Kildare?' he asked. 'You were all thumbs today!'

'What the hell of it?' said Kildare.

'Are you saying that to me?' demanded Reichmann. 'You confounded – '

Kildare walked away. A thing like that was enough to smash a young doctor's career, he knew. The oldsters will take anything rather than impertinence. He was very tired. Nothing mattered.

He got back to his room. Someone announced a telephone call.

He went to the telephone. A deep voice said over the line, in a guarded tone, 'Is this Doctor Kildare?'

'Yes.'

'There's a man lying here with a bullet through his lungs. Can any doctor in God's world do anything about it?'

'No,' said Kildare.

And then he remembered the new work in chest surgery. There was a doctor who had saved the lives of policemen shot down by thugs in line of duty. In the old days they used to give morphine to men shot through the chest. Morphine, and let them die. But the new doctor had showed another way. Kildare knew about it.

'Nothing?' the voice was saying.

'Yes. Maybe,' said Kildare. 'Why?'

'That's all,' said the voice.

Fifteen minutes later, Kildare was called out to the reception room. There were two fellows neatly dressed in brown suits, both wearing bow ties, both with the same hard, casual look.

'You telephoned to me fifteen minutes ago,' said Kildare.

'That's right. Will you come try your hand on our friend?'

'Have you reported that *accident* to the police?' asked Kildare.

The pair looked steadily at him.

'Will you come?' said the first man.

'And compound a felony?' asked Kildare. 'And smash my reputation?'

'There's money in it, Doc,' said one.

And then Kildare remembered. There was no one in the world from whom he could get money except Pat Hanlon. And Hanlon had disappeared.

'Wait a minute,' said Kildare.

He went to Fearson's office. It was late but Fearson opened the door. 'All right. Come in!' he said.

'What's the dead line?' asked Kildare.

'Dead line for what?' asked Fearson.

'That four thousand,' said Kildare.

'Oh, that?' said Fearson. He smiled, his mouth twisting. 'They *do* give me a dead line, like the villains in a book. I have till midnight, Kildare. Now, you go to bed and forget – '

'I've been in jail here for a long time,' said Kildare. 'You're the only right man I've met among the lot. You've been hope to me, Fearson.

And that means life, too. *You* keep on hoping till midnight comes, will you?'

He went back to the two in brown and said briefly, 'I want four thousand dollars for the job.'

'Yeah? That ain't what we heard about you. But I know strangers are different,' said one of them, and he laughed. 'Want to see the money now?'

'No,' said Kildare.

They put him into a fast car and shot across town to an obscure side street.

They unlocked the door of a house with a tall, narrow front and ran up the stairs inside ahead of Kildare. He followed them into a bedroom with a single electric globe glaring from the ceiling.

On the bed lay a man with a bloody bandage about his chest. He was thirty, say, and big and lean. His face was evil, and Kildare thought, 'If I help this man, I'm sold to the crooks forever!'

Where the bandage did not bind the man, the lean of his big arching ribs was visible. He was naked to the waist. He had on trousers and black shoes that no one had thought to take off his feet.

A man rose from beside the bed. 'He's passing out,' he said. 'It's no good. I knew it. Anywhere between the belly and the shoulders, and nothing helps them but morphine to make it easy.'

'You talk like a fool, and I don't want fools around me,' said Kildare. 'Get out of here and heat some water. Somebody, take his shoes off.'

He slit the bandage across. The hole was right in the lungs. It wasn't one of those lucky glancing bullets. It had ripped right through the middle.

The hole in front was quite a small puncture, rimmed with dark purple. The hole in the back was bigger. There wasn't much blood. That was the hell of it. The bleeding would be inward.

Kildare, leaning over the bed, began to listen and tap with a steady, hammerlike finger. He tapped all around and located the place where the hemorrhage was forming. When the blood clot had formed a complete stoppage, then the heart would move across to the other side of the body, and after that, only God could keep the victim from dying.

There was no hope – except what that new doctor had indicated. Kildare happened to know about it because Fearson had pointed out the new work to him.

Here the door to the room pushed open. Kildare looked over his shoulder and saw on the threshold Pat Hanlon and Jeff, with guns in their hands.

One of the fellows in brown had gone into the kitchen. The other two men stood quietly against the wall. One of them said: 'Here's Hanlon. Shooting Dennis Innis here wasn't enough for him. He wants us all. Watch yourself, boy!'

Hanlon said: 'You guys keep your shirts on. Innis had it coming to him, and you know it. Doc, how come you to play with this bunch of louses? Get out!'

Kildare stood up from the bed. He said: 'I want two dishes boiled in water. I want plenty of hot water. Listen to me, Hanlon. If Innis dies, you'll burn. You're going to throw in with these fellows and help me. If you do that, I can pull Innis through, I think.'

'You can't. He's got it through the lungs,' said Hanlon. 'The only right thing I ever done. I'm gunna get you out of this dump. Come on, Doc.'

Kildare cried out in a voice that was strange to his own ears: 'You murdering lot of childish half-wits, give me your guns! . . . Here, you, come out of the kitchen. There's not going to be any shooting. Hanlon, if we don't fix Innis, it's the electric chair for you.'

The man came slowly out of the kitchen, his hands above his head, an automatic dangling from one of them. 'I guess I hear it straight,' he said.

'On that chair!' shouted Kildare, pointing. 'All of 'em.'

Five men piled seven guns in a glistening heap.

'It's a new kind of game,' mumbled Hanlon. 'Only the doc knows the rules.'

'Get that hot water in here,' said Kildare.

Three of them hurried to the kitchen. Kildare began to swab iodine, and he took a big syringe the moment the dishes and the water were brought to him.

'Look at him,' whispered Hanlon. 'Stabbing him through the heart.'

Kildare was shoving the needle right into the lung, two inches, three inches. That was the start of the new idea.

Jeff grunted: 'Back up, you birds. The doc is the only white man in the world.'

Then above the operation leaned hard-breathing shadows, closely grouped, a weight on Kildare's soul. He could feel the cold of sweat on his upper lip. He drew out the plunger of the syringe, and the red of the blood followed and filled the glass cylinder. He squirted it out into the warm dish, with the citrate to prevent clotting. He found a vein in the left arm with the second syringe, and injected the blood back into the arm.

Hanlon said: 'I get it! Look, you dummies! He pulls the blood out of the lung so's Innis can't suffocate. Then he shoves the same blood back into his body. A regular blood transfusion. What he loses one place he gets another, and the old lungs don't fill up. Oh, does this doc know damn near everything!'

'Be quiet!' said Kildare and went on working.

Jeff said: 'When you think what the kid can do! Look, Hanlon! Color is coming back into Innis' face already. Why'd you go and sock lead into this bum, anyway? Even if he knifed you, you could let it go at that, couldn't you?'

'I thought he was too thick with my wife,' said Hanlon. 'Hell, I see how dumb I was. Quit talking, Jeff, will you?'

'Yeah. All I say is it's a damn good thing you got a buddy like me to keep you in with the brainy birds like the doc here,' said Jeff. 'You took and socked him the other day, didn't you?'

'All right! All right!' said Hanlon.

Then it was an hour later, and Kildare was saying: 'Innis, stop talking. If you talk, you'll kill yourself. Lie still. I've given you morphine to make you sleep, and you'll sleep. Just lie still, will you?'

Innis whispered, with eyes closed, smiling: 'Hanlon always was a damn fool. I never could get near the gal.' Then he stopped talking.

'Is it gunna be all right, Doc?' asked Hanlon.

'He has nine chances out of ten,' said Kildare. 'That's all I can tell you.'

'Nine of your chances is better than ninety of the next dirty mug,' said Hanlon. 'Doc, I wish you would stand up and take a couple of good swipes at me! I'd thank you for it, while you was paying yourself back.'

Kildare leaned back in the chair. One of the men brought a cold glass and put it in his hand. It was a stiff Scotch-and-soda. He drank it like beer.

The neatness was gone from Innis' friends. Their brown suits were bunched around the shoulders. They looked at Kildare as one might stare at a being from the other world.

'This'll make you feel better, Doc,' said one of them, pulling out a wallet and counting bills from it. 'Here's the four thousand. We make it five for luck.'

Kildare leaned forward. And then Jeff stepped between him and the money.

'Buddy,' Jeff said, 'if you make a mug of all of us by trying to bribe the doc, I'm gunna sock you myself.'

'Back up, Jeff,' the man said. 'He asked for it, didn't he?'

'He was kidding you, you big stiff,' said Jeff. 'Listen. He's an interne. He can't take anything. He won't take anything. He's too clean for that. He's the only white man I ever seen. Now, get him out of here, Hanlon.'

The money had disappeared while Kildare's hand was still reaching for it. He thought of Fearson and started to protest. But he was helpless when Jeff and Hanlon put hands on him.

They got him quickly down the stairs. Behind them, the man with the money called: 'If Innis gets well, we can all the old stuff. We're friends, Hanlon.'

Out on the street Jeff said: 'Thank God we got the tip and followed you. Don't ever trust yourself with a lot of yeggs like that.'

'I've got to get back!' cried Kildare. 'I've got to get that money.'

Hanlon said: 'Doc, did you want that dirty money?'

'Fearson – ' blurted out Kildare.

Jeff growled: 'Quit it, Doc. Fearson is safe. Nobody ain't gonna worry him. Not after the chief knew he was your friend. You know who he owed the money to? McGuire! The dummy of a doctor had tried some gambling, was all.'

Kildare stopped short. 'You mean it's all fixed?' he asked.

'Listen! McGuire would fix *hell* if you said the word,' declared Hanlon. 'Come on, Jeff. The doc needs a drink.'

They rushed across town in Hanlon's car to McGuire's saloon. It was shut and empty. Jeff opened it up.

'Whisky?' he said.

'Yes,' said Kildare.

Jeff clinked out three glasses on the bar. He brought out a squat bottle and filled the glasses from it.

'Will you have this on me, Doc?' asked Hanlon.

Kildare turned and saw Hanlon's eyes wide open, almost frightened.

Hanlon said, 'I'd like to be able to tell the wife that you'd been having a drink with me – '

'Leave him alone, dummy,' interrupted Jeff. 'He's never taken anything from us yet, has he?'

'Will you have it on me?' pleaded Hanlon. 'Or would you like to smash in my dirty face first?'

Kildare, looking through the dim plate-glass window, saw the glare of the night lights over the top of the elevated. 'What time is it?' he asked.

'It's eleven-forty-five,' said Pat Hanlon, still waiting.

'I've got time for this one,' said Kildare, 'and there's nobody I'd rather drink it with. Here's to you, Pat.'

Fixed

Sometimes called an Irish story (though it is much more), 'Fixed,' first appeared in *Collier's* on June 13, 1936. It belongs to the sport-story genre to which Faust contributed football, horse racing, and boxing stories. He loved sports of all kinds and, though denied much participation in them as a youth because he had to work, he played golf and tennis regularly in later life. He even subscribed to New York newspapers while living abroad so that he could follow the careers of sports teams and stars closely.

Fighting abounds in Faust's work. Nearly every known weapon can be found somewhere in Faust's writing. In *Marbleface* (Dodd, Mead, 1939) Faust devotes ten and a half pages to one epic boxing match. Fighting represented for him the essence of the struggle for survival. 'At the nineteen different schools I attended there were always the fistfights until I found my place,' he said. 'I went for years with a swollen and scarred face because the fights at one school had hardly healed before I had to begin them again in another.'

Faust's youth was in the golden age of boxing – of Corbett, Fitzsimmons, Jeffries, Johnson, and later Dempsey and Tunney, nearly all of whom shared Faust's Irish blood and desire for upward mobility. Faust learned to box early, and continued to box until adult responsibilities and heart trouble forced him to enjoy the sport only vicariously. During his New York years he regularly attended boxing matches at Madison Square Garden. There he became acquainted with many fighters, most notably world heavyweight champion Gene Tunney.

Tunney's knowledge of Shakespeare and fine wines, often criticized in the media as unbecoming a he-man champion, was partly the result of his friendship with Faust. Faust's own experiences in the New York boxing world provided authentic background and detail for stories like this one.

A S HE GOT OUT of his limousine, Big Bill pulled a mahogany-colored leather cigar case from the inside pocket of his dinner jacket and lighted an excellent perfecto, for when he went to a fight at Madison Square Garden he always kept some of the fragrance of good living between him and the crowd. On the sidewalk, in the crowd, he waited a moment, straightening his dinner jacket around the carefully fitted whiteness of his front while he saw and was seen.

He spoke to a police officer. 'Hello, McNally. What you got for tonight?'

'I like Slam Finnegan, sir,' said the officer. 'Whatta you think yourself?'

Big Bill looked at him and smiled. Then he winked. In this manner he conveyed to McNally, delicately, his acceptance of the officer as one of the inside circle who 'know,' but he dropped not a morsel of information in the way of the hungry policeman.

Big Bill looked upon himself as a sort of expensive bomb which, if his news were exploded, would reduce the entire Garden to a rioting shambles. The greatness of his knowledge increased his dignity from the bulges of his neck to the gleam of his shoes and bestowed upon him an inner strength somewhat akin to the virtue of the good and the great; for among all the thousands there was not one who knew that he had wagered fifty thousand dollars on 'Little David' LaRue, that black magician with the gloves; only two others in the entire world knew that ten thousand more of his dollars had been spent to make his profit certain. The truth was that he had bought young Slam Finnegan; in about the eighth or the ninth round the Irishman would 'take a dive.'

Rosenbloom appeared, suspended sidewise in the crowd like a fish in water as he undulated rapidly toward Big Bill. He held up his hat as a signal flag above his bald head, which shone no more brightly than his smile, for Sammy Rosenbloom was never too proud to show his joy when he saw his chief. In spite of his hairless head, which gave his opinion unusual weight with many people, Sammy was only thirty, but already he knew his way around New York so well that Big Bill often forgot to be amused and was amazed outright by the precocity of the boy. He pushed his way through to Bill.

'Where you get 'em, Sammy?'

'Third row,' said Sammy, swiveling his head about, 'where the blood won't splash on your shirt front, Bill.'

After seven years of almost Biblical service, Big Bill had permitted this faithful man Friday to use the shortened name which was familiar on the lips of the wise. As for the row in which he sat, Big Bill only wished it to be close enough for his features to be seen when a flashlight was taken in his direction. God had given him such a nose and chin and he had improved on nature by adding such a pair of jowls that in a group photograph he looked like two-in-one.

They passed the ticket kiosk, entered one of the roped alleys leading toward the entrance door. Sammy began to walk sidewise with his usual skill, giving all his attention to the chief.

'How are things?' asked Bill.

'Two and a half to one,' said Sammy.

'They think Slam is going to take him, eh?' asked Big Bill. 'What *you* think, Sammy?'

'I think Slam has got the old sleep-syringe in both hands,' answered Sammy, 'but I don't think he knows as much as the chief.'

He winked and laughed.

'What *d'you* know?' asked Bill.

'Not enough to answer questions,' said Sammy. 'There's the big guy! There's Harrigan!'

He got his hat off and began to wave it above his spotlight of a head. If attention were attracted his way, his master could benefit by it if he chose. In the meantime a group of men advanced three aisles away toward the entrance, a policeman going ahead to smooth the way of the great Jimmy Harrigan, the chief of chiefs, the boss of bosses. He was a little man with a face putty-white and the eyes thumbed into it with soot. Smiling was not enough. He never stopped laughing.

This group passed into the building ahead of Big Bill in spite of Sammy's fishlike efforts to advance. Bill panted out a cloud of smoke. His fat lips, which glistened almost like a chorus girl's, were saying: 'See us? Did he see us? Did he walk us down or didn't he see us?'

The sweat of Big Bill ran cold upon his flesh. The answer of Sammy

Rosenbloom was sweeter than milk and honey: 'Didn't you see? That was Ike Fishbein alongside of him.'

'What does that mean?'

'Fishbein is gunna find out in a day or two. They're gunna open him up and clean him. That's why Harrigan can't see anything now. He's too busy getting the can opener ready to use on that boneless sardine!'

Big Bill filled his lungs and sighed forth the smoke and the relief.

'You sure the chief didn't see me? You sure he didn't pass me up?' he queried again.

'Sure he didn't see you. I watched every eye in that mob. They were all full of Fishbein.'

'Ike has always been right up there,' said Big Bill.

'We don't know him any more,' answered Sammy. 'Account of that funny job he done in Jersey. He thought account of it was Jersey he could eat all that honey; and now they're gunna clean him.'

They entered a Garden which already seemed full although the several thousand who were jamming toward the gates still had to be poured into the interstices. Big Bill drew toward the ringside as into a family circle. Everyone was there. Levi Isaacs turned with a wave and a laugh. Pudge Murphy loosed a shout of recognition. Old Harry Blatts had a seat just down the row.

'Everyone knows you, Chief,' said Sammy. 'And the ones that don't know are asking. You *look* like something.'

The lights went out through the arena, leaving only the many cones of brilliance above the ring. Beneath that luminous fountain the faces of the crowd weltered away into the outer dimness while Bill still recognized important names here and there. He knew them all; they all knew him; everything was all right. He felt at last a human sympathy, a warm pity for the Police Commissioner off at the left. What was it that the poor devil made in a year? And yet how useful the fellow could be! In the mystery of the metropolis nothing impressed Bill more than the men of small salary in key positions. Their industry was incomprehensible, like that of the bees and the ants.

A hand was laid from behind on the shoulder of Bill. The voice of Snipe Dickinson said at his ear, 'Which one of these you like, Bill?'

'Why should I like one of 'em?' asked Bill.

'I've got a spare hundred at seven to five on McGuire,' said Snipe.

Big Bill, with the easy indulgence of the great for the small, gave some of his attention to the pair of featherweights who were struggling in the ring.

'They all got the forward stance, these days,' said Big Bill to Sammy. 'Which is McGuire?'

'The one in the red trunks,' said Sammy. 'He's a baby, ain't he? Look at that left! Look at that baby go! Oh, socko! He's got Choochoo Lavine as red as Santa Claus.'

The face of Lavine dripped blood but his eye was clear; he was waiting through the storm.

'Lavine's holding something out,' said Big Bill. He added over his shoulder, 'Snipe, make it two hundred at ten to five.'

'Why should I?' asked the Snipe.

'And why should I give you something for nothing?' asked Bill.

'All right, you robber,' said Snipe Dickinson. 'It's two hundred against one hundred, and you've got Lavine, you sucker. . . . Hai, McGuire! The old one-two, kid!'

The round ended. McGuire danced back to his corner. Lavine remained for a moment in the center of the ring, looking thoughtfully after his opponent. The crowd laughed.

'Get an adding machine, Lavine!' yelled a wit.

'Lavine is gunna take him,' said Bill to Sammy.

The girl in front of him turned. She had black hair and blue eyes and a neat, saucy face. Bill winked and beckoned but she became aware of him only to drift her eyes critically up and down his swollen body before she turned away again.

'Listen, Sammy,' said Bill. 'Let that kid know who I am, after this bout.'

'Is this gunna be a pickup?' asked Sammy.

'We'll see, Sammy.'

The next round was already under way. McGuire kept shooting his one-two. But Lavine kept on waiting. The round almost had ended before he slipped a straight right and came in with a body blow. McGuire clinched and held on.

'He's gunna kill McGuire,' said Bill.

One round later the thoughtful Lavine feinted for the body, the hands of McGuire dropped to the hurt section, and through an opening a yard wide Lavine drove the finishing punch to the chin.

'I'll take it in tens and fives,' said Big Bill to the Snipe. 'I need some small change.'

He went over to see Gipsy Connor.

'Whatta *you* want?' asked the Gip.

'Money, Gip,' said Bill. 'I want your money. How are you laying the main go now?'

'A dollar on the nigger gets two from me,' said Connor.

'It's three to one all over the house,' said Big Bill.

'To hell with the house,' said Connor.

'The nigger hasn't got a chance,' said Big Bill. 'Five to one would be more like it.'

'If he hasn't got a chance, why would *you* wanta lay money on him?' asked Connor.

'Sympathy with a downtrodden race,' answered Big Bill. 'Make it two and a half and I'll talk to you.'

'I don't like your lingo,' said Connor. 'I never did.'

'Two and a half, Gip?'

'How far?'

'Five, let's say.'

'Grand?'

'Why should we be pikers?'

'It's ten to five,' said Gip.

'You'd rob your grandmother of her glass eye,' remarked Big Bill. 'But I'd rather have ten of yours than a hundred of somebody regular.'

He went back to his seat where Sammy greeted him with a wink and a nod. Big Bill laughed. He leaned forward and said over the girl's shoulder: 'Why should I remember you so well?'

She moved to face him. At the base of her young throat a gardenia was pinned. It had three big, green, lustrous leaves.

'Why should I remember you so well?' repeated Bill.

'How could you ever forget?' asked the girl.

He laughed again. He felt warm, at ease.

'You really own that nice horse, Dinner Gong?' she asked.

'Why not?' asked Bill.

'I don't see any resemblance,' said the girl.

He had to laugh again.

'That's not bad,' he said. 'That's pretty good. Was Dinner Gong ever right for you?'

'He made my day at Aqueduct,' she answered.

'That was when he gave ten pounds to Topsy Turvy,' remarked Big Bill. 'Was he carrying much for you?'

'He carried a pair of shoes and turned 'em into a fur coat,' said the girl.

'Remembering you so well, why shouldn't I remember your name?' he asked.

'Some people call me Jap. Are you one of them?' she said.

'Japs cheat but they don't have blue eyes,' replied Big Bill.

The gong rang. She turned from him slowly, leaving her smile behind her, as it were.

'Okay?' asked Sammy.

'Sure. What you think?' replied Bill.

'I dunno how you do it,' said Sammy. 'Whatta you say to them?'

'It ain't what you say. It's the way you say it,' said Big Bill. 'Having good intentions is what counts.'

'How good are your intentions?' asked Sammy.

'Why d'you keep on talking when you got nothing to say?' said Bill.

A pair of lightweights struggled through eight dull rounds. Battling Miller had youth; old Jim Cross had a head on his shoulders and a long left that won for him and Big Bill; Snipe Dickinson counted another two hundred into the hand of the lucky man.

'It's gunna be your night, Chief,' said Sammy.

Welterweights were next. Big Bill bet a thousand on the red head of Dick Roach, and young Dick plastered Lester Grogan in the fifth round during a mix-up in his own corner.

'I'm going to take a walk but I'll be back,' said Big Bill to Jap.

'Don't lose yourself, Big Boy,' she said.

He found Gip Connor again.

'Rub the trouble out of your eyes, Gip,' said Big Bill.

Connor looked at him without answering.

'Another five grand the same way,' said Big Bill.

'That's it, is it?' asked Connor.

'That's what?'

'I might have known,' mused Connor.

Big Bill bit into a fresh cigar.

'What you say, Gip?' he asked.

'I say you're a dirty dog,' answered Connor.

'What!' cried Big Bill.

A horribly familiar sickness of heart overwhelmed him; his knees loosened; he remembered out of the great distance a March day, a windy corner, and a young lad screeching insults at him while a crowd of their schoolmates waited for the fight to start. The fight had not started and therefore, from time to time, the giddy nausea returned upon Bill.

'Get out of my sight, you yella rat!' said Connor.

Big Bill got out of his sight. He still was trembling when he returned to his seat. By that time the principals for the main bout were in their corners, Pop Finnegan pushing the gloves home over the hands of his son. Pop had a featureless blear of a face with a mouth that slopped to one side or the other when he talked, but he had been tense and bright-eyed enough when Big Bill talked money to him and put the five thousand advance into his hands.

Now the red old bathrobe was worked off over the gloved hands; now young Slam Finnegan was on his feet with the robe loose on his shoulders as he tested the spring of the top rope and shuffled his feet in the resin. He picked out people he knew at the ringside with a wave and a smile.

This calmness before a fight in which Slam was to 'take a dive' gradually restored a regular rhythm to the heartbeat of Big Bill. He could breathe again. In place of the cigar he had thrown away he lighted a new one and could enjoy the taste of the smoke. After all, the time had passed when he needed to fear physical violence. There are other forms of courage, of moral courage. He skipped from the word 'moral' and found refuge in the phrase 'strength of spirit.' Take a fellow like himself who was always one of the boys and who never let down anyone who was in the know. . . . Besides, he would be a fool to take to heart anything that Gipsy Connor did or said. By this force of inward persuasion, like a sensible man, Big Bill put fear behind him and concentrated upon the present moment, the pleasant expectancy of the future.

'What are you doing about this?' asked Snipe Dickinson.

'Ah, nothing much,' answered Big Bill.

'The nigger's been coming on,' said Snipe. 'You heard what he did to Jeff Millard out on the Coast. Two rounds! . . . These people are all nuts, around here, betting two to one on Slam. Maybe he'll win, but he hasn't got a walkaway. This nigger is another Joe Louis, and he's better every time he starts. If he don't take on too much weight, he'll be the middleweight champ, one of these days!'

Everyone was standing now, near the ringside, getting the cramps out of legs before the final bout. Slam Finnegan waved suddenly straight toward Big Bill, who closed his eyes and almost groaned aloud. It was the last thing that Slam should have done – to recognize his money-man on this night of all nights. But the Irish are dumb, decided Big Bill. That's why they're useful, they're so dumb.

When he opened his eyes again, Jap was waving and shouting at Finnegan.

'You like Slam?' asked Big Bill.

'Oh, he's a honey, isn't he?' she demanded, turning her bright face on him.

Big Bill considered her with a smile. He leaned over and took the gardenia on her breast between thumb and forefinger.

'I better take this before you get it all messed up, waving your arms around,' he said.

She looked down at his hand, then up at his face. Something that might have been almost disgust vanished with her smile.

'All right, Big Boy, you take it,' she said.

He pushed it into his buttonhole. People were calling: 'Down! Down in front!'

'I'll be thinking of you, Jap,' said Big Bill. 'I'll be breathing you, beautiful.'

She gave him her smile over her shoulder as she sat down, and while Big Bill settled into place Sammy was saying: 'The way you do it, Chief! . . . That nigger looks good, don't he?'

'Did you watch the gal's face just now?' asked Big Bill.

'Sure I watched it.'

'You didn't get a flash, did you?'

'You got the flash, Chief.'

'I mean, she had a kind of a look for a second. Maybe she's stringing me.'

'Stringing *you?* That'd be a scream, wouldn't it?'

'Well, women are all kind of nuts,' said Bill.

'The nigger looks like something, don't he?' asked Sammy.

The two had met in the center of the ring to shake hands, receive the final instructions. Now they came out fighting, as different in style as in build and color. Slam Finnegan, hardly more than a lightweight about the hips and spindling legs, had his weight layered around the shoulders and drawn down over his capable arms. He stepped in a light, mincing dance. The Negro was carefully muscled in every part; he wore a gravely studious air as he glided in and out with his stance rather low as against the tip-toe alertness of the white boy.

They came to the danger line, shifted away from it, met again with a sudden darting of gloves. Finnegan shook his head, stepped back; the Negro wove in after him; the whole Garden yelled with delight, seeing that this was to be a fight and not a sparring match.

Sammy said: 'What I tell you? Notice the way that coon let 'em slide off the back of his head? See that left he stuck into Finnegan's belly? That didn't do Slam any good!'

Slam Finnegan, backing away, pecked at a distance. The punches missed the bobbing head of 'Little David' LaRue.

'He can hit when he's on his heels, is what Finnegan can do, can't he?' pleaded Sammy.

'You'll see,' grunted Big Bill.

He turned his head and surveyed the crowd, particularly the working faces along the near-by benches. Their eyes were wide, glaring; some of the men worked their shoulders to help home punches; some made little automatic gestures as though they were blocking hard blows. No one in the great house sat immobile, at ease, except Big Bill, a deity raised above the pitiful human concerns of the millions. For he alone had knowledge of what the end must be.

He watched young Finnegan take the initiative suddenly, hammering home short blows to the body as he backed the Negro into a corner. The crowd yelled, the dry tinder of its enthusiasm for a favorite flaming up suddenly. For from exactly such an attack Finnegan knew how to shift a blow to the head and end a battle.

The round ended. Finnegan sat with his head down a little, his father handling him, sneering out words from the drooping corner of his mouth. Across the ring Little David had begun to laugh. Still laughing, he patted his body, looking up at his trainer. It was plain that the punches of Finnegan had not injured him.

'The nigger's tough,' said Sammy Rosenbloom. 'He sure can take it. Out on the Coast . . . .'

'Ah, shut up for a minute,' said Big Bill. He leaned forward. 'What you think, honey?' he asked.

'I don't know. . . . Slam isn't right,' said the girl. She turned her troubled face. 'There's not so much of the old "I be damned" about him. He studies around too much. What's he think he's doing? Reading a book?'

'No, counting money,' chuckled Big Bill, settling back into his place.

That was, in fact, his explanation. For of course as Finnegan pulled his punches he was thinking of the ten thousand dollars. Not so much that, either, as the avoidance of certain dangers at the hands of the law. It was a practice of Mr. Bill's to investigate the past lives of prominent people in all lines of work, from time to time. It was true that the detective agencies often sent in big bills, but it was equally true that he managed to reap large profits now and then. Besides, the knowledge gave him that divine power over other men which he relished more than all else in the world.

In this instance what he had learned was so unimportant and so outlawed by time that it would have amounted to nothing, except that he had been able to reinforce his knowledge with a powerful bluff. That bluff had turned Pop Finnegan white with fear. He was crumbling under the attack when Big Bill turned to the sweet music of a cash offer. He felt, after the interview ended, that he might have bought out the Finnegans for five or six thousand. In that respect he had been careless, for, having victory in sight, he had named the figure upon which he already had planned.

It was the second or the third round. He cared not which. Finnegan, dancing through his usual maze, was caught by the gliding Negro with two blows that sent a smacking impact through the loud-speaker.

Finnegan covered, stabbed feebly at the black whirlwind, retreated, felt the ropes against his back, and hit through an opening with all his might. The punch caught LaRue high on the chest. Even when he was stung, Slam dared not strike at a vital spot for fear of abrogating his agreement with a knockout punch!

Big Bill laughed a little. It always amused him, in fact, when he considered how money controls men in love and hate, in war and peace. He, for ten small thousands, was able to insure the winning of fifty. Of course it was not a matter of the ten thousand but the leverage he had given to that sum, so that it outweighed the fifty, in the minds of the Finnegans. It outweighed the chance at the championship for rising young Slam Finnegan; it outweighed his pride in three score honest battles. Ten thousand dollars was a quicksand that imprisoned his feet and left him helpless before the Negro.

The joy of command brimmed the very soul of Big Bill. His sense of power was no less great because it was secret.

Snipe Dickinson yelled out, somewhere along in the seventh round: 'Yella! Yella! Finnegan's yella. . . . See that dirty Irish Mick, Bill? He's yella as a dog! He won't fight!'

But Sammy Rosenbloom said a moment later: 'He ain't yella. He's doing about his best, but the nigger's too good for him. The nigger's lefting him to death. . . .'

It was true. Whatever Finnegan might have done with an honest start, he seemed hopelessly out of it now. The left hand of Little David was hitched to his head with a strong elastic and could not miss the mark. It kept the hair of Finnegan leaping up. Now the Negro began to throw the right. The blows glanced. They cut a gash over Finnegan's left eye; they swelled the entire left side of his face; now and then they plumped home deep in the body, shots to the wind that would have brought down a giant, eventually.

Well, the next round was the eighth and then, according to agreement, Finnegan could make his dive and be out of his misery. Only an Irishman, thought Big Bill, would have endured so patiently and made the fight seem so real. In his heart he registered a vow never to forget the Irish — never to forget to use them and to pay them liberally. He felt about the entire Irish nation as a great general feels about the stout fellows who go over the top for him.

The round ended with Little David dancing to his corner, sitting laughing on his stool, while Slam Finnegan stumbled back to his place on loose knees and with hanging head.

'Little David, play on your harp!' shouted the ringside jester.

A few people laughed. Most of them turned sour faces, for Finnegan was a great favorite.

Sammy said: 'When there ain't no jump to the spark, any more, what can they do? Look at Dempsey in Philadelphia. In there with Firpo he was a tiger; down there in Philadelphia he was a tame pup and got clawed to pieces. The best of 'em . . . . They just bog down all at once. But to see Slam go this way, eh?'

Jap had leaped to her feet with her hands cupped at her mouth. Her thin young voice cut through the muddy roar of the crowd.

'Hey, Slam! Hey, Slam, Slam, Slam!'

Slam Finnegan was lying back against the ropes, his body newly drenched and polished with water, his back bent in under his own weight, his flaccid belly lifting, falling with his breathing, while a handler snapped a bath towel to give him a cooling breeze and his father worked on his wounds to stop the bleeding. But it seemed that the voice of the girl reached clearly to the punch-drunk brain of Slam, for now he lifted himself, waving his father aside, and stared down through the dazzle of the lights straight toward her.

Big Bill, at that moment, had risen to say at the girl's ear: 'Take it easy, Jap. He'll be out of pain pretty soon.'

She only screeched: 'Slam, wake up! Wake up, Slam!'

Slam seemed to be waking up. He shaded his dazzled eyes with a glove and stared again. Then the fifteen-second gong was rung and the seconds left the ring. Slam Finnegan rose, but still with turned head he studied the distant figures as though he had forgotten all about the Negro who was slithering across the ring to meet him.

'Stop it!' yelled someone close to the ear of Big Bill. 'Hey, stop it! He's out on his feet!'

'Stop it!' roared Big Bill, and yet he felt like laughing except that the face of Finnegan was puckering strangely almost as though he were about to weep, or shout in a frenzy. He turned at the last instant to meet Little David.

The Negro popped in his left three times. He was hitting perfectly, well accustomed to an unresisting target.

Then something happened. The trained eye of Big Bill could not have missed it and did, in fact, see that Finnegan countered just inside a driving punch; but his mind refused to believe that he was watching Little David walk backward on his heels toward the center of the ring while an Irishman with a bleeding, convulsed face rushed after him.

Those punches were very wild. LaRue, though badly dazed, instinctively wrapped himself in a perfect defense. Finnegan stood up on his toes and with a right fist that was a leaden club beat on the side of LaRue's head.

LaRue gave ground. He began to run. Finnegan swung himself off his feet and landed on the canvas full length. When he rose, LaRue was able to fight again, though still in full retreat.

The air of the Garden was no longer a smoking mist but a continual explosion with an endless siren screaming through the mist. Big Bill felt that he was going mad. The Finnegans had sold him out, and yet that could not be the case, for when he climbed onto his seat as every man in the house had done before him, he was able to see the face of Pop Finnegan as he crouched, making himself small, an animal fear in his eyes.

Big Bill looked up, as though for superior guidance, and beyond the glaring cone of the ring lights he saw the dim upper galleries with the pallor of crowded faces through the shadow like stones under water. It seemed to Bill that this world had no mountains except heaps of human flesh and that no winds moved upon its face except the insane screaming of human voices. A mind had been in control only a moment before and that was the mind of Bill, but now the contact was lost, all was rushing to witness ruin.

The gong sounded the end of the round like a small voice in the distance.

No one sat down. Snipe Dickinson screamed: 'You see it, Bill? The kid was holding it all the time. Like a Bonthron sprint finish. He let the nigger wear himself out, and then he started. . . .'

That was what the sports writers were getting into words as fast as their fingers could work; that was what the announcer was broadcasting; but it held no meaning for Big Bill. Pathetically, with the eyes of a child, he looked up to the misty rafters, he looked back into the ring. Three men with fear-tightened faces were working over Little David, who lay back on the ropes while Finnegan sat alert on the edge of his stool. Pop, on one knee, poured advice at him with a savage leering mouth, and shook a fist under his chin, but Slam pushed the old man off to the end of his long left arm and rose with the gong.

Then Big Bill partly understood. Old Pop was all right. It was Slam who had gone mad. That, thought Bill, was the trouble with the Irish. You never could tell. A lot of sparkle like champagne, and then a hell of a headache.

But fifty thousand dollars . . . a year's profits . . . a year of wasted life . . . .

'There oughta be a law . . .' shouted Big Bill, and found that his voice was the babbling of a voiceless child beside a roaring sea.

For Little David could still fight and did fight. He met the Irishman almost in the middle of the ring, stopped him with a stone wall of straight lefts and then crossed his right to the head, to the cheek, to the jaw.

Finnegan fell on his back so hard that his head bounced from the canvas.

Bill said through the tornado of screeching, to the profound stillness of his heart: 'What a beauty . . . on the button! He can't get up. Oh, God, don't let him get up!'

The referee, down almost on one knee, used his left hand as one half of a megaphone to make the shouted numbers reach the ear of Finnegan. His whole body swayed gracefully in rhythm with his long arm which beat out the count.

'Three . . . four . . . five . . .'

Finnegan stirred.

'He can't get up!' said Bill to his heart.

He reached out his hands. The spiritual weight of them would press Slam back to the canvas.

Finnegan turned over on his face.

Something burned the mouth of Bill. It was his cigar. He spat it out. It hit the back of Jap's fur coat and dropped to the floor.

'Eight . . . nine . . . .'

Finnegan thrust himself up on his arms and swayed to his feet. He was half turned from the Negro and LaRue, seeing that wide target, forgot all the years of gymnasium instruction and risked a wide swing. It landed with a jarring thud – on the lifted shoulder of Finnegan!

And then came the clinch.

'Shake him off!' screamed Bill. 'Push him away . . . and kill him! Kill him!'

LaRue pushed Slam Finnegan away and smashed with both hands, his face grown apelike with the grin of effort. The blows skidded off the ducking head of Slam. He fell into another clinch. The referee worked hard to pry them apart; they separated; and as LaRue smashed with his right again, Finnegan's leaden fist banged home inside the punch. A perfect counter. With dull eyes Bill watched Little David's knees sag.

It was his time to run, now, but apparently he could not believe that a man who one moment before had been helpless was now formidable. So he went in with flailing gloves to the attack.

'Keep away from him!' screamed the sore throat of Bill. 'He's ready again . . . keep away . . . you nigger fool, don't you know he's *Irish?*'

Someone was beating his shoulder. His hat was joggling over awry on his head. But the trained eye saw everything. It watched the two stabbing lefts with which Finnegan staggered Little David back to the right distance. It saw the right poised with a tremor of dreadful power.

Big Bill wanted to close his eyes but he was crucified and had to see fate fulfilled. The blow landed. It seemed to take Little David by the chin and pull out his face to twice its normal length. The Negro fell straight forward and knocked himself out a second time against the floor.

Sammy said: 'Wasn't it great? Ever see anything like it? . . . Hey, Chief!'

Big Bill did not answer. He only smiled as in death he would smile.

Jap was jerking the lapel of his dinner coat.

'Give me back the flower,' she was crying. 'Slam pinned it on me his own self. I forgot! He'll wanta see it on me!'

He let her take the gardenia but still he held her by the arm with his shaking hand.

'Slam Finnegan . . . *he* pinned that stinking flower on you? Slam did that?'

'Sure he did! What's eating you, Papa?'

But Big Bill could not answer, for again he was seeing the picture of young Finnegan in his corner at the end of the seventh round peering under his shaded eyes at the girl. How clearly Slam must have seen the familiar face of Big Bill, large as two in the crowded picture, and beneath it, almost brushing the fat of the throat, the little white gardenia with its three big shining leaves, for luck.

'Let's go home, Sammy,' he said. 'Why do we care a damn about the wind-up fight?'

The noise of the storm had not abated a great deal when Sammy Rosenbloom went with him up the aisle.

'Are you gunna leave the gal, Chief?' asked Sammy. 'Are you gunna chuck her?'

'Doncha see she was only stringin' me from the start?' demanded Big Bill, in a feeble rage.

'Stringing . . . you?' gasped Sammy.

'Yeah, me, me, me!' groaned Bill. 'She's Slam Finnegan's girl. She was only building things with a big shot so's to help Slam.'

'You mean that Slam . . . you mean a classy kid like her . . .' protested Sammy.

'Ah, shut up!' commanded Big Bill, and to himself he muttered: 'Am I getting old, or something?'

They got out into the lobby. Other men came with them, slowly, weak in the knees. Some of them carried their coats and the faces of all were streaming with perspiration. Torn programs littered the floor and the sidewalk. Rain was falling, silver bright, a veil that only half covered the face of this wretched world. He was as sad as Monday morning, as lonely as a telephone ringing in an empty room. His chauffeur, signaling from the distance, was a ghost half lost in the gloomy chaos of time and space.

'The trouble with you, Sammy, is you don't understand,' said Big Bill, sadly.

'Understand what, Chief?' asked Sammy.

'Gardenias, you fool!' shouted Big Bill.

Wine on the Desert

Faust once recalled that when he first began writing stories each idea seemed the last he could find, but then by degrees his story-finding faculty increased. 'You spot stories in the air, flying out of conversations, out of books.' Stories also arise, he said, out of the inversions of things as they are found. 'You sit at the rich man's table; well, what if he were broke and this were the last time he could entertain?' Or: 'When you read a story, pause when halfway through; finish the story in detail out of your imagination; write it down in brief notes. Then read the story through to the end. Often you find that you have a totally new final half of a story. Fit in a new beginning and there you are.'

Faust believed that good prose, fictional or nonfictional, 'should be clear, economical, and should express movement.' He usually wrote with zest, filling his pages with action. 'I enjoy seeing the pages pile up,' he said. Sometimes they piled up at the rate of forty to fifty a day. 'All that can save fiction is enormous verve, a real sweep, plus richness of character, blood that can be seen shining through.' Though he disparaged his prose, he could not help pouring his deepest psychic and moral concerns into it, or refrain from using the action he loved so well.

Frank Blackwell, editor of *Western Story,* told Faust, 'There are only two kinds of plots, "pursuit and capture" and "delayed revelation," and the latter is merely a variant of the former.' In 'Wine on the Desert' there are, in muted form, the plot elements noted by Blackwell, in addition to Faust's precepts of clarity, economy, movement, verve, and richness of character. The story appeared in the

Sunday newspaper magazine *This Week* (June 7, 1936). At the time, *This Week* claimed the largest readership of any magazine in the world – 25 million Americans of a total 125 million at that time – thus perhaps making Faust, author of ninety-two books and over 600 magazine stories, one of the world's most widely read authors.

The focus here, as in many of Faust's westerns, is the struggle between good and evil. Good prevails but only narrowly. As David L. Fox and other students of Faust's work have pointed out, Faust's treatment of good and evil is often ambivalent (perhaps most notably in *Silvertip's Trap* [Dodd, Mead, 1943] which pits a strong hero against a similarly strong villain named Barry Christian). Written when he was doing his best work in many genres, 'Wine on the Desert' is Faust's best known and most anthologized western story.

T HERE WAS NO hurry, except for the thirst, like clotted salt, in the back of his throat, and Durante rode on slowly, rather enjoying the last moments of dryness before he reached the cold water in Tony's house. There was really no hurry at all. He had almost twenty-four hours' head start, for they would not find his dead man until this morning. After that, there would be perhaps several hours of delay before the sheriff gathered a sufficient posse and started on his trail. Or perhaps the sheriff would be fool enough to come alone.

Durante had been able to see the wheel and fan of Tony's windmill for more than an hour, but he could not make out the ten acres of the vineyard until he had topped the last rise, for the vines had been planted in a hollow. The lowness of the ground, Tony used to say, accounted for the water that gathered in the well during the wet season. The rains sank through the desert sand, through the gravels beneath, and gathered in a bowl of clay hardpan far below.

In the middle of the rainless season the well ran dry but, long before that, Tony had every drop of the water pumped up into a score of tanks made of cheap corrugated iron. Slender pipe lines carried the water from the tanks to the vines and from time to time let them sip enough life to keep them until the winter darkened overhead suddenly, one November day, and the rain came down, and all the earth made a great hushing sound as it drank. Durante had heard that whisper of drinking when he was here before; but he never had seen the place in the middle of the long drought.

The windmill looked like a sacred emblem to Durante, and the twenty stodgy, tar-painted tanks blessed his eyes; but a heavy sweat broke out at once from his body. For the air of the hollow, unstirred by wind, was hot and still as a bowl of soup. A reddish soup. The vines were powdered with thin red dust, also. They were wretched, dying things to look at, for the grapes had been gathered, the new wine had been made, and now the leaves hung in ragged tatters.

Durante rode up to the squat adobe house and right through the entrance into the patio. A flowering vine clothed three sides of the little court. Durante did not know the name of the plant, but it had large white blossoms with golden hearts that poured sweetness on the air. Durante hated the sweetness. It made him more thirsty.

He threw the reins of his mule and strode into the house. The water cooler stood in the hall outside the kitchen. There were two jars made of a porous stone, very ancient things, and the liquid which distilled through the pores kept the contents cool. The jar on the left held water; that on the right contained wine. There was a big tin dipper hanging on a peg beside each jar. Durante tossed off the cover of the vase on the left and plunged it in until the delicious coolness closed well above his wrist.

'Hey, Tony,' he called. Out of his dusty throat the cry was a mere groaning. He drank and called again, clearly, 'Tony!'

A voice pealed from the distance.

Durante, pouring down the second dipper of water, smelled the alkali dust which had shaken off his own clothes. It seemed to him that heat was radiating like light from his clothes, from his body, and the cool dimness of the house was soaking it up. He heard the wooden leg of Tony bumping on the ground, and Durante grinned; then Tony came in with that hitch and sideswing with which he accommodated the stiffness of his artificial leg. His brown face shone with sweat as though a special ray of light were focused on it.

'Ah, Dick!' he said. 'Good old Dick! . . . How long since you came last! . . . Wouldn't Julia be glad! Wouldn't she be glad!'

'Ain't she here?' asked Durante, jerking his head suddenly away from the dripping dipper.

'She's away at Nogalez,' said Tony. 'It gets so hot. I said, "You go up to Nogalez, Julia, where the wind don't forget to blow." She cried, but I made her go.'

'Did she cry?' asked Durante.

'Julia . . . that's a good girl,' said Tony.

'Yeah. You bet she's good,' said Durante. He put the dipper quickly to his lips but did not swallow for a moment; he was grinning too widely. Afterward he said: 'You wouldn't throw some water into that mule of mine, would you, Tony?'

Tony went out with his wooden leg clumping loud on the wooden floor, softly in the patio dust. Durante found the hammock in the corner of the patio. He lay down in it and watched the color of sunset flush the mists of desert dust that rose to the zenith. The water was soaking through his body; hunger began, and then the rattling of pans in the kitchen and the cheerful cry of Tony's voice:

'What you want, Dick? I got some pork. You don't want pork. I'll make you some good Mexican beans. Hot. Ah ha, I know that old Dick. I have plenty of good wine for you, Dick. Tortillas. Even Julia can't make tortillas like me. . . . And what about a nice young rabbit?'

'All blowed full of buckshot?' growled Durante.

'No, no. I kill them with the rifle.'

'You kill rabbits with a rifle?' repeated Durante, with a quick interest.

'It's the only gun I have,' said Tony. 'If I catch them in the sights, they are dead. . . . A wooden leg cannot walk very far. . . . I must kill them quick. You see? They come close to the house about sunrise and flop their ears. I shoot through the head.'

'Yeah? Yeah?' muttered Durante. 'Through the head?' He relaxed, scowling. He passed his hand over his face, over his head.

Then Tony began to bring the food out into the patio and lay it on a small wooden table; a lantern hanging against the wall of the house included the table in a dim half circle of light. They sat there and ate. Tony had scrubbed himself for the meal. His hair was soaked in water and sleeked back over his round skull. A man in the desert might be willing to pay five dollars for as much water as went to the soaking of that hair.

Everything was good. Tony knew how to cook, and he knew how to keep the glasses filled with his wine.

'This is old wine. This is my father's wine. Eleven years old,' said Tony. 'You look at the light through it. You see that brown in the red? That's the soft that time puts in good wine, my father always said.'

'What killed your father?' asked Durante.

Tony lifted his hand as though he were listening or as though he were pointing out a thought.

'The desert killed him. I found his mule. It was dead, too. There was a leak in the canteen. My father was only five miles away when the buzzards showed him to me.'

'Five miles? Just an hour. . . . Good Lord!' said Durante. He stared with big eyes. 'Just dropped down and died?' he asked.

'No,' said Tony. 'When you die of thirst, you always die just one way. . . . First you tear off your shirt, then your undershirt. That's to be cooler. . . . And the sun comes and cooks your bare skin. . . . And then you think . . . there is water everywhere, if you dig down far enough. You begin to dig. The dust comes up your nose. You start screaming. You break your nails in the sand. You wear the flesh off the tips of your fingers, to the bone.' He took a quick swallow of wine.

'Without you seen a man die of thirst, how d'you know they start to screaming?' asked Durante.

'They got a screaming look when you find them,' said Tony. 'Take some more wine. The desert never can get to you here. My father showed me the way to keep the desert away from the hollow. We live pretty good here? No?'

'Yeah,' said Durante, loosening his shirt collar. 'Yeah, pretty good.'

Afterward he slept well in the hammock until the report of a rifle waked him and he saw the color of dawn in the sky. It was such a great, round bowl that for a moment he felt as though he were above, looking down into it.

He got up and saw Tony coming in holding a rabbit by the ears, the rifle in his other hand.

'You see?' said Tony. 'Breakfast came and called on us!' He laughed.

Durante examined the rabbit with care. It was nice and fat and it had been shot through the head. Through the middle of the head. Such a shudder went down the back of Durante that he washed gingerly before breakfast; he felt that his blood was cooled for the entire day.

It was a good breakfast, too, with flapjacks and stewed rabbit with green peppers, and a quart of strong coffee. Before they had finished, the sun struck through the east window and started them sweating.

'Gimme a look at that rifle of yours, Tony, will you?' Durante asked.

'You take a look at my rifle, but don't you steal the luck that's in it,' laughed Tony. He brought the fifteen-shot Winchester.

'Loaded right to the brim?' asked Durante.

'I always load it full the minute I get back home,' said Tony.

'Tony, come outside with me,' commanded Durante.

They went out from the house. The sun turned the sweat of Durante to hot water and then dried his skin so that his clothes felt transparent.

'Tony, I gotta be damn mean,' said Durante. 'Stand right there where I can see you. Don't try to get close. . . . Now listen. . . . The sheriff's gunna be along this trail some time today, looking for me. He'll load up himself and all his gang with water out of your tanks. Then he'll follow my sign across the desert. Get me? He'll follow if he finds water on the place. But he's not gunna find water.'

'What you done, poor Dick?' said Tony. 'Now look. . . . I could hide you in the old wine cellar where nobody . . . .'

'The sheriff's not gunna find any water,' said Durante. 'It's gunna be like this.'

He put the rifle to his shoulder, aimed, fired. The shot struck the base of the nearest tank, ranging down through the bottom. A semicircle of darkness began to stain the soil near the edge of the iron wall.

Tony fell on his knees. 'No, no, Dick! Good Dick!' he said. 'Look! All the vineyard. It will die. It will turn into old, dead wood. Dick . . . .'

'Shut your face,' said Durante. 'Now I've started, I kinda like the job.'

Tony fell on his face and put his hands over his ears. Durante drilled a bullet hole through the tanks, one after another. Afterward, he leaned on the rifle.

'Take my canteen and go in and fill it with water out of the cooling jar,' he said. 'Snap into it, Tony!'

Tony got up. He raised the canteen, and looked around him, not at the tanks from which the water was pouring so that the noise of the earth drinking was audible, but at the rows of his vineyard. Then he went into the house.

Durante mounted his mule. He shifted the rifle to his left hand and drew out the heavy Colt from its holster. Tony came dragging back to him, his head down. Durante watched Tony with a careful revolver but he gave up the canteen without lifting his eyes.

'The trouble with you, Tony,' said Durante, 'is you're yellow. I'd of fought a tribe of wildcats with my bare hands, before I'd let 'em do what I'm doin' to you. But you sit back and take it.'

Tony did not seem to hear. He stretched out his hands to the vines.

'Ah, my God,' said Tony. 'Will you let them all die?'

Durante shrugged his shoulders. He shook the canteen to make sure that it was full. It was so brimming that there was hardly room for the liquid to make a sloshing sound. Then he turned the mule and kicked it into a dogtrot.

Half a mile from the house of Tony, he threw the empty rifle to the ground. There was no sense packing that useless weight, and Tony with his peg leg would hardly come this far.

Durante looked back, a mile or so later, and saw the little image of Tony picking up the rifle from the dust, then staring earnestly after his guest. Durante remembered the neat little hole clipped through the head of the rabbit. Wherever he went, his trail never could return again to the vineyard in the desert. But then, commencing to picture to himself the arrival of the sweating sheriff and his posse at the house of Tony, Durante laughed heartily.

The sheriff's posse could get plenty of wine, of course, but without water a man could not hope to make the desert voyage, even with a mule or a horse to help him on the way. Durante patted the full, rounding side of his canteen. He might even now begin with the first sip but it was a luxury to postpone pleasure until desire became greater.

He raised his eyes along the trail. Close by, it was merely dotted with occasional bones, but distance joined the dots into an unbroken chalk line which wavered with a strange leisure across the Apache Desert, pointing toward the cool blue promise of the mountains. The next morning he would be among them.

A coyote whisked out of a gully and ran like a gray puff of dust on the wind. His tongue hung out like a little red rag from the side of his mouth; and suddenly Durante was dry to the marrow. He uncorked and lifted his canteen. It had a slightly sour smell; perhaps the sacking which covered it had grown a trifle old. And then he poured a great mouthful of lukewarm liquid. He had swallowed it before his senses could give him warning.

It was wine!

He looked first of all toward the mountains. They were as calmly blue, as distant as when he had started that morning. Twenty-four hours not on water, but on wine!

'I deserve it,' said Durante. 'I trusted him to fill the canteen. . . . I deserve it. Curse him!' With a mighty resolution, he quieted the panic in his soul. He would not touch the stuff until noon. Then he would take one discreet sip. He would win through.

Hours went by. He looked at his watch and found it was only ten

o'clock. And he had thought that it was on the verge of noon! He uncorked the wine and drank freely and, corking the canteen, felt almost
as though he needed a drink of water more than before. He sloshed the
contents of the canteen. Already it was horribly light.

Once, he turned the mule and considered the return trip; but he could
remember the head of the rabbit too clearly, drilled right through the
center. The vineyard, the rows of old twisted, gnarled little trunks with
the bark peeling off . . . every vine was to Tony like a human life. And
Durante had condemned them all to death!

He faced the blue of the mountains again. His heart raced in his
breast with terror. Perhaps it was fear and not the suction of that dry
and deadly air that made his tongue cleave to the roof of his mouth.

The day grew old. Nausea began to work in his stomach, nausea
alternating with sharp pains. When he looked down, he saw that there
was blood on his boots. He had been spurring the mule until the red
ran down from its flanks. It went with a curious stagger, like a rocking
horse with a broken rocker; and Durante grew aware that he had been
keeping the mule at a gallop for a long time. He pulled it to a halt. It
stood with wide-braced legs. Its head was down. When he leaned from
the saddle, he saw that its mouth was open.

'It's gunna die,' said Durante. 'It's gunna die . . . what a fool I been . . . .'

The mule did not die until after sunset. Durante left everything except
his revolver. He packed the weight of that for an hour and discarded it,
in turn. His knees were growing weak. When he looked up at the stars
they shone white and clear for a moment only, and then whirled into
little racing circles and scrawls of red.

He lay down. He kept his eyes closed and waited for the shaking to
go out of his body, but it would not stop. And every breath of darkness
was like an inhalation of black dust.

He got up and went on, staggering. Sometimes he found himself
running.

Before you die of thirst, you go mad. He kept remembering that. His
tongue had swollen big. Before it choked him, if he lanced it with his
knife the blood would help him; he would be able to swallow. Then he
remembered that the taste of blood is salty.

Once, in his boyhood, he had ridden through a pass with his father
and they had looked down on the sapphire of a mountain lake, a hundred
thousand million tons of water as cold as snow . . .

When he looked up, now, there were no stars; and this frightened him terribly. He never had seen a desert night so dark. His eyes were failing, he was being blinded. When the morning came, he would not be able to see the mountains, and he would walk around and around in a circle until he dropped and died.

No stars, no wind; the air as still as the waters of a stale pool, and he in the dregs at the bottom . . . .

He seized his shirt at the throat and tore it away so that it hung in two rags from his hips.

He could see the earth only well enough to stumble on the rocks. But there were no stars in the heavens. He was blind: he had no more hope than a rat in a well. Ah, but Italian devils know how to put poison in wine that will steal all the senses or any one of them: and Tony had chosen to blind Durante.

He heard a sound like water. It was the swishing of the soft deep sand through which he was treading; sand so soft that a man could dig it away with his bare hands. . . .

Afterward, after many hours, out of the blind face of that sky the rain began to fall. It made first a whispering and then a delicate murmur like voices conversing, but after that, just at the dawn, it roared like the hoofs of ten thousand charging horses. Even through that thundering confusion the big birds with naked heads and red, raw necks found their way down to one place in the Apache Desert.

Virginia Creeper

Like some of the more unusual work of Faust's mature period, this story had difficulty finding a publisher before it appeared in *Elk's Magazine* (August 1937).
It could be set anywhere, yet rarely in Faust's westerns is geography stated so
specifically. Typically the locale is a never-never land, like that found in myth
and fairy tale; it is sometimes referred to as the 'mountain desert' or sometimes
an undesignated place, but clearly somewhere in the West. 'Virginia Creeper' is
specifically set in the Stockton area of the San Joaquin Valley, the region where
Faust grew up.

The story has love, courage, humor, compassion, melodrama, and touches
of poetic beauty – all typical of Faust – as well as deft portrayals of such minor
characters as Champ, the hired man, and the farm animals that Faust knew and
loved with deep affection. The story also has the ritual passage from youth to
manhood, a favorite Faust theme, and the need of a son to idealize his father.
Like his hero Steve Tucker, Faust had mixed feelings about his unsuccessful,
authoritative father with whom he clashed yet needed to idealize. Like Steve,
young Frederick was poor, he sympathized with underdogs (such as the Baccigalupis of this story), and he longed to attend college at Berkeley (where Faust
did go). Faust wanted a girl like Mildred Vincent and found one. And against
the facade of the villa in Florence where he was living when he wrote 'Virginia
Creeper' he planted and lovingly tended a similar vine.

S TEVE TUCKER pitched on; old Champ, the hired man, did the loading. Tucker's back was too narrow and his legs were too long for the neat handling of sacked wheat or baled hay, but his very length gave him a greater leverage on a pitchfork. They were getting in the last of the hay crop on the land John Tucker had rented from the Mullihans. It had been planted for wheat but the crop had suffered for the lack of spring rains. The growth had been cut for hay which ran about a ton and a half to the acre. Now the sun was still high, but Steve Tucker hurried his work because there was a three-mile haul to the home barn and all the chores to do before dark. He leaned well over the shocks of hay and drove his fork straight down until the tines grated on the hard dobe soil; then he swayed back, got the end of the fork under his leg, and made a final heave. Sometimes, though he almost sat down to his work, the shock would only be staggered by the first effort; but the second one would bring it up, though his left arm shook like a wire in the wind and his knees turned sick with weakness.

The great forkful, rising high above him, crushed down on top of the wagon load where Champ walked back and forth, building the sides as straight and true as though he were constructing a stack to stand out all winter. He had a knack for doing this.

They got the last shock aboard and the tines of the fork shivered and sang as Tucker raked together the last wisps of the hay and tossed it up.

'I seen Dago Joe when he was good, and Jump Watterson, too, but all I gotta say is you sure can pitch hay,' said Champ.

'Go on,' protested Tucker. 'Anybody with two hands and a back can pitch hay, but a stacker is born, not made. You've got three tons and a half on top of that old rack.'

He looked with admiration up the straight, shimmering sides of the load; then he climbed up to the driver's seat, stepping on the tongue of the wagon, then on the croup of the near wheeler, and so to the high seat. Champ, with a pitchfork on each side of him, already had sunk down on the crest of the load. That was why Champ had not got on in the world. His brain stopped as soon as his hands had finished working.

The four horses looked absurdly inadequate for starting such a mountain of hay. The forward thrust of the load hid half the length of the wheelers.

'Hey, boys. Gittup!' called Steve. 'Hey, Charlie, Prince! Hey – Queen!'

He always saved her name for the last. The old bay mare on the off wheel needed a moment for digging her hoofs into the ground and stretching her long, low body. The other three already had their traces taut and their hipstraps lifting, but the wagon was not budged until Queen came into her collar. As she made her lift, the near wheeler came back a little, fairly pulled out of place by her surge; then the wagon lurched ahead.

It was a stiff pull because the wheels were cutting well down through the surface of the dobe. The horses leaned forward, stamping to get firmer foothold. Tucker could hear the breathing of the off leader, Charlie, who was a bit touched in the wind; he could hear the crinkling of the sun-whitened hay stubble under the wheels. The hay load jounced over the bumps, throwing up a sweet breath.

They passed the shack, the staggered corral, the broken-backed barn of the old Stimson place where that family had lived until the last generation, when the banks got them. The banks got everything, sooner or later. Two bad crops in a row would make the most provident farmer go borrowing and after that life was poisoned. The Stimson place, like a gloomy prophecy, was soon out of sight, but never out of mind. But now they came from the field toward the road. From the height of the field there was a big dip and a sharp rise to the top of the grade. Tucker sang out loudly, cracked the long lash of his whip, and got the team into a trot on the downslope. The wagon rolled easily almost to the crest, but there was a need for Queen's sturdy pulling to get them safely out on the top. It was always an exciting moment, that descent from the field and rise to the road, with the running gear crackling, and the load atwist and asway. Once on the broad back of the highway, the horses could rest, for though the surface was rutted and the ruts poured full of the white dust, the wheels bit through easily and found a hard undersurface. One ton in the soft of a field was as hard on a horse as two and a half tons on the road.

They were barely out on the Mariposa Road when Mildred Vincent came by on her bay mare and a fellow beside her in real riding togs. His boots shone through the layer of dobe dust with an aristocratic glimmer, it seemed to Tucker.

'Steve!' called the girl, waving. 'Oh, I'm glad to see you. Jerome, it's Steve Tucker. Jerome Bartlett, Steve. Can you come over after supper?'

'Yeah. I'd like to come. Thanks,' said Tucker.

He had taken off his hat and the hot sweat rolled down over his face and turned cool in the stir of the wind. He never was asked out for meals because he had to stay home to look after his bedridden father. Now the two galloped ahead, the stranger sitting well down into his saddle. He looked strong and straight and his tan had been built up on athletic fields and beaches; it was not the dark mahogany which comes out of work in hay and harvest fields. He rode not like a Californian, but holding the reins in both hands with his elbows close to his ribs.

'That feller if he had some gold lace on him would look like a general,' said Champ, from amidst the rustling of the hay. 'Wonder if Millie is gunna take him? Maybe he's a millionaire from San Francisco. She's come to the marryin' age, all right. There was a time when I thought you was gunna have her, Steve, but what with all that college education under her belt, I guess she'll look pretty high.'

Five years ago Steve Tucker had given up his entrance into college in order to spend one year on the ranch. His father had pointed out that one good year would make everything easier and, besides, he had gone so far in higher mathematics that he could do the four-year engineering course in three, without trouble. So Tucker had remained on the ranch, while one year lengthened to five and loss matched profit with every crop. Mildred, who had been with him in the country school and who had been two years behind him at Stockton High School, would be a college senior that fall. She was the symbol and indicator of the distance he had been left behind by life which flows so softly and travels so far.

He roused himself from that thought to find that the team was picking up speed; in fact, they were nearing the home corral and the roof of the little house showed beyond the top of the fig tree. Now they swept from the crest of the road into the corral; the side of the hayload made a rushing sound against the barn and he jammed on the long, iron-handled brake when the center of the wagon was just beneath the door of the mow.

The sun was growing large in the west, now. 'We'll pitch off the hay in the morning,' he said to Champ. 'You take care of the team and I'll get the cows milked. Put some salve on the shoulder of Queen. Dig out the padding so the collar won't press on the sore tomorrow.'

'She oughta be laid up till that shoulder heals,' said Champ. He was always solicitous of Queen's well-being.

'I know she should, but what can we do?'

The cows were already waiting at the pasture gate. Old Red was lowing with impatience, and Whitey was dripping milk into the dust. She must lose two or three quarts a day. Steve pulled the creaking gate open and watched the five cows, the three heifers, the four knock-kneed calves come hurrying for water. The youngsters galloped, the cows went with a long wallowing shamble.

Tucker walked to the house, scrubbed his hands with yellow soap, got the milking stool and two three-gallon buckets. They rattled together as he went back down the boardwalk to the corral.

'Stevie!' called his father's voice from the upstairs window.

'Hey, Dad,' he called.

But his face did not light until he noticed the green pattern of the Virginia Creeper which was opening a beautiful green fan along the unpainted side of the shack.

'Hurry it up!' called John Tucker.

'Yeah – hurrying,' said Steve, and went on in a gloom.

The weighted rope slammed the gate to the corral behind him and sent a long, mournful echo through his heart. Over at the Vincent place Millie and that neat young fellow, Jerome Bartlett, would be sitting out on the green of the lawn, laughing and talking.

It seemed to Tucker five years at least since he had laughed.

The cows had finished drinking. They stood about switching their tails at flies or streaking their sides with saliva as they reached back to lick away the itch.

'So-o-o, Boss!' called Tucker. 'So-o-o, Red! Old Red! Come, girl! Come on, damn you! So-o-o, Red!'

The old cow waddled out of the mud near the watering trough and ambled towards him. She looked like the model of some fat-bellied merchant tub with a queer figurehead carved at one end and the hafts of four slender oars at work out of all time with one another. After her drifted the other cows, stopping to kick at flies and then forgetting what they had been about. But at last they were all gathered in a lower corner of the corral. He milked old Whitey first because she was losing in a steady trickle. Under the big grip of his hands, it gushed out of her. It ran as if from two faucets. He held the pail between his feet and he could feel the vibration of the tin as the heavy streams thumped against it. They made loud, chiming sounds. Even when the pail was almost full, the milk plumped through the inches of froth with a resonant pulsation. And a steaming sweetness rose into the face of Tucker.

The roan-colored two-year-old heifer was the hardest and the most fidgety to handle. She held up her milk. He had to squeeze so hard that it hurt her and she kept lifting a hind foot and kicking out behind her. Steve's hands and forearms were aching when he finished with her and carried the two brimming buckets back toward the house. The sun was a great red face over the blue of the Coast Range; in the eastern sky the twilight color was gathering before the sunset.

He strained the milk into wide-mouthed gallon tins which he placed in the cooler outside the house. It was a tall frame of shelves with burlap nailed about it and water siphoning over it day and night from a big pan on top. The evaporation kept butter fairly firm even when the temperature was a hundred degrees in the shade.

He started the fire in the kitchen stove, put on the kettle of water, and heard his father calling, 'Steve! Oh, Steve!'

He went upstairs and entered the room. It was the best in the house but that was not saying a great deal. Rain seepage had stained the roses of the wallpaper and the ceiling had never been plastered. One looked through the crisscross of the laths up to the slanting rafters of the roof. The window, which faced west, was filled with the brillance of the sunset and one little branch of a green translucence had crawled a foot or so across the screen.

'Look at this. It just came this afternoon,' said John Tucker, heaving himself up in the bed. Sometimes he seemed to Steve stronger than ever above the hips but below them his legs were dead, whitened shanks with the feet like great deformities at the ends of them. He held out a letter in a hand that had grown so white that the veins across the back of it showed as blue as ink.

Steve read:

Mr. John Tucker,
R. F. D. No. 4,
Box 188.

Dear Sir:

We beg to confirm our letter dated 18 May and regret that we have had no reply to our request.

While we beg to remit you herewith enclosed your bill up to the end of May, we again ask you the favor to remit us cheque in settlement of same, as we cannot at all, wait no longer for this payment on account of great difficulties we are crossing in trade.

Trusting to be favored and to save us further corrispondence on this matter, we beg to remain

Yours obedient.
THE FIVE MILE STORE
Baccigalupi and Baccigalupi.
(Signed) Joseph Baccigalupi.

As Steve lifted his eyes, his father growled through his beard, 'There's no Dago as bad as a damned Portuguese Dago.' He smoothed the sleek of his bald head with one hand and added, 'They want to be saved further correspondence in this matter, eh? They can all be damned!'

'They're better to deal with than a bank,' answered the son. 'The interest is no higher and they don't stick a gun under your nose when the money comes due. The Baccigalupis are all right.'

'Don't tell me what's right!' exclaimed John Tucker. 'I can remember back when there were *business* people to deal with in California. I can remember when I could go into Stockton and have any bank in the damned town glad to give me five thousand dollars. Why? Because my name was good. That's why. They loaned money to *men,* in those days. Now they lend it to machines and dirt.'

'I'll go down tomorrow and see Joe Baccigalupi, but – ' said Steve. He clipped his teeth together.

'What were you going to say?'

'Nothing,' said Steve.

'No, you'd rather go down in the kitchen and snarl behind my back, wouldn't you? Why don't you come out with what you've got to say?'

'I haven't anything to say,' said Steve, swallowing hard.

'That's a lie,' said his father. 'But before you go, pull the screen open and tear the vine off. What is it, anyway?'

Steve went to the window and looked down at the tender shoot.

'It's a Virginia Creeper,' he said. 'I planted it the autumn before last – and look where it is already!'

'You planted a creeper? Want to fill the house with dampness and bugs? Want to give us all malaria and rheumatism? Haven't I told you that I'd never have vines growing on my house?' shouted John Tucker.

He banged his hand on the table beside his bed so that the lamp jingled and his pile of books shook over aslant.

'Yes, I've heard you say that,' admitted Steve.

'Then what in hell do you mean? Do I have to drag myself out of the house and go around spying on you? Tear that damned vine off the screen now; and dig it up by the roots tomorrow.'

Steve tapped his fingers against the screen. It gave back a dull chiming, a flat note without resonance.

'I'd as soon – ' he murmured.

'You'd what?' barked his father.

'I'd as soon,' said Steve, 'tear out a handful of hair.'

'What are you talking about?'

Steve walked to the door.

'Come back here and tell me what the devil you mean!' roared John Tucker.

'I'd better not talk,' said Steve. 'I'm worn out, like the ground. Barley and wheat, wheat and barley for sixty years. Now nothing but tar weed and wild oats – I'd better not talk.'

'Speak up what you mean. You talk like you're drunk!'

'I'll go down and cook dinner.'

'Dinner can wait and be damned. What are you driving at? Worn out like the ground?'

'Worn out,' said Steve. 'That's what I mean. Tired out like the soil. All it gives us is trouble, now. And if I talk, all I'll give you will be trouble, tonight.'

'You will, will you? Let me hear what kind of trouble you can give me. But the first thing is – tear that damned vine off my window!'

Steve walked through the doorway and down the hall.

'Come back here – by God!' cried John Tucker. The bed creaked. There was a thumping and trailing sound across the floor, but it did not issue into the hallway as Steve went down the stairs.

He fried thin beefsteak and boiled potatoes with their jackets on. Some corn pone he had made that morning he broke into roughly triangular shapes and piled on a platter. There were mustard greens which he had picked in the field though the season of their tenderness had passed, and he had some clabber cheese. Part of this food he put on the table for Champ and himself; the rest he arranged on a tray and carried up the stairs as he had done every night for four years.

When he came into the room, the lamp was lighted. It was not as bright as the glare in the eyes of John Tucker. He cleared the table and put the tray on it.

'Now I'm going to hear you apologize.'

'For what?' said Steve, and looked straight into the electric gray of John Tucker's eyes.

It was the first time in his life, he realized, that he had dared to face that glance; but there was a hard wall of anger in him that shielded him from fear.

'The time has come,' said his father, 'when there's got to be a showdown. There can't be two captains on one ship. You'll be the boss or I'll be the boss, and as long as I own this ranch, by God, I'll do the running of it.'

Steve said nothing. He could not have unlocked his jaws for speech.

'If you don't like my way, get out!' shouted John Tucker.

'Aunt Sarah,' said Steve, slowly, 'has always wanted to come over and take care of you, and Champ will do the work on the place pretty well.'

'I'd rather have vinegar poured into milk than Sarah's face poured into my days!'

'You'll have to have somebody to look out for you.'

'You're going, are you?'

'I'm going,' said Steve.

'Sell the place tomorrow and take your share and get out, then!'

'I own Queen and Bess and the Jackson buck,' said Steve. 'That's what I'll take. I don't want a share of this place. I want to forget it.'

'Forget me, too, then! Get out of my sight and out of my life!'

Steve went down to the table and found Champ halfway through his meal.

'Old man kind of mad?' asked Champ.

'Kind of,' said Steve.

'When he gets to raring, he sure can go,' said Champ. 'I ever tell you about that time up at Angel's Camp when a couple of Dutchmen jumped him in Wilson's Bar?'

'Yeah, you told me about that,' said Steve.

'Aw, did I?' murmured Champ.

He became depressed and silent, while Steve finished eating and started the dishes. Steve went upstairs into his father's room and found that the supper tray had not been touched. John Tucker lay in bed with his big fists gripped, his eyes glaring at some terrible nothingness.

'Done?' asked Steve.

John Tucker said nothing, so Steve left the tray and went out again. He finished the dishes. Champ, who would have despised such woman's work, remained in the dining room smoking. It was his big time of the day.

'You stay on and take charge of things, Champ,' said Steve. 'Father will tell you whatever you want to know. I'm leaving in the morning.'

He put some hot water into a laundry tub on the back porch, undressed, scrubbed himself down, and went up to his room. He put on a blue serge suit, a high, hard collar that hurt his throat, and a pair of seven-dollar shoes that made his feet feel light. The softness and the snugness of them comforted his soul. Then he walked up the road to the Vincent place. A great grove surrounded that big, square, white house and there was a lawn under the trees. In the distance a pair of windmills were clanking musically; and sprinklers whirred on the lawn, filling the air with a noise like a spring wind through trees.

A piano was rousing up a tune in the front room; a lot of young voices took up the air. There was always music in the Vincent house because there was always money in the Vincent bank account.

The front door jerked open.

'Left it out here. Be back in a moment!' cried the voice of Mildred Vincent.

She left the door a bit ajar and a shaft of light followed her, bobbing on the gold of her hair.

'Hello,' said Steve.

'Hai – Steve! You gave me a start. Come on in – Just a minute while I find – '

'I can't come in,' said Steve.

'What's the matter? Is your father ill tonight?'

'No, he's the same. But I have some things to do tonight. I'm leaving in the morning.'

'Are you taking a trip? You ought to, Steve. You ought to have more fun.'

'I'm going for good.'

'Not leaving your father! Not that! But I've always said it was the most wonderful – I've always thought – '

'I'm taking a team and a Jackson buck down to the Islands. They always need men and teams down there in the haying. I can make enough to see me through most of a college year, between now and August.'

'But your father, Steve?'

'We've agreed to it. Aunt Sarah will come over and take care of him.'

'But your Aunt Sarah – '

'So I came over to say goodbye and to tell you – '

A sudden stroke of emotion stopped his voice.

'Well, goodbye,' said the girl.

She held out her hand in a certain way that stopped all talk. He barely touched it and went quickly.

It was three miles across to Aunt Sarah's place but he was glad of the chance to stretch his legs and start breathing again. By leaving home, it was plain that he was leaving Mildred Vincent farther than he had thought. Since those old days when she had been his girl, he had thought that a world of difference had opened between them, but now he could see that they had been almost hand in hand compared with the cold distance that had come between them now. Did she expect that he was to lay down all the years of his life in the service of John Tucker?

He reached the old house of Aunt Sarah and talked to her in the bareness of the front hall with the gleam of the hatrack mirror beside him and the sheen of the balusters climbing dimly up the stairs into darkness. The house was as empty as Aunt Sarah's life.

He said, 'Father and I have disagreed. If you'll come over to take care of him, I'll be glad.'

She looked at him for a long moment before she began to nod her gray head. She had something of the look of her brother, the same grimness on a smaller scale.

'He's drove everybody else out of his life; and now he's drove you, eh?' she said. 'I'll come right over.'

The parting was brief, the next morning. Steve held out his hand and said goodbye.

His father looked at the hand and then at him.

'Get out of my sight!' he said.

Down on the Islands, where the alluvial soil is deeper than wells are dug, where the drinking water is yellow and has a sweetish taste, where the ground is so rich that sometimes a fire will start it burning, where twenty sack crops of wheat are known and where triennial floods wash away the profits of the farmers, Steve Tucker found it easy to get work with his Jackson buck. He got two dollars a day for his own share, two for the machine, and a dollar a head for the horses, with keep thrown in, of course. That made a monthly net profit of a hundred and eighty dollars, minus what he spent for cigarette tobacco and brown wheat-straw paper.

The hours were long and the work was hard. The dust that flew in the

Islands stained the skin and hurt the eyes. The most cheerful men began to grow silent after a few days in that country, but Steve was silent by nature and he had set himself to a long and hard purpose.

The haypress which hired him was run by a big Scotchman with a bush of red hair on his head.

'You a Tucker that's any relation of John Tucker?' said this giant.

'I'm his son,' said Steve, and stuck out his jaw a little. No man in the world had so many enemies as his father.

The Scotchman turned to his partner.

'This here John Tucker, the kid's father,' he said, 'I seen him on Main Street in Stockton, four years back, run out and snatch a kid off the tracks from in front of a streetcar. And the car ran on and smashed him against the rear end of a dray. Your father ever get well, Tucker?'

'He's still laid up,' said Steve.

'He is, eh? Well, we'll hire you.' Then he added to his partner, 'John Tucker was as big a man as me. And he got his hips all smashed in.'

When work begins at five in the morning and ends with the coming of twilight, men are too tired to think. All that Steve recalled out of the past, during a month, was the bobbing, golden head of the girl as she had run down the steps that night, and the clenched fists and the glaring gray eyes of his father. If the work of the others was hard, his task was still more bitter, because long after they were in bed, he was shaping two by fours to take the place of the long, wooden teeth which he had broken on the Jackson buck during the day. He was thin and hollow-eyed that evening at dinner in the cookhouse when a telegram was brought to him by the owner of the farm.

It said:

YOUR FATHER VERY ILL.
PLEASE COME BACK.
MILDRED

Steve returned the next day.

A southeast wind had darkened the sky with a continual march of clouds and he told himself that John Tucker must be about to die. When he reached the house, the windmill was whirling furiously in the storm, the wheel veering from side to side, and he could hear the rapid plumping of the stream into a half-empty tank. That was a sad music fit for death scenes, he thought.

The picture of the veteran lying with gripped fists, silent in his bed, was filling his mind as a mountain fills the sky.

When he pulled open the kitchen door, it was not Aunt Sarah that he saw, but Mildred Vincent in a calico apron. He stood there with the door propped open against his rigid arm and the wind entering behind him. The room had been changed and the cookery was not stale and sour but a light fragrance through the house. He knew these things as he took in a great breath of astonishment.

'Steve!' she cried out. 'You *have* come!'

'How is he?' asked Tucker, pushing the door shut at last.

'He's changed, and thin, and he's set his will like iron. It's going to be a shock when you see him.'

'I'll go on up.'

'Just a moment. Champ is up there now, getting orders about the place.'

'Does the doctor say anything?'

'I can't get him to see a doctor. He wouldn't have your Aunt Sarah in the house. He won't let Champ come nearer than the door of his room. We got a nurse but he wouldn't let her come near him. He doesn't seem to mind having me around, so I come over every day.'

'Why?' asked Tucker.

'You know why, Steve – because every drop of blood in every Vincent should be willing to die for John Tucker.'

'They should?' he repeated, staring.

'You don't know? Do you mean to say that your father never told you the story?'

'Never.'

She drew in a great breath. 'He wouldn't!' she murmured. 'That's how great his soul is! But when my father was alive – long ago when he was a wild-headed youngster – he and another man got into trouble with a single miner – and the miner beat them, guns and all. Nearly killed father – but then the miner spent a month nursing him back to life – it was John Tucker who did that!'

A thousand moments out of his own life came back to Steve.

'Yes,' he said at last, 'he could do that. And that was why you were nice to a great gawk like me?'

'No, I liked you for your own sake. Steve, is it possible he never told you – and we such close neighbors all these years?'

Steve shook his head. An ache that had begun in his heart the day before began to stifle him.

'Has he a fever?' he asked.

'Yes. Not a high one. He won't eat – hardly anything – '

A heavy, slow step on the stairs. Steve, moving into the hall, saw Champ come down. The hired man, turning his hat between his hands, glanced up once and then walked on, blinded by his thoughts.

'I haven't told your father you were coming. I didn't dare confess I'd sent the telegram.'

'Has he mentioned me?'

'No, Steve, not once.'

She came halfway up the stairs with him.

'God bless you for coming so quickly. He's terribly changed. Be gentle with him, please.'

When Steve Tucker entered his father's room it was strangely dim as though a shade had been drawn down. Then he saw that the Virginia Creeper had grown clear across the screen, the one tendril reinforced by many. From the clouded sky, only a green gloom entered through the leaves.

'What in hell are you doing here?' asked John Tucker.

'I've come back,' said Steve.

'Who asked you back?'

'Nobody,' said Steve.

'Then get out of my sight.'

Steve said, 'I'll stay out of your sight as long as you please, but I'm keeping on the place.'

'I'll be damned before I'll have you on my land!' shouted John Tucker.

'All right, then. You'll have to be damned.'

The gray glare of the eyes fascinated him. He turned from them and went to the window. He opened the screen and ripped the little clinging feet of the ampelopsis away from the wire.

'Let that be!' cried John Tucker. 'What you mean?'

'It shuts out the light and the air,' said Steve. 'Why did you let it grow?'

'Because it damn well pleased me to let it grow. What d'you mean by – by God, I'm going to – '

He had heaved himself up on his elbows. Now that more light entered the room Steve saw how great the wastage had been. The square, jowled face was covered with lank furrows.

'What did you mean by it?' demanded Steve, pointing his finger. 'What did you mean by letting that vine cover the window and spoil your reading light?'

His father started to speak; his lips remained parted but made no utterance.

Steve sat down in the chair beside the bed.

'I've been might unhappy while I was away,' he said. 'It was lonely never hearing you growl.'

'There can't be two captains on one ship!' declared John Tucker.

'You're the captain,' said Steve.

'And what I say has got to go!'

'It goes with me,' said Steve.

'Does it?' said John Tucker. He let himself sink suddenly back into the pillows. He was breathing hard.

'I'm going to have a change of air,' he said.

'All right,' said Steve. 'I'll take good care of the place.'

'You'll come with me!'

'All right,' said Steve, 'I'll come with you, then.'

The eyes of John Tucker opened; they were the mildest blue in the world.

'Where do we go?' asked Steve.

'Down to the Bay,' said John Tucker. 'Air's brisker, down there. Down to Berkeley – get a house up there in the hills – up there near the University – '

Realization poured over Steve in floods of cold happiness.

John Tucker said, 'I waited five years for you to grow up. I waited so long that when you *did* grow up the other day, I didn't understand. But you're only a young brat still. Five years is nothing, now that you're a man. You can make up the time.'

'We both can,' said Steve.

When he left the room, a flash of something across the floor made him turn at the door. The tendrils of the ampelopsis, waving like ragged, green flags, framed a sky in which a changing wind had piled the clouds into white heaps that began to blow away like dust. The brightness on the floor had been one sudden pouring from the sun.

He found Mildred Vincent still halfway up the stairs, crying. She made a hushing sign and tiptoed down before him.

Only when she had closed the kitchen door behind them, and then in a stifled voice, did she dare to say, 'I heard everything, and it was beautiful, Steve. I know he'll get well, now. But what did you do to the vines on the window? I tried to clear them away every day, and he never would let me.'

'Well, I did it,' said Steve.

'No wonder he was in a fury! Why did you do it?'

'I needed to let in some light,' said Steve. 'It's an odd thing. I can't explain it. But he and I understand. We both gave in.'

'It makes me feel like an outsider,' she told him.

'After you've brought all this about?'

He made a gesture of wonder which she seemed to understand, for she put her hand in his, and then she was in his arms, his lips on hers, his arms crushing her, never to let go.

Pringle's Luck

'Pringle's Luck' appeared in *Cosmopolitan* (December 1937) and is a case of life imitating art and vice versa. As a boy Faust regularly fought his way into position at various schools, read the Arthurian legends with their heroic deeds of arms, and steeped himself in Scott's novels. He perceived combat – personal or otherwise – as crucial to human experience. He longed to test himself in what seemed its supreme aspect, war.

After leaving college in 1915, Faust enlisted in the Canadian Army hoping to see action in the 'Great War' against a German Kaiser who, for Faust's generation, embodied evil much as Hitler did for a later generation. When his unit, known as The American Legion, stalled at a port in Nova Scotia, Faust deserted and, risking being shot as a deserter in wartime, made his way on foot across Nova Scotia and New Brunswick to safety across the Maine–New Brunswick border. Reaching New York ragged and nearly penniless, Faust tried to enlist in an overseas ambulance unit and then in the British Army. He was rejected by both, apparently because of his shabby appearance or because of his German name.

Two years later, by then a successful writer and the married father of an infant daughter, Faust underwent surgery (at his own expense) to remove a physical disability which prevented his acceptance into the U.S. Army. Under the condition that he be sent into combat immediately, he enlisted, only to be sent instead to an Army camp to dig latrines. Faust was convinced that by not serving in combat in World War I, he had failed himself, his country, his friends, and even his children. Later, the U.S. entry into World War II gave Faust a second chance: he abandoned his lucrative Hollywood writing career and, despite his heart trouble, wangled an assignment as combat correspondent for both *Harper's* and *The Infantry Journal*. He wanted to experience modern warfare in an infantry platoon on an extended campaign and to write articles and a book about infantrymen in action. No one had ever done anything like it.

Set during World War I, 'Pringle's Luck' gives Faust's vicarious experience of battle, which he later actualized under fire.

P RINGLE FELL in the mud and lay still. Everybody else had fallen in the same way, for the sound of the shell as it dropped passed from a roar to a shrill staccato, a long bright needle of sound that drove through the brain. So every man fell flat. Pringle did not hear the explosion but he felt the earth tremble and knew the mud was being bucketed up in tons. A few drops of it struck him. They were warm, which put a horrible thought into his brain.

Then everyone was getting up and going forward again, but Second Lieutenant Walter Pringle remained in the mud; for, when he looked up, he saw through the mist by the flare of the Very light the bomb thrown by a trench mortar coming down like a little whale, sharp-nosed, with steering flanges at the tail. When one of those damned things burst it did not dig a proper hole for itself and then chuck ruin up into the air; instead, it squattered down against the earth, smashing flat and blowing out straight to the side chunks of steel as big as your arm.

On his first day in the trenches Second Lieutenant Walter Pringle saw a man cut in two by one of those flying fragments. This was his second day, and now fear cut his throat and let the courage out of him like hot blood. Nothing but a cold ichor remained stagnating in his arteries. He kept his lips fast shut, but a rapid pulse was beating against them from the inside and the pulse consisted of words, saying: 'Walter Pringle is a coward; Pringle is a coward; Pringle of the Class of 'eighteen, shot for cowardice on the field of battle; Second Lieutenant Pringle, for conduct not becoming an officer and a gentleman . . . .'

He got himself up on his elbow. Legs were going by him, sagging at the knees with labor in the mud. The feet were soundless in the uproar. Soundlessly they were going to their death – thousands, tens of thousands, millions to die in the war as insects die in hosts with the first frost.

A queer sound began to saw into his brain. It came from all around him like the song of bullfrogs in a marsh, but he knew that bullfrogs were not making the music.

He tried to keep remembering that when you hear the noise of a shell you are safe; it already is past you, traveling faster than sound. The big shells overhead left pulsations in the torn air behind them, strange rhythms like the self-starters of motors beginning, ending.

That was almost a comfort to Pringle compared with the rifle bullets singing high and thin, little flashes of wasplike sound flickering past the ears and always close, close, close, whispering intimately. A kiss from one of them, anywhere between the shoulders and the hips, and you're gone.

The hole a bullet goes in by is small; it tears hell out of you when it comes through, however. Remember when you've pricked your finger with a pin or jammed a splinter under a fingernail, and then consider what the pain must be. Pringle kept considering. Most men after they first hear the whine of the bullets lose the panic ecstasy of their terror, but he knew that his own agony never would abate. Yet he had to get up; he had to go on because his father was the colonel of his regiment.

Perhaps that was where the roots of the trouble ran. A strange surgeon is better than a friend when a vital operation must be performed, and the cold eye of discipline with a stranger behind it might have cut through to the fear that was in him and let it out, like a chilly poison. Instead, the near presence of his father sustained him in a mental gesture of reaching out for comfort, for help. Cannot we learn courage like other lessons? But he had not studied long enough; he was not sufficiently prepared when he was rushed into this examination on the battlefield.

A hand caught him under the armpit and lifted. He got to his knees, to his feet. It was Lieutenant Jim Gaffney, so thin that it was no wonder he felt at ease in the midst of battle. As well shoot at the edge of a sword as at Jim Gaffney.

'It's Big Pringle,' said Gaffney. 'Have they got you, Walter? Where?'

It seemed to Pringle that he was being held up by the scruff of the neck for the world to see by Very light a poor dangling scarecrow, a shameful mud-dripping rag of humanity.

'I'm all right,' said Pringle. 'I just – '

'You're all right!' shouted Gaffney. Then scorn twisted his face. 'Ah, hell!' he said, and went suddenly on with that wave of the attack.

Pringle tried to go after him but his feet would not stir. He made out the nature of that noise which had been sawing into his brain like the croaking of bullfrogs. Now he realized that it came from the wounded. They were all around, and some of them were screaming. Something dragged itself toward him on two arms. It had no legs.

Pringle ran forward, bogging his feet, sagging his knees at every step. He wanted to overtake Gaffney and explain; yet he knew that he never would be able to confront that face of scorn again.

Where it wasn't mud, it was up and down of trenches. The place was crazy with trenches. The ground was a junk heap, a garbage pile. There were cans everywhere, most of them untrampled. Barbed wire grew up out of the mud like horrible, thorny weeds.

There were old shoes underfoot, heels or toes sticking up, or else stamped flat on the side. All the old shoes in the world were there; and all the torn-up letters and tattered newspapers were soaking into the wet earth. In the spring a harvest of words ought to grow, loving words, and songs of international hate.

The fog was in his face, in his soul; he breathed of it, and it was like breathing smoke; and through the dreadful confusion the rifle bullets kept kissing the air close to his ear. If he could see death coming – if it would only come at him like a straight left in the boxing ring – if it were a clean, visible thing, he could stand it, but to smother in the dark of a garbage heap, a junk pile . . . .

They had gone on forever. There were no Germans to shoot at. There was no Company K. A counter-flood of noise flowed toward them, split to both sides, washed back toward the river. It was that barrier of water to their rear, he felt, which killed his heart in him. To cross a river and then plunge right ahead into German trenches, with that little river like a knife cutting off retreat – that wasn't generalship. It was madness. He listened with dread to the pouring sounds of battle that moved past them on both sides.

'It's the counterattack, isn't it?' he asked of a face.

'Sure it is, and we've caught hell,' said Lieutenant Mays. 'They've got us blocked off on both sides and in the rear, and we'll never see the Mézigny again – damn little tadpole creek!'

At least there was no more marching through the mud. The men sank down into the bog. They dropped on their backs. They were all mud, anyway, so it didn't matter. Rifle bullets flickered in the air all around them, but they didn't care for that, either.

Pringle lay a little flatter than the rest, trying not to think. If every man of them were killed, still the rumor would be alive in the world to tell people at home that Walter Pringle was yellow; that Jim Gaffney had seen him turn yellow right on the battlefield. A yellow dog who lay down in the mud and let the charge go past him. Perhaps a bullet had reached the colonel. It could not split his heart in two more surely than this news about his son.

Then the men began to drag themselves out of the mud. There was a German dugout right under them, and they were crawling down into it.

By the time Pringle got into it the dugout seemed already full, but more men were still streaming into the long tunnel with its bunks on each side. It was all concrete; the Germans knew how to make things permanent, and safe, safe, safe! He began to breathe again; his heart commenced to beat.

The air turned incredibly foul with the steam from wet, dirty bodies, but that didn't matter because there was warmth, and Pringle realized that he had been horribly cold for hours, for eternities. He began to do what others were doing, raking off mud, but all the while he was waiting, waiting, waiting for the news of his cowardice to spread until faces should turn toward him, sick with disgust. An American, but yellow; a big American, but yellow; and his father was the colonel of the regiment!

He lay down on a bunk. The autumn cold still kept touching him with fingers of ice but by degrees the heat of his body warmed his wet clothes, and the clothes then warmed his body.

In the dugout, the fuming cigarettes had thickened the air to a whiter smoke than the land mist which hung over Mézigny. Some were heating cans of bully beef over smokeless fires; some passed round a stock of Rhine-wine bottles that had been uncovered; a phonograph played German songs. Some worked over the wounded, particularly the German wounded. Some wandered about gaping at the pictures of girls over the bunks and reading aloud the strange German words of endearment that went with the signatures.

Ah, God, how kind and comfortable the Germans could be, with their beer and their music and their family devotions; and what an honest, hard-working people they were; and how could they want to turn butchery loose upon the world? Pringle would not hate them for it.

Shorty Waters was holding up the head of a wounded German, tilting a bottle of wine at his lips. The wine spilled over the fellow's throat. Waters took the bottle away. He laughed, and the German laughed.

They made a nice picture together; Pringle wanted the whole world to be filled with brothers and brotherhood. Was there not one Bach for all the world? Was there not one Shakespeare? Had not the Germans put up a statue to 'Unser Shakespeare'? These tokens of a common humanity of mind and spirit deepened the ache in Pringle's sick heart, as he waited and waited.

Then, suddenly, the colonel was upon him. He was there with Major Carlton and Captain Reeves. Pringle got up. His father laid a hand on his shoulder and bristled his short gray mustache with a smile. The major and the captain moved away from this family scene.

'Muddy business, Walter, wasn't it?' asked the colonel. Then: 'What's the matter? Have you been nicked somewhere? Are you sick?'

The lieutenant smiled a little. He could feel the smile crinkle the drying mud on his face. 'I'm sick,' he said, and waited again. The whole thing had to come out, one time or another. Then he saw truth strike like a shadow across the eyes of the colonel.

It was not until then that he saw his father's left arm was tied up in a sling. The colonel's eyes tried to hold to the face of his son but they slipped and dodged away, staring into far corners of this wretched world.

'I'll try to see you later,' he said. 'I'll try . . . .' Then he was off through the stifling mist.

Pringle's knees gave way beneath him, and he had to lie down on the bunk again. Without looking about him, he could learn from random words the history of their attack and their present situation. The attack had proceeded so swiftly because the colonel had seized on the best possible moment. But by a devil of bad luck under the fog the Germans had an unreported reserve close to the point of attack. It was that reserve which had smashed both wings of the attack.

The whole ground on both sides and behind what was left of the regiment was occupied by German troops. Now, in the thick of the land mist, for the moment contact was lost with the enemy. Colonel Pringle had some four hundred men lodged in the throat of the salient, and when they were found, the Germans would swallow them. It was time to surrender; but to those stupid brutes canned beef seemed more important than the sweetness of life. They went on cooking, eating, endlessly.

Pringle tried to keep them out of his mind but one sound continually tore open his heart. It came from a man who had been shot through the hand. Sometimes he endured for whole minutes, with grinding teeth; then the groans came, and last the horrible noise of sobbing.

The colonel's voice brought Pringle to his feet again. His father said: 'I've found a way out for you – you're going to go back to our lines. You can find the beginning of the communication trench just outside. You follow the general line of it, zigzags and all, and never leave it, because it winds up right at the edge of the Mézigny – and once in the water you're as good as home. You can swim.'

'But if they see me on the way down the trench?' asked Pringle.

'You'll have a German uniform on. We'll take one out of the dugout.'

'So that I'll be shot as a spy if they catch – '

'Don't you see that they won't catch you?' said the colonel. 'You can speak a little German. You know how to swear in it, at least. If you're challenged, start cursing and swagger your way through. Only one of all these men can live; I choose that it should be my son.'

Pringle felt himself choking.

'You'll go back to our lines,' said the colonel. 'The river twists back into them. You'll report to General Bailey that we're established here in the throat of the salient and that if he counterattacks, we'll take them with our fire from behind. Tell him that I am rigging whole lines of machine guns. As a matter of fact, I'm starting to entrench now. Tell him that, if he attacks, he's to send up a cluster of five Very lights; if I don't see the signal, at dawn I attack the Germans anyway. You understand?'

'Can you pick me out like this?' asked Pringle, trembling with hope. 'Can you give me my life like this? Won't it be held against you?'

The colonel paused. Then he said: 'I'm going to put the proposition to the regiment in very stark terms. When I ask for a volunteer to carry the message, you can be sure there'll be no sudden answer. I want you to shout at once. Do you see, Walter? I'll put it in such a way that you'll seem a hero!'

Pringle discovered suddenly that he was alone, for two steps through the mist had turned the colonel into a distant, wavering figure of black through the white, foul smother of the dugout. Now some loudly shouted orders brought the soldiers to attention. The colonel's deep voice seemed to Pringle as big as drum and bugle combined.

'We are stuck here like a fishbone in the throat of the Germans,' he said. 'If our friends across the Mézigny knew we were here, they'd make

the Germans try to swallow – and choke in the process. Our job, now,
is to let General Bailey know where we're located. If we get one man

across the trenches and over the river, I think another attack would be
launched, to help us and to use us. Otherwise, when the day comes we'll
be found and stamped out by the heavy artillery.

'The only way to get a messenger through the lines and across the
river is to put a German uniform on him. He ought to be able to speak a
little German, to help him through a pinch. We don't want a man who's
depressed by the knowledge that he's carrying the lives of four hundred
men with him; we want a fellow who'll be inspired by the thought.'

It seemed to Pringle that all the days of his American life had been
spent in sunshine, with green grass underfoot and drowsy summer hum-
mings of contentment in the air. It seemed to him that all the rest must
be thinking of their country in the same way, and that every man in the
dugout must realize that the colonel was opening a door to safety out of
this hell of mud and fog.

Then he heard the colonel saying: 'Of course a man caught in a German uniform will be shot out of hand as a spy. I don't want to minimize
the other dangers, but I'm asking for volunteers.'

He stopped. And Pringle's heart stopped at the same time. He wanted
to shout out, but his own eagerness filled his throat like a gag. A second
or two went by.

Then Pringle's voice came to him and he sang out. Many heads
turned; a space opened before him; he heard voices saying, 'Who is it?'
and then the unmistakable nasal whine of Jim Gaffney exclaiming, 'It's
Pringle! Pringle, by *God!*'

They were making a hero of him. They didn't understand – because
the colonel had not explained to them how easily the thing could be
done. Shame roused up suddenly in Pringle as he confronted his father.
Major Burnet was saying: 'We can't allow this. You can't let your boy
go, sir.'

He heard that, but he was hardly aware of words or of anything about
him as he was helped out of his uniform and into German clothes. The
dying life which fear had been gnawing at the roots was returning to
him. A mighty river of hope was beginning, a current which seemed
already to be bearing him home.

Then he was shaking hands. He saw eyes widened with admiration
and fear of what lay before him. Then his father was holding both his
hands, and now he was at the entrance of the dugout.

And then there was the mist, the fluttering nightmare battle lights, and the uncertain footing where he began to stumble the moment he took a step. He was remembering his father's face and eyes which in the moment of adieu had seemed to shine with pity, with grief, and in farewell.

He found the zigzag communication trench and followed it. The voices of the battle came and went in great flooding pulses, with moments when the uproar of the great guns trampled all thought from his mind, and again pauses of emptiness during which he was aware of the smaller noises. In those pauses he heard the thin whining of airplanes as they drew little patterns of complaint in the air.

It seemed strange that those tribes of the air should be divided against one another instead of combining in a splendid fury against all the earth dwellers. He knew the song of the three-inch shells and the handstroke of air when they passed. But always the incredibly swift, short whistlings of the rifle bullets ran through his consciousness like the dots and dashes of a telegraphic code, spelling in a thousand ways a single word. But behind and around all these sounds he was conscious of one constant utterance, like the mournful lowing of cattle far off. He refused to put his mind on that sound, because he knew it was the lament of the wounded.

Something flowed through the mist along the ground. It poured like water. He made out the helmets of a thick column of Germans pouring up the communication trench toward the front. Their feet made no sound. They were a column of ghosts already walking to death.

The full sickness of fear returned upon Pringle. He sank into the mud and remained there, hardly breathing. Rain came down with a crash. It washed the manhood out of him; it beat him like a sodden rag into the mud.

When he pulled himself to his feet again, his brain was spinning. He had forgotten in what direction he should be going. Along the communication trench – but which way?

The horizon all around offered a circle of smoky glares. There is no up or down, no north or south in hell.

He almost lurched against a tree trunk. It turned into a solid figure with a rifle at the ready, nearly touching his breast. A German voice was saying something angrily, blurred in the rain.

The prepared words came yelling out of the throat of Pringle. 'Verdammter – Schwarzkopf!' he shouted, and knocked the rifle aside.

He strode on. Fear pierced his side like a thrusting bayonet, but at the edge of his consciousness, he seemed to be aware of the German standing at attention by way of apology. Then he was alone again except for what he was stumbling over. Sometimes the earth grew teeth that tore and cut at his boots; sometimes it was sloshing mud; sometimes it was lumped with soft forms.

The battle noise, all at once, drew far away and became dim, so that Pringle felt he must be fainting. But it was only one of those pauses in the racing heartbeats of a fight.

Out of the fog he heard a voice scream: 'Put me out of it! I can't stand it any more! Kill me, will you? Put me out of the pain – oh, my God!'

And a deep German voice full of a father's gentleness said, '*Sei ruhig, sei ruhig, mein Kind!*'

Pringle fled from the voices.

Here the mud underfoot turned into something kneedeep and cold. He found that he was standing in running water and knew that he had reached the Mézigny. He was on the verge of safety.

He pulled off clothes and shoes, lunged forward, and the water received him with dark, cold arms. He needed only to float. The current was floating him toward his country. Thereafter, he never would look at a stream, he never would hear the music of running water without a sense of gigantic deliverance.

Then a white eye opened in the sky above him. A magnesium light was dropping slowly down under its parachute. Its glare turned the river and its bank to silver, obscurely marked by tangles of ink-black shadows.

Pringle saw this as he dived. Under the water he kept swimming slowly, holding his breath until his lungs burned and were bursting. When he rose to the surface the brightness of the magnesium light was intensified. Then something pierced his leg; a needle-thrust, a hammer-blow, and after that numbness from the hip down.

He swam on, the left leg a senseless weight to drag.

The glaring face of the river was cut with dark whipstrokes. Little wasp sounds flocked about his head. That was a machine gun feeling its way to find him.

He dived again, endowed with extra strength, for the ghost which had haunted him now dissolved into a silly little man-made scarecrow. This was the whole terror of the battlefield, and the bullet-stroke was hardly more, actually, than the ache of a bad tooth!

The thought was like fresh air in his lungs. It had been, after all, mere excess of expectation, like that brief moment of coldheartedness which comes just before a boxing bout commences; and as the first blow dissolves that nervous apprehension, so the bullet had killed the fear in Pringle.

Darkness came over the river like a mercy. He swam confidently on. He wanted to shout his good news. He wanted to print it in great red letters across the sky – to tell everyone that fear is only a fake giant.

The current was swinging him toward the left bank, so that he realized he was rounding the bend of the Mézigny. He was, in fact, already at the verge of the American lines when his reaching hand found sharp teeth submerged just under the surface of the water. He had struck a barbed-wire obstacle in the stream.

Well, it would cost him merely another kind of pain to cross it. He laid out his body with the left side down and so turned himself slowly across the uppermost edge of the wire. Twenty of its teeth entered him, cut, tore, and then he was across on the far side with his whole body on fire with the new pain.

But what was pain of the body compared with the wounding of a man's pride? Now he knew that his spirit would be complete to the end of his days.

He had not even thought of the loss of blood until he tried to drag himself from the water with arms that refused to bear his weight. Then sudden hands were on him.

'Look at this damned Boche tryin' to sneak through,' said a voice.

'Get me to an officer,' said Pringle. 'Get me to him fast before I faint.'

For life, now, narrowed to a single bright thread to which he had to cling with desperate craft. Too strong an effort would break the thread, and the message that might save his father never would be spoken. He understood perfectly, now, the pity, the grief and the farewell in the eyes of Colonel Pringle. He had lied with a good, manly roundness to his son, sending him out to be shot down, certainly, but in such a way that his memory would live for his family and his friends like that of a hero.

But heroism isn't a question of brute courage. It's merely a matter of knowledge; what we know, we don't fear, and Pringle had looked into the whole mystery, face to face.

He was lying on a board in a trench, now. Consciousness widened and showed him the face, the shoulder-markings of a young captain who leaned over him.

'Get word to General Bailey,' said Pringle. 'Lieutenant Pringle reporting from Colonel Pringle – the colonel has four hundred men entrenched, over there. If the general hits out and starts the Germans backing up, they'll back into a wall of fire. They'll be cleaned up. If the general doesn't attack, Colonel Pringle reports that he'll attack on his own, at dawn. If the general attacks, will he please fire five Very lights in a cluster . . . .'

He could not remember, afterward, whether he had spoken those last words or only thought them.

Out of a hazy dream, burning pain brought him back to consciousness, and he heard a voice yelling: 'Look out how you handle him, you louse! Can't you see he's shot to hell?'

But the pain of the body merely warmed his inner soul.

'Five Very lights in a cluster, if there is to be an attack,' said Pringle.

Something shouted in Pringle's ear, afterward. Something of 'Very lights' touched the inward nerve of his being and opened his eyes, and he saw, high above him in the night, lights opening like phosphorescent flowers in a sea of black. He counted one, two, three, four, five in that shining cluster.

'Ah, that's good!' said Pringle.

He fought to cling to consciousness. It came and went, however, like cloud shadows across lovely daylight hills.

He was in a dressing station. The uproar of a thundering sea had withdrawn to a distance; no, it was battle, not the crashing of breakers. Two men in blood-splashed white were doing things to him, and every touch of their hands burned him with agony.

'What do you think?' he asked.

'You're going to have your chance, maybe,' said the doctor. 'What in hell did the dirty dogs do to you?'

'They're not dogs,' said Pringle. He spoke softly, saving his breath, for one great exhalation would sweep away his soul and make it a part of that dark wind which blows between the stars. 'They're like us – just the same. The way I see it, war is a game. It's a sport. We shouldn't fight Germans because we hate them, but because in the game we're on the other side. Germans. Music, singing, black radishes and beer – you can't hate all that.' Then he said, 'Can I give a message?'

The doctor was leaving him. 'Garner!' he called. 'Come here, Garner!'

A little man stood by the cot with a pencil ready above a notebook.

'To Colonel Pringle, if he lives through the attack, from Lieutenant Pringle. Walter Pringle. Tell him, if I die, that I understood.'

'Understood what?' asked Garner.

'He'll know what I mean,' said Pringle.

'All right. Good luck, Lieutenant,' said Garner, turning away.

'I've had my luck,' said Pringle, as the shadow poured over him again.

When he came to consciousness again, breathing was hard.

A voice was saying: 'Nobody knows how. Left leg useless. Body cut to hell. But he got through. How? Nobody knows how a hero does his stuff. Anyway, he's the reason that salient was smashed flat this morning. They got to Colonel Pringle in the throat of it. He still had two hundred men with him; they'll get decorations. One of the damnedest things in the whole war.'

'Is this poor devil going to die?' asked a second voice.

'I don't know. He's got the blue in his face.'

It doesn't matter, thought Pringle.

The cloud came over him again, with the softness of perfect sleep.

The Silent Witness

This tightly knit 'short-short' first appeared in March 1938, in *Black Mask*, the same magazine that published stories by Dashiell Hammett, Raymond Chandler, and most of the best crime writers of the 1920s and 1930s. Many writers of westerns made a successful transition to crime stories. Faust, best known for his westerns, actually began his career with a crime story. As novelist and literary historian William F. Nolan has pointed out, Faust's first professionally published story, 'Convalescence' (*All-Story Weekly*, March 31, 1917), was a crime story.

During the 1920s Faust contributed occasionally to Street and Smith's *Detective Story Magazine* and, from 1933 to 1937, his stories appeared regularly in Popular Publications' *Detective Fiction Weekly*. His crime fiction also appeared in *Argosy, Double Detective, Dime Detective, Cosmopolitan, The American Magazine, Liberty, McCall's,* and *Collier's.* Altogether he wrote some seventy crime pieces for magazines, ten of which have also appeared in book form.

Two of Faust's crime books, *Cross Over Nine* (Macaulay, 1935) and *The Night Flower* (Macaulay, 1936) are among his most popular, though perhaps his finest work in this field is the detective serial ' – Murder Me!' (which appeared in *Detective Fiction Weekly* beginning September 21, 1935 and has yet to see book form). A collection of his shorter crime stories is in preparation. Faust's crime fiction constitutes a significant aspect of his literary achievement without which his fiction as a whole cannot be properly understood or evaluated.

R IDDLE PRESSED the Bentley bell and then held the doorknob while he stared through the glass into the downstairs hallway. It had the nakedly expectant look of all entrances to push-button apartment houses. The lock began to click rapidly; it kept on clicking after he had entered the hall and pressed the elevator button.

Everything happened very slowly. He heard the elevator door slam shut above him, a deep-voiced humming began in the throat of the shaft and descended gradually toward him. The lighted elevator slid past the diamond-shaped peephole. It halted. The inner door was pushed clanging back by the ghostly fingers of the machine.

He entered, pressed the button of Number 6, and watched the door slowly roll shut, obeying the electric mind. With a soft lurch the elevator started up the shaft.

At the sixth floor the automatic brake stopped the car softly and the inner door rolled gradually back. This mechanized precision, this mindless deliberation, screwed up Riddle's nerves to a breaking tension. He had to set his lips and his lean jaw and make ready to endure what he knew was ahead of him.

Then the outer door of the elevator was snatched open by Gay Bentley. She leaned against the edge of it with her eyes so big and dark that she looked like a white-faced child. Riddle put his arm around her and closed the door while she clung to him, saying: 'Dick. . . . Dick. . . . Dick. . . .'

He took her through the open door into the living-room of her apartment. It was exactly in order, disappointing the horrible expectation with which he had entered. The floor lamps cast two amber circles on the ceiling and two white pools on the floor. The huge litter of a Sunday newspaper lay scattered on the davenport and on the table there was a tall highball glass, almost full.

'Where?' asked Riddle.

She pointed toward the bedroom door. 'I'll come with you,' she said.

He shook his head. 'You sit here. No, lie down.'

'I'll go mad if I lie down,' said Gay. Her lips began to tremble and her eyes rolled, so he picked her up and laid her on the davenport amid the rustling of the newspaper.

'You be quiet. Will you be quiet? Close your eyes!' commanded Riddle.

She closed her eyes and he crossed the floor with the sense of her light, firm body still making his hands feel strong. He needed that strength of spirit when he entered the bedroom and saw Tom Bentley lying on the bed, far over against the wall with his right arm stretched out, pointing an automatic at his friend in the doorway. But Bentley's half-open eyes were drowsily considering something on the white of the ceiling instead of Riddle, and a spot of deep purple appeared on his temple with one thin, watery line of blood running down from it.

Riddle went back into the living-room where Gay Bentley already was off the couch and sitting on the piano stool with her face in her hands. She started up to face Riddle. He wandered to the table and picked up the unfinished highball. When he tasted it, he found the whisky good but the drink was tepid; it had come to the room temperature.

'The police?' whispered the girl. 'Do we have to call the police?'

He sipped the tepid highball again before he put down the glass.

'I want a drink, Gay,' he said.

'Take this. It's mine but I don't want it.'

'This? *This* is yours?' he asked, looking suddenly at her.

'Ah, but you like a man's drink,' she nodded, unobservant. 'I'll make you a fresh one.'

She passed him on the way to the pantry, and clung close to him again for an instant.

'Oh, Dick,' she whispered, 'think what animals we are! When I found him, my mind stopped, and all I could do was to come out here and go through the motions of mixing a drink. . . . Think of that! And then I remembered you. Thank God for you! Thank God for you!'

She went on to the pantry.

'How do you want it?' she called.

'Just like yours,' said Riddle. He saw his own pale, thin face in the glass above the fireplace and stared at the gloomy image entranced.

'Just like mine?' she repeated, surprised. 'But two lumps of ice, you always take.'

'No. Just like yours. One lump. That will do,' said Riddle.

She brought the drink back to him, and he sank down into a chair at the table. He put his chin on his fist and stared at nothingness. The girl stood behind him with her hands on his shoulders.

'Poor Tom!' she said. 'I know you loved him, Dick, but try not to take it too hard. He *was* unhappy, you know.'

'I knew,' said Riddle, 'and I kept away from him for a month. . . . Was it money, Gay?'

'No,' she answered.

'It had to be debts that drove him to it. There was nothing else,' insisted Riddle.

'There was something else,' she replied.

'What under heaven?' asked Riddle, jerking up his head so that his face almost touched hers.

'Jealousy, Dick,' said the girl.

'Jealousy?' cried Riddle. 'Jealousy of you, Gay?'

She made a pause, with her face still close to his, before she answered carefully and gently, as though to a child: 'You know we haven't been so very happy together, lately.'

'After a few years, the bubble and zip goes out of most marriages,' said Riddle.

'Ah, it was more than that,' she answered.

'You mean there *was* a definite reason for his jealousy?' demanded Riddle. 'You mean that there was another man?'

She was silent again before she answered just above a whisper: 'Ah, Dick, you blind, blind fellow!'

Riddle reached up and caught one of her hands from his shoulder. 'What the devil do you mean, Gay?' he asked.

'He knew I loved someone else,' said the girl.

'Who?' asked Riddle.

She pulled to get free. 'I don't want to talk about it. I can't talk about it,' she said. 'Not to you.'

Riddle let her hand go.

'You mean that I'm the man?' he said.

She gave him no answer but walked across the room to the window and stood there looking out. A breeze came in from moment to moment and set her bright hair shimmering over the smooth and soft of her neck. She stood there an eternity of minutes. The silence between them – between her beauty and his friendship with the dead man – that silence sang on for minutes.

He tasted her drink on the table then, quickly, took a small swallow from his own glass. After that he glanced at his watch. The silence drew out in length like a dark thread. . . .

'You know that Tom was my best friend?' he asked.

'I know everything,' said the girl. 'It was because he cared about you so much that I first began to care – too. . . .'

Her voice broke a little. Riddle went to her and took her by the shoulders. He seated her firmly in a chair.

'That's all to be talked about afterward,' he told her. Then, walking up and down the room, he said: 'Tell me what you know about it.'

She lay back in the chair with her head partly turned away from him and her eyes almost closed and sometimes a smile that was characteristic of her when she talked appeared on her lips. Now, at thirty, wrinkles pinched her eyes a little at the corners but her smile was still very lovely. She talked slowly.

'I went out just before five. I couldn't remember but I thought I had a tea engagement with Martha Gilbert and I couldn't get her on the phone. I didn't find Martha. I ran into Jud Mowbray a little later, and he insisted on cocktails. I didn't want one, but I sort of had to. . . . After a while I left him and got back here at around a quarter to six. And I found Tom – like that; and then I telephoned to you.'

Riddle nodded.

'You saw Tom and he was dead – of his own hand. Then you poured yourself this drink and then you telephoned to me.'

'What does the drink matter?' she asked, with a sudden curiosity.

'The police always want to know everything,' said Riddle. 'They eat up every detail. And I'll have to ring them in a moment. You poured yourself this drink about forty-five minutes ago, let's say?'

'Yes. Almost exactly.'

He sipped her drink, carefully, and then tried his own. He said nothing – endlessly.

'Then by the time I arrived,' he finally said, 'your drink hadn't been standing more than twenty minutes, had it?'

'No. Of course not! . . . Dick, what's the matter with you?'

'Nothing,' said Riddle, standing up and seeing the white of his face in the glass again. Then he glanced at his wrist. A half hour had come – and gone.

He went to the telephone but paused there for a long moment until she asked: 'What's in your mind, Dick?'

'I was thinking of the first days out of college when Tom and I were fighting our way up.'

'*You* fought your way up,' said Gay Bentley, 'and Tom kept sliding back in spite of all his scratching. He was a derelict before the end and the only thing that drew him along was the towline you threw to him, Dick, darling. . . .'

He picked up the receiver and began to dial.

'I want the police,' he said.

'Not so soon, Dick!' cried the girl. 'I don't want their dreadful, blunt faces near me. I couldn't stand them!'

'This is One Forty-two East Hargreave Street,' said Riddle. 'On the sixth floor, apartment D, Thomas Bentley is dead. It is murder. . . .' He hung up.

'Murder? Murder?' cried the girl. 'Dick, what are you talking about?'

'About a man I loved, and a woman I used to love, too,' said Riddle, 'and an alibi rotten all the way through.'

He sipped from the glasses on the table, one after the other.

'This drink of mine has been standing here for half an hour, but it's still cold,' he said. 'It still will be cold when the homicide squad arrives and hears me testify that your glass was room temperature when I came in. . . .'

'Dick, what do you mean?' she gasped. 'What crazy idea is in your head?'

'My idea,' said Riddle, 'is that you *were* out of the house to collect your alibi, but you poured your drink, here, before you left, and all the time you were away the highball was going ahead like an automatic machine gathering warmth and registering murder. *You* killed Tom.'

She went to pieces, flew at him, beggingly.

'Dick, throw the stuff out of the window! Dick, you wouldn't kill me, would you? Not like a rat; you wouldn't kill me, Dick, would you?' she sobbed to him. 'I needed a drink – to do it! But, Dick, because I love you – Oh, throw it away!'

He covered the glass with his hand. He could not look at her but he knew she was shrinking away from him now – toward the door. And then that she had slipped out into the hallway, running.

Now she would be pressing the button of the elevator frantically; but he knew with what an unhurried steadiness it would respond.

A siren screamed out of the distance and turned loose its howling in Hargreave Street. Riddle opened his eyes as he listened, and in the mirror the white image stared back at him in astonishment and horror.

Miniature

Faust had a remarkable capability to write eloquently about horses. In his first published story, which appeared in the Modesto High School literary magazine *The Sycamore* in 1910, the narrator is a horse. Horses gallop through the pages of Faust's stories as he once galloped on horseback through the unpaved streets of Modesto or on nearby farms and ranches. To a poor orphan, horses represented excitement. Perhaps they symbolized escape to worlds beyond the San Joaquin Valley. As an adult he often attended professional horse races and steeplechases in the United States and Europe and rode for pleasure whenever possible. A fall from an Irish jumper near Dublin resulted in a broken leg, and kept him from a scheduled series of conversations with C. G. Jung in Zurich (a follow-up to an earlier series in London).

'The horse is the noblest animal,' Faust said repeatedly. Many kinds of horses appear in his pages – cowhorses, plowhorses, draft horses, war-horses, racehorses, steeplechasers, stallions, geldings, mares, colts. Sometimes they are major characters. Satan in *The Untamed* (Putnam, 1919) is one aspect of the supernatural that his master, Dan Barry, embodies. The horse, too, can perform a kind of magic. Moonshine in *Galloping Danger* (Dodd, Mead, 1987; the title has since been restored to *Lee Garrison's Quest*) symbolizes the Holy Grail and the human quest for the highest and best. Similarly, Sky Blue in *Lucky Larribee* (Dodd, Mead, 1932) helps Larribee realize his inner self. A horse is equally important in 'Miniature,' another of Faust's unusual stories that had some difficulty initially finding a market (eventually appearing in *Good Housekeeping*,

September 1939). The horse is frequently the means by which Faust's heroes and heroines are able to transcend themselves, an American version of the mythic Pegasus.

I T WAS PLAIN to Count Lanskoi, who knew women and horses, that Mariette Willoughby once had been a gem of loveliness, and though time had flawed her deeply, she continued to enshrine herself like a jewel in a rich case. Time, like a hungry fish, begins to swallow us by the head; but Count Lanskoi looked upon Mariette Willoughby as a collector looks upon a Chinese print. He shut the face from his attention and devoted his appreciation to the robes, background, color, and design.

Viewed in this manner, Mrs. Willoughby was quite a satisfactory subject for study, for her Parisian designer kept her imagination under some control and her French maid knew how clothes should be worn. Powerful corseting poured the spacious body of Mrs. Willoughby into a classic mold, which was filmed over by an afternoon dress that had cost several times its weight in gold: it looked like a delicate drapery bestowed upon a statue. Diamonds lighted her hands and clasped the fat of her wrists as she sipped sherry and examined a little miniature.

'You were more beautiful then, Dmitri,' said Mrs. Willoughby. She looked up at Lanskoi and rested her eyes on the thin black sheen of his mustache. 'But not so manly, my dear,' she added.

Count Lanskoi bowed from the hips with youthful suppleness and speed. He had a military way of coming to attention and bowing that American women found entirely irresistible; but until he met Mrs. Willoughby he never had used his graces to get on in the world. It was only when he found himself forty-four, the age of great reason and smaller hope, that he turned at last to the ultimate resource of the poor.

'And what was the regiment again, Dmitri?' asked Mrs. Willoughby.

'The Lancer Guards,' said the count.

'Did they use lances?' she asked.

'They did,' said Lanskoi.

'Fancy!' said Mrs. Willoughby. 'How sweet and medieval! How did they use them?'

'They stuck them into the enemy,' said Lanskoi, 'and left them there. Then they used the sword.'

'Really?' said Mrs. Willoughby. 'It's a darling little patent-leather cap, too. I thought that only hussars used them.'

Lanskoi answered with another bow, for sometimes he found no words with which he could express himself to his lady. He took a slightly deeper breath and allowed his glance to pass out the window, already blue with the evening, across the yellow lights of Central Park and the naked shimmering of the frosted trees. Then, as though after repose, he returned his smile and his slightly downward regard to Mrs. Willoughby.

She found something enchanting in his lowered head, as though he dared not quite lift his gaze to his queen. She, glancing down in turn, saw the ruby pendant shine and tremble on her bosom. She was beginning to adore Count Lanskoi, because she never felt so well as when she was in his presence.

'But how strange,' she said, 'to have a blue uniform with a red breast to it!'

'Those are the lapels,' he pointed out.

'And such epaulets! Fit for a general, at least!'

'I was only a captain,' said Lanskoi, who rarely lied except when he was very hungry.

'Oh, how very odd to wear a red flower on your sword, Dmitri!' cried Mrs. Willoughby, bringing the miniature closer to her eyes.

'It is the scarlet sword knot of St. Anne,' said he.

'Ah, does it mean something, then?' she asked.

'It is a decoration,' said Lanskoi, with his bow.

'But Dmitri! You never told me about decorations!'

'But you know, Mariette, one does not speak of such things.'

'Does one not? Does one not?' said Mrs. Willoughby, almost fiercely. 'Well, we shall see about that! . . . Dmitri, kiss me!'

Count Lanskoi bowed, clicked his heels together, lifted her hand, and pressed his lips against a large solitaire diamond.

Mrs. Willoughby continued to gaze upon her hand afterward. 'Dmitri,' she said, 'you are a really sweet . . . boy!' She laughed a little and, laughing, turned her attention to the miniature again. 'But ah, ah – what's this?' she asked, putting the picture very close to her nose. 'Speaking of decorations, what's this, Dmitri? This red enamel cross on your breast with the crossed swords on it?'

'It is the cross of St. Vladimir,' said Count Lanskoi, bowing once more.

'Is it just a part of the uniform, dear?' she asked.

'No,' answered the count. 'It is not just a part of the uniform.'

'But what, then? You know, Dmitri, you have a silly way of holding back. Please tell me about it!'

'It was the second highest decoration that could be awarded to a Russian officer in the Imperial Army,' said Lanskoi.

'Dmitri!'

'My dove!' said Lanskoi, and his black mustache bristled with his smile. It was characteristic, when he was with Mrs. Willoughby, that his smile turned on like an electric light and turned off in the same manner.

'But even that isn't all,' said Mrs. Willoughby, narrowing her eyes as though for the finest print. 'Here is a lamb of a little white cross right over your heart. Does that mean something, too?'

'It does,' said Lanskoi.

'What is it, then?'

'It is the Cross of St. George,' answered Lanskoi.

'It's a pretty little thing,' she remarked. 'My dear, what are you looking at on the ceiling?' asked Mrs. Willoughby, with some impatience. 'Now, Dmitri, tell me exactly what it means.'

He submitted. 'It is the highest decoration of the Empire, madame,' he said.

'The highest? Oh, Dmitri!' she cried, and rose suddenly from her chair, thrusting herself up with both hands. She stood at her full height and extended her arms.

Count Lanskoi drew a slight breath and embraced her.

'I have made up my mind,' said Mrs. Willoughby. 'I am going to marry you!'

He tried very hard to make an answer but for the moment his mind was possessed by visions of the country house, the huge, warm, quiet rooms, the servants so perfectly trained, the terraced lawns and their great trees, the stables like a separate mansion, and above all the sheen and silk of the thoroughbreds.

'Dearest, don't be overcome,' said Mrs. Willoughby. 'I *mean* it. You are going out to the country with me this very evening. . . . Hurry downtown and pay that wretched hotel bill; then meet me here at seven, and we'll motor out. And Sunday, Dmitri, we'll be married in the village church. Don't say a word. My mind is made up. . . . Hand me my purse from that table, Dmitri. . . . Here is five hundred. It will put the miserable hotel out of your mind, at least. And then hurry back – my angel!'

Count Lanskoi did not take a taxicab because he felt that it would be better to walk himself into a clearer understanding of the position which was about to be his. Plainly the five hundred dollars was no more than the first sheaf from the harvest field. But it was not cash that he had in mind; rather he looked forward to the ending of pain than to the beginning of pleasure.

As he walked rapidly down Fifth Avenue, the golden heights of Central Park South shone loftier through the twilight. Men never have built another such face for fairyland as that chain of towers in the half-light of the day. It had been to Lanskoi, since his arrival from Russia, the symbol of all that New York contained which was locked away from him. Now he was to have the key that would open those mysterious doors. As for Mariette Willoughby – when he conceived of her as 'Countess Lanskoi,' he could not prevent a tremor of cold conscience. The image of another Countess Lanskoi, his mother, was like an eagle in his mind and kept watch over his guiltiness. Russian titles were far too commonly adrift in the world, and even a silly woman like Mrs. Willoughby must know that they could be bought for a song. What she really wanted was the miniature and the count's past life, which the picture represented like a young ghost in an old house.

The walking heated his blood in spite of the evening cold. He began to recall, with the cheerfulness of one who has escaped, all the situations that had imprisoned his spirit in the great city. He had been a doorman, a uniformed dancer in a Russian restaurant, a street laborer, and so on through a dwindling perspective of misery. He was changing all this – and paying his honesty of soul as a price for the alteration. Yet for the moment he was not sold, for the miniature he had presented to Mariette Willoughby was worth at least the five hundred dollars she had given to him. Therefore he walked lightly, one enjoying his last moments of liberty. He left the avenue and headed for his hotel. That was why he came past the entrance of the old riding academy just as half a dozen horses trooped into it. Lanskoi stopped to watch them with an eye trained in the old Russian cavalry school. He was about to step on when he saw the exposed hip of the last of the troop. The blanket had twisted a little awry on the chestnut mare, and he saw on her bright hide a little patch of darkness like the shadow of a crawling beetle.

Lanskoi whistled, for it was the singular birthmark which the great Russian stallion, Bayan, transmitted to his progeny. Strange to find that mark on a horse in America! Bayan had stood for years in the government stud of the Soviets, and this mare was young.

Lanskoi drew near the entrance as the mare walked through, jerking back against the lead rope and dancing sidewise with flattened ears.

'Kassatik!' said Lanskoi.

The mare stopped her dancing. She stood still and turned her head toward Lanskoi until the groom wrenched her forward.

'Kassatik!' murmured Lanskoi again, as though he were speaking to a woman.

There had been no horses in his life for fifteen years – since the night a battered column dragged through the darkness toward Vladivostok with the guns of the Reds still audible to the rear. A bullet through his left arm had drained much of Lanskoi's strength and brought him to a fever that made him almost glad of the snow that whirled into his face. But his horse was more deeply wounded by weariness, so he walked at the gelding's side, letting it lead him blindly. That had been his last day with a horse; and he remembered the proverb: 'A Cossack without a horse is like a man without a soul.'

He went suddenly in behind the horses to the big tanbark arena of the riding school. The troop of horses he was following disappeared down a side chute as the count asked the doorman, 'Do you know that mare? That last one of the lot?'

The doorman pulled back his cap by its visor. 'I know her. I know the devil inside her, too,' he said. 'But I suppose she'll be knocked down to some damn fool that likes a picture in his stable instead of a horse he can use. Katya is her name, and there's a lot of cat in her, all right.'

'She's about to be auctioned off?'

'Here's the list,' said the doorman, and gave to the count a thin printed folder.

Lanskoi looked at his watch. It was only a little after five; he still had two hours before he presented himself at the crossroads of his life to take the final way with Mariette Willoughby. He kept remembering the bright head of the mare as she had paused to look him in the face. 'I have time,' said Lanskoi to himself. But a chilly sense of guilt, and expectation of disaster, worked in his blood and along his nerves.

There were ten or twelve score people in the gallery. The auctioneer was saying, 'Now, my dear friends, I ask you to pause and think again. I conceal nothing from you. I announced in the beginning, and I tell you again, that this gelding is a trifle over in the knees. Gentlemen, do I hear a thousand? To sell him for less is a shame to your intelligence as horsemen and horse lovers.'

'Six-twenty-five,' said a voice.

A few people laughed, and the auctioneer threw up his hands in despair.

'Six-thirty!' called another bidder. There was louder laughter than before.

'Seven hundred!' called a woman.

'Seven-fifty!'

'Eight hundred!'

'Nine hundred!'

The bidding stopped there, and the gray was knocked down at that price.

A pale young man beside Count Lanskoi said, 'The horses know how to sell themselves. Did you see that gray look us in the eye just now?'

'I saw!' agreed Lanskoi. He looked suddenly and hungrily at the pale youth and then sighed, for the man had the dead eye of a professional horse dealer.

A sleek bay mare went for fifteen hundred, and a chunky gelding able to gallop under two hundred pounds brought an even two thousand.

Lanskoi was moved. He held out a gloved hand and said, 'They don't want horses; they want safe machines. *That* horse should pull a plow.'

He felt his neighbor's eye upon him.

'My name is Hudderson,' the stranger said.

'Lanskoi,' said the Count.

'Mr. Lanskey,' said Hudderson, 'when you want some of the right stuff, I hope you'll remember me. I'm in the telephone book.'

Lanskoi answered, 'I have exactly five hundred dollars in my pocket – and that's bonanza for me. I would make a poor customer.'

Hudderson looked at him with that dead eye and nodded his head with understanding, almost with approval. 'But you like to see a gentleman mounted as a gentleman should be,' he said.

'Ah – there!' said Lanskoi. 'Something like that, I'd say!'

A big dark bay gelding danced into the arena, shaking his bridle-wise head, curving his neck, asking leave to go.

The auctioneer said briefly, 'Castleton by Commander out of Serene. I won't insult this horse by describing him. Where shall we start, my friends?'

He began to walk up and down his short platform quietly. No one made an offer. And then Hudderson said in a conversational voice, 'Five thousand.'

No one turned to look at the bidder. Count Lanskoi felt chilled. The auctioneer said nothing. The silence continued.

'Six thousand,' said someone.

'Seven.'

'Eight.'

'Ten,' said Hudderson.

The auctioneer paused for an instant. 'I think that's about all,' he said. 'Going and gone to Mr. Hudderson.'

A sound as of a softly blowing wind passed through the gallery, and the gelding was led off.

'Did you waste a thousand in there, perhaps?' asked Lanskoi.

'You see that fat fellow over there?' said Hudderson. 'He would have gone to twelve or fourteen, I think. But after my last bid he felt it was no use.'

'How high would you have gone?' asked Lanskoi, feeling like a child.

'Not a hundred dollars more,' said Hudderson.

'I hope you get your money out of Castleton,' remarked Lanskoi courteously.

The pale man laughed. 'I know a fat banker in Philadelphia,' he said, 'who'll pay fifteen thousand for the sake of hacking Castleton along bridle paths.'

Lanskoi dipped into his past and rode again over the windy ridges of the Lanskoi estate and saw the birch trees merge with speed on either side of him. In those days he had not even known the prices of the horses that carried him; for money had not counted, then, in his life. It had been an essential, like the air he breathed, unasked-for and always present.

Conscience thrust a cold finger into the small of his back, and he looked at his wristwatch a little later, when a few more horses had passed under the hammer. Amazed to find that it was six-forty, he turned to leave. He walked down to the foot of the gallery as a flashing chestnut mare swept into the riding hall, plunged past the groom who held her, and whirled about as she came to the end of the long rope with which he anchored her.

The auctioneer took a look at the mare and braced back his shoulders. He frowned upon the crowd. 'I want to speak seriously to you about this imported mare,' he said. 'The bloodlines may not be familiar to you, but Bayan is standing in the government cavalry stud in Russia, and Katinka, the dam, is a registered Thoroughbred. You see Katya for yourselves. Flawless lines. Plenty of foot. A bold jumper – '

'So bold she doesn't care where she lands,' interrupted a man in the middle gallery, and the crowd laughed heartily.

'I see your minds are set against her,' said the auctioneer. 'A great pity, too, I would have said,' he continued, straightening himself and peering into the gallery.

Lanskoi looked at his watch. The time gap was narrowing with wonderful speed; but he still had time to rush down to the hotel, pay that bill, and arrive at Mrs. Willoughby's apartment house on the stroke of seven. With her, delays were dangerous, he knew; for she had made enough out of three successful marriages to enable her to consult nothing but her pride during the rest of her life. He had a most inward foreknowledge that her automobile would depart punctually at the hour of seven, with or without him.

So he left the gallery and hurried across the riding hall toward the street exit.

He could hear, as he went, further eloquence on the part of the auctioneer: '. . . if I were a younger man, I would want that mare for myself.'

Lanskoi turned his head as he walked and saw Katya on her hind legs, striking at the air like a stallion.

'I am open to bids for Katya,' concluded the auctioneer in some disgust.

A voice called: 'Twenty-five dollars!'

Lanskoi, already at the arched, dark vault of the exit passage, turned suddenly about when he heard that bid. The people still were laughing about it, but not a soul raised the offer. He felt that time was slipping away and was carrying him with it toward disaster. But he could not help calling out. 'Fifty!'

The auctioneer, turning toward him, said, 'Ah, the gentleman has a proper eye for horseflesh. He cannot endure seeing quality of this sort sacrificed for a song. Friends, Katya is a nervous creature, to be sure, but all she needs is the proper handling.'

More laughter and a few shrewd comments from the gallery interrupted him.

'Make it seventy-five!' sang out a voice.

That was the fat man whom Hudderson had pointed out. Lanskoi hated him.

'You amuse yourselves, ladies and gentlemen,' said the auctioneer bitterly.

Katya at the moment again was rearing and pawing the air. The mare looked to Lanskoi as wild and tireless as one of those winter storms that rush across the thousand-mile levels of Russia.

'A hundred,' said Lanskoi.

He leaned against the wall of the exit passage with his heart going fast. He would have to give up going to the hotel, now, for there was barely time to catch a taxi and get back to Mariette. And if he did not pay the hotel bill, he would be without necessary clothes for the ceremony which – He stopped his mind. He could not allow it to carry him forward into the dark entanglements of the future.

'The gentleman by the door offers a hundred,' said the auctioneer, 'a hundred for this beautiful, high-blooded – '

'Fifty,' said the fat man, yawning.

'Ah, thank you, sir,' said the auctioneer. 'Thank you very much, Mr. Perkins. I see you all have been amusing yourselves at my expense. I am offered for Katya a hundred and fifty dollars – less than a farmer would have to pay for an old mule.'

'Sixty,' said Lanskoi, gripping his left wrist to conceal the wristwatch.

'I thank you again, sir,' said the auctioneer.

'Two hundred,' said the fat man.

'Three,' said Hudderson.

The brain of Lanskoi reeled with the successive shocks.

'Three-fifty,' said Perkins.

'Seventy-five!' called Lanskoi.

A pause followed. And Lanskoi's heart stood still. The hotel bill was a hundred and fifty-odd dollars; if his bid for the mare stood, his luggage would have to remain unredeemed and he would present himself to his lady with only the single suit in which he stood! He saw fat Mr. Perkins wave his hands and turn one shoulder. He had abandoned the bidding in profound disgust.

'I knew it!' cried the auctioneer. 'I knew that there were horsemen in this crowd tonight. Would it be America if the riders were to turn their backs on such a flier as Katya?'

To illustrate his words, she bucked in a flying circle at the end of her rope.

Lanskoi looked at his watch. It lacked one minute of seven o'clock. There was still a hope –

'Going at three-seventy-five,' said the auctioneer. 'At three-seventy-five going, going, and – '

'Four,' said Hudderson.

Lanskoi turned and fled down the exit tunnel with a sick heart.

And then, behind him, he heard the auctioneer saying, 'Well, the opposition gives up and withdraws, Mr. Hudderson.'

Count Lanskoi reached the edge of the pavement, and the cold night air cut into his face. Above the twinkling, yellow walls of scattered lights he saw the stars like a pale whirl of mist. And it seemed to Lanskoi that he saw the lovely head of Katya at his shoulder, the translucent lens of her eyes clouded by divine blue.

He turned and ran back up the passageway. The rank smell of the horse ring passed up his nose and into his brain like the pungency of whisky.

'Going, going, to Mr. Hudderson,' cried the auctioneer briskly.

'Four-ten!' cried Lanskoi.

'Ah-ha, and here we are in a little duel,' said the auctioneer.

'Fifty,' said Hudderson.

Lanskoi bared his wristwatch and looked down at it. It was five minutes past seven. He could see Mariette leaning back against the cushions of the car while the chauffeur tenderly tucked the robe around her. It was far too late. It seemed to him that the wind of the closing gates of fortune was in his face.

'Sixty!' he called.

'Seventy-five,' said the hard, even voice of Hudderson.

Lanskoi cried out, 'Five hundred!' and his voice cracked on it just a little. Taking a step out from the shadowy archway into the light of the ring, he peered earnestly up into the gallery to hear his fate pronounced by the pale lips of Hudderson.

'Five hundred offered,' said the auctioneer, delighted. 'And now let us enter on the real phase of the bidding. Five hundred, Mr. Hudderson; and do I hear – '

Hudderson, a cigarette between his lips, stared at Lanskoi.

'Going at five hundred. Going – '

Hudderson lifted his hand a little as though to signal another bid; but the gesture remained incomplete, and Lanskoi felt the eyes of the horse dealer hold him for an instant of profound understanding.

'Well, let him have her,' said Hudderson, and Lanskoi felt that for the first time in his life he had received mercy.

'Too bad,' said the auctioneer, shaking his head. 'But she is yours, sir!'

Lanskoi took the money from his wallet, the five little hundred-dollar bills, and passed them over. The end of the rope was placed in his hand.

'Hold hard on her!' said the sweating, panting groom. 'I'd like to bust her one!'

Katya made a plunge, her ears back.

'*Stoyat!*' called Lanskoi.

The mare stood still with her flanks heaving, her legs braced. Lanskoi gave the rope a slight pull. It was like pulling at a stone pillar.

'Give the gentleman a hand to get her out,' said the auctioneer.

'Never mind,' said Lanskoi. 'She'll come quietly, I think.'

'If you'll leave your name and address – ' said the auctioneer.

'I'll take her off your hands at once,' said Lanskoi. He pulled gently on the rope again. '*Poshli!*' said Lanskoi, and Katya stepped briskly out after him as he turned toward the exit. He felt her breath snuffing at his shoulder as he paused on the sidewalk. The gallery was still applauding.

The doorman called after him, 'Are you a horse charmer, sir?'

Lanskoi said nothing, for the cold wind, striking through his clothes, made his sweating body seemed naked to the night.

He went up the street with the green light, waited at Fifty-ninth for the traffic to change. Katya crowded him all the way across Central Park South until they entered the bridle path of the park. It dipped down into a darkness under a footpath bridge, and came out on the other side among trees all delicately silvered with frost to the tips of the finest twigs. The beaten snow underfoot was darkened with the soot of New York; but the banks on either side of the path shone like newly cloven marble, all the crystals freshly glistening. Then snow began to fall.

Lanskoi stopped. The shoulder of the mare nudged him as she paused at his side. 'Where, Katya?' he asked.

She turned her head, her eyes wide with a lustrous confidence.

'*Kassatik!*' said Lanskoi, slipping an arm about her neck. He looked about him again and saw a world turned into white iron. It would be long before the spring softened it again to life, for winter was only beginning. The falling snow clouded his future in a smothering mist of white.

Even the miniature, which had been his passport and credential in many a bitter time, was gone now forever. He had come to an end of stratagems and of all gentlemanly resources, and yet in that nakedness of mind he felt a strange comfort, as though his soul had come back to him from exile. As for the future – he could be a groom in some rich man's stable.

A bitter wind out of the north blew against Lanskoi and seemed to freeze and to cleanse him at the same moment.

'*Poshli!*' he commanded.

The mare stepped forward, and Lanskoi walked at her shoulder with one hand resting on her withers and the lead rope dangling loosely; for he needed to think, and in the meantime it seemed as well for Katya to lead the way.

Our Daily Bread

This story was written for the first Max Brand collection, *Wine on the Desert and Other Stories* (Dodd, Mead, 1940). It was inspired by Faust's youthful experience in New York in 1916 when he was working for two dollars a day handling freight in the basement of John Wanamaker's department store and dreaming of becoming rich and famous. A friend remembered an evening spent with Faust at the Bowery YMCA, where he was living in a cubicle 'just big enough to accommodate him, a table, a chair, and the inevitable typewriter. We went up to the roof, where we could see the glow of the great city and feel, rather than glimpse, the shapes of great buildings on the horizons. Frederick poured out his ambitions: to write great verse, to make money out of his prose writings, to marry and rear a family. He was doing most of his eating at Busy Jack's on Skid Row where ten cents would buy you a meal of spoiled hamburger and damaged potatoes.'

Faust learned about the big city from the bottom up. He walked its streets, gazing with admiration and envy at the glittering Plaza Hotel where he would one day stay in style, accumulating real-life material he would later use in stories and poems. He absorbed the urban environment, as he had once absorbed the rural San Joaquin Valley. The city helped provide the realistic mainstream subject matter, tone, and language that would become Faust's hallmark as a popular writer.

For a time Faust lived in a rented room in the home of a rabbi on the Lower East Side. This story of a family and a neighborhood he almost certainly knew may be, among other things, an act of grateful remembrance. That he should have chosen a vaguely Jewish pen name as early as 1917, when anti-Semitism was widespread, says something about Faust as rebel and innovator. 'Max Brand the Jewish cowboy' he sometimes humorously called himself. His attitude toward Jews was characteristically ambivalent: sometimes he denigrated them; sometimes he celebrated them, as here.

M
RS. SIDNEY M. LESTER used to come into the grocery store of Kahn & Seidelman every day in the busy time about five-thirty. She looked things over, from the boxes of red apples to the rich hams and golden-brown chickens under the glass of the delicatessen counter. Those bologna sausages, broadly sliced across, those glittering heaps of potato salad, overstrewn with parsley, and the various new touches which came into the store from the kitchen of Minnie Seidelman. Sometimes, but that was in the early days before Kahn & Seidelman understood, one of them asked Mrs. Lester if she were being served. On those occasions she priced some of the delicacies and learned with undying interest, over and over again, that the little tubes of anchovy paste were sixty-five cents and that the dabs of *pâté* cost seventy-five; and three dollars and a half for one tiny little jar of caviar always caused Mrs. Sidney M. Lester to nod her head and look out of the corner of a speculative eye, as though she were telling herself that she must remember this when she gave her party next week.

But the party never came, and in six months of constant patronage Mrs. Lester never bought five cents' worth of provisions of any kind from the store of Kahn & Seidelman. But every day, at about five-thirty, she stole a loaf of bread and walked with dignity into the street.

It would not be easy for most women to steal a loaf of bread. A loaf is about the most clumsy object in the world to conceal. But Mrs. Sidney M. Lester wore a short cloak of black silk, and when she picked up the loaf, she held it between her hip and the pinch of her left elbow, so that it was very well concealed by the cloak. These loaves, you understand, were not the ordinary blocks, soft, pulpy, cellophane-wrapped articles which you get in most stores. Instead, they were long, brown-crusted French loaves which come out of the oven of Minnie Seidelman's own kitchen. If you know what good bread is, go over there to Lexington Avenue this very day and buy a loaf of Minnie Seidelman's bread. It has a good smack to it, I can tell you; with a bottle of milk and an apple, it will make you a fine meal. And every day, at about five-thirty, when the store was filled with shopping women who had finished their day's work and were getting food for supper, Mrs. Sidney M. Lester stole a loaf of that beautiful bread and took it away.

Bernie Kahn saw it first of all.

Bernie is a good boy. He is in high school now, when a lot of youngsters begin to put on airs; but Bernie has no nonsense about him, and when he comes home from school he rushes through with his homework and then hurries over to help at the store during the rush hour. His cousin, Abe Seidelman, is following that good example, shamed into it. And of course Ruth Kahn and sweet little Rose Seidelman are always around to help out. It's a wonderful thing, the way the Kahns and Seidelmans work together and in their own families find all the help that they need for everything. By the way, Rose Seidelman is the pretty one with the high color. If you say that the apples are not as red as *her* cheeks, she lifts up a quick hand and touches one of them and looks as surprised as though she never had heard this remark in her life before.

But to go back to Bernie, he was the one who discovered the thefts. He was not one of those headlong young fools who shout out the first guess that comes into the head. The first day he suspected. What did he do? The second day he counted every loaf in the stack just before Mrs. Sidney M. Lester went out past the bread counter. And then he counted them again after she went by and found out, as he suspected, that the store was one loaf shy. Any other boy would have talked then and there, but Bernie is really a boy in a thousand. He waited until the next day, and the next day's theft, and then he trailed Mrs. Sidney M. Lester around the corner to the old place which had been turned into a rooming house. When she went in, he looked at the names under the mail boxes and discovered that she lived on the west side of the top floor. When Bernie was thoroughly equipped with this information, he went back to the store, took his father aside, and told him the news.

The brow of his father darkened, but he said nothing. Bernie did not talk about it to the others. He watched his father and kept his mouth shut.

You never saw a boy like Bernie. Nothing can keep him from getting on in the world.

His father, Jake Kahn, is unlike the physical tradition of his family. Martha Kahn has cooked for her entire family with wonderful success all the days of her married life, but she can't put a pound on Jake. He remains as thin as a thinker, and his shoulders bend forward over a narrowing chest.

That night after supper they all went in, as usual, to sit for a half hour with Grandfather Oscar Kahn in the front room. Grandfather Oscar sits there in a brown leather chair and smokes a long pipe that has a China bowl with a cap of silver filigree. It curves down out of the white beard of Oscar and rests comfortably upon the top fold of his stomach, as upon a shelf.

The half hour almost had ended when Jake Kahn said, 'Well, we've got one at last.'

Grandfather Oscar opened one eye and lifted the white shag of one eyebrow.

'What have you got, my son?' he asked.

'A shoplifter,' said Jake, quietly.

The stir in the family circle was immense. Grandfather Oscar opened both eyes wide. Only Bernie, rich in knowledge, sat still and said nothing, but watched. He is that kind of a boy.

'An old scoundrel of a woman,' said Jake, 'who steals a loaf of bread from our store every day of her life!'

His indignation put fire in his sunken eyes.

As for Grandfather Oscar, he sank back in his chair and the mouthpiece of his pipe slipped from his lips and the pipe itself sank down to the second fold of his stomach, where it rested again as upon a shelf.

'*Himmel – Gott!*' said Grandfather Oscar.

'There's a jail for such people!' cried Martha Kahn.

'*Himmel – und Herr Gott!*' said Grandfather Oscar.

'I know that sly old thief – I know the very one!' cried Ruth, inspired by afterthought.

Only Bernie Kahn said nothing. He is really a remarkable boy.

Then Grandfather Oscar groaned again, his voice like a rumbling of distant thunder: '*Heilige Himmel – unter Herr Gott der Vater!* A loaf of bread!'

The last four words were unexpected. They struck the rest of the family to a sudden silence. They were rich in surprising implications. They attacked the whole Kahn family of the younger generations as from the rear.

Grandfather Oscar said, 'Every day of her life – to steal – a loaf of bread!'

There was such an accent upon 'bread' that a shudder ran through the listeners.

After that, Oscar Kahn closed his eyes, lifted his pipe to the uppermost fold of his stomach, and restored the mouthpiece to his lips.

His family stole quietly from the room.

The next day they were changed people. No one said anything to anybody else; and every one of the Kahns had the same idea.

That very afternoon, Abe Seidelman came running to Jake Kahn shortly after five-thirty and cried out, 'That old woman – the one in the black cloak – she's a thief!'

'Yeah?' said Jake. He looked down upon Abe not from a superior height of inches, but from a superiority of mind and soul and time. 'What did she steal?'

'She stole a loaf of bread!' said Abe. 'I saw her put it up under her cloak as slick as you please!'

'She stole a loaf of bread. And so what?' asked Jake.

Bewildering light dawned upon the brain of Abe.

'Geez!' he said, and laughed a little, embarrassed.

'Yeah, sure,' said Abe, and he laughed a little again, very softly.

The Kahns and the Seidelmans have lived and worked together for so many years that their mutual understanding is remarkable. In a flash they now knew what their attitude should be toward Mrs. Sidney M. Lester. And that attitude never faltered.

When she came in, always wearing the same dress of black silk, upon which time had shed a sort of dust, almost impalpable, with a collar of black lace concealing the indignities which the years had worked upon her throat, she was sure to get a cheerful greeting from the Kahns and the Seidelmans – not too much, not so much attention that she might become embarrassed, but just enough to warm the air with a touch of neighborliness. Her pleasure was always asked. She always had a chance to price the caviar or the sliced white chicken, or the lobsters, or the *pâté*. And at the moment when she started from the store again, all the Kahns and all the Seidelmans were suddenly very busy, with their faces turned to the rear of the store. At that moment even a flash of lightning would not have been seen by those good people.

As I was saying, this went on for upward of six months before Mrs. Sidney M. Lester failed to appear at the store. Her absence was noted at once. It was the subject of a telephone conversation between the house of Kahn and the house of Seidelman that evening. On the second day again she was missing. And when the third evening did not bring her between five and five-thirty, Bernie went around to the rooming house and rang the porter's bell. A sour old woman said, 'Mrs. Lester must be in because she ain't gone out!'

'She's sick, I guess,' said Bernie, when he went back to the store.

The Kahns and the Seidelmans were confused and worried by the thought.

Then Jake Kahn did something about it. Jake is a dry, hard-faced man and he is apt to surprise his entire family by the unexpected workings of his brain.

They were about to close the store; the last clients were gone; and Jake's loud, dry voice said: 'Ruthie, get a jar of that caviar out of the icebox, and a couple tubes of anchovy paste, and some of them anchovies, and a jar of *pâté*. Bernie, get a dozen of those Southern California navels. Select. No, maybe you better make it half a dozen. Some of those Spanish olives, Abe . . . .'

He went on with additional selections.

The unanimity of the Kahns and Seidelmans never was shown to better advantage. The mind of Jake instantly was apparent to all the rest, and in ten minutes every Kahn and Seidelman in the store was walking around the corner on that cold November day – for it was nearly Thanksgiving and there was ice in every breath they drew. And every Kahn and every Seidelman of the lot carried something in hand to the little rooming house where Mrs. Sidney M. Lester lived.

The sour-faced woman opened the door again.

'Top floor west,' she said. 'And help yourself!'

She stood at the bottom of the stairs, sniffing, as the procession climbed.

When they came to the top floor west, Jake tapped. There was no response. The smiles died upon the faces of the Kahns and the Seidelmans.

Then Jake tried the door. It opened at once. He peeked and the Kahns and the Seidelmans peeked behind him. They saw a neat little living room with a round table in the center of it, and the center of the table was crossed by an embroidered runner; and on the runner stood four or five books, upheld by bronze book ends; and on the wall there was a picture of a dignified gentleman in tails, making a gesture as though he were in the midst of a public address. They knew, instantly, that that was Sidney M. Lester, and that he was dead.

"Good!" said Jake, seeing that the inner door to the bedroom-kitchenette was closed. 'We'll get everything on the table and surprise her. . . .'

They got into the living room. Their eyes gave warning to one another to make no sound. When Ruthie dropped the spoon out of the potato salad and it clattered on the floor, the whole group looked upon her as upon a mortal sinner, and she was frozen with fright.

But presently they had everything laid out so that it would have done you good to see that caviar, packed in glistening ice, and the silver white of pure chicken breast, sliced by Abe – he really has a perfect touch for carving, Grandfather Oscar says; and there were grapes frosted with cold and sweetness and the fragrant big California oranges, richer than the fabled apples of the Hesperides; and so on, through item after item, almost every article that Mrs. Sidney M. Lester ever had priced in the store was represented by that array upon the table.

Then Jake, after taking a final survey of the table, advanced toward the inner door. The Kahns and Seidelmans, unbidden, ranged themselves in a straight line, beginning with Martha Kahn and ending with Bernie, who is the smallest of the family, though of course he more than makes up for inches with brains.

Jake rapped delicately upon that inner door. He waited. He rapped again. Suddenly he rapped very loudly indeed. Martha Kahn caught her breath.

Martha said, whispering: '*Gott mit uns . . .* !'

And then Jake turned the knob, slowly, and slowly pushed the door open. He and all the families behind him could look through the door to the chair where Mrs. Sidney M. Lester sat beside the western window with a time-yellowed old letter in her hand, and her head bent thoughtfully to the side, and her eyes looking askance out the window for all the world as though she had just been pricing the caviar or the *pâté* in the store of Kahn & Seidelman.

Jake Kahn did not speak. He turned slowly, and slowly he closed the door.

He crossed the room. He opened the door into the hall. Through it filed the Kahns and the Seidelmans, stepping soundlessly. So perfectly were they of one mind that it did not occur to any of them to take even the perishable caviar away; but all remained as they had brought it and arranged – what was to have been a feast, but became a sacrifice. The caviar with its glistening ice, the rich *pâté*, uncovered, the snow-white slices of chicken which Abe had carved, all stood there in order, and the

California oranges, at a dollar and twenty-five cents a dozen, gave into the air an aromatic fragrance purer than the purest incense in a church.

The Kahns and Seidelmans went noiselessly down the stairs with big Martha Kahn weeping silently all the way and Jake comforting her, for he understood the nature of their loss.

Honor Bright

A sense of honor pervaded Faust's life and work. It forms a chief element in his writing. Like Adrienne in this story, Faust's heroes and heroines do not achieve or preserve honor without undergoing painful ordeals. Though he was apparently fearless, this story reveals how deeply and intimately he understood cowardice and shame. 'Honor Bright' was found among his papers after his death and first appeared in *Cosmopolitan* in November 1948.

Faust liked to remind readers that love is a central force in human experience. 'Golden Lightning' was his favorite name for it. It strikes many of his heroes and heroines as it struck him at the moment he first saw his future wife. He wrote eloquently about many kinds of love: male-female, male-male (but not homoerotic), human love for animals and vice versa, love of danger, love for country, for ideas, for ideals, and, as here, love of a surprising kind. 'My Adrienne, your Adrienne, every man's Adrienne' is one of his unforgettable heroines. His daughter Judith Faust named her only child Adriana.

ADRIENNE STEPPED into the library through the French window – her family's garden adjoins mine – and sat down in the red tapestry chair near the fire. My Adrienne – your Adrienne, every man's Adrienne – selected that chair because it made a perfect background for her black velvet evening wrap, and she wanted to be near the fire so that the bright blaze of it would throw up little golden lights into her hair. I got up and poured her favorite drink, which is a bit of plain water without ice, just stained with Scotch.

'This is very pretty, Adrienne,' I said. 'With your profile just so and your head leaning a little, you look like a child.'

'When you know the truth, does it matter how I look?' she said. 'How is your poor back, Uncle Oliver?'

I had been moving some great heavy pots of hydrangeas a few days before on the terrace and had given myself a wrench, but it was not sympathy that caused Adrienne to ask that question; something in my speech had annoyed her, and she wished to remind me, in her sweetly poisonous way, that the first sign of age is weakness in the small of the back.

'I'm perfectly well,' I said.

'I'm very glad, *darling*,' said my Adrienne, 'but don't insist on being so strong and manly just now, dear.'

I looked up from filling my pipe and waited.

'You know you prefer cigarettes,' she explained.

I put the pipe aside without a word and picked up a cigarette.

Adrienne rose and came, rustling, to stand over me with her fragrance while she held the lighter. 'Isn't that the wrong end, dear?' she suggested.

I reversed the infernal cigarette, and she lighted it. These near approaches or forays of Adrienne's often make me nervous, and of this truth she is exquisitely aware.

'Are you angry?' she asked.

'Just enough to give you my full attention,' I told her. 'It's your usual system.'

'But I don't come here to annoy you, *do* I, Uncle Oliver?' she wanted to know. 'You don't really feel that I come here to annoy you, Uncle Oliver?' she said sadly.

'You come here to think out loud, because I'm so old and safe,' I answered.

'Oh no; not really so *safe*,' she said.

'Well, well! Who is it this time?' I asked.

'Something terrible happened,' she told me.

'What's his name?' I asked cannily. 'And who is he?'

'It's not so much a "who" as a "what,"' decided Adrienne. 'Will you help me, *dear* Uncle Oliver?'

'I suppose so,' I said.

She went back to her chair and held out one hand to be gilded by the firelight, yet I felt that only part of her attention was being given to the composition of this picture and that she was in real trouble. I was astonished and touched.

'I have an appointment for eight o'clock,' she said. 'You won't let me be late? It's frightfully important.'

'Very well,' I answered. 'I won't let you be late. But now let's get on with your problem. What's his name?'

'Gilbert Ware,' she said.

I felt a shock of loss and regret. For years I had realized that my Adrienne was growing up, but still it had remained easy for me to think of her in short skirts and with her hair in braids. A child belongs to every man; a woman belongs to one only; and so my heart shrank at the name of Gilbert Ware. He filled both the imagination and the eye. If he was not one of the richest ten men in the country, he was not far behind them. On his mother's side he went back to the best of Massachusetts, and by his father he was Old Virginia; placed in the diplomatic corps by the Ware dynasty, he had tasted the best the world offers by the time he was thirty; and finally he had the beauty, together with the raised eyebrows, of one of the Founding Fathers. I daresay that he was the catch of the whole country. Such a man did not waste his time on children, which meant that my Adrienne was now a woman.

She explained, 'He gave a week-end party at his house in the country, and I was there.'

'At his country house?' I said. 'Why, Adrienne, you really are getting on.'

She did not answer but continued to look sidelong thoughts, so that I understood she was about to tell her story. I took my drink in hand, comforted my sight with her, and prepared to listen. Of course, 'uncle' is merely a title that she chose for me, but I have watched Adrienne and listened carefully for several years without coming to the end of her. She is strangely combined of warmth and aloofness. Not even her school friends could nickname her 'Addie,' and no one fails to put the accent on the last syllable of 'Adrienne' because she seems, if not a Latin, at least very different. Actually, her blood is mostly of the far north – Norwegian, I think – and those people of the endless nights have gifts of deep brooding and long, long dreams.

Adrienne is continually in and out of love like a trout in sun and shadow, but the net never seems to take her. When I thought of the name and place of Gilbert Ware in the world, I wondered if this might not be the time. I wondered also how much truth might be mingled in this story with the fictions of Adrienne, for, though I hope she is not a deliberate teller of untruths, she is at least a weaver who loves to have many colors in her web. With the question there came to me a sudden surety that tonight, at least, I should hear nothing but the truth. Also I knew, for no proper reason, that she was to speak of a great event. At this point in my thoughts she began to talk in that voice so light and musical that more than once, it surprises me to say, she has talked me to sleep.

She was quite excited, she said, when the invitation came, for she had seen Gilbert Ware only a few times and, though she had done her very best, she had not been sure that he noticed her. Now she put her mind thoroughly upon the future, as she laid out the things for her maid to pack. She hesitated particularly over the jewels for, if she took none, she might seem dull, and too many might be pretentious. At last she hit on a diamond bracelet – a mere thread of light – and a little ruby pendant of the finest pigeon's blood. The two together might be worth some thirty-five hundred or four thousand dollars. (Adrienne is very good at figures.)

Long before her packing was finished or her thoughts arranged, young Harry Strode stopped by to drive her down to the country. She permitted this service from him, but not with pleasure. She had been quite fond of Strode at one time and, during an extremely dull evening, she had permitted herself to tell him so. But, since Adrienne cannot endure sulky men with long memories, her liking afterwards had turned the other way.

Once in the car, she was as pleasant as possible. However, this was a dark afternoon with such a roar and rushing of rain that conversation meant straining the voice. She had intended to be kind to Harry, but not in the face of such difficulties. Adrienne, who has more than one of the talents of a cat, found herself, while considering the next subject for talk, so comfortable that presently she was asleep.

She roused when Harry paused to take a hitchhiker in out of the downpour. He was a pale man of about my age, she said, with his head thrust forward at the end of a long neck like a caricature of all the bookkeepers in the world. A certain restless hunger in his eyes intrigued her for a moment, but then, in spite of the best intentions, she was asleep again; and the fellow sat quietly in the back seat.

At the entrance to Ware's driveway, Strode let out his extra passenger – the lights of a town were only a short distance down the road –
and Adrienne remembers how the poor fellow stood in the rain with his
hat in his hand, thanking them and waiting for the car to pass on. This
roused her so that she was wide awake when they entered the house.

The place was quite a disappointment to her for it combined two
faults: it was both baronial and new. Yet she could understand that a
man like Ware might simply pick the best of architects and say to him,
'Here is the land. Select a proper site and build me an appropriate country house. Suppose you take a year to do it, gardens and all.' But the
moment she went into the living room she was warmed by the realization that Ware was giving the party entirely for her. Every one of the
dozen or more house guests had been chosen from among her younger
friends. It was only a pity, said Adrienne, that he had not included some
of the older ones. Saying this, she smiled at me.

In the great living room, huge as a Tudor hall, tea was being served
in delicate porcelain with faint chimings of silver; and there was Gilbert
Ware, as ingratiating and observant a host as though he were by no
means the catch of a continent. Adrienne made up her mind to have
him. Her tactics were to strike at once and to keep on striking.

When Ware asked her about the trip down, she said, 'I don't want to
think about it.'

'Why not?'

'No – please! It was only a hitchhiker we picked up, and I simply
started imagining things about him.'

'Something is bothering you,' said Gilbert Ware, 'so let's have it out.'
He had a doctor's air, attentive for humane reasons even to foolish
stories.

'It was like something you're afraid of seeing by night,' said Adrienne.

The storm jumped suddenly at the house and set the tall windows
trembling. Since it was only twilight, the curtains had not been drawn,
and she looked out over a shimmer of lawn into the green gloom.

'Harry had his eyes glued to the road,' she said. 'He's such a careful
driver, but it seemed to me that he *must* have known what I was seeing
as I sat there, pretending to be asleep. In the mirror I could see the man's
face; I think I'll always see it.'

'The hitchhiker's?'

'It was so pale,' said Adrienne. 'It was so long and dead and white. . . .
Please don't make me remember.'

'Don't talk about it; you look sick,' said Ware.

'I'll be all right. It was only a dream. There wasn't any reality about it. Nothing so evil *could* be real. You know, the sort of horror that smiles at you in the dark?'

Ware was listening to her but with plenty of reservation in those raised eighteenth-century eyebrows. She realized then that, if she married him, she might find herself playing a part forever. The thought excited her as she went on with the embroideries of her little story. Actually there *had* been something strange about the hitchhiker. Now she enlarged upon him.

She said she had seen the devil wake up in the eyes of the man when, as she raised her hand to her hat, her sleeve fell back and showed the diamond bracelet; she had seen the beast of prey in him appear like some grisly shape that floats up under water, never clearly seen. It wasn't the thought of mere robbery and loss that troubled her but that brooding sense of a monstrous presence.

Gradually the man leaned forward in his seat, preparing to act. She was trying desperately to convey a warning to Harry Strode. If it were too overt, the signal would bring the attack on them instantly. She tried to signal with her eyes, with her hand. She slipped her foot over and touched Strode's. But he remained impervious, simply fixing his eyes on the road and singing a song, said Adrienne, which declared that for alma mater he would stand like a wall and never, never fall; also, when he took the field, he would never yield.

When she talked about the college hymn, something melted in Ware's eyes. A barrier fell, admitting her, and whether or not he believed all the tale, plainly he enjoyed the art of it.

She made a quick ending. A police car, she said, suddenly came up behind them, used its siren, and went by. This was enough to make the hitchhiker change his mind. Perhaps the sight of the uniforms recalled to him certain unforgettable years of punishment. He relaxed in his seat, and a moment later they were letting him out at the entrace to the Ware place. She never would forget him standing in the rain with that faint white mockery of a smile, thanking them for the ride. She had reached the house still half sick, but what saved the day for her was a desire to laugh, because Harry Strode had gone through it all aware of nothing but a desire to rally around a banner and, with a heart so true, die for the red and blue.

Ware chuckled at that. Then he said that the guestrooms of the place were cottages scattered through the grounds but, if she were nervous after her experience, she should have a place in the main building.

'No, no!' said Adrienne. 'I've talked it all out now, and I won't think of it again. You were *so* right to make me tell you everything. I didn't want to say anything about it before the rest of them; there's something so ugly about that kind of a story, don't you think?'

Ware's eyes dwelt on her for a moment before he agreed; then he let the general conversation flow in upon them, and Adrienne found the eyes of the other girls fixed on her a little grimly. They took it for granted that she merely had succeeded in putting herself on trial, but her resolution was hardening every instant. She would take this man, to have and to hold; she would take him – if for no other reason – because he was hard to get.

Everyone went to change, and Adrienne was shown to her cottage. There were a number of these cabins, each tucked into a special environment: one by a pool, another drenched in vines, one lost in towering woods, and a fourth sunning itself on a little green hilltop, though there was only rain streaming down when Adrienne was taken to it. It was built snug and tight as a ship's cabin, but it was a complete job even to a sunken pool in the bathroom.

When she had dressed – in black, she said, with only her ruby pendant – she put on overshoes and a featherweight cellophane slicker which were provided and went back to the house with a flashlight. There was only a misting rain, by this time, but the trees still looked a little wild from the storm.

A few moments after her return to the house dinner was announced. When they went in, she found herself at the right hand of Ware and felt that the game was half won. Yet he made no particular effort at the table; he preferred to watch her and smile.

She was surprised when suddenly he asked her what she thought of the house.

'Doesn't it need something?'

'Does it? What would you say? More color?'

'No, but more time.'

This seemed to please him. For an instant he came out of the distance and sat within touch of her, his eyes clear and keen, but after that she felt that he had drawn away again. She did not feel that she had failed but that he needed more leisure to make up his mind. She determined to give it to him, so she pleaded a frightful headache and went off to bed early.

By this time the storm had slid away down the sky and out of sight, but a few clouds were flying. The moon hit one of them and dashed the whole weight of it into a shining spray like a bow wave. Adrienne enjoyed these things. She knew that she was on trial – for fifty million, so to speak – but her eye was turned confidently to the future.

She decided, as she lay stretched on her bed in the cottage, looking at the apple-green ceiling, that Gilbert Ware probably wanted a restful creature for a wife. He was an unhurried sight-seer in life, determined to take nothing but the best. She, with her imaginings and her acting, had amused him for a time. She should have adopted an entirely different role and made herself, like him, a quiet observer, a little tired by the game. Adrienne decided that in the morning she would show him a change of pace.

The moment she reached this intelligent conclusion she grew sleepy, but as she yawned, her arms wide open to welcome the aching drowsiness, she heard a slight sound and observed that the knob of her door was turning. She had locked the door, but a thrill of horror froze her heart. Not since she was a child and ghosts had haunted her in dark corridors had she felt such a thoroughly sufficient chill. She reached for the telephone and turned the dial. The bell in the main house began to buzz with a deep, soft voice. The buzzing continued, a far-away sound on the wire and a hollow echoing in Adrienne. Then not a servant but Ware himself spoke.

'It's Adrienne Lester,' she whispered. 'Someone is trying to get into my cottage!'

He said, with his eternal calm, 'Someone with a long, white, evil face, no doubt?' He laughed and rang off.

She could not believe it, but there it was. Her play-acting had been perfectly patent to him.

The doorknob no longer was turning. Instead, there was a very discreet sound of metal scratching on metal. She remembered now not the sins of her past but the old fable about the little boy who had called 'Wolf! Wolf!' once too often. For an instant she thought of being merely beautiful and helpless; instead, she got up and seized the heavy poker which stood in the brass bucket beside the fire. At the same time the door opened.

A gust of night air came in along with her hitchhiker who looked 'like a caricature of all the bookkeepers in the world.' He closed the door with his foot and pushed his hands into his coat pockets. He was very wet. When he moved, his feet made squashy sounds in his shoes. The rim of his hat, which he did not remove, hung down around his long, pallid face. A thin purple dye, which soaked out of his coat, had streaked the white of his shirt and, since the coat collar was turned up, had left a mark like a cut across his throat. He looked at Adrienne and at the poker she held, then turned his back on her and went to the bedside table where her jewels were lying. He dropped them into a coat pocket.

He was quite hunched and so thin that she could almost count the vertebrae through his coat, but in spite of his apparent weakness she put the poker back into the brass bucket. She was young, swift, strong, but only as a woman. And, though he was by no means a big man, she knew that he could pluck the weapon out of her hands with ease. The knowledge sickened her a little; for the first time she was insufficient in an emergency. My Adrienne slipped quietly toward the door.

'No,' said the hitchhiker, and shook his head at her.

She turned for an instant toward the blackness of the outer night, but she dared not flee because of the nightmare that might pursue her. She went back to the fire.

A small pool was collecting around the man's feet; she watched the growth of it on the Chinese rug across the tongue and lower jaw of a little dragon.

'How do you feel?' he asked.

'I'm all right,' said Adrienne.

'You're not afraid?'

'I was, terribly. But it's better now that you're talking,' she said.

She thought that it was a pleasant remark, and she made it with a smile, but all the time the sickness of the fear was deepening in her, thickening like a new taste, because the hitchhiker was aware of her from head to foot and from foot to head. It was only for a moment that his eyes touched her in this fashion, but the screaming muscles began to tremble in her throat.

He kept nodding his head up and down in understanding. He ran the tip of his tongue over his lips. 'It always makes me kind of laugh,' he said, 'the way you people get scared. Once I got into a place and in the first bedroom, where I didn't expect it, there was a young fellow lying reading. He'd heard something. He knew I was inside the room, but he didn't dare to turn his head. I stood there and watched. The magazine was resting on his chest, and his heart was thumping so hard that it made the pages keep stirring like leaves in a wind. He was young, and he was twice as big as me; but nothing is as big as the things that come out of the night.'

'What happened, then? What did you do?' asked Adrienne.

'Don't scream or nothing,' said the thief. 'I'm gonna turn out the light.'

He turned out the light so that there was only the fire to send his shadow and hers up the wall and over the ceiling in waves and tremblings.

Adrienne picked up the poker again.

'Yeah, you'd fight, wouldn't you?' he said, and laughed a little. 'Got anything to drink in here?'

'No,' said Adrienne.

'What's over here?' and he pulled open a small door set into the wall.

Two flasks of cut glass glimmered inside the niche. He sniffed at them.

'Brandy and Scotch. Funny how you people never know that bourbon is better than Scotch . . . Have some?'

'No,' said Adrienne.

'Here's down the hatch!'

'Don't drink it!' cried Adrienne.

'Why not?'

'Please don't drink it!' she begged.

'Ah, that's what you think, is it? Well, here's down the hatch!'

He took a good swallow, and while his head was back, his eyes half closed, she freshened her grip on the poker, but still she could not act. She put the poker back in place for the second time, because it came to her that all the danger she dreaded was, in fact, closed in the room with her and that she would have to meet it with a different kind of force.

He wiped his mouth on the back of his hand, which made a smear across his face, and then he sat down beside the fire. Adrienne sank into the opposite chair.

'They spent some money on *you* all right,' he said. 'I remember hearing a rich feller say, once . . . I used to be a plumber, and plumbers hear what people say, but a length of cast-iron pipe rolled on me, and it gave me a kind of a twist in the back, so I wasn't any good, after that. I had to use the old bean, so I used it . . .' He seemed to have lost his place in the conversation. 'Where was I at?' He took another drink.

'You were about to say how much money is spent on us.'

'This feller was saying that his girl cost ten thousand a year from twelve years up. Travel, governess, maid, school – he said ten thousand wouldn't cover it. Ten thousand for ten years. That's a hundred grand. How many languages you got?'

'French and Italian, a little. And a bit of German.'

'You don't look like you would know any German.'

'They sent me to Vienna for a year. To study singing.'

'I guess you can do that pretty good.'

'Not very.'

'Sing "Home on the Range," dead soft.'

She sang 'Home on the Range' softly. He finished the flask of Scotch while he listened. He hummed the last part of it in unison with her.

'I never was West,' he said, 'but I like that song. It's kind of American. It reminds me how big we are . . . I've heard plenty sing it better than you.'

'Of course you have.' She managed to smile again.

He stared hard watching for the end of the smile, but she kept it, after a fashion, in the corners of her mouth and in her eyes.

'There ain't hardly a good swallow in one of these flasks. Go fetch me the other one, will you?'

'Certainly,' said my Adrienne.

She rose and went to the little cupboard. As she turned with the flask of brandy in her hand, she saw that the plumber sat a little higher in his chair, and then she was aware that his body was rigid as she came up behind him. He was waiting, tense and set, for whatever she might attempt to do, but he would not turn his head an inch toward her. She went slowly by him and gave him the flask – and her smile.

He relaxed in his chair. 'You feel better, don't you?'

'A lot better,' she said.

'I guess you been scrubbed clean every day of your life. I guess you never wear anything but silk?'

'Oh, yes. Oh, lots of other things,' she said.

'You don't mind me now if I drink this?'

'I don't mind at all.'

'Look,' he said.

'Yes,' said my Adrienne.

'Maybe there's better singers, but I never heard nobody talk so good. You bet I never heard anybody talk so good.' He stood up. 'You been pretty all right, and I sort of hate taking your stuff. You know?'

For the first time, in a way that was strange to Adrienne, he opened his eyes and looked at her with an appeal for understanding. He was apparently about to go, and she would not have to keep on smiling. She felt she had done enough acting in those few minutes to last her the rest of her life.

'It's all right,' she said to him. 'We all have to get along somehow.'

'Thanks. I believe you're on the square, but I'll fix this first.' He pulled the telephone wire from the wall socket. Then he lifted a finger at her. 'You won't budge out of here for ten minutes?'

'I won't budge.'

'Ten whole minutes? Honor bright?'

'Honor bright,' said Adrienne, and crossed herself automatically.

'Well, I guess that's all right then. Good night to you.'

He went out of the cottage.

There was a little clock above the fireplace. She noted the hands at five past eleven and resolved to wait for the ten whole minutes, honor bright; but all at once, said Adrienne, she thought of what a scene there would be when she rushed into the big house and told them, how everyone would be roused, and there would be calls for the police, and Gilbert Ware looking frightfully mortified and, for once, thoroughly alert. She thought of these things and ran from the cottage, but before she had taken three steps, the man moved out from behind the corner of the little building. He came straight toward her, slowly, with his hands in his coat pockets, and his black shadow slid silently over the ground beside him, like a man and his ghost or a man and the black devil, said Adrienne. I wonder why she did not use those quick feet of hers to fly away to the big house, but all she could do was to creep away from him through the open door of the cottage. She backed up until the wall stopped her. Her knees gave way. My Adrienne crouched with her eyes closed, because she dared not look for another instant at the long, white, deadly face of the hitchhiker. But she could feel his shadow falling over her, cold on her face and breast, she said.

'Well, so there isn't any honor bright,' he said. 'I thought maybe you were one of the things for the country to be proud of. But you ain't. You ain't all right at all. You're dirt. You're just dirt.'

It seemed to Adrienne that the chill of his shadow still was falling on her, but when she looked up, after a long time – after a long time when the breath seemed to be stopping in her body – she saw that he was gone, and she was able to get to the chair by the fire and drop into it.

Only a moment later Gilbert Ware came in. He looked at the black, wet footprints on the floor, and then dropped on one knee beside her chair. She was reminded dimly of other young men who had taken the same position – my Adrienne always is reminded of someone else, no matter what a man does.

'I've been a fool – I've been a goddamned fool!' said Ware, in just as trembling a passion of regret as any other man. 'What happened? What has he done?'

My Adrienne said nothing, not because she was incapable of speech, nor because she was remembering the theft and her fear, but because she was thinking of a loss far more vital, for which she could not find a name. So she kept on thinking until her thoughts went jogging all the way back to childhood, which was the last time 'honor bright' had troubled her soul. She was holding out her hands to the fire which, against all nature, gave her no comfort.

Gilbert Ware took those hands and turned her suddenly toward him so that she had to see his face, all savage with resolution. There was no trace now of that astute and critical spirit which had looked so carefully through her. 'When did he go? Has he hurt you? Tell me. Do you hear me, dear Adrienne? What has he done?'

There was one word in this speech which could not help partially reviving such a practical girl as my Adrienne, and yet she still was half lost in that unhappy dream as she answered, 'He took the bracelet and pendant. I don't know when he left. The hitchhiker . . . .'

'Was it *that* fellow? And I thought it was only a story!' cried Ware.

He jumped for the phone, found it was disconnected, sprang back to her.

'Let him go!' she said. 'I don't want ever to see him again. Don't make me see him again, Gilbert.'

Gilbert Ware threw a blanket around her and lifted her to her feet. He helped her along the path to the main house.

'You won't have to see him. Of course you won't have to see him. Don't talk, my sweet girl, my Adrienne. You've had a frightful shock. Will you be able to forgive me?'

Miserable as she was, she could not help thinking how easy it might be to forgive fifty million and Gilbert Ware.

The party at the house had not broken up, and everyone hurried to be of help. Faces leaned over Adrienne as she lay on the couch wrapped in the blanket. Someone chafed her feet. Her fingers were around a mug of hot toddy that warmed her hands and her lips and her throat but could not melt the ice around her heart.

She was conscious of much telephoning back and forth, but she was not prepared for the return of her philosophical hitchhiker, flanked by a pair of proud policemen. In that frame he was a wretchedly starved picture of a man. He had left the muddy country lanes for a highway, and the police had picked him up at once. Ware, bending close beside Adrienne, was saying, 'There's only one word for you to speak, and then it's all over. Simply identify the jewels and the man. The law takes on after that. Don't move, Adrienne. Don't sit up.'

She did sit up, however, because it was mortally necessary for her to face again those eyes which had looked into her so shamefully far. But the inquiring mind was gone from the thief. All that had been free and dangerous and of the night now was faded into a dim creature who had suffered before and was prepared once more to endure.

'I guess this is the stuff, Miss?' said one of the policemen, holding out the jewels in the palm of his hand. 'You just identify it, and he'll take a trip.'

She kept trying to catch the glance of the thief, but he stared straight forward at the years of labor, of silence and of shame. His wet hat, now a shapeless sponge, was crushed in one hand, and it was upon this hand that Adrienne was forced, most unwillingly, to focus her attention. There was something abnormal, misshapen and oversized about it. By contrast, Gilbert Ware had such slender fingers, such a rounded but in-adequate wrist, that one wondered how he could swing a polo mallet. The thumb of the hitchhiker, for instance, was broadened, thickened and fleshed on the inside to a surprising degree. Across his wrist lay two forking veins as big as her little finger, and all at once she penetrated the mystery. It was simply that the thief had been a laborer. By swinging sledge hammers, by tugging with all his might at powerful wrenches, he had deformed and desensitized his hands until they were merely gross tools, vaguely prehensile.

'. . . just a matter of identification,' a policeman was saying.

'They aren't mine,' she said.

The smiles of the policemen persisted a moment, wavered and went out like lanterns in a sudden wind.

'But wait – but, Adrienne!' said Gilbert Ware.

She shook her head. 'Not mine.'

'But this is the very fellow you were talking about!' cried Ware.

'I never saw him before.'

'My dear Adrienne,' said Ware, looking hard at her, 'if you're doing this out of charity, please remember that the law has a rightful place in this affair.'

She lost track of his voice, watching comprehension break up the calm of the plumber, but even as the hope entered him, and he saw that after all she seemed to be giving him some chance of escape, the manhood seemed to go out of him. Something of his spirit came leering, groveling at her feet.

Ware asked everyone to leave the room. Then he sat down beside Adrienne. 'Now what's it all about?' he asked, and he looked at her as a dealer might look at a picture of uncertain authentication.

'I don't know.'

'I'm sure you always think your way through before you do anything.'

'I try to,' she admitted, and she kept searching her mind only to discover that the deeper she went, the more unknown was this new Adrienne.

He was waiting.

'I don't know what the whole truth about this is,' she said, 'but I have a horrible, naked feeling that I'm going to tell it.'

After all, he had lived a bit. He showed it now by saying nothing.

'Did you see his hands?' she asked. 'They were real, don't you think?'

'Real?'

'He's worked like an honest man, and he's been a thief. He's been in prison, too, and that's real enough. He could see that I'm all make-believe. I'm not even honestly looking for a husband. I'm just as honest as a cat that wants kittens. I try to be clever, but I'm only silly and young. I've never even made a beginning. I hate it. Oh, you don't know how I hate it.'

'There's something pretty final about this,' he said. 'I think you're writing me down as one of the people who never have made a beginning.'

And now, in this interval, Adrienne found that she could not tell a pleasant lie. She knew that every second of the silence was saying good-by to fifty million dollars but, instead of speaking, she could only remember the voice of the thief saying, 'You're dirt! You're just dirt!'

After a while Ware stood up slowly, still with something between anger and entreaty in his eyes, but when that frightful silence continued, he said, 'I'll tell them the hitchhiker isn't the man.'

He left the room.

A fortune vanished with him, but with a very convinced longing Adrienne wanted to be out of that house. That was what she told the doctor, when he came a few minutes later.

He said, 'You've had a shock, my girl.'

'Have I? I'm going to be better, though, now.'

'You'd better stay in bed for two or three days.'

'Oh, no; I won't need to do that. There's someone I have to see.'

'You'd better do as I say, though,' he advised.

'But I know me so well,' said my Adrienne.

Here she finished her drink, and I knew that her story was finished also; her timing is so perfect.

I blew some smoke upward and watched it vanish. 'Fifty million dollars all gone?' I said, but then I saw that there was a shadow on Adrienne, a strange dimness.

'Now tell me about everything,' she said, looking at the place where the smoke had vanished.

'Why, it's not difficult, my dear,' I told her. 'You're unhappy about it because you don't understand the big, quick movement of your own heart; when you saw Ware bearing down with all the dogs of the law on that poor, hunted devil – '

'Oh, nonsense,' said Adrienne. 'Just as poor and hunted as a wolf. You don't *know*. I mean, a wolf that's perfectly at home in the woods, snow or shine. Don't you see? What am I looking for? Why, I'm looking for a *man,* and that evening I thought I'd found him. But I hadn't. I'd only found a sort of beautiful social legend, or something. The hitchhiker was more of a man.'

'Well, yes. Well . . . of course,' I said, and gave myself a twist that hurt my back. 'I hadn't thought of that. But – just to return a bit – who was it you wanted to see in the pinch? You remember you spoke to the doctor about him.'

'Oh, an old, old friend,' said Adrienne. 'His voice was with me all through it. He's the one I'm to see tonight.'

'Better be on your way, then,' I told her. 'It's ten to eight now.'

'Really? Is it as late as that? Then may I ring for Jericho?'

She was pressing the button as I said, 'What the devil do you want with *him?*'

Jericho came in. He is made of white hair, yellow parchment, and heavenly spirit.

'Jericho dear,' said Adrienne, 'is there any cold, cold champagne?'

'There is one just barely turnin' to ice,' said Jericho.

'Then we'll have that for an aperitif,' she told him. 'And is that pheasant big enough for two?'

'Just perfect, Miss Adrienne.'

'Then serve it that way, please,' said Adrienne.

'Do you mean that *I'm* the appointment?' I asked, when Jericho left.

'You're the only person who knows enough to tell me what's wrong with me,' she said desolately. 'But I don't need the telling actually. I know already. Say something or I'm going to cry,' said Adrienne, who now was sitting on the arm of my chair.

Jericho brought in the champagne and paid no attention to Adrienne as he began opening the bottle.

'Well, I'll tell you a fact that's better than a story,' I said.

'I hate facts,' said Adrienne.

'When the Arab mare comes out of the tent in the morning – because the Arabs value their mares most, you know . . . .'

'What silly people!'

'They're not silly at all.'

'Oh, aren't they?'

'No, they're not. But when the mare comes out of the tent, she looks away off beyond the tribe and over the heads of the family that owns her, and across the desert to the edge of the horizon. She has her tail arched and her head raised, and there's a tremendous expectation in her eyes that makes her master sad.'

'But why?'

'Because he knows she's saying to herself: "When will the real master come!" '

'How rather lovely,' said Adrienne.

Jericho had placed in my hand a glass in which the bubbles broke with a crisping sound. 'Here's to the real master, my dear,' I said.

'Will you find him for me?'

'This is just nonsense, Adrienne,' I told her with severity.

'But I'm tired – oh, I'm tired to death!' she said. 'I want my life to start.'

'Come, come! Let's have this drink.'

'Not until you promise me.'

'But what?'

'Either find me a husband – I'll ask no questions – or marry me your-self.'

'Adrienne!'

'Are you really so shocked?'

'But I'm old enough to be – '

'You *are* old enough, you see. Shall we drink to it!'

'I *shall* find you somebody,' said I.

'Of course you will,' said Adrienne, raising her glass slowly as though waiting for permission.

I lifted mine in turn and, looking up, saw her all shining and golden through the color of the wine.

The King

Faust arrived in Hollywood in 1938 with high hopes of bringing his beloved Arthurian legends to the screen. Instead he was assigned the mundane though well-paying task of script doctor, repairing other people's work. Though he broke out of this role from time to time, his creativity as an artist suffered. During his Hollywood years Faust produced little writing of note other than the Kildare stories, a short poem in *Harper's* (January 1942), the crime serial 'Dead Man's Passport' in *The American Weekly* (beginning January 12, 1941), and a story or two like 'The King.' Written in the last year of his life, 'The King' first appeared posthumously in *This Week* (November 21, 1948).

The story is set during Hollywood's golden age of big studios, big pictures, and celebrity writers. At the time, Faust's college friend, Pulitzer Prize–winning Sidney Howard, was writing the screenplay for *Gone With the Wind* (M-G-M, 1939). Aldous Huxley was doing likewise for *Pride and Prejudice* (M-G-M, 1940), and they resumed an acquaintance begun in Florence. Faust may also have met F. Scott Fitzgerald when both had offices at M-G-M. Later, at Warner Brothers, Faust collaborated with William Faulkner on a story about Charles de Gaulle that never reached the screen – although between 1918 and 1993 seventy-nine other stories from Faust did.

Faust left Hollywood and financial success (his salary had reached $2,000 a week) for his assignment as a war correspondent. He said he could no longer continue writing in comfort and safety while others risked their lives in combat for values he cherished. There was an escape factor, too. He was tired of screen work and felt himself a failure as a writer and person. Though his prose was widely accepted, his beloved poetry was not. He also held a long-deferred desire to experience battle. Dorothy parted from him with the conviction she would never see him again.

'The King,' found among Faust's papers after his death, is a story about illusions. The aged Etherton, legendary king of Hollywood actors, is under the illusion he is superior to what he considers the vulgarity of the screen. Zandor, the producer, is under the illusion he possesses the real story of Etherton. The narrator is under the illusion he knows the truth about the entire situation. 'We live by illusions,' Faust often said. His favorite movie was Jean Renoir's *Grand Illusion* (French, 1937), his favorite play Shakespeare's illusory *The Tempest*. Professor Leo A. Hetzler, who studied Faust and Shakespeare, found entire scenes in Faust's work paralleling scenes in Shakespeare. Faust's passionate interest in the bard began in high school when he memorized thousands of lines from Shakespeare's plays. Etherton is a Shakespearean character, regal, legendary. He also represents Faust the poet, far removed from Faust the script doctor.

When Faust was lying wounded on a battlefield in Italy on the night of May 11, 1944, he was asked if he were in great pain. With a gesture worthy of a Shakespearean character, he replied, 'I'm all right. Take care of them,' indicating other wounded lying nearby. When the stretcher-bearers found him, he was dead. That night Dorothy had a dream in which she heard him calling out for her.

Frederick Schiller Faust is buried in the American Military Cemetery at Nettuno—Anzio, among the young men with whom he served and at whose side he died.

I T WAS a big day when Rudy Zandor consented to dine with me at Chasen's because those were the years when he was astonishing Hollywood with a series of super productions. He was another Sampson whose strength lay not in his long hair but in his perfect self-confidence.

The country he loved, the flag followed, the God he worshiped was Rudy Zandor. So I put in the whole day working on my plot and reached the restaurant rather full of hope.

Zandor was hardly an hour later, which seemed a good sign, and then he came in with a yes-man named Gregg and Jimmy Jones, whose real name is Jonascsky. Zandor raised quite a buzz with his entrance because he always dressed for public appearances. This time he wore corduroy trousers, a riding coat buttoned high around the throat, and four days' whiskers. His friends were in dinner jackets for contrast.

Rudy was almost at my table when another murmur started. All eyes left him, and in came Raymond Vincent Etherton in his black coat and white stock like an eighteenth century ghost. It was rather hard on Zandor to have his entrance messed up like that, for he was completely forgotten as the old man went by, looking straight ahead and failing to see the people who spoke to him. He went to his usual corner, waited for his coffee and cognac, and contemplated the dignity of space.

When Dave Chasen in person brought the brandy, Etherton became gently and kindly aware of him, for he was really abstracted, not merely high-hat. Thirty years before, when he consented to be King Arthur for D. W. Griffith, he must have been a glorious man.

Some of the glory hung about him as Henri Quatre in 'Ivry' or as Richard the Lion-Hearted in 'The Talisman.' He never was cast except as a king and he moved through his parts without the slightest acting, merely lending his presence, as it were. The whisper had it that there *was* a dash of real royalty in his blood but no one even in Hollywood dared to suggest the bar-sinister to Etherton.

Even Hollywood was surprised by the appearance of such a man on the screen. He was more a rare legend than a fact. That was why Chasen's buzzed so this evening.

Zandor, in eclipse, looked pretty sour.

'That man,' he said, pointing at Etherton. 'Who is he?'

Jimmy Jones winked at me. It was the yes-man who gave the answer. A celebrity in Hollywood can't help accumulating them as the north side of a tree gathers moss.

'That's Raymond Vincent Etherton,' said Gregg.

'I want him. He has a hungry look. I want him to play Shylock,' said Zandor.

'The "Merchant of Venice" after the big western?' I asked.

'Before,' said Zandor. 'I'm not doing the western.'

My hopes went crash; and at the same moment I heard Gregg ordering caviar.

Jimmy said: 'You can't buy an Etherton, Rudy. He doesn't need money, but he acts now and then to raise the level of the screen and show the world what royalty should be.'

Zandor waved his hand at Jones. 'You bother me,' he said. 'Go away.'

Jimmy Jones went away.

'Now get Etherton. Offer him seventy-five thousand,' directed

Zandor.

His Number Two boy went over to Etherton and I felt a little sick about Zandor and about myself for being with him.

Etherton was sipping his brandy when the yes-man leaned over his table and started talking. The old fellow showed no sign that he heard a syllable. Presently he laid a bill on the table, stood up, and walked through the Number Two boy as though the fellow were a thin mist. He passed out of Chasen's and Gregg came back to Zandor, astonished.

'Nothing could stop him – not even *your* name, Rudy,' he said.

'Why didn't you raise the bid?' asked Zandor, furious. 'I don't care what sort of blood he has in him; *nobody* walks out on me. Why didn't you offer him one hundred thousand?'

'But I didn't have the authority,' said the yes-man.

Zandor looked him over from his chin to the sleek of his hair and turned his shoulder; it was plain that there was one parasite less in his life.

It was a rotten dinner. I tried to be bright for a while but gave it up after Zandor had snarled a few times. The great man was preoccupied. In the middle of his chicken *cacciatore* he jumped up and left the tableware jingling.

'Show me where this Etherton lives,' he commanded.

I paid the bill and took him to Etherton's house – small, sedate, withdrawn from the vulgar world behind a formal Italian garden. The California moon, for we have a special variety out here, was laying cool silver over everything and the fountain statue left a perfect shadow on the pool.

The door of the house was open. I don't know why this shocked me so much. It was like seeing the great Etherton with his mouth agape. Zandor leaned on the bell. It made a thin chime of music far inside and we had no other answer. Zandor went in.

'You'd better not do that,' I protested. 'The old man won't stand intrusions.'

'Look!' said Zandor. 'I knew it . . . hungry!'

I followed him a step and saw him pointing to the living room; there was enough slanting moonshine to show that it was empty. The waxed floor shone like water, but there was not a stick of furniture. Zandor strode through the open door beyond and into the kitchen. There was a rusted gas stove. Something scurried away on a shelf and I saw a bit of nibbled cheese rind and cracker crumbs. But Zandor was moving on through a naked dining room and into a bed chamber that was furnished with box springs on the floor, a pier glass, and a big, gilded chair in front of the mirror. In the chair sat Etherton wrapped in a black cloak with his white head thrown back and his right hand at his breast, supported by something.

He looked at us with deeply veiled eyes of contempt and seemed about to make a gesture of silent dismissal. It needed another glance to see that all his gesturing had ended, for what supported his hand was the hilt of the little medieval dagger he had driven through his heart.

I looked away from him to the three big photographs which hung on the walls and showed me Etherton as the Lion-Hearted in heavy chain mail, as Henri Quatre with the famous white plume in his helmet, as King Arthur bearded like a saint.

Understanding grew in me. Those rare appearances of Etherton on the screen had not been a casual amusement but the nerve center of his whole life. His parts never had been large but they had made him a king, and with a child's pitiful sincerity he had enclosed himself within a dream. Rather than step outside it, he had starved. I could imagine with what care he dressed himself this evening, borrowed the last possible dollar from a pawnbroker and went out for the final time to see if Hollywood once more would give him a shadowy throne. Instead, it preferred to see in him the wicked moneylender, so he came home and erased himself from the page.

Zandor was triumphant.

'You see? You see?' he roared at me. 'I was right. I *did* spot the hunger in him. He's been on a throne for thirty years but when he got the Shylock offer, he knew that I'd seen the starvation in his face. The seventy-five thousand scared him. He was tempted and he almost fell. The hundred thousand would have bought him, lock, stock and barrel. But that fool of a Gregg didn't know how to bargain.'

I got out into the garden. It was a warm June night, but I was shivering. Zandor followed me. The bigness of his voice made the fountain pool tremble.

'He wanted to be a king or nothing, you see?' roared Zandor.

'So he came home and ended his reign. You get it? It's big stuff. It's new. It's a picture. And it's mine.'

Acknowledgments

Grateful acknowledgment is made to the Dorothy S. Faust Trust for permission to reprint the stories in this book as follows:

'John Ovington Returns' originally appeared in *All-Story Weekly*, June 8, 1918. Copyright © 1918 by Frank A. Munsey Company. Copyright © renewed 1946 by Dorothy Faust. Reprinted by arrangement with the Golden West Literary Agency. All rights reserved.

'Above the Law' originally appeared in *All-Story Weekly*, August 31, 1918. Copyright © 1918 by Frank A. Munsey Company. Copyright © renewed 1946 by Dorothy Faust. Reprinted by arrangement with the Golden West Literary Agency. All rights reserved.

'The Wedding Guest' originally appeared in *Harper's*, January 1934. Copyright © 1933 by Harper & Bros. Copyright © renewed 1961 by the Estate of Frederick Faust. Reprinted by arrangement with the Golden West Literary Agency. All rights reserved.

'A Special Occasion' originally appeared in *Harper's*, February 1934. Copyright © 1934 by Harper & Bros. Copyright © renewed 1961 by the Estate of Frederick Faust. Reprinted by arrangement with the Golden West Literary Agency. All rights reserved.

'Outcast Breed' originally appeared in *Star Western*, October 1934. Copyright © 1934 by Popular Publications, Inc. Copyright © renewed 1962 by the Estate of Frederick Faust. Reprinted by arrangement with the Golden West Literary Agency. All rights reserved.

We wish to thank Jon Tuska, William F. Nolan, Charles Schlessiger,
William Bloodworth, Sandra K. McDonald, and Mariette Risley among
others for their help in making possible this centennial selection of
Faust's stories. We are also grateful to the late William J. Clark, prime
mover among Faust enthusiasts and collectors, and good friend.

R. E. and J. E.

MAX BRAND is the best-known pen name of Frederick Faust, creator of Dr. Kildare, Destry, and many other fictional characters popular with readers and viewers worldwide. Faust wrote for a variety of audiences in many genres. His enormous output, totaling approximately thirty million words or the equivalent of 530 ordinary books, covered nearly every field: crime, fantasy, historical romance, espionage, Westerns, science fiction, adventure, animal stories, love, war, and fashionable society, big business and big medicine. Eighty motion pictures have been based on his work along with many radio and television programs. For good measure he also published four volumes of poetry. Perhaps no other author has reached more people in more different ways.

Born in Seattle in 1892, orphaned early, Faust grew up in the rural San Joaquin Valley of California. At Berkeley he became a student rebel and one-man literary movement, contributing prodigiously to all campus publications. Denied a degree because of unconventional conduct, he embarked on a series of adventures culminating in New York City where, after a period of near starvation, he received simultaneous recognition as a serious poet and successful popular-prose writer. Later, he traveled widely, making his home in New York, then in Florence, and finally in Los Angeles.

Once the United States entered the Second World War, Faust abandoned his lucrative writing career and his work as a screenwriter to serve as a war correspondent with the infantry in Italy, despite his fifty-one years and a bad heart. He was killed during a night attack on a hilltop village held by the German army. New books based on magazine serials or unpublished manuscripts continue to appear. Alive and dead he has averaged a new one every four months for seventy-five years. In the U.S. alone nine publishers issue his work, plus many more in foreign countries. Yet, only recently have the full dimensions of this extraordinarily versatile and prolific writer come to be recognized and his stature as a protean literary figure in the 20th Century acknowledged. His popularity continues to grow throughout the world.

This book was typeset by
Tseng Information Systems, Inc.
The text type is Sabon and the
display type Futura light condensed.
It was printed by Bookcrafters, Inc.,
and designed by Dika Eckersley.